Reviews of DR

MW01228830

"DREAMS & DESIRES feat
from sweet to sizzling and penned by some of the leading ~g
in today's romance and erotica genres. Buy it to help a great
cause, read it for the great stories!"

~ Lauren Baratz-Logsted, author of VERTIGO and HOW NANCY
DREW SAVED MY LIFE

"With a story to suit every appetite, DREAMS & DESIRES is a
delicious collaboration. Kudos to the authors for taking readers
on a delightful journey while promoting a wonderful cause."

~ Joanne Rock, author of THE KNIGHT'S COURTSHIP and
DON'T LOOK BACK

"From the first story to the last, these stories are filled with hope,
love, and the promise of the future... I highly recommend
DREAMS & DESIRES for those of you who cherish your
romances... a fantastic read..."

~ Rose, Romance At Heart, http://romanceatheart.com/

"(DREAMS & DESIRES) an unforgettable anthology that will
warm you right down to your toes... The nineteen beautifully
written stories will capture your heart..."

~ Zoë Knighton, Sensual Reads, http://www.sensualreads.com

"(DREAMS & DESIRES) a wonderfully diverse collection of
stories... something for every mood... When you reach the end of
Dreams & Desires, you'll be left craving more..."

~ Deborah Barone, Romance Divas,
http://www.romancedivas.com/

"(DREAMS & DESIRES) a fabulous sampler of many very talented authors... a breadth of display of love to warm the heart, heat one's thoughts, inspire wonder, and provoke contemplation... a varied, grand and guiltless indulgence..."

~ Lil, Love Romances and More,
http://www.loveromanceandmore.com/

Dreams and Desires:
A Collection of Romance & Erotic Tales

Freya's Bower.com ©2006
Culver City, CA

For information on the cover illustration and design, contact
secondmediauk@aol.com.
Cover illustration © 2006 Freya's Bower. All rights reserved.

Editor-in-Chief: Marci Baun

ISBN: 1-934069-22-1 – Paperback, ISBN: 1-934069-23-X – Cloth
ISBN: 1-934069-36-1 – eBook

This book is a work of fiction and any resemblance to any person, living or dead, any place, events or occurrences, is purely coincidental. The characters and story lines are created from the author's imagination or are used fictitiously.

Warning:

This book contains graphic sexual material and is not meant to be read by any person under the age of 18.

If you are interested in purchasing more works of this nature, please stop by http://www.freyasbower.com.

Freya's Bower.com, P.O. Box 4897, Culver City, CA 90231-4897

Printed in The United States of America

Works are arranged alphabetically by the last name of the author.

TABLE OF CONTENTS

Acknowledgements

Freya's Bower would like to thank all of the authors who donated their works to make this charity anthology possible. We would also like to thank all of the men and women who volunteer and work in the battered women shelters throughout the United States and the world. Without you, many women would still be trapped in dangerous and demeaning relationships. May your work continue to shine light on this important issue.

Foreword

Abuse is an ugly little word; it paints a million pictures. The dictionary looks at it this way: v. abuse (past and past participle a·bused, present participle a·bus·ing, 3rd person present singular a·bus·es)

1. maltreat somebody: to treat a person or animal cruelly, whether physically, psychologically, or sexually, especially on a regular or habitual basis
2. misuse something: to use something in an improper, illegal, or harmful way
3. insult somebody: to speak insultingly or offensively to somebody

Over time, the perception and acceptance of the definition has changed. In most countries now, if a pet is abused, the animal protection people come and take the dog away, they arrest the offender and put him/her in jail, fine them, maybe even prevent them from owning another pet. Even a hint of child abuse, and again the authorities rally around. They take the child away, put the offender in jail, make the offender get counseling— even if the accusation isn't based on the truth, but hearsay. Someone's reputation and parental rights come into question.

Yet, the woman in the ER with a black eye, the one who "fell down the steps" or is bruised and battered in ways that could not result from accident or self-injury becomes the center of a world of silence. The silence of domestic abuse. The authorities, if summoned, arrive with their hands tied. The beaten victim must press charges.

Does the beaten pet? Does the beaten child? Does the guy on the street that someone robbed and beat? No.

Domestic abuse is about the only crime where the victim is blamed. Rape as well, but that so often falls into the category of a crime against women – that women somehow asked for it. Abuse is not just about hitting.

Often, the only escape a woman has is to leave everything behind – her home, her pets, her family (many have been separated from their family), her job, if she has one – and flee to a shelter or underground railway for abused women. All her hopes and dreams rest on those who put their own lives at risk and donate their time to help others.

One in four women will experience some sort of abuse in their lifetime. From a spouse, a boyfriend, a father, or even on a casual date. One in four. Yet, it is an underreported crime. The women are made to feel that the abuse is their fault. Society once supported a husband's right, a father's right, a brother's right to make his woman behave. (And still does in some cultures.) Haven't we grown past that? Haven't we grown past blaming the victim?

Abuse is hard to understand. TV and print ads scream – don't use drugs, talk to your kids about smoking, sex is worth the wait – maybe there should be commercials warning the generations to come of the signs of abuse, telling them to not close it in a blanket of silence.

Society needs to stop blaming the victim. Punch someone and the offender goes to jail for battery. This same law needs to be applied to women and men in their own homes. Nothing "domestic" about it. It should be across the board – assault is assault no matter where it happens or between whom.

Our children need to see abuse for what it is. Classes are offered in high school on what it's like to have children. We need to have classes on healthy relationships. Step up and ask your school system to offer girls and boys these classes. While this should be taught at home, abuse is a cycle learned at home. Those that need it the most won't learn it there and will be stuck in the vicious cycle unless they get help, advice and support.

The staff of Freya's Bower, and the writers who have so graciously donated their work, want to do what they can to stop the cycle, to bring awareness of the world these women and children must live in, and to keep those avenues of help open to all women, children and men who need them.

The authors in these pages write stories about hopes and dreams, about romantic dreams, and life's wishes. By buying this book, you are doing your part in breaking the cycle.

To break the cycle, everyone needs a clearer understanding of what abuse is. The following is a list of warning signs and characteristics common to abusive situations and relationships. Pass it on to your daughters, your sisters, and anyone else you think can benefit from it. It may open their eyes and save their life.

1. **'Jeckel and Hyde Behavior':** Your partner is wonderful and caring for a while and then will do an about face and be angry about things that they thought were fine at an earlier time. They switch back and forth between behaviors for no apparent reason.

2. **'Life Would be so Good If':** You frequently think that your relationship would be perfect if not for his or her emotional storms. The storms seem to be coming more and more frequently. Between times, life is wonderful, but when a storm is coming, you can often tell by that 'Walking on Eggs Feeling'.

3. **'That Walking On Eggs Feeling':** You feel at times that any action on your part will cause your partner to erupt into anger. You try to do everything you can think of to avoid it, but the longer the feeling goes on, the more likely the blowup will happen, no matter what you do.

4. **'I Can't Stand You, But You Better Not Leave':** Your partner keeps telling you that you aren't worth having a relationship with, but will not consider breaking off the relationship and acts more outrageously when he or she finds out you are attempting to leave the relationship.

5. **'So Much, So Fast':** Your partner just met you and doesn't know much about you, but he or she has to have you, so you must commit now.

6. **'It's You That's the Problem':** Your partner never seems to consider his or her own part in your domestic disputes. You get blamed for all problems because of the most ridiculous things.

7. **'This Happened to Me and It's All Your Fault':** You are blamed for your partner's problems even when it was his or her responsibility to not make mistakes. This could be things like him or her not getting to work on time and getting in trouble, not getting a job, not paying the bills in a timely manner, etc.

8. **'It's Their Fault':** Your partner is never the cause of his own problems; if it's not your fault, it was somebody else's.

9. **'Overreacting':** Your partner overreacts to little irritations. Small offenses like leaving the cap off the toothpaste

cause him or her to have huge anger scenes or act out in an outrageous manner.

10. **'I Will Get You for That':** Your partner doesn't try to negotiate a better relationship, but retaliates by doing something to you that he or she knows will hurt you emotionally.

11. **'All the Fights are about What I Do Wrong':** You never seem to be able to talk about his or her wrong actions; the discussion always seems to be about what you did wrong, and there always seems to be something new that you did wrong.

12. **'You are Worthless':** Your partner keeps telling you that all your problems are because you can't manage to do anything right.

13. **'Unrealistic Expectations':** Your partner is dependent on you for all his/her needs and expects you to be the perfect mate, lover and friend. You are expected to meet all of his/her needs.

14. **'Blames Others for His/Her Feelings':** You are told, "You make me mad," "you're hurting me by not doing what I ask," or "I can't help being angry".

15. **'Intense Jealousy':** Your partner tells you that expressing jealousy is a sign of love. Jealousy is a sign of insecurity, not love. You are questioned about who you talk to and you may frequently receive calls or unexpected visits during the day.

16. **'Isolation':** He or she has attempted to cut off your family, friends, and independent financial resources. Your friends and family are put down, and you are put down for socializing with them. You or they are accused of ridiculous motives.

Abusive people have problems with handling anger. They try to control their environment with aggressive behavior, not assertive behavior.

Aggressive behavior is characterized by: Asserting his or her own rights at the expense of others; engaging in inappropriate outbursts or badly overreacts; intending to humiliate or to get even, to put down others; feeling superior to others; verbal behavior of interrupting, threats, uses name calling, demands, put-downs – in short, judgmental; and saving up anger and resentment and using them to justify later blowups.

Assertive behavior is characterized by: Standing up for legitimate rights in a way that does not violate rights of others; emotionally honest, direct, expressive; working to enhance self; confident, feeling good about him or herself now and later; verbal behavior of direct statements, "I" statements (I think, I feel, I want); speaking in cooperative terms (let's, how can we); statements of interest (what do you think?); valuing him or herself and others so that needs are met; and owning his or her own behavior.

Last, there are some numbers every woman and every teen should have:

The National Domestic Abuse Hotline:
1-800-799-SAFE or 1-800-799-3224 TTY

Coming in February 2007, there will be a teen dating abuse line. Verizon phone service offers a quick dial number **#HOPE — dial from any Verizon phone**.

National Domestic Abuse Hotline web site: http://www.ndvh.org/

Please enjoy our book and the stories within. And if you or anyone you know or even think is in a bad situation, get them the above numbers and give them the above list—but most of all, reach out, let them know they are not alone and not to blame.

S.R.Howen

References: Family Advocacy handout
"Learning to Live without Violence"
by Daniel Jay Sonkin Ph.D. and Michael Durphy, M.D.

The Forest for the Trees

by

Jenna Bayley-Burke

Rating: Sweet

Genre: Contemporary

Ryan jerked to a stop, his arm shooting out, keeping Brenda from barreling past him on the overgrown trail.

"We're lost." Her brown eyes widened with worry. She looked up, the wind moving the treetops. Little sun made it past the fragile spring leaves.

"I told you not to follow me." A flash of irritation showed in his bright blue eyes, and his handsome, wind roughened features twisted in annoyance.

He spun around, leaping over the decaying log that must have stopped him short. Old leaves crunched under his bare feet as he broke into a long stride, dodging boulders as he jostled down the shaded path.

Brenda followed. Her anger kept her warm in spite of the chill in the air. Only birds and animals disturbed the quiet of the forest, squawking away. Twigs snapped under her sneakers as she kept pace with him, a defiant clench to her jaw.

She'd been so excited to come here last year, a city girl finally camping. He'd laughed that she thought a cabin with indoor plumbing and cable was roughing it.

Today began harmlessly enough. Then she'd asked him an innocent question. Well, not so innocent, but after two years, she deserved to know where he saw their relationship going. And alone at his family cabin at Lake of the Woods seemed like the best place. No distractions, just an honest talk about their future.

"I'm not lost." Ryan's deep voice carried through the woods. "But you're ruining this."

"I'm ruining this?" She shouldn't have gone after him, she realized now. But she couldn't bear to see him go, now or ever. He always said he admired her feisty independence, but his support was what gave her the courage to be so brave. "Because I refuse to let you walk out of a very important conversation?"

"Exactly." A sloppy smile crossed his face.

Her answering grin was automatic. Brenda reminded herself she was angry and scared and a million other things that would keep her from being taken in by his charm. It didn't work, never did.

"I don't suppose you brought my keys?"

She shook her head, long brown hair rustling about her ears.

His keys? Ryan's truck was in the public lot by the campground. They'd left it there after meeting up, using her SUV to drive the two miles to the cabin.

Ryan extended a hand to her, and she took it, holding tight to his chilled fingers. Tugging her forward on the barely there path, she matched him step for step. Lights brightened around them as the forest thinned and the sun struck their faces. The screeching of the birds grew fainter when they approached a grassy knoll, overlooking the parking lot.

"We'll have to hurry to make it back before nightfall. Unless you brought a flashlight?"

"I didn't bring anything, Ryan. I followed right behind you."

He sighed deeply. They walked hand in hand over the grass towards the parking lot. "At least you put your shoes on."

She looked down at his feet, dirty and red from the cold. Why hadn't he slipped into shoes before bolting? Did the future really send him into such a cold panic he'd hike two miles in the woods without shoes?

"Close your eyes." Ryan squeezed her hand and stepped away, hoisting himself into the bed of his pickup truck. His fingers slowly worked the dial on the metal gearbox by the cab. "Please?"

With a huff, she did as he asked and wondered if it was so he could run away again. Maybe he kept a spare set of keys there. She tamped down the memory of hearing her father's car leave the house late one night. She never heard that precise roar of engine again. Tears burned her eyelids at the thought, and she opened her eyes so not to let them fall.

Ryan spun the dial of the lock and hopped out of the truck. A smile stretched from ear to ear. Sun glinted down on his blond hair, and he took her hand, pulling her back towards the forest.

"That's it?" she asked as the scent of the trees enveloped them, the sun at their backs. "You were walking to your truck?"

"What did you think I was doing?"

"Running away." She squeezed his hand tighter to keep him from doing just that.

"Ouch. Thanks for thinking so much of me."

"Can you blame me? You shot out of the cabin like a rocket and led us on a rambling tour of the woods."

15

"I told you not to follow me."

"I'm not letting you get away."

"I'm not going anywhere."

Relief flooded over her. Choosing their path carefully through the woods, they made it back to the cabin. Ryan retreated to the bathroom to wash up, and Brenda slipped out of her shoes, kneeling in front of the hearth. As he'd taught her, she arranged the kindling into a teepee over strips of paper and lit it with a long match.

"You've turned into quite the girl scout," Ryan said from behind her. He set the first log into the fireplace.

She smiled as he sat down, wanting to ask why he'd ran, what he'd taken from the truck, but not wanting him to flee again. "I'm a fast learner."

"I'm not. I'm sorry about that." Brenda raised an eyebrow, but his finger against her lips silenced her questions. "I thought you wanted the perfect story. I've been waiting a year for the right moment to spring this on you. I've planned it out twice, only to have some minor emergency derail my intentions. Even right now, I'm thinking this would be better with you sitting in a chair."

"What would be better?" The words were a puff of breath, her self-preservation barely reining in her hopes.

"Brenda, I've never been happier in my life. When you asked where I saw us going, I knew I'd found our moment. But idiot that I am, I left the ring in the truck. And stubborn woman that you are, you couldn't let me run down there to get it.

"I can't wait for another perfect moment, so I'm telling you now. In the future, I see you and I building a life, growing together until we are strong enough to be our own family."

From his pocket came a small black box, which he opened to reveal a diamond ring. She giggled with nervousness. Of course, he saw the same future she did; it had been that way for a while. She'd just been so lost in her own insecurities and keeping up in the game of life she'd missed the forest for the trees.

"Ryan Granger, we're getting married!"

His laughter rose to match hers as he slipped the ring on her finger.

Biography

Jenna Bayley-Burke soaked up a steady stream of romance novels as soon as she found them on her grandmother's bookshelf. Taken by the exotic locales (Minnesota) and interesting jobs (flight attendant), her world blossomed and dreams of happily every after outside the confines of her small town took root. Her first stories lacked emotion and depth, but most eight-year-olds don't get the concepts of motivation in literature. She tried on other careers, but realized she only wanted to write romance stories and read bedtime stories to her two blueberry-eyed baby boys.

Jenna is the author of JUST ONE SPARK (Mills & Boon, 2006) and COOKING UP A STORM (Mills & Boon, 2006). To see what is keeping Jenna busy now, check out www.jennabayleyburke.com

Song Without Words

by

Faith Bicknell-Brown

Rating: Sweet

Genre: Contemporary

The melody drifted through the home like pipe smoke. Nancy sat at the baby grand piano, her back straight, yet flexible, her shoulders squared to her body. Her head bobbed slightly as her hands glided over the piano keys. She ended the piece and sat quietly mulling over her next choice.

"What do you think Robert would prefer I play next?" Nancy asked the feline laying sprawled across the leather ottoman a few feet away. The cat blinked its gold eyes, trilling softly in response. "You're right as always, Euphoria." Nancy nodded, placing her hands on the appropriate keys. "I must keep my promise to Robert and play Tchaikovsky's *Song Without Words* every day."

The haunting notes floated through the sprawling Victorian home. Nancy's talent for the piano rivaled the most prestigious concert pianists of the world, but the only ears that heard Nancy play belonged to Euphoria, Nancy's housemaid Janine, and Bradley, Robert's brother. However, Robert was the one for whom she actually played.

Magic dwelled within every note produced by Nancy's fingers. The melodies instilled warmth on the coldest of days, healed weary hearts, and revived exhausted minds. *Song Without Words* undulated from room to room, melding with the scent of cinnamon-flavored coffee and ginger snaps that Janine prepared in the kitchen.

When the doorbell chimed, Nancy didn't hear it. She played for Robert, and until the melody ended, her heart remained with him.

"Mrs. Alexander."

Nancy continued to play, losing herself to the notes, her mind and music one entity.

"Mrs. Alexander."

The music ended. Nancy breathed deeply, then allowed the air to slip from her lungs slowly, delicately, as if the song's conclusion caused her great pain.

"*Mrs. Alexander.*"

Startled, Nancy looked up. "Janine! How long have you been there?"

The matronly woman regarded Nancy with concern. "Long enough that I listened to the last minute or so of *his* song."

Janine slung a dishtowel over one shoulder, then stuffed her hands into her apron pockets. "Your brother-in-law is waiting in the foyer. Shall I let him in?"

Nancy grimaced, her gaze locking briefly with Janine's. Sighing, she nodded.

"Here we go again, eh, Euphoria?" Nancy leaned over, rubbing the orange tabby's neck. The cat purred thunderously in response. "I'm not up to this tonight. He knows how he makes me feel, but he's my brother-in-law for God's sake."

Behind her, a man politely cleared his throat. Nancy turned, offering him a wan smile.

Bradley Alexander stood tall and proud in the doorway. His assessing gray gaze slipped over Nancy sitting at the piano. "Do you ever do anything else except play piano in your free time?"

"No."

"Are you angry with me?"

"No."

He chuckled. "Would you like for me to leave?"

"Now you're starting to pique my interest."

Bradley's chuckle transformed into deep laughter. He slipped out of his suit jacket, tossing it across the back of a leather loveseat. "Your talent for piano is nearly surpassed by your sarcasm."

"Coming from you, I'll take that as a compliment." Nancy gathered up the sheet music scattered on the carpet like wind-blown leaves. "What do you want, Bradley?"

"You know what I want."

"The answer is still no."

"Why?" His question didn't come out as a whine or a plea, but acute curiosity.

"Do you want me to answer that question honestly?" She turned, facing him, unconsciously straightening the music she still clutched in her hands.

"That would be nice," he said, still amused. Mischief danced in his eyes, and Nancy hated him for it. His mischievous nature was one of the things that drew her to Bradley—and reminded her of her husband.

"You are a pain in the ass, Bradley. Plain and simple."

"So?"

With an exasperated sigh, Nancy tossed the sheet music inside the piano bench. Closing it, she sat down hard as if her legs had given out. "Look, we've known one another since I met your brother. Robert has been dead for nine years now. I play for no one except him. I have no intention of recording my music nor traveling abroad giving piano concerts. My music is for Robert alone." She stood up and walked to the heavily draped window. Gazing through the part in the curtains, her mind didn't register the rolling, snow-covered field behind the house. "You're not going to change my mind."

"Damn it, Nancy! Robert is dead!" His footsteps traveled across the carpet, and then one warm hand grasped her shoulder. He turned her around, forcing her to look at him. "You know this has nothing to do with your music. It's time to move on with your life."

"You're wrong," she said tersely. "I promised Robert I would play his favorite songs so he could hear them wherever he traveled to after he succumbed to that damn cancer!" She sucked in a deep breath, reigning in her emotions. "I'm keeping my promise."

"You have, Nancy." Robert's gray gaze locked with hers. "Don't you think my brother would want you to be happy?"

"And what makes you think *you* can make me happy?" Pulling away from him, she saw Janine standing in the doorway with a serving tray. "Set the tray on the table by the window, please." She glanced at Bradley and motioned toward the two wing-backed chairs on the other side of the room.

The glass top table mirrored the serving set placed in its center. As Nancy seated herself, it occurred to her that she was merely a mirror image of the woman she had been when Robert was alive. Would Robert mind if she succumbed to his brother's touch?

When Janine left the room, Bradley leaned back in his chair with a pastry in one hand, watching Nancy pour the coffee. "I suppose you still believe that Robert will send you a song without words."

"Why not?" She glanced across the table at her brother-in-law. "Anything is possible."

"He's dead, Nancy."

"So you keep reminding me."

Bradley sighed and reached for his cup. "It's as if you expect my brother to come knocking on the front door one day and hand you sheet music for that damn *Song Without Words* he spoke of before he died." He accepted his cup and saucer from her, promptly dropping two sugar cubes into the dark liquid. "It doesn't work that way, Nancy. My brother's promise was the ramblings of a man in pain, teetering on the precipice of death."

"Bradley, please shut up."

Pausing, he met the pain and anger of her icy gaze. "Forgive me. You could only understand if you saw yourself through someone else's eyes."

"And you would only understand if you walked around in my body with its heart ripped out, knowing there is nothing that will ever relieve the pain."

"Let me take away your pain."

Nancy raised her cup to her trembling lips. It would be so easy. The attraction between them had been there even while Robert was alive. Finally composing herself, she leaned back in her seat.

"Let's change the subject," Bradley suggested.

"Best idea you've had since arriving."

He grinned. "How about allowing me to take you out to dinner tomorrow evening?"

"I don't think that's a good idea." Nancy patted a curl back into her upswept hair, deliberately avoiding his eyes.

"Oh, that's right. You wouldn't want to miss playing the piano for my dead brother." Bradley stood, placing his cup back on the serving tray. "Have a nice evening *alone*."

"You bastard!" she shouted, snatching the creamer and hurling it at him.

He dodged the porcelain. The creamer exploded against the doorframe. Milk splashed across the wall, floor, and upon a lamp and its stand. The startled cat leaped to the floor. Hissing, Euphoria disappeared into the hall.

A smirk cavorted upon Bradley's lips. "Your aim is as good as your excuses."

"OUT!"

"Out of this house, or out of your life?"

They stood facing one another, two people denied what they desired, armed with barbed dialect and fueled with hostility.

"Take your pick," Nancy said quietly, a note of agony in her voice.

Bradley turned, walking down the hall. Faintly, the door clicked shut in the foyer.

As always, Nancy sought solace at the piano. Sobbing, she played for several minutes, pausing only long enough to wipe her nose with the hanky she pulled from her skirt pocket. *Für Elise* slipped through the home followed by *Moonlight Sonata*. Janine entered the music room, and quietly cleaned up the mess of creamer and shattered porcelain while Nancy hammered out *Bagatelle* with vengeance.

Melodies and dirges consumed the big house throughout the remaining late afternoon and into the evening. When a brief lull occurred, Janine poked her head into the room.

"How does baked lemon chicken sound for supper this evening?" Janine asked.

Nancy didn't turn around. She placed her fingers on the keys in preparation for Robert's melody. "That's fine, Janine."

A third of the way through *Song Without Words*, Nancy's fingers faltered. Stunned, she stopped and began again. Her fingers stumbled in the same place, striking the wrong key. Several unsuccessful attempts to finish the song resulted in a fresh round of tears.

Exasperated, she sat sobbing softly, her fingers poking the occasional key. A new sound grew from the exploration of her fingertips. Mystified, she flipped over a photocopied piece of sheet music and began writing the experimental notes on the back.

She remembered meeting Robert at a flower shop. He had been buying roses for his mother's birthday, but after a brief conversation with one another, he had her phone number, and then handed her the roses instead. Their first date had been at a coffee shop where she had bumped the table, dumping a scalding cup of cappuccino into Robert's lap. Nancy smiled at the thought of him jumping up and down.

Nancy quickly jotted down a few upbeat music notes on the paper. Pausing, she recalled how three months later, their wedding had been small and simple, spending their honeymoon in Maine in autumn. Scrawling more notes, she mused about their walks through the field behind their home during heavy snowfalls. Every summer she had collected wildflowers in the tall grass, and Robert had braided them into colorful chaplets for her hair.

Then, she recalled how their good doctor friend had told them Robert had cancer. The disease had taken Robert quickly. Before he sighed his last breath, Robert told her he would give her a new song one day, but until then, he asked if she would play *Song Without Words* often and think of him.

Sobbing uncontrollably, the empty spot in her chest aching as if afire, Nancy wrote long expanses of music through a haze of tears. She used her handkerchief once more, gulping down her grief, wishing his brother's arms could comfort her.

With trembling hands, she set the crude sheet music in front of her. Slowly, Nancy began playing what she had composed, then the pace quickened, her fingers and inner senses growing more sure of the notes. The slow, mournful parts soughed through the piano room and into the big, empty house.

As Nancy worked, she stopped several times, erasing notes, replacing them with changes, her fingers playing and re-playing. She never heard Janine announce that her supper was ready or hear her place it on the coffee table behind her.

As the evening waxed later, an urgency to complete the music replaced the ache in Nancy's heart. She played the song one last time, listening for inconsistencies. As she keyed through the mournful section, her soul returned to her, lightening her fingers, adding another section of rebirth to the crudely written sheet music.

Shocked and excited, Nancy scribbled furiously. She dropped the pencil and began playing in earnest, the piano shouting happiness into the house followed by sorrow, then salutations of life and healing.

Her hands fell into her lap as she listened to the last notes echo throughout her home. The scrawled sheet music in front of her told about her life with Robert. Now Robert had a new song, but this song had words her heart could hear. He had known. How, she didn't know. Although she had loved Robert and had never been unfaithful to him with Bradley or any other man, she'd always felt guilty for the attraction she felt towards his younger brother. It was time to move on, and she knew without a doubt that Robert wanted her to follow her heart.

When she turned around, Bradley stood in the doorway.

"What are you doing here?" she asked, her heart leaping at the sight of him in his tailored jeans and rugged button-up shirt.

"I don't know." He stepped into the room, his hungry gaze meeting hers. "I was compelled to come here, as if someone were telling me to get into my car and drive over here to see you."

Standing, she waited for him to reach her. Nancy looked up at him, hoping he saw the message in her eyes. She offered him her heart and her body.

Bradley cupped her cheek, his other hand drifting to the opening of her blouse, one finger tracing the swell of her breast. "What changed your mind?"

"Robert's song."

He lowered his head, capturing her lips. When he released her, he said, "I want you, Nancy. I've waited a long time to have you body and soul."

Fire flamed throughout Nancy's body. An intense need built in her loins. All she could think about was lying naked against Bradley as he thrust deeply between her legs.

"I'm all yours," she replied, her breath ragged.

"No regrets?" he asked, his eyes deepening with desire.

"Not a single one." She placed her hand into his and followed Bradley upstairs.

Biography

Faith Bicknell-Brown's work has appeared in a wide range of genres such as: *Would That It Were, Touch Magazine, GC Magazine, Ohio Writer Magazine* (non-fiction), *Waxing and Waning* (Canada), and The Istanbul Literature Review (Turkey) just to name a few. She was a regular contributor to *Gent* under her pseudonym, Molly Diamond. She has also had fiction published in *Hustler's Busty Beauties, Penthouse Variations, Twenty 1 Lashes,* and has become a regular contributor to *Ruthie's Club*. Faith's first erotic eBook, WOMAN OF UNKNOWN ORIGINS, debuted with Freya's Bower.com in March 2006.

For two years, Faith served as the co-editor of *The Tenacity Times*. In October 2001, she took the position of romance and horror editor for *Wild Child Publishing* and now serves as the managing editor. In 1980, she represented Switzerland of Ohio at the *Young Writer's Conference* held at Athens University.

Life in the Appalachians as a minister's daughter serves as Faith's inspiration for nearly all of her fictional work. She resides with her husband, four children, a chocolate Labrador, and a cat named Chloe on a 123-acre farm just outside the small rural Appalachian town of Beallsville, Ohio.

Love @ First Site

by

Amanda Brice

Rating: Sweet

Genre: Chick Lit

That's it. I'm done with dating.

Yeah, I know I've said that before, but this time I mean it. Really. I've completely had it with men. Arrogant assholes, all of them.

I knew my most recent announcement would give my mother *agita*, but I didn't care. The second I graduated from college, Linda Antonelli began parading an endless stream of friends' sons and friends of sons' friends in front of me. For the past seven years, I've had to endure her endless passive-aggressive symphonies about how nice it would be to have a grandchild before she died. I'd even resorted to making up a fake fiancé to get her off my back, but she caught me in that lie. I swear, the woman is omniscient. I bought myself a ring and everything, but she caught on.

Damn her.

I mean sure, I wanted to get married. Eventually. I mean, who doesn't want free Cuisinart and china? But being the poster girl for the "Workaholic of the Year" award wasn't exactly consistent with meeting the types of men you'd be proud to take home to Mom, if you know what I mean. And because leaving my love life to fate wasn't working, about six months ago, I signed up with an online dating service.

Big mistake. Huge. Enormous.

I wasted a good half year of my precious time going on countless dates with the various men I'd met on the website. Doctors, lawyers, teachers, Congressional aides, police officers, salesmen, engineers, lobbyists, and even an artist. Some looked liked they'd walked right off the cover of a romance novel. Others probably had some pretty heavy duty Photoshop work done on their pictures. Some I went out with more than once. With others, one date was one too many.

Unfortunately, a very large percentage of them fell into that last category.

Was there a single decent guy left in D.C.? Sadly, given its reputation as the city of phallic monuments and dirty politicians, I had my doubts.

Last night was the worst. Hindsight may be 20/20, but my foresight was in desperate need of a visit to the optometrist.

You'd think by now I could spot a loser from a mile away. And you'd certainly think that I'd know to avoid certain professions.

Apparently I'm a slow learner because I agreed to go out with yet another guy from DCDating.com. It started out promising, but doesn't everything?

Thinking back to that train wreck of a date, I checked the clock on my computer screen. Seven-forty-five. Sweet – it was early! I couldn't remember the last time I'd left before eight. It had to be weeks, months even.

I closed my Microsoft Word document and left the office, looking forward to another night at home utterly alone. Alone, but not lonely, mind you – I'd penciled into my schedule a bubble bath with a steamy paperback, a glass of merlot, and a box of gourmet chocolates.

Really, who needed a man?

I'd just passed the homeless man who specialized in an out-of-tune trumpet rendition of "When the Saints Go Marching In" (for some reason, he was playing "America the Beautiful" today – go figure) when my cell phone rang. I dug it out of my purse and peered at the screen.

Dave?

"Hey, what's up?" I asked.

"Jules, you have to meet me at The Big Hunt."

I sidestepped to avoid being run over by the crush of tourists coming up the escalator on the wrong side. "No can do."

"You have a hot date or something?"

We both laughed at that idea. "Oh yeah, and it's a kinky one," I said.

"Did I hear that right? Julie Antonelli, the celibate queen, kinky?"

"With Ghirardelli and Robert Mondavi." I waggled my eyebrows suggestively, even though he couldn't see me. "It's a threesome."

I could hear him sigh on the other end of the line. "It's Friday night."

"Your point?"

"Okay, not Big Hunt. How does Tryst sound?"

"You propositioning me?" I joked, knowing full well that Tryst was the name of a popular nearby coffee house.

"Uh—"

"Kidding!" I switched the phone to my other ear while I pulled my Metro card out of my wallet. "See you in twenty minutes?"

* * *

My best friend peered over the top of his steaming mug. "So, how's that online dating thing going? Meet anyone good?"

I sat down at the table and motioned for the server to bring me the usual – a double mocha skim latté with three shots of raspberry syrup. "Quite to the contrary. All men are jerks."

"Present company excluded, I hope."

"Of course."

The latté arrived in record time. I lifted the mug to my lips and sipped deeply. Mmm... Seriously, who needed a man when you had something as exquisite as this? Okay, so it wasn't Ghirardelli, but it was pretty darn close. Awash in the heavenly aroma, I looked up and saw that Dave was staring at me intently. Putting down the mug with a sigh, I braced for the inevitable interrogation.

Dave didn't disappoint.

"So, what happened this time?"

I began ticking off the stats on my perfectly manicured fingers. "Derek Michaels, screenname Barrister. Never married. First in his class at Harvard Law. Partner at Cohen, Kelly. Has a condo in town, a house on the Bay, a yacht, and a German Shepherd."

"So what's the problem?"

"Loves himself." I sighed. "A lot."

Dave took a bite of his panini. "I thought you guys really hit it off over e-mail."

"I thought so, too. It was great until we met in person."

"So who's next on the list?"

I stirred my drink, letting the steam condense on my hand. "Nobody. I'm off men. So done with this whole dating thing."

"For good?"

I nodded. "Absolutely. So, any news on the romantic front for you?"

Dave shifted in his seat. "Uh..."

"What about that cute Anna?" I took another sip of latté. "The one you met at the gym?"

Dave shrugged. "What about her?"

"Are you gonna ask her out?" I asked.

"Nah," he replied.

"Why not?"

Dave pushed his sandwich to the edge of his plate and swallowed the last drop of coffee before he answered. "I don't know. Just not interested."

"You done with dating, too?"

"No. I'm just not interested in her," he replied.

I smiled. "So there's someone else..."

Dave's brow furrowed. "I thought we were here to discuss you."

"I wasn't aware that was the point of tonight. I thought we were here to hang out and enjoy each other's company."

"Julie..."

"There's nothing to discuss." I laughed. "I'm done with dating, remember?"

"Please," Dave said. "You know you're not. Isn't there anyone else?"

There was.

Okay, so I lied when I said that all guys were assholes. Other than Dave, who was really more like a brother than a guy, I could think of at least one decent one. I've been e-mailing for two months with someone who called himself NiceGuysFinishLast. Unlike the other men I'd met on the website, NiceGuy only e-mailed and never actually suggested that we meet.

But that was fine. I found that whenever I actually met one of these guys in person, it all went downhill. The charming gentleman from the lovely e-mails morphed into an arrogant, self-centered cretin with no personality. It was better to just keep it from getting to that point. I was fine with faceless, impersonal flirting. I couldn't get hurt that way.

Nothing to ruin the fantasy. And boy, was my imagination fertile.

But if I was completely honest with myself, I'd have to admit that I was beginning to really like NiceGuy. Never before had I met someone with whom I got along so well, so quickly. Our "conversations" were so easy. I woke up every morning hoping I'd find a new message from him. Reading his e-mails always put a smile on my face and could brighten even the worst day.

Thinking about it now, I realized that I'd developed feelings for NiceGuy. It was totally nuts, I know, because we'd never met. But the connection we shared was deeper than most other relationships. We actually got to know one another, and from what I'd seen, I really liked him. But there was no way I was going to admit that.

Especially not to Dave.

The waitress came over to refill Dave's coffee. Thank God for distractions.

But Dave wasn't distracted. "So, *is* there anyone?"

I coughed heavily to clear my throat. "Anyone who?"

Dave laughed. "Anyone else on the dating site. I think your reaction just gave you away."

I sighed. He wasn't going to let up, was he?

"Well, there *is* this *one* guy," I began.

"Spill it."

I took the last remaining sip of my latté. Pity. "There's nothing to tell. He's just a guy I've been e-mailing."

"What's his name?"

"No idea. I only know his screenname, NiceGuysFinishLast."

"Ain't that the truth?"

"I already told you, I'll happily set you up with Shonda from my office—"

"Stop changing the subject, Julie."

I swear, the guy was so attuned to my feelings that he made a better girlfriend than my girlfriends. "Why do you care?"

Dave's deep blue eyes were pools of concern. "I don't care about him, Julie. I care about you. You deserve to be with someone great."

Dave was such a good friend. We'd known each other since sixth grade. Almost twenty years later, and through countless significant others, he was still my favorite confidant. I often wondered how a great guy like Dave could still be single. It gave me hope that maybe not all the good ones were taken.

"Thanks. That's sweet, but really, I'm fine," I said.

"But isn't there anyone you're interested in?"

I laughed. "Nope. I don't need a boyfriend." I reached out and touched his hand rather dramatically. "I've got you."

Dave pulled away and gulped down his coffee. "So, tell me about NiceGuy."

I paused. "I don't know what to tell you. He's just like his name – a nice guy."

"Do you like him?" Dave stared intently, his eyes boring into me, making me slightly uncomfortable, but in a good way.

I shifted, trying to break eye contact, although I couldn't. "I don't know. I guess. But it's not worth pursuing."

"Why not?"

"Because every guy I've ever met on there turned out to be a jerk and I don't want that to happen with him. I want to keep the fantasy intact."

"But you haven't even met him yet."

I sighed. "What's the use? He'll just turn out like the rest of them."

Dave reached across the table and placed his hand on my arm. Shivers of pleasure went up my spine at the connection. *What's that about? Dave's my friend.*

"I just want you to be happy," he said, leaning in so that I could feel his breath warm on my nose.

I smiled. "I am."

"Why don't you go out with him?" Dave asked, his eyes still locked with mine.

I turned away to break their gaze. "Because I'm done with online dating. It's not worth it."

"But didn't you just say you thought you'd made a great connection with him?" Dave pressed.

I could feel a hot flush spreading over my cheeks. "Did I say that?"

"You said you liked him. Don't you owe it to yourself to at least try? If it doesn't work out, you can just cancel your membership with that site."

"I don't know..."

"Go out with him, Jules."

I turned away. "He hasn't even asked me."

"But if he did, would you?"

I smiled, thinking back to our e-mail conversations, and the way he made me feel. "Yeah, I would."

Dave's midnight blue eyes danced with excitement. "That's all I needed to hear."

He drew me in for a long passionate kiss, his arms holding me tight, sending my senses reeling. I've been kissed many, many times, but never before like this. Every inch of my body was on fire, like molten lava bubbling to the surface.

Normally, I'm not one for PDA, but for some reason, I completely drowned out the noisy coffee house and just focused on him. I felt the kiss in every extremity, from the hairs on my head to the tips of my toes, if that's possible.

Finally, he sat back, tenderly brushed a curl away from my face, and said, "Julie Antonelli, would you go to dinner with me?"

Biography

Amanda Brice lives just outside the nation's capital. She is the author of SHE'S GOT LEGS, a 2006 release from Freya's Bower. When not writing fiction, Amanda is an intellectual property attorney and divides her free time between dancing, cooking, traveling, and an unnatural obsession with Duke Basketball. You can keep up with Amanda at her website: www.amandabrice.com, or her blog: www.amandabrice.blogspot.com.

The Christmas Prize

by

Sela Carsen

Rating: Sweet

Genre: Contemporary

Julie Corrigan stood on the rickety stage, staring out at the crowd of strangers and her throat locked. Completely. Forget singing, she couldn't even breathe.

Greg's voice in her head drowned out the sound of holiday shoppers at the mall.

"Julie, stop singing! You're making my head hurt."

"Good grief, woman. Quit that yelling and finish making supper."

"Could you just, for once, shut up?"

The center court was packed with people passing through, frantic to pick up that last present on the night before Christmas Eve. The night of the Kristmas Karaoke Kompetition sponsored by WLBJ radio in Columbus, Ohio.

Greg was long gone, along with most of her self-confidence, but Julie's knees nearly buckled as the memory of his slashing remarks rushed back to her.

"Are you ready?" Another voice cut in, business like and indifferent.

She nodded, forcing breath past the block in her throat, feeling the air flow from her diaphragm. The quiet notes of the piano began from the speaker beside her and she sang.

O Holy Night, The stars are brightly shining...

The music filled her, reverberating through her body before she sent her voice out to the crowd, floating over the noise of commerce. People stopped to watch and listen. She finished the song and the last, lingering note fell into silence. Peace. Good will toward men.

An old man near the back of the gathering began to clap and others joined in. Julie flushed hot, then cold, then hot again as the sound registered. They were clapping for her.

She whispered "Thank you" into the microphone, then stepped aside for the next singer. She couldn't sit down yet – couldn't bear to listen to the others, certain their talent surpassed her pathetic attempt.

The Christmas decorations looked brighter now, people seemed friendlier. Even if other contestants were more talented, she knew she had done well. A woman with two babies in a stroller stopped her with a hand on her arm.

"Thank you. That was beautiful," she said before moving off to finish her shopping.

Julie stood rooted to the spot. She couldn't remember the last time anyone had said anything so nice to her. Tears burned her eyes and nose and she sniffled, patting her jeans pockets for a tissue she knew she didn't have.

One appeared before her and she took it, blotting at her mascara before it ran and trying to blow her nose without sounding like a startled goose.

"Thank you," she said, tossing the tissue into a nearby waste bin. Julie looked around at her rescuer and, for the second time that night, was struck dumb.

Tall and handsome, he seemed like something out of a fairy tale or a romance novel. But fairy tales princes and romance novels heroes never noticed women like her.

"You're welcome," he answered. "I heard you sing. It was wonderful."

Julie's mouth opened, but nothing came out. This was worse than singing. "I..."

He smiled at her, unphased by her sudden descent into muteness.

"That's one of my favorite songs."

"Mine too." Finally, she could talk. Not that she sounded that bright, but at least they were words.

"My name is Mark Kincaid."

"Julie Corrigan." She stuck out her hand and his warm palm engulfed hers for a moment.

"Sorry," she said. "My hands are cold."

"No problem. You know what they say – *Cold hands, warm heart.*"

They smiled at each other, and she felt a little steadier.

"Out getting some last minute shopping done?" she asked, unable to think of anything brilliant.

"Yeah." He held up a bag from a gourmet cooking shop. "It's for my sister-in-law. I couldn't decide what to get her and she's a foodie, so I figured I couldn't go wrong."

"Good choice, then."

An awkward silence descended. Julie didn't know what else to say. She wanted to stay and talk with this dream guy, but he was so out of her league, she didn't want to embarrass herself.

Greg's memory intruded again. "*I could have done better than you.*"

Julie straightened her spine. No, he couldn't. He didn't. The pre-nup he'd made her sign had come back to bite him on the backside when he left her for another woman, incriminating himself under the adultery clause. Julie had sold the house – all hers now – and the useless roadster he'd bought so she would fit into his image, then used the money to start fresh in a new town.

She had a new job, a new condo, and she was finally starting to live again. If only she could summon the courage to talk.

"I think they're about to announce the winners now," he said, breaking in on her thoughts.

"Hmm? Oh!" Julie turned back to the stage, feeling the stranger's warmth at her side.

Third place went to a seven year old girl who had sung "All I Want for Christmas Is My Two Front Teeth." The gap in her own dental work was obvious when she picked up her prize.

A guy dressed as Elvis won second place for singing "Blue Christmas." Julie was frozen. She'd either won first or not placed at all.

Greg's voice boomed loud in her head. "*You're useless, Julie. I'm leaving. At least I won't have to listen to you squawk anymore.*"

She'd lost. She just knew it. The failures of the past swamped her, and she swayed on her feet before she felt a warm touch at her elbow. Julie looked up at Mark.

His mouth was moving, but she couldn't hear him while fear and shame pounded a tattoo in her brain. She shook her head.

"What?"

He spoke again, then her ears popped. Noise rushed in with one word.

"Won."

"One what?"

"No, Julie. Not 'one.' Won. You won."

Mark grinned at her before he leaned down and placed an impulsive, celebratory kiss on her cheek.

Her fingers flew to her face, and a smile grew.

"I won? I won!"

"Can I get the winner a cup of coffee after you're done here?"

A new life really was starting for her. And the prize that waited for her on the stage, the symbol of her victory over the past, took second place in her mind to a kiss on the cheek and a cup of coffee.

"Yes, I'd love that."

Biography

Sela Carsen was born in Houston, Texas, but as the daughter of an oil company engineer and then an Air Force wife, she's lived all over the world. She has a bachelor's degree in French and another in Communication. She has worked as a tutor, a reporter, a magazine writer, at an advertising agency, and met her husband while working at an airline ticket counter. Her first novella, a paranormal romantic comedy entitled NOT QUITE DEAD, was released by Samhain Publishing in August 2006.

Romance For One

by

Rachelle Chase

Rating: Spicy

Genre: Chick Lit

Mary fiddled with her wine glass. As her fingertips circled the lip of the glass, her gaze traveled around the room, resting briefly on the occupants at the other tables, before moving on to the couples slow-dancing on the dance floor. Bodies swayed, pressed close together – chest to breast, cock to pussy.

Hips gyrated, hands stroked, lips touched.

Need coiled in Mary's stomach. Why had she stopped by Giddeon's on the busiest night of the week? To prove to herself that she was over Scott? That she could sit in their favorite restaurant – at their old table – and not feel an inkling of remorse or nostalgia? Well, to that end, she had succeeded. Not once had she yearned for Scott. Instead, desire was winding its way through her body, circulating longing for the next man – the one who had not yet made his appearance in her life

So what *was* she doing here?

Being silly, *that's* what she was doing here. Desire and longing for the next man, indeed. Mary shook her head in disgust and yanked her gaze from the couple with moves straight from *Dirty Dancing*, looking for her waiter, instead.

Ah, there he was, a couple tables away from her, setting a plate of fried plantains with sour cream in front of the man—

Mary's breath stuttered in her chest, jolting her desire up a notch and sparking heat in her stomach – as her gaze zoomed in on the man.

Charcoal black hair glittered under the soft light, perfectly complimenting his bronze skin. Long black lashes framed his chocolate brown eyes. Faint lines appeared at the corner of his eyes when he smiled. Brilliant white teeth dazzled below his neatly trimmed mustache. And those lips – they looked...Full. Soft. Moist. Kissable.

He tipped his head back and laughed.

Mary leaned forward and stared. Heat spilled from her stomach, swirling downward, over her lower abdomen to her inner thighs, moving inward...

His companion smiled faintly and raised a spoonful of mousse to her lips. Her gaze appeared slightly bored. How could any woman look into those smoky eyes from across a table and not feel the lust that percolated in Mary's veins from across the room? If Mary were his date, the sensation buzzing through her body, causing her to press her legs tightly together, would put a sparkle in her eyes that would blind her fellow diners.

Mary stopped fiddling with her wine glass long enough to take a sip. Her hand trembled. As the ruby red liquid slid down her throat, the longing that she'd shrugged off in disgust slithered through her body, flooding her mind with images of *her* as the man's dinner date...

* * *

The rumble of his laugh stroked her ear, sending waves of desire roiling through her. Though his eyes crinkled with amusement, his gaze was unwavering, burning with an intensity that belied his humor. He seemed to see what was going on inside her.

Mary shifted in her seat, suddenly hot. "What's so funny?" *She hoped her smile looked natural, that the passion building within her was masked.*

"You."

She grimaced. Funny was not the way she wanted him to find her.

Still smiling, he gestured toward her fingers tracing the rim of the wine glass. "Do I make you nervous?"

Oh. That is what he finds funny.

She dropped her hand to the table, resisting the urge to fiddle with her silverware. "A little."

"Why?"

"Because I haven't done...this in awhile."

He raised a thick, naturally arched, brow. "This? Had dinner?"

No, not dinner. It's been awhile since I've really wanted a man.

But Mary didn't say that. While thinking of her answer, her gaze drifted to the table. This time, he was the one toying with his glass. Only the long, lean fingers circling the base of the flute seemed to caress, toying with her *instead of the crystal.*

44

She imagined his fingers drawing circles on her flesh as they moved up and over her ribcage, grazing the swell of a breast, before dipping into the valley separating them. His strokes were feather-light, causing her skin to prickle, to crave a deeper caress and yearn for his touch on her nipple. To rub and pinch.

Mary blinked.

The feel of his hands on her disappeared, yet the tingling in her body, the moisture that dampened her panties, remained. She watched his fingers move slowly up the stem of the glass and back down. That made her imagine his hands on his flesh, stroking his cock, making it lengthen and thicken before her eyes, driving more wetness between her legs as she imagined him there, as she—

"Are you going to answer the question?"

Once again, her attention was jerked from her fantasies. "Um...yes, of course...uh, it's been awhile since I've been on a date.

"Hmmm." His lips quirked, as if he knew she was not being honest. He leaned forward, resting his elbows on the table and forming a steeple with his hands.

Mary watched, mesmerized, as his fingertips rested against his chin before moving upward and stopping at his lips, which were pursed in thought.

She wanted to trade places with his fingers, wanted to lean across the table and feel her lips pressed against his, wanted to take his lower lip in her mouth and suckle lightly, before releasing it and outlining his lower lip with her tongue, stopping to plant a soft kiss. His lips would press forward, seeking more than her whisper of a kiss. She would pull back and resume her exploration with her tongue, tracing his upper lip—

He interrupted Mary's imaginary kiss as he moved his fingers down, where they stopped at the underside of his chin.

His lips moved, no longer pursed, which sent Mary's thoughts back to her kiss. She imagined his mouth moving under hers as she captured his lips, no longer nibbling, no longer teasing, instead giving in to his need for more, slipping her tongue inside his mouth, tasting the wine he'd sipped mingled with the heat of his desire for her—

"...better?"

She blinked, instantly realizing that his lips were moving because he was talking. I really must pay attention. *Her face burned as she lifted her gaze to his.*

His eyes burned with awareness, as if he knew what she had been imagining, as if he had been an active participant in her mind.

"Excuse me?" Her voice was shaky.

"Can I do anything to make you feel better?" His voice was a husky purr, confirming the sexy thoughts she'd imagined she saw reflected in his eyes.

She could think of a hundred things he could do to make her feel better, beginning with the kiss she had imagined and moving to the hands caressing her skin in places she had not yet imagined – her neck, her back, her sides, before moving to her hips—

Mary stopped the direction of her thoughts, for they fanned the fire that was spreading through her body, scrambling her words, and making simple sentences difficult. Her gaze moved from him, seeking to focus her thoughts on his words, and landed on the dance floor that had started the longing within her. She had her answer, though it would turn the fire burning within her into a blaze.

Her gaze darted back to him and she smiled. "Yes. You can dance with me."

He smiled back. She thought he said, my pleasure, *but she wasn't sure, for she was once again mesmerized by his lips, which had parted – yet again – into a smile that dazzled. She liked his smile, almost as much as his imaginary kiss, for it affected her the same way, sending a jolt through her body that made her want him.*

To make love.

To have sex.

To fuck.

She'd take any or all of the three.

She stood on shaky legs and he took her hand. This first touch sent a bolt of lust up her arm, where it zipped over her shoulders, to her breasts. Her nipples tingled, straining to press against his back, as he led her onto the dance floor.

Miraculously, she managed to make it through the crowd without stumbling. He stopped, turning toward her just as the band began to play Steve Cole's Stay Awhile. *It was the perfect title, since that was exactly what Mary wanted to do.*

His hands circled her waist.

She rested her hands on his shoulders.

"Better?" he asked, his breath rustling her hair and warming her ear.

She shivered. The fire within her raged. "Yes," she whispered. Because she was better. Lust had overwhelmed her nervousness.

"Good." He pulled her closer. Her breasts brushed his chest.

She inhaled sharply.

His hands slipped to her back, caressing upward, then back down. His leg dipped between hers, brushing against her thigh, breaking the thin thread that she'd been clinging to – the thread that held her resistance in place.

She wound her hands around his neck, tangling her fingers into the silky strands of hair at the nape of his neck, while pressing her body against his. Her breasts rubbed against his chest, giving her nipples a taste of the touch they craved. Her hips moved lightly against his, teasing her pussy with what she wanted to feel inside her.

His cock was hard against her.

Her pussy lips throbbed.

He groaned softly.

She exhaled loudly.

Their bodies continued to move together, but now, Steve Cole was forgotten. Instead, they moved to their own music, created by the heat arcing between them, pulling them even closer.

Mary no longer wanted to Stay Awhile.

"I don't either," he said in her ear.

Shudders rippled through her body. Excitement surged through her blood. Had she spoken the words out loud?

"I want to feel you naked against me," he said.

His hand slipped underneath the waistband at the back of her skirt.

"I want to hold you..." His fingertips grazed the top of her ass cheek. "...and pull you close, burying my cock inside you..."

Mary gasped. Her pussy twitched, wanting what his words promised.

"...and I want to taste you..." his tongue flicked lightly against her ear, before swirling down her neck – pressing against spots that sent jangles of sensation straight to her pussy – mixing licks with a trail of light kisses.

Mary moaned, stumbling.

His hands on her tightened, keeping her upright, pressing her closer against him

"Do you want to leave now?" His voice was hoarse.

"Oh yes." Her voice cracked. She so wanted to feel what his words – and his actions – created. She wanted the lips now kissing her lower neck to suckle her breasts. The hair threaded between her fingers to caress her breasts, instead. Their clothed bodies, unclothed, naked. His hands gripping her ass, squeezing, guiding. His cock—

* * *

"Excuse me."

Mary jumped, her attention jerked from the image of sex playing out in her mind to the waiter standing in front of her.

With a polite smile, he removed a glass of wine from his tray and set it in front of her. "This is from the gentleman at table four." He turned slightly, motioning to a table behind him.

Mary followed the direction of his hand with her eyes. The man from her fantasy quirked his lips, just as he'd done in her mind, and tilted his head in greeting.

Her face grew hot. *Oh my God.* Had she been staring at him all this time? And even worse, had her face revealed the nature of her thoughts? Before she jerked her gaze away, she noticed he was alone at the table

"He also said to give you this," the waiter continued, placing a card in front of the wine glass. With a parting smile, he walked away.

Mary glanced at the card. It was a business card with the name "Bryan Andrews" in bold lettering. She looked up from the card at him – Bryan – again.

Still smiling, he held up a card of his own and rotated his hand vertically.

Face still flaming, she looked down and mimicked his gesture, turning the card over.

> *"My sister says I'd be a fool to let you leave*
> *without a word. May I join you? Smile for*
> *"yes"; stick out your tongue for "no."*
> **Bryan**

Without thinking, she laughed at the image of her "saying" no. She could not imagine sticking her tongue out at him, though she *could* imagine running her tongue along his body, tasting the naked flesh she'd just fantasized about – lips, chest, stomach...cock...

This time, the heat rushing to her face was not due to embarrassment. Still smiling, she raised her eyes.

He was striding toward her table with a smile of his own.

Biography

In between writing her current books and fantasizing about the next one, Rachelle Chase works as a business consultant in the unromantic, though sometimes comic, corporate world. Her first published erotic romance novella, *Out of Control*, appeared in SECRETS VOLUME 13 in July 2005. Coming in 2007, SEX LOUNGE (May 2007) and SIN CLUB (December 2007) will be released by Kensington in the Aphrodisia line. For more information about the author and current projects, please visit her at http://www.rachellechase.com/.

Confessions of a Bombshell Bandit

by

Gemma Halliday

Rating: Sweet

Genre: Chick Lit

All I ever wanted was a little freedom. They say money can't buy everything, but that's not entirely true. Money buys you freedom. Freedom from worry, freedom to retire, freedom from the mortgage monster. Freedom to pick up and fly off to the Bahamas should you get the tropical urge. Or, in my case, freedom to park your car on the street without worry that the repo man will tow it away by morning.

My best friend, Quinn, majored in psychology at UCLA and she says my obsession with this whole money-equals-freedom thing probably stemmed from a deep-rooted issue in my childhood.

She could be right.

When I was four years old my father went to prison for holding up a convenience store in North Hollywood. He robbed the Indian clerk at gunpoint and left with thirty-two dollars and sixty-one cents before his Volkswagen Beetle sputtered and died two blocks away. He got five years for armed robbery. While inside, he got into a fight with another inmate over the Sunday mystery meat and stabbed him with a plastic spork. They added another five years to his sentence. While he was serving those out, a riot broke out in my father's cell block, which ended up with a guard getting killed and everyone in cell block D got another four years.

By the time I was eighteen and finally leaving my mother's cigarette-stained doublewide on the college scholarship I'd worked my butt off for, my father was doing his last six months in San Quentin. That is until he was caught smuggling contraband bubble gum into the yard and held over for another eighteen months. Which quickly stretched into three years when he refused to do the mandatory ten minutes of jumping jacks per day, resulting in an altercation with an overweight guard who couldn't do a jumping jack to save his life.

So you see, the price of my father's freedom was thirty-two dollars and sixty one cents.

As for me, my trappings are less penitentiary but no less constraining. I thought a college education would buy me some freedom.

Nope. Just student loans.

Quinn, who rides public transportation – an almost unheard of phenomenon here in Los Angeles – says that having a car gives me freedom.

Nope. Just a car payment that I can't afford, gas prices that go up every three seconds, and a game of cat and mouse with a repo guy who looks like Harvey Keitel in coveralls.

And Lynette, my co-worker with a mortgage, an out-of-work husband, and two kids in diapers, says that being a single twenty-something renting a one bedroom apartment in Chatsworth should be all the freedom any woman needs.

To me it just means having to cash in my meager paycheck the first of the month, signing 90% over to the apartment manager, Mr. Chen, and spending the remaining 10% on lots of Top Ramen for one.

Not my idea of footloose and fancy-free.

Then again, neither was an eight by nine cell, which is why I made Quinn go over our plan one more time.

"You're going to leave the car idling, then we loop around on Pico and take La Cienega straight down to the ten. No stopping."

Quinn nodded, her eyes shining as her hot pink bangs bobbed up and down in the seat beside me. "Here, Carrie."

Lynette reached her arm between the console and handed me a .22.

I checked the chamber. Fully loaded.

Lynnie handed another gun to Quinn, who twirled hers like a wild west sharpshooter, almost dropping it on the upholstered seat of Lynnie's mini van.

"Ready, ladies?" Quinn asked.

Lynnie and I nodded as one.

Quinn pulled her Marilyn Monroe mask on. Lynnie and I followed suit, becoming Mamie Van Doren and Jayne Mansfield.

My vision instantly blurred as I tried to see out the tiny plastic eye holes.

"Just like we rehearsed," Quinn instructed. "They'll be so distracted, they won't even know what hit them."

"Right," I said.

Lynette nodded.

Then we all stripped down to the matching black and pink polka dotted bikinis we'd purchased at Wal-Mart the day before. We tore open the mini van doors, streaking across the parking lot of the Los Angeles Mutual Bank on Fairfax and Pico, guns drawn.

Quinn was the first to hit the front doors. She plowed in, her gun stuck out in front of her like an Al Pacino movie. "Everybody on the ground, hands behind your heads! Nobody moves, and nobody gets hurt. I'm fucking serious!"

She waved her gun in the direction of a guy in a Jerry Garcia tie and Dockers who was making a move for his cell phone. He froze, dropping to the floor along with the other people in line on their lunch break. Lynette came in a close second behind Quinn, aiming her gun at the security guard by the door who looked like he'd just started shaving yesterday.

His wide eyed gaze bounced between Lynette's boobs, barely contained by the triangles of polka dotted fabric, and her gun, leveled at his chest, not sure if he should be scared or turned on.

I came in behind Lynette, making my way across the floor of stunned people to the third teller window on the left. I set my plastic, flowered beach tote on the counter and pulled it open.

The man behind the counter stared at me, his jaw stuck in the open position, eyes looking from the tote to my generous size C chest, the one thing I'd been happy to inherit from my mother.

"Hi, there" I said. "Empty the drawer into my bag, don't even think of pushing your panic button, and keep your hands where I can see them. And," I added as an afterthought, "stop staring at my tits."

Score one for the Bombshell Bandits.

* * *

We were making good time, the warm desert sun beating down on my face as the wind flipped my loose hair back over my shoulders. Not that we had a schedule. Not that we were really going anywhere in particular. The man in the seat beside me held the tiniest hint of half smile on his face as he looked at me across the console.

"So," he said, his eyes laughing, "you're telling me that you just woke up one day and decided to start robbing banks?"

I bit my lower lip and looked out the front windshield, watching the barren landscape fly by us. "Well, no. That's not exactly how it happened."

I could feel him watching me, his eyes intent as his hands gripped the steering wheel of his black jeep. The top was down, warm, dry air swirling around us as the speedometer registered ninety.

"So?" he asked.

"So what?"

"So, spill it. What made you turn to a life of crime?" I could hear the hint of humor in his voice again.

"It's a long story," I answered truthfully.

He grinned at me, gesturing to the wide open stretch of road ahead of us. "We've got all the time in the world, baby."

I couldn't help it. I felt the corners of my mouth curve up. We did, didn't we? "You really want to know?"

His eyes crinkled. "I want to know everything."

I took a deep breath. "Okay. You asked for it."

* * *

Banks have always been some of my favorite places. I love the hushed tones, the calm in the air, the smell of crisp dollar bills being counted out in neat little piles. In a world where everything is debit cards, travelers checks, and automatic transfers, real money is hard to come by.

Unless you're in a bank.

Between a father in prison and a mother in a doublewide, cash was scarce growing up. And what we did have didn't take more than an empty Folgers can to hold.

I was seven the first time I went into a bank. My great aunt Harriet had choked on a Dorito while watching *Judge Judy* and died at the ripe old age of 94, leaving my mother her collection of glass rodeo clown figurines and four hundred dollars in the form of a check from her estate attorney.

I remember standing in line with my mother waiting to cash her check and staring at the wall of brochures that touted the bank's services. Retirement plans. College loans. Home loans. 'Finance your next vacation with a second mortgage' the brochure advised, showing a picture of two happy people, hand in hand on a white, sandy beach that belonged in a Corona ad.

I decided then and there that banks were the places where dreams were made. It's not surprising that as soon as I graduated from college, I took a job at Los Angeles Mutual Bank, home of the famous L.A. 'Moo' dancing cow ads. And I would have probably been content for many years with my just-getting-by life there, too, if it hadn't been for Mr. Leeman.

"So," the woman across from me said, leveling her even gaze at me above stylish wire rimmed frames. "What exactly is the issue you have with Mr. Leeman?"

I looked down at my hands, twisting themselves together to gather courage. "He's inappropriate."

The woman, district manager for L.A. Mu, raised an eyebrow at me. "Inappropriate how?" she asked. "Please elaborate?"

I took a deep breath. "He calls me 'muffin.'"

"Muffin?"

I nodded. "And 'sugar cakes' and 'honey buns' and sometimes even 'dumpling pie.'"

The district manager pursed her lips, but it was impossible to tell what she was thinking.

So, I plowed ahead. "And it's not even that he just calls me these degrading things, but he does it to my chest. He always talks to my chest."

The DM looked down at my chest. Luckily, I'd had the forethought to dress in a high-necked sweater.

"Now, I've always been a sticks-and-stones kind of girl," I continued. "So, I've tried to shrug it off. But, last Monday he..." I paused. I did another deep breath. "He touched me."

This got the DM's attention.

"Touched you?" she asked leaning forward, her pen hovering expectantly over her clipboard.

I nodded again. "Yes. He..." I paused, trying to think of a genteel way to say this. Then gave up. There was nothing genteel about it. "He grabbed my ass."

She narrowed her eyes at me. "I see." She scribbled something on the clipboard.

"I don't want to make waves," I assured her, knowing that the last person who'd complained against the all powerful Leeman had been transferred to the South Central branch of L.A. Mu, where she had to go through a metal detector every morning, "but I just want him to stop. It's... inappropriate."

"I see," she repeated. Still scribbling.

"We all went to the sensitivity training session last month and they said we had a responsibility to the team to report any inappropriate behavior."

"Uh huh."

"So, um, I'm reporting it," I said, craning my neck to see what she was writing.

'Grabbed my ass' seemed like a pretty quick thing to jot down, and she was now working on paragraph three. She quickly slapped a hand over her clipboard, obscuring her notes.

I cleared my throat. "Right. So, um, I just want him to stop. Okay?"

"Thank you for bringing this to my attention, Miss Cabot. I'll look into it."

Hmm. I noticed she hadn't actually said what she'd do. I rose and shook her hand, trying in vain to get a look at her notes, then hopped in my little red Civic (parked two blocks down and behind a dumpster to avoid Mr. Repo) and left the district office for my own L.A. Mu branch, where, I realized looking at my dash clock, I was already five minutes late for my shift.

I hated having to tattle on my lunch hour.

* * *

"So, what did she say?" Lynette asked. "Are they going to fire The Octopus?"

Quinn rolled her green eyes up toward her spiked hair. Blue today. "Geeze, Lynnie. The guy grabs Carrie's ass and suddenly he's an Octopus?"

"He touched my booty, too! In the break room yesterday. My husband hasn't even had his hands on my booty in six weeks," Lynette mumbled wistfully.

"TMI, honey." Quinn flicked cigarette ash onto the pavement behind L.A. MU. "So, what *did* she say?"

I took a long sip from my Diet Coke before answering. Ever since I'd gotten back to my teller window (ten minutes late, Mr. Leeman had irritably pointed out) I'd been running the conversation with the DM through my head. Three hours later, on our mandatory five-minute coffee break, I was no closer to a conclusion.

"She said she'd look into it."

"What does that mean?" Lynette asked, popping the rest of her fat free muffin into her mouth. After dropping two babies in twenty months, Lynnie lived on a fat-free diet. "Does that mean he's going to get fired? He should get fired. He's a total perv."

"And he talks to my chest," I reminded her.

"He talks to all our chests," Quinn added, making the most of her bee bites in a low cut, V- necked blouse today.

"God, what I wouldn't give to see him fired." Lynette got a far away look in her eyes, imagining a Leeman-free workplace.

I had to admit, the thought filled me with the warm fuzzies, too.

David, the security guard, stuck his head out of the back door. He was clean shaven, clean-cut, and I'd bet his butt cheeks squeaked when he walked, he was so clean. Rumor had it he'd wanted to join the army – hence his quarter-inch crew cut – but they'd turned him down because the vision in his right eye was only 50%. Lucky us, they let him walk around our branch with a gun instead.

"Break's over, gals."

"Thanks, tiger," Quinn said, giving him a wink.

David blushed clear to his blond roots. "Oh, and Carrie," he added. "Leeman wants to see you in his office. The District Manager is here."

Lynette raised an eyebrow at me. "Wow. That was fast."

Yeah. Almost too fast. I bit my lip. Then realized I'd been doing that a lot lately and made myself stop, knowing it'd look like chewed hamburger by the end of the day if I kept this up.

Quinn crushed her cigarette beneath the toe of one snakeskin pump, and we followed her back into the bank. Lynnie and Quinn took their places at the first and second teller windows, switching out their 'next window please' signs. I passed my window, instead swerving right into Mr. Leeman's big, glass office in the back corner of the bank.

Leeman was standing beside his massive oak desk, his bald head shining in the glare from the fluorescent lights. His pencil thin mustache twitched on his pasty upper lip as I entered the room.

"Miss Cabot," he began in a voice that was all nasal. "I have some sad news."

I looked from him to the stoic DM. "Yes?"

"We regret that we're going to have to let you go."

I blinked. "Excuse me?" My gazed rocketed from Leeman to the DM again. "Let me go... where?"

Leeman cleared his throat. "Terminate your employment here at L.A. Mu. I'm sorry, but we've been going over your last performance review and we both agree that it's substandard."

"Substandard? You've got to be kidding me." Only he didn't look like he was joking. "But... but..." I sputtered, appealing to the DM. "But what about the grabbing? And the 'muffin'?"

She spoke up for the first time. "Miss Cabot, bringing false sexual harassment claims against your manager is no way to hold onto your job. Mr. Leeman tells me your performance has been slipping for months. You're repeatedly late for work and take excessively long lunch breaks. Today's included."

"But I was with you!" I was shouting now, feeling my face grow hot with a mixture of anger and embarrassment. But mostly anger. What the hell was going on here?!

"Yes, you were," the DM replied calmly. "Filing false accusations. For which, quite frankly, I'm appalled."

My jaw dropped open, tears lining up behind my eyes, ready to march straight down my flushed cheeks. They had to be joking. False accusations? Substandard performance? This was not happening.

I realized Leeman was still talking, his nasally voice droning on like an annoying fly.

"... we'll need you to clear out your things immediately. David will escort you back to your window."

David appeared suddenly in the doorway, looking sheepish as if he'd heard every word.

I stood up, my mouth opening and shutting, trying to come up with something – anything! – to say in my defense. But I could tell by the look on the DM's face that she'd made up her mind.

Leeman was the manager, and I was substandard and now I was getting a security escort from the building. Numbly, I allowed David to steer me back to my window. I passed by Quinn, who mouthed me a, "What's up?", her drawn-in brows puckering in concern. I managed to mouth back a, "later."

David, embarrassed by the whole thing, stood back while I gathered my personal belongings. Which weren't many. A couple of clipped cartoons, a pen I'd brought from home, two framed postcards of tropical islands that I'd never have the cash to actually visit. Especially now that I was unemployed.

I heard Quinn ask David what was up. David went into the impression of a lovesick schoolboy that he always did around Quinn, and Quinn ate it up, flirting the way she always did around David. But I tuned them both out.

I was still seething, the embarrassment slash anger thing turning into full-blown pissed-off. How could the DM have sold me out like that? A woman even. What had all that crap about team players been at the sensitivity training? That's it, I was going to get a lawyer. A big, mean, pit bull of a lawyer and sue the whole damn L.A. Mu 'team'. Even the dancing cow!

Had I not been so intent plotting my revenge (and wondering where on earth I could scrape together the cash for a pit-bull lawyer), I might have noticed him sooner. As it was, I didn't even look up until he was already at my window.

He was average height, brown hair, wearing an Anaheim Angels baseball cap pulled low over his eyes. His gym-made build was encased in a non-descript white T-shirt and worn jeans. My eyes lingered a moment on the jeans, tight in all the right places against the guy's fit form.

"Hi," he said.

I snapped my eyes back up to meet his. Blue. Really blue, like that fabled clear blue California sky that I'm told resides just above our smog layer. And they crinkled at the corners just a little. Like at any moment his rock-star gorgeous face might break out into a smile. I wracked my brain trying to think if I'd seen this guy on MTV recently.

"Hi," I said back. Odd. My voice had suddenly gone up about two octaves. I licked my lips.

"Could you help me..." he paused to read my name tag. "...Carrie?"

"I'd really love to..." Oh, boy, would I! "...but, I'm sorry this window is closed. If you'd like to step over to..." But I trailed off as the man slid a piece of paper along the counter toward me. It read:

Empty the drawer. Keep your hands where I can see them. I have a gun.

Oh. Shit.

I looked up at him. He was still doing that casual half smile thing, his blue eyes as friendly as if we were chatting over coffee.

I licked my lips again, my mouth dry for a whole new reason. "Seriously?" I whispered.

His eyes crinkled more and he leaned in close. "Seriously," he whispered back, his voice low and deep. "So, go nice and slowly and just empty the drawer. Okay, Carrie?"

I nodded. Then took a deep breath, my hands starting to shake. I'd been warned about this sort of thing when I'd first been hired, but it hadn't actually happened until now. I tried to remember what the human resources lady had told me. Something about cooperating. Since the blue eyed man apparently had a gun, I was all for that course of action.

I punched in my code to open the drawer.

"This has got to be the worst fricking day of my life," I mumbled under my breath. I glanced behind me, trying to catch David's eye.

Unfortunately it was firmly rooted to Quinn's rising hemline as she leaned over to help a customer.

"Crack security team you have here." The man grinned, nodding toward David.

"L.A. Mu only hires the best."

"I liked the guy in the cow suit outside. Nice touch."

"Our manager has a thing for puns."

"So I noticed."

"Lousy sonofabitch."

He raised one eyebrow.

"Not you," I explained, remembering the gun. "The manager. He just fired me because *he* grabbed *my* ass."

"Hardly seems fair."

"Tell me about it."

"Maybe you should sue him," he offered.

"I was thinking the same thing," I said. I noticed he was oddly easy to talk to for a bank robber.

"I don't mean to cut this short, Carrie, but could you hurry up a little?"

My hands were shaking so badly I was having a hard time getting the cash out of the drawer. I took another steadying breath, trying to keep him talking. If he was talking, he wasn't shooting, right?

"So, what are you going to do with this money anyway?" I asked.

"I thought I might run away to the Bahamas."

I paused, a twenty suspended in mid-air. "Really?"

He shrugged his captain-of-the-football-team shoulders. "Or, maybe I'll buy a llama farm."

"You're pulling my leg."

"You have nice legs."

Crap. The best compliment I'd gotten in weeks and it came from a felon.

"You know, there are seven security cameras in this place," I said, trying to keep the quiver out of my voice. "You're not going to get away with this."

His eyes crinkled again. "Maybe. But I know for a fact that only three are hooked up, the other four are dummies. The three working cameras are trained on the door, your blue haired co-worker's window, and the outer office to the vault."

Crap. He'd done his homework. Even I hadn't known about the camera on Quinn. I made a mental note to warn her not to make rude gestures behind Leeman's back anymore. He probably catalogued them from the tapes after hours.

"Look, if it makes you feel any better," he said, "this place has insurance up the wazoo. They're expecting someone like me to come in and relieve them of a little cash. They'll be fully reimbursed. Heck, they probably won't even bother looking for me."

"It's still stealing."

He grinned, a dimple showing in his left cheek that would have been boyishly handsome if he hadn't had a gun pointed at me. "Hey, I never said I was a saint."

If I'd have been the kind that went for bad boys, I'd have swooned right about then. Luckily a lifetime in a trailer park had cured me of that girlish obsession and my hormones just did a mild 'yowza' at the wicked twinkle in his blue eyes.

Mr. Bank Robber did a quick glance down at his watch. "Okay, Carrie. That's all the time I have to chat. The cash, please?"

I handed over the stacks I'd pulled, surprised to see my hands had almost stopped shaking.

Almost.

He must have noticed them still quivering a little because he covered one with his. "Hey, sorry you're having such a shitty day," he said.

And if he wasn't still pointing that gun at me, I might have said he actually sounded sincere.

"But, chin up," he said, stuffing the money into the duffel bag. "You're too cute for this place anyway." Then he winked one blue eye, pulled his Angels cap down low, and turned to walk out of the building.

I stared after him. Damn. The man with the gun had made me blush.

I waited until he'd cleared the front door and passed the cow handing out interest rate flyers. Then I hit the panic button.

* * *

After the police took my statement and left, David helped me carry my pathetic file box of belongings to my Civic. I drove straight to the nearest 7-11 and picked up a pint of Ben and Jerry's, figuring being fired *and* robbed all in the same day negated any calories consumed that night. I pulled up to my three-story apartment building in the fringy neighborhood of Chatsworth. Two blocks to the east, paradise. Two blocks west, the ghetto. But at least it didn't have roaches. Okay, not *that* many roaches.

I did a slow drive-by of my building, checking the street for the repo man's black van. I didn't see him out tonight, but I circled the block and parked behind a dumpster in the alley anyway. Better safe than sorry.

I climbed the stairs to my third floor apartment and opened the door. Once inside, I found an envelope had been slid underneath. I tore it open while I fished the B&J's out of my grocery bag.

Only I paused as I read the note, that first spoonful of Cherry Garcia hovering halfway to my lips.

"Dear Resident,
We're happy to inform you that the building is going condo.
As of the first of the month, you will have the option to buy
your current apartment at a reasonable market price. If you
do not wish to purchase, please be advised that you must
vacate by said date."

I continued reading the fine print, my mouth dropping open, B&J's dripping onto my linoleum floor. When I got to the bottom, the listed price for my apartment turned condo, I felt tears well in my eyes. There was no chance in Hades. Especially now being unemployed.

I looked up at my Betty Boop calendar. The first was three weeks away. Great. Fired, robbed, *and* Mr. Chen was evicting me. I was so pissed off at Fate I could spit.

Instead, I crumpled up the letter, grabbed my pint of B&J's and went to bed, consoling myself that at least the day was over.

At least life couldn't get any worse.

Famous last words.

* * *

"Well this just sucks big fat donkey balls," Quinn said, rereading the condo notice as she sipped her margarita.

"You know you could always come stay with me," Lynette offered.

But considering she was currently wearing both cupcake colored drool and baby spit up on her blouse, I decided that was Plan B. Or C.

"Thanks," I mumbled. Then did another tequila shot.

I'd been holed up in bed for the past three days, existing on cheese doodle crumbs and ice cream until Quinn and Lynnette had staged an intervention. They arrived with chips and salsa (Lynette's contributions) and margarita mix and a video entitled 'Huge Hung Hunks' (Quinn's contributions). Somewhere between the hunks and the chips, I'd abandoned the margarita mix and switched to straight tequila.

"It's not fair," I said, slugging back another shot. "I've worked hard. I've paid my dues at the bottom. And every time it seems like I might claw my way just a teeny bit closer to the top, Fate knocks me down again. I'm homeless and unemployed. Even my dad has a job making license plates!"

"I'm sorry, honey," Lynette said, patting my arm.

But I wasn't going to be that easily consoled. One of the benefits of tequila.

"And you know what? I think the repo man found my car last night. Bastard."

"Leeman's blaming you for the robbery, you know," Quinn said.

"No!" I poured another shot. "He isn't?"

Lynnie nodded. "I heard him in the break room telling the cops that they should look into the disgruntled employee theory."

"Snake." I threw another shot back.

"I heard that he's sleeping with the DM, " Quinn said, rewinding a particularly interesting section of her video.

We all paused, turning our heads to the side to get a better view of just how hung the hunk was.

"Figures," I mumbled. "No wonder she didn't believe me."

"Well, if it makes you feel any better, at least you won't have to endure the octopus any longer. I'm sure you can get another job at a different bank."

"Not if the cops really do start investigating you," Quinn added oh-so-helpfully.

"Shit."

I did another shot. Was that number four or five? Or fifteen? I'd totally lost count.

"You know what's the least fair thing in all this? He's free as a bird, off to the Bahamas, and I'm stuck here unemployed and soon to be homeless!"

"Who's going to the Bahamas?" Lynette asked, popping another chip in her mouth.

"The guy who robbed me. Mr. Blue Eyes. Twenty five thousand, three hundred and twenty-two. That's the price of his freedom. I know," I said, waving my empty shot glass in the air. "The cops made me count."

Quinn made a low whistling sound. "Wow. I could pay off my student loans with that."

"You know how many diapers I could buy with that?" Lynnie chimed in.

"Well, hell, maybe we should start robbing banks," I said, giving up on the shot glass and swigging straight from the bottle.

Quinn laughed. "Yeah, and we'd start with L.A. Mu. Could you just imagine Leeman's face if you showed up waving a gun?"

Lynette snorted. "He'd pee his pants, the little weasel."

"God, that alone would be almost worth it," I mumbled.

"But wouldn't that be weird? I mean, the same bank getting robbed twice in a row?" Quinn asked.

"But that's the genius of it," I argued. "No one expects it to get hit twice in a row. They're not ready for it."

"We'll need disguises," Lynnie decided.

"Yeah, that robber's disguise sucked. Blue eyes. Pft!" I blew out a puff of air between my lips. "We could so do better than a pair of blue contacts." They had to be contacts, right? I mean, no one had eyes that blue. Almost unnaturally blue. Bright and wide and so clear you could get lost in them...

"Masks!" Lynnie yelled, snapping me back to the present. "We'd need masks."

"I have a Marilyn Monroe one from Halloween last year," Quinn offered.

"Perfect! Let's all be 50's bombshells," Lynnie suggested.

"And we can wear teeny tiny bikinis," I added, doing another shot. "They'll be so busy staring at our tits, no one will be able to describe us later."

This sent the three of us into a round of unladylike snorting that sounded more barnyard than bombshell.

* * *

"So, you hatched your master plan over a bottle of Jose Cuervo?"

"No!" I punched him in the arm, making the car swerve a little on the nearly deserted highway.

We were taking the old route 66, scenic, ill maintained, and less conspicuous.

"We were only joking around."

"But then it became serious."

I looked out the window. "I guess it did."

"When?"

"Right about the time I got evicted and had to go live on Lynette's couch. It smelled like urine. And I wasn't even sure if it was from the golden retriever or the babies, because no one in that house could seem to hold their bladder. Even Lynnie dribbles when she laughs too hard."

"Wow. More than I needed to know."

"You did say you wanted to know everything."

He grinned. "So I did. Okay then, you decided to do it for real. Lynette and Quinn were with you?"

I shrugged.

It took a while, but Lynette started realizing just what that kind of money would mean to her kids and Quinn, well, Quinn said it could be more of a high than when she bungeed naked off a 400 foot bridge in Ojai. Besides, we all figured that after enduring years of Leeman's leers and ass grabs we'd earned this. Call it hazard pay.

"So, here's what I want to know," he said, turning to me. "Where did you get that gun?"

I smirked. "Let's just say I have friends in low places," I said, remembering how my mother's latest honey, a paranoid underground militia member, hadn't even missed the pieces I'd borrowed from his stock arsenal underneath Mom's doublewide.

He rolled his eyes. "Oh please, don't tell me you're one of those girls that goes around quoting Garth Brooks songs? I'll let you out right here."

"You wouldn't dare."

"I might."

"You forget, I have the gun."

He lifted one eyebrow at me and grinned. "Good point."

"Thank you."

I settled back in my seat, pulling one bare leg up to my chest as I let the sun soak into my skin.

"So... you decided to rob the bank to get enough money for your condo?"

I shook my head. "No. We did it out of revenge. On L.A. Mu. And Leeman. We wanted to see him squirm."

"Really? Pure revenge?"

I paused. "Okay, so maybe not pure revenge. There was a little greed in there as well."

He laughed. Deep and low in his throat. It seemed to rumble off the abandoned red-rock canyons surrounding us like a picture postcard. "Greed I understand. So, you convince the girls, you get the disguises, you have a gun. Then what?"

I turned to him and smiled. "Then I met you."

* * *

"Ready, ladies?" Quinn asked.

I felt butterflies rolling anxiously in my stomach as we pulled our masks on.

"Just like we rehearsed," I heard Quinn say.

"They'll be so distracted, they won't even know what hit them."

"Right," I managed through my dry throat.

I stripped off my jeans and tank top and the three of us bolted from the car, earning a confused stare from the guy in the cow suit. Personally, I didn't think he was anyone to judge. Two seconds later we were through the doors, guns drawn. There was no going back now even if we wanted to.

I heard a woman scream, Lynette telling David to 'be cool', Quinn yelling obscenities at the bank patrons. But I blocked it all out, intent on my one mission. I strode purposefully up to the third teller window on the left. Mr. Leeman stood behind it, his jaw stuck in the open position.

"Hi, there" I said in my most cheerful voice. Which wasn't hard to fake. Seeing Leeman scared shitless put me in a pretty good mood. "Empty the drawer into my bag, don't even think of pushing your panic button, and keep your hands where I can see them. And," I added, unable to keep from grinning behind my mask, "stop staring at my tits."

He paused, going a shade of pale just slightly above death. "I... uh... I can't," he said, his nasally voice quivering.

I shoved the gun inches from his nose. "Sure you can, muffin. Just open the damn drawer."

"Oh, Jesus," he squeaked out. He licked his thin lips, a bead of sweat trickling down his face to hover on the tip of his nose.

"Empty the damn drawer."

"I, I, I can't!" he stuttered. "I just emptied it for that guy!" He pointed a shaky finger to the right where a group of bank patrons lay face down on the floor.

I looked over. A man in an Anaheim Angels baseball cap, carrying a bulging duffel bag, stood up. Then trained a pair of California sky blue eyes on me.

"You!" I turned the gun on him. "What the hell are you doing back here?"

He took a tentative step forward. He blinked, taking in my mask, then honed in on my eyes, recognition dawning in his own.

"Hi there," he answered. "I guess I just enjoyed myself so much last time, I thought I'd stop by again."

I shook my head. "You're hitting the same bank twice in a row?

He shrugged.

"That's genius. No one's expecting it." I narrowed my eyes at him. Damn. Nice logic.

"What are *you* doing here?" he asked.

"What does it look like I'm doing?"

He looked down at my outfit. Or lack thereof. His gaze lingered a healthy amount of time in all the right places. Despite the fact that our best laid plans were falling down around me, my body responded with gusto, my stomach clenching and going all fluttery.

"It looks like you're causing a scene," he finally responded. "And what's with the gun?"

"You use a gun."

"I 'say' I have a gun. That's different."

I narrowed my eyes at him. "You mean to tell me you didn't even have a gun?"

He shrugged.

Figures. "Look, let's speed this up. I'm here for the money." I gestured to his duffel bag.

A grin spread across his face. "Looks like I beat you to it, huh?"

"Yay. Goody for you. Now hand it over."

"Carrie," Lynette yelled. She held up her matching flowered beach tote. "All full. Let's go."

Quinn took the signal and started backing toward the glass doors.

I turned back to Mr. Beat-you-to-it. "I have to go now. Give me the bag."

"Nu-uh."

"What do you mean, 'nu-uh?'"

"Hey, I got here first. Fair's fair."

I had never shot someone before, but I was seriously contemplating it now. "Give me the bag!" I yelled, straight-arming the gun at him.

"Okay, okay. Take it easy." He held up a hand up in surrender. "I'll hand it over. Or..." He paused. Then took a step toward me, giving me a long, deep stare that I swore could see right through my bikini, right through my mask, right down to my core. "Or... we could share it." He flashed me that boyish half smile. "The Bahamas are always more fun with two."

I admit, I thought about it for half a second. "You want to share?"

"Picture it," he said, taking another step closer. "You, me, a white sandy beach, big tropical drinks." He reached out a hand toward me. "What have you got to lose?"

I opened my mouth to respond. But I didn't get to. A sound in the distance suddenly paralyzed us both. Sirens.

Quinn heard them, too, because she instinctively started shooting. She took out the entire loan brochure stack in one swoop.

"Sweet, Jesus." Leeman dropped to his knees and covered his head.

I took immense satisfaction in the fact that a tiny dribble of wetness soaked through the crotch of his crumpled slacks.

"The cow must have called the cops!" Lynette screamed.

She bolted for the front door, almost crashing into Quinn.

"Carrie?" she yelled.

But for some reason I was rooted to the spot. Still holding Mr. Bank Robber's blue-eyed gaze. Suddenly I wasn't in the middle of the worst botched bank robbery of all time about to go to prison because a cow ratted me out. I was on a beach, in one of those Corona ads. Palm trees swaying, lazy sun on my face, warm salty air filling my lungs. The repo man, Mr. Chen, Leeman – none of them existed. I was sipping a drink with an umbrella in it. I didn't have a car, didn't have a home, didn't have a job... and I didn't have a care in the world.

"Carrie?" Lynette called again, the sirens getting closer.

I took a deep breath. "Go," I yelled back. I took the cute bank robber's outstretched hand. "I'll catch up."

* * *

We'd put at least 50 miles between us and the city. Another hundred and we'd be across the border, and on a plane to an anonymous island full of mai tais and who knows what.

"You know," he said, turning to face me, one hand lazily caressing the steering wheel, "you're quite a girl."

I grinned. "I know."

"You think your friends are worried?"

I shook my head. I'd called them when we'd stopped for gas an hour ago. They'd pulled the minivan away from the bank seconds before the police had arrived. They'd ditched the guns in a dumpster in North Hollywood, then driven straight to Lynnie's house where they'd disposed of the bikinis and masks in Lynnie's Diaper Genie.

Quinn promised me she'd experienced enough adrenalin to last her the rest of her life. The Bombshell Bandits were retiring.

Lynnie, on the other hand, said she'd never felt more alive. Apparently she'd jumped her husband the second she'd gotten home and finally had her booty in the right hands.

I promised them I'd call again soon.

The wind whipped through my hair, sending it flying behind me, and I stretched my arms above my head, loving the feel of the hot sun on my skin.

"So," I asked lazily, pulling a stack of twenties from the navy blue duffel bag at my feet and inhaling deeply. "I have to know. Contacts?" I gestured to his blue eyes.

He shook his head. "Nope." He glanced at my C's, still barely contained in my bikini top. "Implants?"

I laughed. "Nope."

"What are you doing?" he asked as I pulled out another stack.

"Counting the price of my freedom. God, it better be more than thirty-two sixty-one."

He gave me a quizzical look, but didn't ask.

"So, you know my story now," I said, flipping through the bundles of green. "What's yours, Big Bad Bank Robber? Let's hear your confession."

He did that wicked grin again, his eyes twinkling at me beneath his wind tussled hair. "How much time have you got?"

I leaned back in my seat, watching the landscape fly past us on our way to anywhere-we-wanted. I thought of mai tais, rustling palms, tropical breezes, and those endless white sand beaches. And Mr. Blue Eyes. I smiled.

"All the time in the world."

Biography

In her previous life, Gemma has worked such diverse jobs as a film and television actress, a teddy bear importer, a department store administrator, an English tutor, and a 900 number psychic. She started writing fiction in 2002 and after winning several awards as an unpublished writer, her career kicked into high gear in 2005 when she won RWA's prestigious Golden Heart Award. One month later she was offered her first book contract, saving her from adding another dead-end to her eclectic employment history. This exciting turn of events resulted in SPYING IN HIGH HEELS, a 2006 release from Dorchester. KILLER IN HIGH HEELS will be released in March 2007.

After stints in Oregon and Los Angeles, Gemma now makes her home in the San Francisco Bay Area where she is hard at work on her next book. You can learn more about Gemma on her website at www.gemmahalliday.com.

The Velvet Mask

by

Candace Havens

Rating: Sweet

Genre: Contemporary

Chapter One

The stately, gothic-revival mansion glittered like a beacon on the hill. Peyton Fielding had never seen a more romantic looking home. She and her friends Kat and Melly had been invited to a Valentine's masquerade ball for singles, and the castle, which looked like something one might see set in the English countryside, seemed appropriate for the occasion.

"It looks like something out of a fairy tale." Peyton clapped her hands together. It was her dream home.

"Down girl." Kat laughed from the back seat of Melly's red and white Mini Cooper. "You and your old house fetish. It's probably tattered and musty smelling on the inside."

"Leave her alone," Melly chided as she pulled up into the circular drive. "Let her have her moment." Melly understood Peyton's love for old homes. While Kat preferred everything new, like the condo they shared, Melly and Peyton were fond of homes with character.

Valets dressed as Victorian footmen opened the doors of the car. Peyton panicked. "I can't do this." She suddenly remembered that underneath her sensible wool coat was the sexiest outfit she'd ever worn.

When she'd arrived home from work earlier, her friends had blind-sided her with the party invitation and had even picked out a costume. *Temporary insanity.* That's the only reason she could think of as to why she would even put it on. She took a deep breath. Maybe if she stayed outside and kept her coat on, no one would see the horrendous thing she wore.

Scheherazade. What were they thinking? Peyton pulled the navy, wool coat tighter around her chest. Underneath, she wore a costume made of nothing more than well-placed scarves in an array of pastels. She'd never been more exposed.

"Come on Pey, Pey, time to find your king." Melly, who had picked an angel costume, complete with halo, had come around the car and grabbed her hand. The angel outfit was tight and white, but at least she was covered from head to toe. She'd pulled her blonde curls on top of her head to finish the look.

I should have made Melly switch costumes with me.

"She's not Pey tonight," Kat, her wicked roommate who was dressed in a revealing fairy costume, giggled behind her. "You may address her as Queen Scheherazade."

Peyton rolled her eyes. "I can't believe you guys did this to me." She wanted to shut the door and drive off, but her roommates would never let her. "I'm not going in there looking like this." She gave it one last valiant try. Her friends laughed, and she knew they wouldn't give in. She let Melly pull her from the car, and Kat climbed out from behind her.

"Stop being a wuss. You're beautiful. It's about time this town saw what a babe you are. Besides, you have a mask on." Kat pointed to the soft pink velvet mask covering the upper part of her face. "I bet no one will ever even know it's you."

If only. Peyton hoped. If she was honest, and she didn't want to be, she'd admit she was excited about hiding behind the mask. She'd spent the last year losing more than fifty pounds. She was no longer the "fat lump" her ex-boyfriend had called her just six months ago when she only had fifteen pounds left to lose. *No, I'm not going there.* She hadn't lost the weight to get back at him. She'd done it for herself.

Still, she had a difficult time believing it when she took the time to look in the mirror. Though she was nowhere close to supermodel thin, she had to admit her new curves fit the costume perfectly.

I am powerful, beautiful, and intelligent and I can kick ass in any situation. She repeated the mantra over and over. It had helped her get through some difficult situations over the past year. The worst of course, was dealing with her brother's sudden death. The pain hadn't gone away, but she could now think of him without crying.

I don't want to think about any of it tonight. She stared up at the spires and arched windows and the lights that shone through the leaded glass.

"If you stay out here, you'll never know what it looks like on the inside." Melly always knew exactly what to say.

Peyton squeezed her hand. "Okay."

Passing several people in elaborate costumes from Cleopatra to Wolverine, the women made their way up the grand marble steps to the entry. Double doors opened and warm air encircled Peyton, making her cheeks flush. She took a deep breath and repeated her mantra as an Adonis in a loincloth and nothing else, took her coat.

Mesmerized by her surroundings, she forgot about her costume for a moment. "Holy mother of..." She pulled her jaw back up and gazed at the beautiful room.

In shades of red, gold and brown, the enormous foyer had a medieval feel to it and, at the same time, was sophisticated. A glittering chandelier shed light like crystallized stars against the stone walls. "This place is amazing," she whispered to no one in particular.

"Ain't it, just?" Melly faked a southern twang. "Now, I want you to go and try something new." She paused dramatically. "Have fun. You've done nothing but work in that stuffy office, or workout at the club for a year. Drink some champagne, eat some chocolate."

Kat came up on the other side of Peyton. "Get laid!"

Before Peyton could protest, Kat laughed. "Oh, lord. I think I have to get me some of that," she pointed to a man wearing a Superman costume. "Those biceps and those thighs. My, oh, my."

Peyton had to admit Superman did look mighty good. She turned to tell Melly, but she was already conversing with another hunk dressed in a Batman costume. *My friends definitely have a thing for superheroes.*

Peyton made her way to the drawing room on the right. A large spread of food sat on several tables. Worried that her revealing costume would show every bite she swallowed, Peyton decided to forgo the food for something to cool her suddenly parched throat.

Making her way to the bar, she noticed more than one man staring at her. The looks weren't exactly uninterested. The idea that these men might find her attractive made Peyton feel powerful.

"Milady, what do you desire tonight?" The bartender, dressed in a pirates costume complete with eye patch, asked.

She smiled. *I'd like a plate full of chocolate éclairs, more money than I've ever dreamed of, and a man who adores me.* "Champagne, please."

He filled a champagne flute nearly to the top and threw in a strawberry. Peyton gave him a wink, and he gifted her with a glorious smile.

He's totally flirting with me. Turning away, so he wouldn't see her blush, Peyton fished the strawberry out of the glass and took a sip. She let the bubbles fizzle on her tongue. Moving to the side of the room, she watched as different groups chatted. It was funny to see George Washington hanging out with Lady Godiva, dressed in a nude-leotard, and three guys dressed as the Marx Brothers.

The more sips she took, the faster the tension eased from her shoulders.

Feeling relaxed, Peyton decided to take a bite of the strawberry. She closed her eyes and sighed with delight as the sweetness of the ripe fruit glided along her tongue. *How had they found strawberries this time of year?* She savored it for several seconds before swallowing. *Yummers.*

"That's one lucky strawberry," a husky male voice interrupted her reverie.

Peyton jumped, sloshing champagne on her hand, and tripping on one of the scarves that encircled her legs. Stumbling back, she landed in strong arms. One circled her waist, a hand flat against her belly. The other grabbed her drink before she could do further damage.

"Umph," she grunted and tried to catch her breath. She found herself leaning back in an awkward position. Turning her head, she stared into a pair of cerulean eyes that were dreamy and draped with long black lashes.

The eyes were wrapped in a black mask. Not the cheap plastic kind many of the men were wearing. This one was velvet, with subtle silver trim around it. Then he smiled, and her breath caught again.

"I'm so sorry," she whispered. Embarrassed by his bold stare, she looked down at his jacket lapel, which seemed to be made out of the same material as the mask.

The man deftly turned her so she faced him. "There. That's better." His voice was deep, and there was a hint of a chuckle. The masked hero, dressed in a Zorro costume, smelled like patchouli and sandalwood, and Peyton found herself wanting to nuzzle his neck.

I must be losing my mind. "I didn't see you there."

"Not a problem," he chuckled. His midnight black hair waved away from his face, and she squeezed her fists together to keep from running her fingers through it. Even with the mask, she knew he was *GQ* handsome. "I'm sorry for startling you. I was just very envious of this." He plucked the strawberry from her hand and bit into it; he too savored the taste.

His eyes shut in ecstasy, much the same way hers had, and a sudden heat burned in her core. She melted from sheer lust at the sight of his lips around the fruit.

When he opened his eyes again, he smiled. "Beautiful Scheherazade, I believe we should find some more of these."

Peyton couldn't find the words. Instead, her traitorous mouth lifted up to his, and she licked a tiny bit of juice from his lips. Even as she was doing it, she thought it insane.

Coming to her senses, she tried to pull away. Before she could push back, he bent down and kissed her. It was a soft exploration, and he tasted of champagne and strawberries. He pulled her tighter to him.

Peyton's senses were in overload. Now she really was melting from the inside out; her body hummed with excitement. One part of her brain screamed, "What are you doing?" The other part screeched, "If you stop kissing him, I'll never forgive you." She listened to the latter. She was in a mask, and the stranger would never know who he kissed.

She became aware of the heat at her pelvis and the slight swelling. The power that came with the knowledge she'd given him an erection made her feel bold. She splayed her hands against his soft jacket and pushed away slightly.

"That—was tasty." She gave him her best sexy smile and hoped she didn't have strawberry seeds in her teeth.

He blew out a deep breath, and she could tell he worked hard to bring himself back under control. "Yes, it was." Smiling, he reached for one of her auburn curls and wrapped it around his finger. "I want more."

The words implied so much and they sent Peyton's heart fluttering like a million butterflies in spring.

"So do I," she said simply.

Chapter Two

Nate McClellan stared at the vision before him. He had Peyton Fielding in his arms, and he could barely keep himself in control.

"Let's dance." The surprise on her face made him smile. He pulled her out of the room and across the foyer to the ballroom. Crowded with partygoers. Superman danced with a fairy. Batman had his arms filled with an angel. It was a surreal world, and Nate became a part of it as his arms slid around Peyton.

In love with her for as long as he could remember, he'd often thought about this day. Back then, she'd been his best friend Michael's, little sister and a freshman. He was a senior and, well, seniors didn't date froshies, and Michael would of have killed him. Little sisters were never viable dating material when it came to best friends.

When Nate went away to Yale, he'd tried to forget her, believing it a schoolboy crush, but then he'd seen her a year ago. All soft and womanly, and his heart had melted once again. He loved every inch of her.

But once again she was off limits. This time she'd been engaged to that jerk Joey Martindale. Nate didn't understand what she saw in the guy.

He'd come back for Michael's funeral. She'd lost a brother, and he a best friend. It didn't seem the right time to tell her she was the love of his life.

Still, when he'd heard the way Joey had talked to her, he couldn't let it rest. He'd gone to see the man later that night and told him that if he didn't treat Peyton better, he'd have to deal with him.

Joey had bellowed a bit, but it wasn't long after that the idiot broke off with Peyton. Nate knew the breakup had hurt her, but it was for the best. He'd planned to woo her senseless, but then his mother had died, and Nate had to leave town again.

Nate had only been back a month and hadn't even seen Peyton. He'd thrown this idiotic singles party, hoping she would show up. When she'd walked through the door dressed in the Scheherazade outfit, it took a full minute for him to catch his breath. The scarves had billowed around her legs, arms and chest. Her belly was bare except for the sheerest piece of material. He couldn't wait to touch her.

When she'd stumbled into him, with a bit of help, he'd been like an excited puppy.

He loved that she had no idea who he was, and that the mask was helping her to be bold. She snuggled closer to him, and suddenly the world felt right.

"This is crazy," she said against his chest.

"I know, but it's fun." He kissed the top of her head, and she sighed.

"It is, and magical. Everyone seems so happy. I wonder if they drugged the food."

He laughed. There was a sense of euphoria in the room. "Maybe, it's the strawberries."

She moved her head to glance up at him, her milk chocolate eyes taking him in. "Or the champagne. It's made me," she paused, "or maybe it's the mask, but I feel different – happy and carefree. It's been so long. It's fun that none of us knows who the other is, and I find that exciting."

Oh, I know you Peyton. "That's the reason for a masquerade. To pretend and to be anything you want. Though anyone can tell you are Scheherazade, the woman who could woo an angry king, even with the mask."

She giggled, and the sound tugged at his heart. He knew there hadn't been much joy in her life the past year, and he planned to change that.

"So Scheherazade tell me some stories. First: Do you know who's hosting this party?" Nate couldn't wait to hear her answer.

At first, she leaned back, and stared at him. She shrugged indicating she had no idea. "Hmmm." She chewed her lip. "Oh, yes, now I remember." She laughed again, but stopped herself.

Excited she wanted to play the game with him, Nate twirled her to the right and then moved to the left on the outside of the crowded dance floor. "Go on."

She continued. "We happen to be in the home of a wealthy oil baron." That part was true, the home had once belonged to the McCullough family, but everyone in town knew that. "The Baron, as he likes to be called," she paused, "was heartbroken when his beloved wife Celia died. Most of the time, he had nothing to do with relationships, believing that he could never find what he had lost. But each Valentine's Day he throws a huge party for singles, hoping to at least catch a glimpse of true love." Her last words were said almost whimsically as if true love really were a fairy tale. It made his heart hurt.

"Interesting, and very sad." He couldn't think of anything else to say, and his voice caught in his throat. The music ended, and Nate guided her to the bar where he ordered two more glasses of champagne.

He handed her the glass, and then held his up. "Here's to the Baron and finding true love." Smiling, he tapped the glass against hers.

She smiled, but even with the mask he could see it hadn't traveled to her eyes. She didn't believe. He would have to do something about that.

Taking a tiny sip, she turned away to watch the dancers. "It seems funny to see Satan," a man dressed in a horrible red, velvet devil costume, "dancing with Joan of Arc." She tried to change the subject, and Nate let her.

"No more than Madonna dancing with Jesus." He joked about the couple at the far end of the ballroom. "Are you ready for some more?"

She turned to face him. "Dancing? Champagne? Or did you have something else in mind?" Giggling, she rolled her eyes. "I'm sorry. That's my feeble attempt at being sexy." Setting down her glass, she took his hand. "I wouldn't mind another dance."

As they made their way onto the dance floor, the small orchestra began a slow ballad. Taking her in his arms, he pressed her tight against him. "I didn't think it was a feeble attempt at all," he said about her earlier comment. "In fact, it took my mind into some rather exciting places."

Peyton blushed, and he smiled.

Flustered, she tried to speak. "That—oh. Um, cool." Then she put her head against his chest and let him guide her along the dance floor.

"Peyton, is that you?" A gruff voice interrupted their magical moment.

Lifting her head, Nate watched her blanch when she saw the nuisance.

"Joey?" Her voice quavered.

"No other." Wearing a construction hat and jeans, Joey smirked. "You're lookin' pretty tight tonight, how about I cut in?"

Peyton tensed in his arms. Instinctively, Nate pulled Peyton behind him. "We're busy." He hated Joey, and everything the chauvinistic jerk stood for in life. While the man might be handsome, he had no soul. He would be an enemy for life just because of how he had treated Peyton.

Joey moved his head from side-to-side like a weird bobble-headed dog in the back window of a car. "Well, I say I want to dance. She's my ex, and I have a right."

"You have no rights where Peyton is concerned." Nate moved toward the man. "I think it's time for you to go."

Joey puffed out his chest. "I think it's time for *you* to go. I'm dancing with Peyton."

"No, you aren't." Nate wanted to hit Joey. The dancers had all stopped, and everyone stood in a circle around them. His security team had moved into place, two men to the left, and one on the right, but he didn't need their help with this idiot.

The fairy and the angel, as well as their dance partners Batman and Superman, had moved to stand behind Peyton. Nate assumed the women were her friends since she'd come in the door with them.

"Look, dude, I don't know who you are, but nobody tells me who I can dance with."

"Excuse me?" A small shaky voice came from behind him. "Hello?" Peyton moved out from behind him. "I think I can decide whom I want to dance with." Her voice grew bold. "And it isn't you, Joey. I wouldn't touch you if someone gave me a million dollars." Her friends snickered behind her. "You are small-minded, smarmy man, who doesn't deserve to mow my lawn let alone dance with me."

Joey jumped forward and reached for Peyton. As he did, Nate brought up a fist and plowed it into the man's nose. Joey stumbled back. Blood spurted through the fingers that covered his face. "You bwoke, my nobe. My fwace!" Joey cried.

Nate motioned to his security detail. "Gentleman, please take him away." The men moved in, and a few seconds later, Joey was gone.

Nate turned to face Peyton. "I'm sorry about the violence. I— there's no excuse. I should have just had security haul him away, but when he reached for you, I couldn't let him hurt you."

Peyton looked down at the floor, and he feared he'd lost her. After Michael's murder, he knew how much she detested violence. Her brother had been mugged and then beaten to death. They still hadn't found his killers.

The music began, and everyone danced again.

Peyton's friends surrounded her. "Are you okay?" the angel asked.

Nate stood outside their small circle wondering if she would ever even speak to him again. *Oh, God, I've lost her forever.*

Chapter Three

Peyton couldn't believe she'd stood up to Joey. Her whole life she'd never been able to say what she wanted, when she wanted to. Whenever she was faced with confrontation, she panicked and usually never said a word. But tonight was different. She'd turned a corner and she felt stronger than ever.

So many times Joey had berated her and made her feel like the ugliest woman on the planet. Every time she went home after one of their arguments, she would think of a thousand things she could have said, but didn't.

She hoped his broken nose hurt. Her shoulders bobbed up and down as she laughed hysterically. Tears streamed down her face in sheer joy. Lifting her head, she looked at Kat and Melly.

"I did it," she said to her friends. "I told that idiot exactly what I thought of him. I could never do that when we were together. I just took his crap, but I gave it all right back to him this time."

Kat hugged her. "You sure did. I'm proud of you."

"Hey, me too." Melly wrapped her arms around the other women.

"And how about your masked hero? Now, girl, that's a step in the right direction," Kat joked.

Her hero? Peyton pulled back from her friends and wiped the tears from her cheeks. "He was magnificent." She looked around and worried when she realized he'd disappeared. "Did you guys see where he went?"

Superman stepped closer. "I saw him go through those doors."

Peyton nodded her thanks and headed to the door. She worried what Zorro would think of her. Maybe, even though he'd been terribly kind trying to protect her, that she was too much trouble. She couldn't blame him.

As she reached the French doors, she stopped. Maybe she shouldn't go after him. He probably didn't want anything more to do with her.

Well, if that's the way he feels, he can tell me to my face. She straightened her shoulders. *Man, I am brave tonight. I may wear this costume more often.*

Pushing open the doors, she walked into a gorgeous study. The walls were made of cherry wood, and each was filled with shelves of books. A massive and ornate desk sat in the middle, between two huge arched windows.

She heard a noise and looked to the left. Zorro was speaking with a man at another door on the opposite side of the room. He had his back to her.

Turning to leave, she hit her hand on the brass lamp on the desk. The heavy, ornate object didn't move, but she shook her hand.

"Peyton?" her masked hero called to her.

"Hi. I — um. I wanted to apologize. I'm assuming since you know all the security guys, this is your house. I'm sorry we ruined your party."

He said something to the other man, and then he crossed the room. "You've no reason to apologize. You didn't ruin the party, and that guy was a jerk." He took her hand and kissed her fingers.

There was a strength about this guy. She may have known him for only a few hours, but she knew he was a good soul. "You are sweet, really. Thank you." She smiled at him. "But I really am sorry. You've made this a magical night for me, and everyone else here."

"Peyton?"

When he said her name, it made her realize something. "Hey, you know my name, thanks to Joey, but I don't know yours."

He leaned back so he could sit on the desk.

"Well, you're Scheherazade. Why don't you tell me the story about my life?"

Peyton pulled away from him a moment. So he wanted to keep the game going a little longer? She could do that. Backing away, she waved her hand around the room. "Well, obviously you are a man of great means, with exquisite taste." She walked around his desk and sat in the large leather chair.

88

The masked man shifted so he could watch her. She could tell he was biting back a smile.

"Your father was the wealthy baron, and he left all of this to you. But you've been traveling around the world in search of your true love, and this is your first trip home in many, many years. In order to meet all of the gorgeous, sexy women," she blatantly pointed at herself, "in town. You threw this enormous party this evening, which, I have to tell you, up until Joey interloped, was one of the best nights of my life. And— you are so handsome, even with that mask, you make my heart do very funny things." She whispered the last words, slightly embarrassed by her boldness.

"You think I'm handsome?" He smiled and her stomach joined her heart in a strange dance.

"Yes," she said breathless.

"How about now." He lifted his mask.

"Nate?" She whispered his name.

"Yes, Peyton." He held his breath wondering what she would think.

"I don't understand." Peyton frowned, and he worried that knowing who he was would change her mind. "Did you know the whole time it was me?"

"Yes." He said the word carefully.

"But there are hundreds of women out there, why would you want to – I mean. Why me?"

"Why not? You are a gorgeous, intelligent woman. Though, I had planned to woo and date you for many months before saying this, I've been in love with you for as long as I can remember."

Peyton gasped, and her hand went against her chest.

Nate held up a hand. "Don't freak out on me yet. Please, listen to what I have to say."

He told her what had happened over the past six months, after her brother's and then his mother's death.

"After my dad died, I went to college and Mom moved out to Santa Barbara to be near her friends. I didn't get back here much after that, but I always thought about you. I couldn't get you out of my head. No matter how hard I tried.

"I've spent the last few years building the family business, and I decided it was time to come home. To you. My one big worry was that someone else would have realized how incredible you were and I'd be out of luck.

"Okay, now you can freak." Nate crossed his arms against his chest.

She stood. He could see the shock in her wide green eyes. "You love me?"

"Yes." He nodded.

Biting her lip, she stared at him for a few minutes. "I've had a crush on you since I was thirteen, and you moved into the Carter House. Whenever you came to hang out with my brother, I would watch your every move. I would imagine I was your very first stalker."

Nate didn't think it possible that she might care for him too. He'd developed a long-range plan to make her fall in love with him. This was much better.

"What about now?" He couldn't help but ask the question.

"I still want more." She gave him a devilish grin as she slipped off her pink mask.

Scooping her up in his arms, he squeezed her tight. "Me too. So tell me, Scheherazade, how do you think this particular story is going to go?"

She snaked an arm around his neck and pulled his head toward her. "Oh, I think this has the makings of a Happily Ever After, written all over it," she whispered against his mouth.

Biography

Candace Havens is an entertainment journalist covering film and television. In addition to her weekly columns seen in newspapers throughout the country, she is the entertainment critic for 96.3 KSCS in the Dallas/Fort Worth area.

She is the author of CHARMED & DANGEROUS, the newly released CHARMED & READY, the upcoming June 2007 release CHARMED & DEADLY, and the non-fiction biography JOSS WHEDON: THE GENIUS BEHIND BUFFY, as well as several published essays.

CHARMED & DANGEROUS was nominated for two RITAS, a Holt Medallion and a Write Touch Readers Award.

A Road of Misgivings

by

Zinnia Hope

Rating: Sweet

Genre: Contemporary

A Road of Misgivings

Indian summer graced the Appalachian foothills. After a golden day in the upper seventies, the temperature began sliding down the thermometer. The sun hid behind the hillside, in search of foreign countries to warm. A creek followed the state route, winding through a long, shallow valley. Caleb tried to keep his attention on the curvy asphalt, but his gaze kept straying to the trees. He couldn't recall ever having seen such an incredible autumn display.

His brother, Jake, snored in the mini van's passenger seat. His head lolled back on the headrest, his mouth splayed open like a largemouth bass, windpipe imitating the squeals of a damaged French horn. Caleb turned on the radio, but its signal faded like a bad dream. He reached for a CD. Classical guitar filled the van. Jake's wounded animal sounds crested over the sweetly plucked notes.

Caleb pushed the volume button again and jerked the steering wheel hard to the right and back again. Jake's head flopped to the side.

He sat up with a start. "What?"

"You sound like someone choking a cat," Valerie, Caleb's daughter, said from the back seat

He twisted in the seat to look at his niece. "Was I snoring?"

"If that's what you call those horrific noises you make while your eyes are closed," Caleb commented and braked for a hairpin turn.

"Sorry."

"Darn," Valerie said. "Uncle Jake drank the last Coke."

"Wow, I'm getting slammed today," he muttered and settled back in the passenger seat.

"We'll get more soda and snacks before we leave Powhatan." Easing off the gas pedal, Caleb hugged the roadside as a semi rushed by loaded with coal. "Your mother has to be back at work tomorrow, so we won't be staying."

"Who's this friend Leslie's visiting?" Jake asked. He fished around in the storage space housing the compact discs.

"Dottie, her best friend, is moving to Germany to live with her military husband," Caleb explained. He noted a dark blot on a straight stretch about half a mile ahead. "One of Leslie's co-workers was driving to Philadelphia this weekend, so Leslie hitched a ride with her.

"I guess that makes more sense." Jake pointed. "What the hell is that?"

Gradually, they approached a black box upon carriage wheels, pulled by a bay horse wearing blinders. Caleb slowed to a crawl behind the Amish buggy, checked ahead for approaching traffic, and moved over into the other lane to pass slowly. The Amish man waved. Three small girls wearing dark blue bonnets poked their heads out of the back. The whir of metal rims on asphalt and the clop of horse hooves faded behind the van.

"Cool!" Valerie said.

"Man, can you imagine driving something that farts in your face?" Jake said.

Valerie giggled.

His brother switched CDs, but Caleb said nothing. Los Lonely Boys filled the van. He didn't care much for his wife's taste in music, but he had to admit he liked this group. He listened to the beat of the first song. Daylight marched toward evening, and in another hour, they would reach Powhatan. By midnight at the latest, they would be back in their suburb on the outskirts of Cincinnati and return to their mundane life.

Caleb heard faint, garbled music from Valerie's Walkman and smiled. A devoted hip-hop fan, she had little tolerance for any other music. Since she couldn't hear anything above Black Eyed Peas, he decided to broach a private topic.

"So have you and Olive set a date yet?" Caleb asked his brother.

"No, but Olive is really pushing the issue."

"What's the hold up?"

"I dunno." Jake stuck his hand out the open window, his fingers splayed. "I want to marry her, but I don't want to do it right away. Olive thinks that if we don't get married within the next year, we'll never marry at all."

"Maybe she senses something."

"And what would that be?"

Caleb glanced at his brother. "That deep down you really aren't ready for that sort of commitment."

A snort escaped Jake. "Well, I'm not—at least not now. I want to wait."

Braking, Caleb grimaced at another coal bucket that roared past. The van swayed in its tail wind. "Wouldn't it have made more sense just tell her you would like to get married in the future, but only when you're ready for it?"

"Are you kidding?" Jake said. "To Olive, it's one and the same. I should have kept my mouth shut about marriage, but I was afraid she'd get tired of waiting for me to pop the question."

"Then she should have asked you."

"Asked me?" Jake raised his eyebrows.

Caleb tapped his fingers on the steering wheel in time to another song. "Why not? Women believe in equality, so why should the man always be the one to propose?"

"Because," Jake chuckled and pulled his hand back into the car, "men are less inclined to marry. If a woman pops the question, it means she's desperate and a sure sign for the guy to run far, far away."

"You have a weird sense of logic," Caleb stated.

"Maybe, but I don't think so."

The clock on the dash read six-fifteen. Tired of driving, Caleb shifted in his seat. He glanced in the rear view mirror and saw that Valerie had fallen asleep with her headphones still on.

"What if Olive *had* asked you to marry her?" Caleb continued in an effort to forget about his cramping muscles. "What would you have said?"

"I would've told her I wanted to get married, but not right now."

Shooting his brother a bemused look, Caleb said, "What's the matter with you? I just said that."

"I don't know."

"I do. You really don't want to marry Olive."

Sighing, Jake stared out the window.

A thread of guilt wormed its way through Caleb's gut. "I'm sorry. I can't keep my own life straight, so I shouldn't tell you how to take care of yours."

"Forget it."

Caleb maneuvered the Windstar out of a curve. He accelerated, but the engine coughed and died.

"What the—?" Dread fell over Caleb. He watched the roadside for a wide, safe place to coast the van to a stop. "I don't believe this!" He hit the steering wheel with his fist and steered the Windstar as far off the road as possible. Dried weeds scraped the passenger side and undercarriage; pollen plumed into the air and settled like golden dust on the windshield. Each time Caleb turned the key, the ignition produced a faint click, but the CD player continued filling the vehicle with Los Lonely Boys.

"Maybe it's the fuel pump," Jake suggested.

"Why are we stopping, Daddy?" Valerie asked.

"The engine quit." Caleb shrugged out of his seatbelt and opened the driver's door. Releasing the hood latch, he got out and raised the hood. What was he doing? His total knowledge of a vehicle consisted of how to drive it, how to refill various fluids, and how to change a flat tire. "Shit," he whispered. "Now what?"

Jake stepped into the roadside weeds. "I tried to use my cell phone, but there's no signal in this valley."

"This just gets better and better." His nerves frayed, Caleb shut his eyes for a moment.

"I'll take a look under the hood," his brother added, "but I don't know much more about mechanical stuff than you do."

After poking around under the hood, Jake stepped back, wiping his hands on his jeans. "I guess we'll have to walk to the next house. One of us can go while the other stays with Valerie, or we can all go together."

"I want to go, Daddy," Valerie said. She had climbed into the front passenger seat and stuck her head and shoulders through the open window. "I've been in the van forever."

"Okay." Caleb motioned at her to get out. "Let's leave the hood up and lock the van." He waited until his daughter had her CD player and stood with her uncle on the roadside. Flipping on the hazard lights, Caleb rolled up the windows and locked the doors. "Let's get going."

They walked for several minutes in silence. A few yards away, the creek burbled and a breeze sighed in the treetops full of twittering birds. Valerie clipped the Walkman to her jeans. She placed the headphones on her head and strode alongside Jake, her sneakers crunching on the berm, their glittery red stripes sparkling in the late evening light. Caleb watched his daughter keep pace with Jake, strawberry blonde ponytail swinging in time to her movements. Once she reached maturity, she would certainly mirror her mother.

Thoughts of Leslie made him uncomfortable. He needed to talk to his wife, to tell her what was bothering him, but how did he talk to her when even *he* didn't know what was?

They hadn't made love for… He thought back and couldn't remember. Oh, how he missed Leslie's smooth, creamy skin and the way she always smelled like peaches and honey. His groin stiffened, so he tried to think about something else—anything else, but thoughts of Leslie's ripe breasts and satiny folds wreaked havoc on his sex drive.

He wanted to run his hands over his wife's body, investigate her sensitive places, and trail kisses down her belly to her legs kept slim and toned by her racquetball sessions. For a second, he shut his eyes. Every time he slid into her hot, wet, receptive body…

"When will we find another house, Daddy?" Valerie asked over her shoulder. She removed her headphones.

His eyes flew open. "I have no idea, honey. We could be walking for a long time." Caleb regretted that he didn't possess any mechanical knowledge, but since it was easier for a garage to fix car problems, he never learned anything about vehicles. "I have Triple-A, but who knows how long it will take a tow truck to find us out here?"

Valerie said, "I'm getting cold."

"You should have got your jacket out of the van," Jake told her.

"The longer we walk," her father said, "the more your body will warm up."

The sound of a loud engine and tires whirring on the pavement reached them. Caleb grabbed Valerie's shoulder and pulled her into the roadside weeds. In moments, another coal bucket barreled toward them. It shot by in a blur of dusty metal, roaring like a resurrected beast from eons past. The overpowering aroma of diesel and coal dust enveloped them in a toxic cloud.

"Since when did a rural route become the Indianapolis 500?" Jake asked.

"Since there seems to be so little traffic on this road, I'd say the truckers keep the trucks running wide open to make good time," Caleb answered.

Jake stared at his brother for a moment. Finally, he turned and watched the semi disappear down the long stretch of highway.

"Let's pick up the pace," Caleb said. "It'll be dark soon."

The shadows deepened, and early evening crickets chirred backup for the mourning doves cooing their melancholy song somewhere in the undergrowth. They rounded a wide curve and started down a slight incline. The creek veered off to the far side of a field; it flowed under a bridge a quarter mile ahead. Pale gold fox grass fluttered in the breeze, offering sparse concealment for a flock of wild turkeys feeding a few yards from the edge of the creek. Faintly, the soft cluck of the hens reached them.

"What are those, Daddy?" Valerie stopped and pointed across the meadow.

"Wild turkeys," Caleb answered.

"Mom always buys a Butterball for Thanksgiving."

Caleb and Jake laughed.

Grinning, Valerie settled the headphones over her ears again.

Looking at his pocket watch, Caleb noted that they'd been walking for twenty minutes and still hadn't seen a house or a car. Somewhere, a crow cawed angrily and another answered it. A disagreement arose between the two birds and they began squabbling like an unhappy married couple.

They traveled another ten minutes along a relatively straight stretch of road with trees encroaching on each side. His pace slowing, Jake lagged behind his niece. He unbuttoned his shirt, his chest damp with perspiration, and fell into step with his brother. "Maybe this wasn't such a good idea after all," he said.

"We had no choice." Caleb unfastened his shirt cuffs, pushing up the flannel sleeves. He caught his brother's sober look and added, "What were we supposed to do? No cell service and no one around for miles. If we had stayed with the van, who knows how long it would've been before someone other than a truck driver came along."

Having wandered several feet ahead of them, Valerie paused. "Daddy, what kind of bird is that?" She removed the headphones and leaned across the guardrail.

The landscape changed from the crowding tree line to a sharp road bank skirted by a guardrail. Below it, a waterway gurgled along. Large flat rocks lay helter-skelter in the creek. A tall sycamore sprawled from the nearby bank nearly reaching the far side, its roots probably forced up by a recent summer storm. Several of its branches trailed in the current like a young woman dipping her fingers in a pool. Near the cascade of half-dead leaves, a slender gray-blue bird stood upon one stick-like leg, its other drawn up against its off-white breast.

"That's a crane, Valerie," Caleb answered.

"Can I see if I can get closer?" his daughter asked. "There's a path down the bank to the water."

Caleb stopped next to her and saw that there was indeed a footpath over the bank. "Okay, I could use a rest. I'm sweating so badly your mother will probably smell me before we even get there." He straddled the barrier and sat down. "I'll be right here, watching, so be careful."

"I will," Valerie promised and stepped over the guardrail. She scrambled down the worn path.

Caleb watched his daughter walk hunched over to look less threatening. She waited, gauging the crane's reaction to her. She took a few more steps closer to the creek's edge and crouched to watch the bird.

"If I ever have a daughter, I hope she's as great as Valerie," Jake said.

"She's my little sweetie," Caleb said. "We're the best of friends."

"You're lucky. Most of the guys I work with at the factory hardly know their children. Either they have no interest in them or they're too wrapped up in advancing up the corporate ladder to pay attention." Jake sighed, shifting his position. "Half of them are divorced and seldom see their kids."

Jake's comment pierced Caleb's façade. He sensed his brother's gaze upon him. He said nothing, knowing Jake would push the topic.

"What's on your mind, Caleb?"

He stared at the crane. "What do you mean?"

"You're my brother. I can tell when something is bothering you."

"I'm still trying to sort it out."

"Is everything okay between you and Leslie?" Jake asked bluntly.

"Yes."

"Yes?"

"And no." Taking a deep breath, Caleb let it out slowly.

"What's the no part?" his brother pressed.

"That's the part I'm still trying to sort out."

"And you criticized me for my views on marrying Olive."

"What's that supposed to mean?" Caleb looked at him askance.

"I sense you're having doubts about Leslie, but you offered me advice regarding Olive."

Caleb frowned. "Are you calling me a hypocrite?"

"No, I'm saying you're screwed up."

Snorting, Caleb said, "You're probably right."

"Are you two fighting?"

"No."

"One of you banging someone else?"

Caleb repositioned himself on the rail, his watchful gaze on Valerie, who had given up on the crane and began skipping stones. "Neither one of us is that type of person."

"Hey, it's human nature," Jake said. "The grass is always greener on the other side cliché. Infidelity is growing more common nowadays."

"I'm not having an affair, Jake. I love Leslie."

"Is your sex life okay?"

Caleb shot him a withering look. "That's none of your business."

"For God's sake, Caleb." He sighed. "I'm your brother, not some barfly looking for gossip while throwing peanut shells on the floor!"

Caleb sighed heavily. "It's been weeks since we've had sex." Throwing a stone into the water, he added, "It's just that..." He paused, searching for the right words. "Leslie's always distracted, always working on a new project for the radio station, always on a business trip..."

"Are you pissed that she makes more money managing the station than you do teaching at the U?"

Shaking his head, Caleb stared up into the trees. "No, it's not that."

"Then what is it?"

Sighing loudly, he shook his head again.

Jake said, "Back to my earlier question: do you think Leslie's messing around?"

"I don't know. I don't think so."

"And you think I'm weird for avoiding marriage," Jake stated.

Caleb shot his brother an annoyed look. "I bet Olive would love to hear your outlook on marital relationships."

His brother's laughter echoed up and down the creek bed. Startled, the crane lifted its gawky frame into the air and flew out of sight. Valerie watched it flap away.

"What's so funny?" Caleb asked.

"I'm only being honest. That's where you and I are very different. You like to sugarcoat everything, even to yourself. I'm brutally honest. It's better that way. "

Caleb ignored his brother's comment and caught his daughter's attention, motioning for her to return. "Let's get going, Valerie. It's getting late."

"How much longer do we have to walk, Dad?"

"I have no idea, but let's hope it's not much farther."

The evening light weakened as a candle flame starved for oxygen. Caleb worried they would still be walking after dark. The air grew steadily cooler and insects whined in the dimness. Perhaps he whined too much, too, Caleb mused. He had a good life, an enjoyable profession, a great kid, and a lovely, talented wife. His brother's views startled him; he knew that people had affairs all the time, but he had never really thought about just how many people committed adultery. In the back of his mind, he'd been wondering if Leslie had lost interest in him. Making love to Leslie wasn't boring; she invigorated him. He wanted more even when he was spent. After her pregnancy with Valerie, Leslie had whipped herself back into shape and had maintained her weight and body tone for the past ten years. In her mid thirties, she had the body of a twenty-five-year-old. Had someone else noticed what an attractive woman she is?

The thought of another man touching her, thrusting deeply between her lovely legs prompted an insane rage to rip through him. She was *his* wife!

Valerie let go of her father's hand and jogged ahead. She discovered a large, glittery sandstone at the roadside and began kicking it along the pavement. Kick, walk several steps, kick, walk... She wore her headset again, and faintly, Caleb could hear the beat of the music.

Shoving his unfounded jealousy aside, he called loudly, "Valerie! Turn the volume down!" She didn't respond, and he sighed, momentarily giving up the fight.

At his side, Jake chuckled.

Single file, they hugged the guardrail with Valerie about twenty feet in the lead. They trudged up a slight incline that slipped into a blind turn going left. The barrier lined the edge of a steep hillside, falling away to a swampy area full of nettles and briars, the perfect environment for rabbits to thrive, Caleb noted.

Lost in his thoughts, he finally noticed a sound growing steadily louder. It filled the valley, the noise ricocheting from hillside to hillside. Caleb stopped, and Jake bumped into him.

"What are you doing?" asked Jake

"Hear that?" Caleb asked. He glanced both directions along the road. "Which direction is that coming from?"

The headphones!

Caleb and Jake started running.

"Valerie! Get off the road!" Caleb shouted.

She kept walking, her headphones snugly over her ears. She kicked the sandstone again; it rolled out into the center of the right hand lane.

"Valerie!" they screamed in unison.

The girl stood in the middle of the lane, staring down at her feet. She kicked the rock along. Her head bobbed to something in her headset. She performed a little jig and punted the sandstone again.

The roar around the bend intensified; the coal bucket sped onward. Caleb's heart slammed painfully against his ribs. He had to reach her, had to make her hear him over the booming music! His Converse sneakers slapped the pavement in time with Jake's Nikes. If he didn't reach her in time, if the truck driver speeding toward them didn't see her...

"VALERIE! Get off the road!" Caleb bellowed so loudly it hurt his throat.

She stopped, turned slowly, and pulled her earphones off. "Did you say something, Daddy?" she asked. Upon seeing her uncle and father pounding toward her, Valerie's expression turned to one of fear.

She heard the approaching truck and spun on her heel. The semi rounded the bend like a medieval monster, its grill bared in a grotesque snarl of angular metal teeth and amber eyes glowing in the dusky atmosphere. Caleb watched in horror. His daughter stood in the beams, mesmerized as death thundered toward her, her feet rooted to a path leading straight into the mechanical beast's hungry maw.

At his side, Caleb dimly heard Jake cry out, "Please, God. No!"

One of Caleb's feet caught the edge of the gravel berm and his Converse shot out from under him nearly spilling him face-first onto the ground, but somehow, he righted himself. The truck's headlights illuminated a cloud of gnats swarming above the cooling pavement, the metal grill gobbling up each insignificant life.

He looked up at the driver. The truck drifted left of center. Shadows cloaked the driver's face; the dark outline of a person behind the wheel sent a finger of fear poking at his heart as if he were watching Death himself driving a load of souls to the next world. The blast of the air horn snapped Valerie out of her horrified stance. She stumbled backward, her feet slipping in the roadside gravel. Caleb watched her scramble to keep her balance and stagger against the guardrail. The force of her impact against it flipped her end over end. She landed on her side in a cluster of dried hay and wildflowers.

The coal bucket streaked by Caleb and his brother, the tail wind buffeting them and the scent of hot rubber and diesel trailing in its wake. Reaching Valerie a mere step ahead of Jake, Caleb leapt the barrier and knelt next to his daughter, who lay dazed but breathing. Locks of hair pulled loose from her ponytail lay over her face.

"Valerie? Honey, are you okay?" Caleb smoothed back the strawberry tresses, creating dirt smears on her cheeks.

"Valerie?" Jake gasped, his voice full of terror.

She blinked. "I'm okay."

A cry of relief burst from Caleb and he scooped her into his arms. He saw Jake grab the guardrail for support, his head bowed, chest heaving.

"I thought I was a goner," Valerie said against his shirt.

"Me too." Caleb checked her for injuries and found only a scraped elbow and a rip in her jeans. "Thank God you're all right." He sighed in relief and helped her stand. Jake lifted her over the rail.

They sat on the barrier for a few minutes, catching their breath. His heart rate finally slowing, lethargy seeped into Caleb's limbs.

"I hear kids playing," Valerie said.

Caleb listened. She was right. Somewhere ahead there was a residence with children, and hopefully, an adult who would let them use the phone.

A crow cawed in a treetop across the road. Scanning the limbs in search of the bird, Caleb heard another coal bucket approaching.

"How do people with children stand living on a stretch of road where those trucks roar up and down it all day?"

"How do city folk deal with their children playing on the sidewalks of busy streets?" Jake countered.

"Look!" Valerie said, pointing at the crow. It glided out of the tree and settled on roadside opposite them.

The crow's black, beady gaze studied something in the road. The bird hopped onto the highway, snatched up a wooly worm and snapped it in two. Half of the worm fell to the asphalt.

The semi drew closer, the steady crescendo of its engine and tires echoed throughout the valley.

Caleb picked up a rock and hurled it at the crow. "Get lost before you get flattened!" he yelled.

The stone missed the crow, landing in the weeds. Snatching up the other half of his snack, the bird swallowed it whole. The coal bucket sped around the turn. Flapping its wings, the crow started to lift off just as the truck smashed into it. A flurry of black feathers embraced the semi's grill, and the truck roared down the road. Only a single black feather swirled in the tailwind.

"Bye-bye, birdie," Valerie said forlornly.

"Looks like the wooly worm was his last supper," Caleb mused.

Valerie's gray eyes stared at the lone crow feather drifting along the asphalt. "The trucks are hungry tonight."

A shiver slithered through Caleb. He hugged his daughter, never wanting to let her go.

"Well, you're okay," Jake said. "I'll take you over a crow any day."

Half a mile later, they found a farmhouse. To Caleb's immense relief, the man of the house turned out to be a mechanic employed at a local garage. The man drove everyone back to the van, and after a cursory investigation, he discovered it only needed a new ignition fuse. Caleb offered to pay the man for his kindness, but he refused.

"Be a Good Samaritan to someone else one day," the fellow said. He got into his car and drove away.

Back on the road, Caleb kept glancing at Valerie, who sat in the passenger seat, having traded places with Jake so that he could stretch out in the back. She looked up at him, grinned, and returned her attention to a video game on her uncle's cell phone display. The Walkman lay on the floor between their seats.

Darkness descended on the valley. Flipping on the headlights, he heard his brother stir behind him.

"I'm going to talk to Olive about this December," Jake said.

Caleb slowed down for a deer standing close to the roadside and replied, "What changed your mind?"

"Life's too short."

"Do you think three months will give her enough time to plan the wedding?"

Sighing sleepily, Jake answered, "I don't want to deal with all the stress and expense, so I'm going to talk to her about using the money for a nice honeymoon instead."

Next to Caleb, the cell phone snapped shut with a faint click, and Valerie said, "I'm tired."

"Me too," Jake replied. "I'm going to take a catnap."

Valerie leaned her seat back, closing her eyes.

Within moments, Jake's snores filled the van. Smiling, Caleb pushed the button on the CD player in hopes that Los Lonely Boys would drown out the strains of the mangled French horn behind him.

Leslie's simple directions were impeccable. Caleb found the address without any trouble. He parked the van, but didn't wake his brother or Valerie. Caleb got out and walked up to the house, ringing the doorbell.

Leslie opened the door. "Hi, honey," she greeted him, her face lighting up.

"Where's Dottie?" he asked, taking her purse and suitcase from just inside the door.

"Oh, she was due at a baby shower for her sister, so I told her to go on, that you'd be here any time." She slipped her arm through his and they walked down the brick path to the van. "What took you so long?"

"Had some mechanical trouble, but it's fixed."

She paused and made him put the purse and case down. She slipped her hands into his. Looking up into his eyes, her gray gaze probed his soul. "I missed you, baby. This weekend made me realize how much I've been neglecting you. Dottie said that if I wasn't careful, I could lose you, that you might get the wrong ideas because I've been running to out-of-town meetings, brainstorming at the office for new station promotions, and numerous other things I have going on. I didn't realize how much

I've been gone lately, and when I did, I missed you so badly I could barely stand it. I'm cutting back my hours at the station. You and Valerie need a wife and mother, not a career gal." She glanced towards the van, but looked back at her husband with a mischievous smile cavorting upon her lips. Placing her hand against Caleb's crotch, she rubbed it gently. "And I'm dying for a romp in the sack that will make me walk funny for the next two days."

At that moment, a knot of emotion surged up out of Caleb's gut. He started to say something but his words lodged in his throat and a small, strangled sound slipped from his lips.

Leslie rose up on tiptoe, her lips brushing his. He slipped his arms around her, drawing her close.

She smelled like peaches and tasted like honey.

Biography

Until recently, Zinnia Hope wrote category romance fiction. Her work has appeared in several online and small print magazines. A year ago, one of her friends, who is an avid reader of erotic romances, read one of Zinnia's longer works and swore she'd whack her over the head with her keyboard if she didn't finish it and submit it for publication somewhere. That short story of over 8,000 words turned into the novella, FREE SPIRITS, published by Freya's Bower in March. Now the erotic romance bug has bitten Zinnia pretty hard, and she has three other books with Freya's Bower: HONEYSUCKLE AND WILD ROSES, the first e-book to be published in their Goddess Freya Series, SEXUAL SCIENCE OF WITCHERY, and CONSPIRACY OF ANGELS. Visit Zinnia at www.zinniahope.com/.

To The Core

by

Jackie Kessler

Rating: Tangy

Genre: Paranormal

Wendy, darling, are you there?

Grandmother's thought-probe jolted me away from my essay. I grumbled as the idea I had been toying with regarding McLuhan's global village faded into dream-stuff. Grandmother's timing never ceased to amaze me. It was always horrible.

Humph. You should talk. You were the one who decided to take ten months to emerge from your mother's womb, dear, so I don't want to hear you complaining about my *timing.*

I sighed. *Grandmother, haven't you heard? Alexander Graham Bell invented this wonderful device called the telephone.*

Grandmother chortled. *That's my darling. Always trying to modernize me.*

"This is a very bad time, Grandmother," I said aloud. Luckily, my roommate was out. It can get a bit embarrassing to be caught talking to "myself" when other people are around.

What's that? Darling, you're not coming in clearly. Are you taking drugs again?

Grandmother!

Well, you know drugs don't exactly help you focus your thoughts. Oh, unless you're working on a Moon ritual.

Grandmother, I'm sorry, but I don't have time for this. Call me on the phone like a normal person, please.

I blinked up a mind-block, effectively putting a shield over my thoughts and cutting off Grandmother's presence. Then I blew out a sigh as I scanned my assorted notes, trying to recapture my thoughts about McLuhan. He'd famously announced that the medium was the message. Hah. He had no idea about mediums. Media, as in plural technologies, sure. But mediums? Not so much. We *Zintal* were a temperamental bunch. Years of working in both the spiritual and physical planes could do that to anyone.

My mother had "tuned in" about a half-hour ago, interrupting my schoolwork and ranting about my "Chosen Time," whatever that was. It had taken me fifteen minutes to convince her that I was truly busy, and that we'd pick up the conversation tomorrow.

"But your Time won't wait for you!" she had insisted.

I'd replied that if, indeed, it was my Time, it most certainly would wait for me.

Of course, I had no idea what she was referring to, but I didn't give it much thought. I had to concentrate on my term paper. None of my relatives had ever been to college, let alone graduate school. None of them had any idea how stressful the whole academic process could be, and they certainly did not take my pursuit of a doctorate seriously. "Sweetie," my Aunt Jillian had crooned to me last year, "why on earth would you want to be a doctor? You've never been any good at healing, you know." When I'd explained to her that my degree would be in communications, she'd asked why telepaths needed their own special doctors. Aunt Jillian was even more archaic than Grandmother.

The phone rang. That was fairly interesting, considering that I had unplugged it to discourage any interruptions. Resigning myself to fate, I walked over to my nightstand. The only things on it were my telephone and my fern plant, Fido. Fido hadn't spoken to me in over a week. It was still annoyed with me for going away during Thanksgiving break without taking it along for the ride. Ferns could be incredibly moody.

I picked up the receiver. "Hello, Grandmother."

"Really, Wendy. That was horribly rude of you to disconnect me like that."

I closed my eyes as I sank down on my bed. "Grandmother, I'm in the middle of a final paper right now. Could we please continue this some other time?"

"Sorry, darling, but this is important."

"So's my paper."

"Young lady, I happen to be over six hundred years old. If I say something is important, it is important!"

"Yes, Grandmother." I sighed.

Grandmother had been the Family Grandmother for a dozen generations. I didn't know if it was an elected post, or if it got delegated to the oldest living female relative. Either way, Grandmother had been around for a long, long time.

"Humph. Are you certain you have time to listen to an old woman?"

"Yes, Grandmother."

"Good. It's your Chosen Time, dear."

I groaned. "Grandmother, did Mom put you up to this?"

"Your mother told me about how you dismissed her, yes." Her disapproval dripped from the telephone. "Why don't you come by so we can discuss what you need to do?"

I opened my eyes. "Grandmother, with all due respect, I have other obligations."

"None more important," Grandmother said, "than those of the *Zintal*."

"But I don't *want* to be *Zintal*." Was that a whine in my voice? *Ugh. Grow up, Gwendolyn.*

"Dear, the world needs the *Zintal* to keep the spirits at bay and the Elements in line. It's an honor."

"I don't want the honor," I said. And no, I was absolutely not pouting. "The world has plenty of mediums and witches in it already." Okay, maybe a little pouting.

"Wendy, we've been through this. You are *not* just a medium or a witch. You speak Words and cast fire into the sky. You have *power*. Remember what happened when you were twelve?"

"I was going through a Dungeons and Dragons phase."

"You nearly incinerated Chicago."

You did something *one* time; you could never live it down. "I've apologized like a million times for that!"

"You're missing my point, Wendy. You are *Zintal*. You can't change who and what you are. And your Chosen Time has come."

The sooner I got off the phone, the sooner I'd finish my term paper. Maybe I couldn't escape being *Zintal*, but I certainly could avoid it as long as almost-humanly possible. "The time for what, Grandmother?"

"The time for you to marry."

The world shifted two degrees to the left. "Excuse me?"

"You are to be married, darling," she said this with obvious pride. "I have the perfect dress for you."

Married.

I bit back my anger as I motioned with my left hand, making a "come here" gesture. In response, my cigarette pack flew off my desk and into my palm. A cigarette popped out of the box and inserted itself between my lips. Muttering a Word of power, I lit the tobacco via a passing Fire Elemental. The Elemental growled at me and tried to set my hair ablaze.

Holy God, I wasn't even *dating*. Now I was supposed to get *married*?

"Darling? Are you there?"

When the Elemental realized it couldn't harm me, it showered me in rather imaginative curses and disappeared in a waft of smoke. Nasty little bugger. But at least it could high tail it when things got tough. Me, I was trapped by what I was.

Zintal. Forever.

I hated my life.

"Wendy? Hello?"

Trying not to sound bitter, I said, "Don't I get a say in this?"

"You are *Zintal*."

"I take it that means no."

She sniffed. "You shouldn't smoke, by the way."

"Now that you've confirmed my life is not my own," I said, dragoning smoke through my nostrils, "can I *please* go back to being a graduate student for a little while longer?"

There was a pause. "How long do you need?"

My sarcasm was completely lost on her. Speaking with a person who took everything literally could be damned infuriating. "Since you ask, I need another ten credits. That translates to about another six months. Then I earn my master's and begin my doctorate. I should get my Ph.D. about two years later."

"Oh. Sorry, darling. You're to be married at midnight tonight."

"*What?*"

"He's a nice enough fellow, so try to fall in love with him during the ceremony. Why don't you come by now, and we'll talk about the details?"

* * *

"Let me get this straight. You're getting married? Tonight?"

I shot Randolph a baleful look. He might have been my best friend going on ten years, but at times I didn't think he knew me at all. "Of course not. I told Grandmother as much."

"You know, you haven't had a date in forever. Or sex in longer."

Maybe I should rethink the best friend thing. "Keenly aware of both, thanks. Your point is what, exactly?"

He shrugged. "You get married; you get laid."

"You're going to start singing 'Matchmaker' from *Fiddler on the Roof*, aren't you?"

"I'm just saying."

"What, you think a forced marriage is a good thing? Specifically, *my* forced marriage?"

"More like making lemonade from the lemons, Wend."

"I'll stick with grapes. Hit me again."

He eyed me from behind the counter of the bar. "You've had a lot of the vino tonight. Don't you have your paper to finish?"

"Hey, if Grandmother threatened to hog-tie you to your own wedding, you'd be working on a drunk, too. Now hit me."

With a sigh, he uncorked a bottle of Pinot Grigio and poured the wine into my empty glass. Randolph had been working at the Voodoo Café for two years. Given that he startled easily, I didn't know how he managed to tend bar at the best interdimensional pub this side of the Astral Plane. Some of the clientele leaned toward the exotic. And otherworldly.

Pushing the glass to me, he asked, "So how'd your grandmother take the news?"

I frowned. "Surprisingly well." It still bothered me that Grandmother had given up so easily. That wasn't like her at all. When one lived for the better part of a millennium, one became an extraordinary plotter. She was up to something, I just knew it.

Me, cynical? Absolutely. Unlike the rest of my family, I had no desire to be *Zintal*. Never had. Sure, having an affinity for controlling Elementals made daily chores easy to deal with. But my family was too firmly entrenched in the dealings of the spirit world. I liked my politics to involve the President and my local congressman, not the Emperor of Ice-Cream and the Queen of Sleep. I liked the Internet and my cell phone; my family preferred Tarot and telepathy. And it was very embarrassing whenever I'd bring over a new boyfriend, and my folks would ask, sweet as you please, whether he was from the physical plane or if he was a spirit within a temporary mortal shell.

Although it looked like that last wasn't exactly a cause for concern any longer.

Married. God spare me.

I knocked back my drink, treating my wine like a shot of tequila. Chosen Time, my fanny. Yet another shining example of how my family would conveniently forget to mention important milestones in my life. Like the *Zintal* version of a Sweet Sixteen, which had included a spot-exam of three rituals. Grandmother had given me all of twenty minutes' warning before the first ritual. By the time I'd finished all three, exhausted and cursing the day I'd been born into a family of magic-wielding maniacs, I had successfully created six new Words of power. Since then, I tried to take eleventh-hour notices of Major Turning Points with as much grace as I could muster. But sometimes, I resented it more than anything.

Like this Chosen Time thing. No way was I getting married tonight—especially not in some spiritual version of an arranged marriage. Maybe deep down I was a sap, but I believed in true love. To my mind, a wedding vow was eternal. Ever since I was a little girl, I'd had a picture of a boy with a red rose in hand, on bent knee, asking me to be his wife.

A magical shotgun behind my head sort of shattered the illusion.

I'd sooner turn my back on my heritage and never utter another Word of power again than be forced to say "I do." But the power was part of me; I could no more do without it than a normal human could exist without breathing. Through my magic, I could topple small mountains without breaking a sweat. But even with all of that power—no, *because* of that power—my life was not my own.

Randolph's voice pulled me out of my unhappy thoughts. "You're moping."

"Not moping," I said. "Fretting. There's a difference. What time do you have?"

He glanced at his wrist, noted the lack of watch, then looked up at the wall clock. "Just about the witching hour. Three, two, one—there it is, on the nose."

Midnight. I sighed in relief. Whatever Mom and Grandmother had intended for me was moot—my so-called Chosen Time was moseying on past me. Maybe now I could get back to my term paper.

Just as I was ready to celebrate with another glass of wine, my nose itched. I felt the blood drain from my face as I realized what that meant. Oh, no, she couldn't—she *wouldn't*—

"Wend?" Randolph peered at me, his eyes wide. "You okay?"

A monstrous sneeze ripped through me...and flung me out of my body.

I hurled through the Astral Plane, tearing through spirits and slamming past visiting corporeal bodies. I desperately tried to stop, but I'd have better luck trying to halt a speeding jet plane with my pinky. Kicking and screaming, I fought against the magic hook that had dug deep into my being, but to no avail—something was reeling me in, and fast. And I couldn't sever the line directly without running the risk of stranding my soul forever between dimensions. So I tore at the hook with all of my power, working feverishly to nudge it free. No good—it was stuck tight.

Seconds later, I burst through the spirit plane. With an unceremonious thump, my astral body landed hard on the floor. Groaning, I rubbed my bruised shoulder as I sat up. And froze.

I'd been summoned to a place where spirit took on physical form, where the soul was just as real—and just as fragile—as a beating heart: my parents' living room. Besides my parents and Grandmother, there were about twenty people squeezed into the cramped space. All looking at me.

That's when I remembered that in astral form, I was naked as the day I was born. Gah.

Covering my breasts with one arm and my groin with the other, I stared bloody murder at my grandmother.

"Sorry to do it like this, Wendy," she said, not looking at all sorry, "but it's your Chosen Time. Would you like to meet your betrothed now, or during the ceremony?"

* * *

"Gwendolyn?" Another knock at the bathroom door. "Come on, sweetie. Everyone's outside, waiting for the blushing bride."
"I'm not going out there," I said, flushing the toilet out of spite.

The only room in the entire house that was warded against spiritual intruders and magic spells was the bathroom. Getting interrupted by a vengeful mage or an obnoxious Elemental while sitting on the can is a mite embarrassing. Therefore, it was a rule that all bathrooms in the house of a *Zintal* were safe zones. In my case, it was the only refuge I had. I'd lied my head off, saying I wanted to freshen up before the ceremony. So I'd locked myself in, and there I sat. And would continue to sit for all eternity if I had to.

"Sweetie," Aunt Jillian said from the other side of the door, "you're being silly. It's just a wedding."

"It's *my* wedding, and I don't want one!"

"So have more than one," she said with a giggle. Easy for her to say; Aunt Jillian's been married more times than I could count. When I didn't respond, she said, "Come on, sweetie. Let everyone see how beautiful you are."

"I'm naked," I shouted. "I'm not going out there naked."

"They already saw you naked."

"Once is all they get."

She sighed loudly. "If I conjured a spirit slip, one with some lovely bead work, would that make a difference?"

"No. Tell everyone to go home."

A pause, then a man's voice said, "Wendy? My name's Jason. Can I talk to you?"

Jason? I didn't know any Jason. He gave Good Voice, though—deep, melodic. Warmth inducing, in some very low places. Astral body mine, behave. Aloud I said, "Your dime."

"I didn't want it to be like this." I heard him blow out a breath and I could picture him running a hand through his hair, whatever color it was, as he thought of what to say. "I wanted to introduce myself properly, give us a chance to at least know each other a little bit before exchanging vows."

Ah. That would be the fiancé, then. "Tell my family that I'm happy to do a blind date, but I'm not going out there to marry you. No offense," I added.

"None taken." I heard the smile in his voice. I wondered if his cheek dimpled when he smiled. He said, "Anything I can say to convince you to come out?"

"Nope. But points for asking."

"You know, it doesn't have to be all bad." He paused, and in my mind I saw his smile turn bemused, imagined a mischievous twinkle in his eyes. "My folks, they met each other at the alter, and they've been married now for fifty years and the honeymoon's still going strong."

Despite myself, I smiled. "Sounds like they're part rabbit."

"Horny as toads." Jason chuckled, and I felt my belly flutter. I liked the sound of that chuckle. Forget the chuckle; I liked the sound of his voice: rich and thick, like verbal hot chocolate.

For a moment, I pictured that voice's mouth—the lips would be full, sensual; the teeth would be just a touch crooked, a hair south of pure white. That mouth pressed against mine, sucking out my breath, bruising my lips with kisses. The tongue now, darting inside, copping a feel and snaking back; inside again, bolder, thrusting between my lips and prodding, exploring...

Stop. That. Now.

He said, "They learned to love each other. If they could, we can."

"Jason," I said, somewhat breathless, "are you promising me a lifetime's worth of honeymoons?"

He laughed again, and the sound shot straight to my core. If I was in my real body, my panties would have been drenched. I shivered, closed my eyes, begged my astral body to behave.

His voice sinfully sexy, Jason said, "I'm willing if you are."

My body was willing; no doubt about that. If he could bring my astral form close to orgasm just by his chuckles, imagine what he could do to the real me. Yummmmm.

No, no, absolutely not. You're a *Zintal*, Gwendolyn, not a sex-starved succubus. Ignore the way your nipples are aching and how there's this heat simmering between your legs, and tell the medium on the other side of the door that you're not interested.

Go on, tell him.

"What do you say, Wendy? Come on out and take my hand."

I imagined his hands—they'd be large, with gentle fingers—roaming over my body, dancing over every inch of me...sliding over my...

...my God...

"Jason," I panted as the center of me quivered with anticipation, "you sound"—feel—"really"—amazing—"nice..." My voice broke as I felt an orgasm building inside.

"But?"

"But I don't do forced marriages."

"Ah."

My body began to curse out my brain as the wave of sheer pleasure receded into still waters. In the throes of not-climax, all I could manage to say was, "Sorry."

"I understand," he said. "I really do. Gwendolyn," he said like a sigh, and hearing that voice say my name almost sent me over the edge again.

Back, orgasm! Back! Come on, yucky thoughts! Right now!

He cleared his throat. "Um, your Grandmother is here."

Yep, that'll do it. "Okay."

"Bye, Wendy."

Before I could say good-bye, or beg him to stay, my Grandmother snarled, "Gwendolyn Ker, you come out here *this instant.*"

"I don't think so." If I wasn't opening the door for the man whose voice was better than foreplay, I sure as hell wasn't opening it for her.

"It's hard enough to stop Time so that it's still midnight. I don't need the extra aggravation of steering my headstrong granddaughter to her own wedding."

"Grandmother, I don't want to get married now."

"But you're *Zintal,*" she said, as if that were the end of it.

"If being *Zintal* means that I need to get married at this very instant to a man I don't know"—even if part of me wanted him—"then I don't want to be *Zintal.*"

"Stop that," she said. "Stop that *now.* Don't say such things."

There was an urgency to her words that made me pause. Grandmother, nervous? Why was that?

I asked, "Why not? You know this is how I've felt for a long time. I don't want to be *Zintal*."

"Stop!" She pounded the door and tried the lock, but the ward still held. "Wendy, don't say that again! I'm warning you!"

Equal parts of hot rage and cold despair shot through my soul. My life wasn't my own, and I hated that more than I could ever say.

Slowly, deliberately, I said, "I don't want to be *Zintal*."

The room began to tremble. Uh oh—

In an explosion of tile and sulfur, a form burst through the bathroom floor. Shielding my eyes from the flying debris, I felt the sting of shattered tile against my astral form. The sound died down, and the rubble settled into place.

Telling myself not to panic, I lowered my arm. And proceeded to panic.

A three-faced woman loomed above me, a mountain of femininity with ice-capped hair floating up in a smoky beehive. Her massive head hovered above her shoulders, with no neck to speak of; her head rotated continually, slowly, like a planet revolving around the sun. The first face tuned past me, showing a young woman's pout, a maiden's sharp, calculating gaze. The second face sneered at me, drowning me in a mother's penetrating look, her frown threatening to swallow me. But the third face was the worst—wrinkled, knowing, and arrogant in its wisdom.

Maiden, Mother, Crone—the Hecate, goddess of witchcraft, patron of all *Zintal*.

Wards and safe zones didn't mean a thing to deities.

I threw myself on the ground, offering complete supplication. Never, never, never anger a goddess. It really could screw up your life. Whatever was left of it, that is.

In my mind, three voices boomed: WHO CALLS US WITH THE RULE OF THREE DURING THE CHOSEN TIME?

Outside the bathroom door, I clearly heard my Grandmother curse.

I swallowed thickly. She'd known this was going to happen. Of course she'd known; Grandmother knew everything. This was just one more thing she'd hidden from me. Fury extinguished my fear, and I said to the goddess, "I do. Gwendolyn Ker."

TELL US YOUR PURPOSE.

In for a penny, and all that. "I no longer want to be *Zintal*."

I felt three sets of gazes riddle my astral form, and I tried not to squirm.

AT THIS, YOUR CHOSEN TIME, YOU WOULD FORFEIT YOUR BIRTHRIGHT?

Clenching my jaw, I said, "Yes."

A light voice, resonating with youth and promise: TELL US WHY.

"I don't want to marry now."

A deeper voice, a stern contralto: TELL US WHY.

I licked my lips. "I'm tired of my life not being my own."

A cold voice, filled with the frostbite of age: TELL US WHY.

My momentary rage evaporated, leaving a bone-gnawing dread (and never mind that I didn't have bones in this form). But it was too late to back out now—far too late. Looking up at the three-faced goddess, and hoping I sounded braver than I felt, I said, "I want to be free."

She seemed to consider my words; it was hard to tell between her rotating faces and my all-consuming fear.

Finally, the Crone announced: TO REMOVE THE MARKS OF THE *ZINTAL*, YOU MUST GO WITHIN YOUR CORE.

TO GO WITHIN YOUR CORE, said the Maiden, YOU MUST PASS THE DOOR, THE GUARDIAN, AND THE CROSSROADS.

THE RULE OF THREE HAS BEEN, WILL BE, INVOKED, said the Mother. THREE CHALLENGES, THREE CHANCES.

Together they said, THREE BLESSINGS UPON YOU.

Then the world disappeared.

* * *

I was in a black room. I tried to call out, but there was no sound. *Um, hello?*

Nothing.

Next time you decide to act impulsively, Gwendolyn, keep in mind that deities may be waiting in the wings. Or bathroom. Whatever.

Okay then. A door, the Hecate had said. I glanced around, rubbing my arms. A door. Terrific. As if I could see anything. What I needed was a light—

The room lit with a blinding force. Crying out, I shielded my eyes. *Too bright! Tone it down!*

Just like that, the light dimmed.

Mind over matter. Duly noted.

Blinking, I looked around. Everything was a purplish-black, and the walls, if they could be called walls, pulsed to a soft beat. Before me stood a plain, wooden door, apparently attached to nothing. A quick circuit around it confirmed that it was a door, floating—and closed.

I guessed the next thing to do would be to open it and see what waited on the other side. Except there was no knob. I tried to magic one up, but nothing happened. No problem; I was still in astral form, so I should be able to just walk through the wood. I moved forward and—

Ow!

Crap. It looked like the same physical rules applied here (wherever that was) as they did in my parents' house: astral, but with solid form. Nothing like being a walking contradiction to shake things up. With a wordless cry, I hurled myself against the door. The wood didn't budge, but something in my shoulder did. Tears in my eyes, I popped the dislocated bone into place. Just another reminder that even though I was in spirit form, I felt everything as if I were in my physical body.

I hissed in frustration. Think this through, I told myself. You can't just ghost your way through. And brute force, not so much. I pursed my lips as I considered the door. Maybe being polite would be the way to go.

With that thought, an elaborate silver knocker appeared on the door. Excellent.

I pulled back the handle. It was heavy and stiff, as if reluctant to be lifted away from the wood. With a grunt, I pushed the knocker to the door once, twice, then let it go.

I stepped back and waited.

Nothing happened.

Candygram, I called out. *Hello? Anyone there?*

Still nothing.

I knocked a third time. After a moment, the door inched open. Rule of three, I reminded myself. That's the magic number of the day. Taking a deep breath, I stepped inside.

And immediately turned upside-down. Something unseen held my ankle in a deathgrip as I spun slowly, my free leg dangling, arms flailing. *Hey! Not funny!*

The pressure on my ankle grew. Around me, the blackness thickened, and as the air started to solidify, I felt myself begin to choke.

NO TRESPASSING.

The voice thundered around the sound of blood thrumming in my ears. I thought as loudly as I could: *Not trespassing! I was sent!* The pressure abated somewhat, and I managed a shaky breath. *The Hecate sent me here!*

WHO GOES THERE?

I swallowed before giving my name. *Gwendolyn Ker.*

The unseen hand dropped me, and I landed on a floor cushioned by inky mist, almost like a black cloud. In my mind, the voice asked: WHAT IS YOUR PURPOSE?

I no longer want to be Zintal.

The fog moved up my legs, caressed my thighs, inched toward the V of my crotch. *Whoa there, sailor...*

A whisper against my most sensitive spot—breath misting, fingers tickling.

Eeeee...

My legs buckled, but invisible hands gripped my arms, propped me up as something probed me, explored me. Up that vaporous touch moved, now over my belly, now under-around-over the swells of my breasts. Air blew against my nipples, cool and moist, and a liquid heat bloomed between my legs. The ghost fingers splashed in my wetness, stroked.

Nearly lost in pleasure, I closed my eyes as my body reacted to the spiritual seduction. Back arched, I made contented noises as the mist enveloped me, soaked every inch of me with smoky kisses...

The voice, purring, full of sex: WHAT'S THE PASSWORD? My eyes snapped open. Wrapped in its cocoon of sensuality, my body tensed. *You're kidding, right?*
WRONG!

The bubble of pleasure burst as fetid breath washed over me. Before I could move, a knife sliced into me, grazing my ribs. With a yell, I twisted, rolling until I landed on the balls of my feet.

A large creature slobbered over me, hairy and naked and hungry. At least twice my size, it stood, panting, its gray pelt filthy, its round eyes glowing with an amber light. Between its legs, its maleness saluted me.

A troll. Gah.

Remembering the misty caress against my body, I shuddered. Please tell me that a troll didn't just bring me this close to orgasm. I knew I was hard up, but really, a gal has to have some standards...

As my mind berated my body for getting sexed up by a monster, the creature lunged at me. I leapt to the side. Its long arms snatched at the space where I'd been. With a grunt, I landed hard on my shoulder—the same one I'd dislocated before, ouch—then rolled to the right, barely avoiding getting jackhammered by the troll's huge feet.

I yelled, *This is not the best way to impress a lady!*

Grinning, leering, the troll spread its fingers—impressively. I realized I hadn't been sliced by a knife at all, but by its claws. This was very bad. Think, Gwendolyn!

Three challenges, the Hecate had said. Three chances.

Rule of Three, I called out. *Another try!*

The troll paused, the blades of its fingers winking in the darkness. WHAT'S THE PASSWORD?

I had no idea. *The Hecate sent me!*

WRONG! The troll burbled laughter: a wet, smacking sound. Round eyes sparkling, it drew back its hand for another strike.

I shouted, *Rule of Three! A last try!*

Again pausing in violence, it asked, WHAT'S THE PASSWORD?

My head pounding, I tried the direct approach. *It's the word that lets you in! That's the password!*

The troll lowered its arms. CORRECT. Looking hungry and disappointed, it vanished in a puff of smoke.

I literally breathed a sigh of relief. My back and shoulder were painfully tight, and my side burned. I'd gotten lucky. If not for the Rule of Three, I'd be troll food.

A white, misty path stretched forward, and I began to walk. After a small eternity, I stopped by a crossroads: the final challenge before reaching my core.

Terrific. What was I supposed to do—flip a coin?

I stared off to the left, then off to the right, and finally straight ahead. All roads seemed to stretch on forever. Wondering which direction to pick, I stared at my feet.

And stared.

It wasn't a crossroads. It was an X. An X marks the spot.

Okay—door, check. Guardian, check. Crossroads, check. So...core.

I looked around. Nothing particularly screamed out "core" to me. Why couldn't there be a note or something...

By my feet, something tiny caught my gaze. I crouched down for a better look. A small white circle with silver writing rested snugly in the center point, where the two paths of the crossroads met. Squinting, I saw the words "PRESS HERE."

I couldn't help it; I grinned. Go, go, mind over matter. Then I touched my index finger to the circle and pushed.

The area glowed, and a slow rumble sounded. Smoke poured out of the circle, and I stepped back, covering my eyes as a column of light erupted from the ground.

I waited until the rumbling stopped. Then I counted silently to ten. Finally, I uncovered my eyes.

She hovered above me, pure and light. Her skin was white gold, her white hair cascading over her shoulders. Her eyes were silver with white flecks, large and liquid and loving. She wore a gown of stars, and it billowed around her, floating with her, caressing her. Laughing, she reached out to me. HELLO, GWENDOLYN.

I stared at myself—a perfect, pure aspect of my true Self: the Core of my very being. My mouth dropped open as I felt love flowing from her, surrounding me and beckoning me. I breathed in, taking in her scent, spicy and warm, like brandy. Tears rolled down my cheeks as I stared at her in awe. Falling to my knees, I opened my arms to her. *You're so beautiful.* The thought didn't do her justice; she was the epitome of Beauty.

She blushed, a soft gold darkening her face. I AM YOU. I shivered as my Core touched my hands, helped me to my feet.

The Hecate's words resounded in my mind. I had to find the marks of the *Zintal*, and somehow remove them from my Core. I closed my eyes, drinking her with every breath. See the marks of *Zintal*, I told myself. Don't be blinded by love, or beauty, or memory. See the truth, and begin.

I opened my eyes. My Core still floated before me, but now I saw hundreds, thousands, of tiny hooks piercing her form. They were a dull black, but the tips glowed red where they touched her skin. They went on forever, covering every part of her.

How was I supposed to remove them all?

She smiled at me. YOU MUST BE TRUE TO YOURSELF. DO WHAT MUST BE DONE.

I reached out and gently touched one of the hooks nestled in her left shoulder. My fingers clammy, I nudged the hook until I pried it free. It disappeared after it left my Core.

Her smile faded as she let out a cry of pain.

I hurt you! A white welt had already formed on her shoulder, was quickly fading.

She touched my hand, and I tore my gaze away from her healing wound. My heart cried out to see tears brimming in her eyes. DO WHAT MUST BE DONE.

Blinking away my own tears, I touched another hook. There were so many—hundreds, thousands, of ties that bound my Core to the *Zintal*. I whispered, *Forgive me.*

THERE IS NOTHING TO FORGIVE.

I went about my work, cringing every time I removed a hook, hating the welts that I caused. She tried not to cry out, but every now and again a wail escaped her, piercing my soul even as the hooks pierced her form. I pulled, and pulled, and pulled, and her cries gave way to moans. By the end, my Core gasped with every touch of my fingers, winced with every approach of my hands.

Finally, finally, it was done. I pressed her fingers to my cheek and held them there. *I'm so sorry.*

Her other hand reached out and lifted my chin until I looked into her eyes. She smiled at me—a tired, loving smile. YOU ARE TRUE TO YOURSELF. THERE IS NOTHING TO FORGIVE.

I wrapped my arms around her and sobbed into her hair as I hugged her, hugged myself. She caressed me, her breath warm on my cheek, as I cried for my Core, for a loss that I would never be able to forget. Her lips brushed mine—

—and my eyes snapped open. I was back in my parents' ruined bathroom. I felt an ache deep within my heart, as if it had been hollowed out. With a Word, I tried to unlock the door. But the power that had been part of me since I could remember was gone.

Gone.

The world spun madly, then the bathroom melted into the Voodoo Café. I blinked at Randolph, who turned fuzzy, transparent. I reached out to him, but humans without magic could not remain between dimensions. With a snort, the universe put me firmly back where I belonged: in my dorm room.

Shaking, I collapsed onto my bed, feeling lost and sad and so very tired. I mumbled a greeting to Fido, who said nothing. Worse than any of the fern's previous silences was that now I could no longer sense it. Biting my lip, I tried to touch Fido with my mind. Nothing—not even the faint, background hum of its life.

I was truly *Zintal* no longer.

Burying my head under my pillow, I cried myself to sleep.

* * *

Bleary eyed, I glared at my door. That didn't do any good; whoever was outside continued knocking. My head throbbed, and my body felt empty, drained. Groaning, I pulled myself out of bed and stumbled to the door. I even unlocked it by the second try. Restraining a sigh, I opened the door, expecting to see my roommate, who was quick to forget her key.

Instead I saw a blond-haired man standing in the hallway. Tweed jacket, tan slacks, nice shoes...and a rose in his hand.

"Wendy?"

Even without being muffled by my parents' bathroom door, I recognized his voice. "Hi, Jason." I tried to give him a smile, but between my exhaustion and my complete surprise, the best I could manage was a twitch of my lips. "What're you doing here?"

"I..." He ran a hand through his hair, just like I'd pictured. "I wanted to tell you that what you did was amazing. Tearing yourself free of the *Zintal* like that... I'm sorry I was the cause."

"Oh, Jason." This time, the smile stayed on my face. His voice was just as sexy as it had been at my parents' house, but I was too exhausted to enjoy its effects. "It wasn't you, not really. I needed to be in control of my own life. That's all I ever wanted." I rubbed my arms. "I just didn't think I'd feel so...empty."

His brow crinkled, and I saw concern and sadness in his brown eyes. Something in me melted a bit from that look, and I suddenly wanted to feel his arms wrapped tight around me, have him fill the emptiness at my core.

He said, "Are you sorry you did it?"

Sorry to finally get my heart's desire? "No. It's just going to take some getting used to." Well, a lot of getting used to. "I guess now I have to learn how to just...be."

He stared at me, his eyes brimming with emotion. After a moment, he cleared his throat. "I realize my timing's not the best. But I wanted to give this to you." A smile on his face, he offered me the rose. "If you ever want to go on that date, I'd be honored."

My voice almost too full for me to speak, I managed to whisper: "Even though I'm not *Zintal?*"

"You're you, Gwendolyn Ker. And I wouldn't have it any other way."

Marshall McLuhan said that the medium is the message. In my case, he was spot on.

As I took the rose, our fingers touched. And in that moment, I knew that not all magic came from Words of Power.

Biography

Jackie Kessler is the author of HELL'S BELLES (Kensington/Zebra Books, January 2007), a humorous paranormal romance about a succubus who runs away from Hell, hides on Earth as an exotic dancer, and learns the hard way about true love. Sex, strippers, and demons — what's not to like?

Her short fiction has appeared in *Wild Child Publishing*, *Farthing*, *From The Asylum*, *Ruthie's Club*, *Byzarium*, and *Allegory* (previously called *Peridot Books*), with another story due to appear in an upcoming issue of REALMS OF FANTASY. She also had a book review published in *Ténèbres*, but it was translated into French, so she can't read her contributor's copy.

Jackie lives in Upstate New York with her husband, two children, two cats, and 9,000 comic books. Yes, it's true that Jackie and her husband scoped out a gentlemen's club when doing research for HELL'S BELLES. No, it's not true that Jackie interviewed a real succubus to get the dirt on Hell. As to whether Jackie worked her way through college by moonlighting as a stripper, that's how rumors get started. (Actually, she worked in the campus cafeteria, which is closer to working in Hell than in a strip club.)

For more about Jackie, visit http://www.jackiekessler.com.

Taking the Alleys

by

Susan Lyons

Rating: Sweet

Genre: Contemporary

The radio – my sole companion for many hours now – announces that it's four in the morning when I hit the outskirts of Vancouver. This is the first time I've seen this city anything other than abuzz with its own weird energy.

Even at this hour, there are a few other cars on the street, a few people on the sidewalks – the kind of people who make me punch the door lock button.

Traffic is so light that I could go straight in on the main streets, but instead I take the alleys. Call me crazy, but it feels to me like the only possible route to Jeff's.

I'm sick of the radio, so I flick it off, and now it's just me and my thoughts filling the truck.

Catherine Elizabeth Jefferson. A gal who chooses a guy's name, but Jeff surely is all woman. Unlike any other woman I've ever met, though. Any other person. She's absolutely, totally, unquestionably unique. Yeah, I know that's redundant, but just "unique" doesn't get it across.

She's so special, that's what I'm trying to say.

She's special and unique – and me, I'm just an average Joe. Well, actually, I'm an average Frank, because that's my name.

"Silly old Bear," she says when I talk this way – she's Christopher Robin to my Pooh, in case you haven't got the picture – "silly old Bear, you're a fine person. Truly fine."

Fine. Now there's one of the biggest say-nothing words of modern English. "How you feelin'?" "Oh, fine." "How's the weather out there? The new job? Your relationship? Your kids?" Yeah. Everything's just *fine.*

I'm just fine. And Jeff is awesome.

So I'm not feeling so fine right now, to tell you the truth. About as scared as I've ever been in my life, if you really want to know.

I'm hyper-alert, easing the truck over speed bumps and around dumpsters, though I've been driving since ten in the morning yesterday. Straight arrow, as straight as a crow could fly if it had to do it in a truck, all the way from my place in Red Deer, Alberta, to Jeff's. Straight, at least, until I cross over the Georgia Street Viaduct and hook off to the first available alley. Tracing, superstitiously, the memory-worn route to Jeff's.

It's really simple, why I'm doing this. Got up yesterday morning, had my usual juice and cereal, toast and coffee, looked around my sunny little two-bedroom bungalow, and decided I just couldn't live without her any longer.

Oh, she's been in my life, but not really. Not enough. You know what I mean?

I met her when I went to an accounting seminar in Vancouver. That's what I do – I'm an accountant for the school board. See what I mean, about being just an average Frank?

Anyhow, the seminar was more of an excuse for a holiday in Vancouver than something I really needed for my work. Had to pay for it myself, but I drove down and stayed at a cheap hotel, leastways as cheap as you can find downtown.

So, there I was on the first morning, needing some food in my belly. I've never used room service in my life, and the coffee shop looked...well, like any coffee shop looks in any cheap hotel in any city, I'm guessing. Didn't do anything for me. Besides, I'd come here to do some exploring.

I walked toward the Hotel Vancouver where the seminar was booked. Passed lots of coffee shops. Seemed like there were at least three in every block, most of them busy and intimidating. Gals in business suits and sneakers, guys carrying on animated conversations with cell phones, Asian kids with backpacks and jeans hanging off their skinny hipbones.

Too much for me, so I turned onto a side street, and there was a nice-looking, kind of laid-back place called Higher Ground. I checked out the menu. No cereal and toast, but I was playing at being cosmopolitan. Ordered a couple of croissants and a cappuccino, settled down with the "Visitor's Choice" booklet I'd found in my room, and then hooked eyes with this woman at the next table.

She really was eye-catching: attractive face, bright turquoise shirt, dangly earrings, some kind of sketchpad spread in front of her with what looked like fabric and paint samples stuck all over the open pages.

But I was more interested in her face than her weird collage. Especially seeing as that face was smiling, all bright and open. "A tourist, I see," she said.

Surprised at finding friendliness from a pretty girl in the big city, I said, "Well, kind of. I'm here for a course" – I didn't say it was on accounting, or she'd know immediately how dull I was – "but I'm taking a couple of extra days so I can explore. It's my first trip to Vancouver." For some reason, she had me feeling like I was back home where folks talk to folks, and I added, "Is there anything special you'd recommend?"

Her face crinkled up. She's a little gal with a pixie face. Stubborn jaw and dark wingy eyebrows, but in between, there's sparkling brown eyes, an upturned nose, and a mouth that can take on most any shape you can imagine.

She said, "Oh, there are things I'd recommend, but I'd bet they're not in your book."

I frowned. Was she into some weird, kinky stuff? But she didn't look the type, what with her pixie eyes and mouth. "What kind of things?" I asked dubiously.

"Jeff's things," she said. "That's me, Jeff. Just personal things like the best oyster bar in town, the place where you can get a glass of dessert wine and watch the sunset, the funkiest bookstore, the most out-there theatre group. Fabulous sushi. Do you like sushi?"

"Uh, that's raw fish and rice? Well, I'm from the prairies…"

"Oh, a *beef* person." She gave me a knowing look. Like she was teasing though, not insulting.

Me, I got defensive. "Beef's good, and don't get me started on that whole mad cow ruckus. But I like fish too. If it's real fresh." A memory got me smiling. "Used to go to the lake with my family when I was a kid, and we'd catch trout. Mom would fry' em up with butter and slivered almonds. Or Dad'd do them on the barbecue, with just lemon slices."

I slid down in my chair and grinned wider, caught up in the remembering. "We'd be exhausted, my brother Brian and me, from all the fresh air and exercise, and somehow no one would get organized to make supper until late, and we'd sit outside at a picnic table, slathered up with bug dope, yawning until we thought our jaws would break, eating trout and those little new potatoes, maybe some corn on the cob. Didn't want to go to bed, didn't want the day to end, yet there was no way we could stay awake any longer."

This woman – did she really say her name was Jeff? – was watching me with wide eyes. I came to my senses and got embarrassed. "Sorry, you didn't need to know that, did you?"

"Maybe I did." She smiled. "It's a wonderful picture you just painted for me. Thanks."

Painted? "You're welcome," I muttered. I'm never at my best with pretty women. Quickly, I said, "I'd like to know about your special places in Vancouver. It's more fun getting away from the standard tourist spots. I mean, you stand there with all the folks off the tour buses, and everyone's snapping pictures of everyone else snapping pictures and…" Lord, I'm not usually anywhere near this talkative. "So maybe I could write down names of the places you mentioned? And anything else you'd recommend."

She tilted her head, a curly-haired elf, and put on a face like she was thinking really hard, but I got the feeling she already knew what she was going to say. "There's always Wreck Beach."

"Wreck Beach? Is that a shipwreck?"

The corners of her mouth twitched. Her eyes were holding steady, but I could tell she was struggling to hold back a laugh. I figured I'd been had, but I didn't know how.

"It's a nude beach," she said.

I felt the blush rising up my chest. It was going to hit my neck, then my cheeks, and I couldn't stop it. She was going to realize what a hick I was. As if she didn't already know.

She laughed, a quick burble. "Sorry, that wasn't fair." Then she said, straight out, "So, do y'all from the prairies feel adventurous enough to check out the sushi with me tonight?"

Oh boy, did I, if it meant spending time with Jeff! So we did – though the sushi wasn't a patch on the lake trout I'd been remembering. Then we went for dessert wine from the Okanagan Valley. It was like summer in a glass, so good I wanted to drink it in tiny sips and make it last forever – or maybe it was Jeff's company that I wanted to last forever. We watched the sunset, and it was damn fine too. And the long and the short of it was – well, let's just say we saw a lot of each other during the week I was in town.

When I wasn't at my course, and she wasn't working as what I'd call an interior decorator but she calls a living space designer, she showed me Jeff's Vancouver. And I was hooked, harder than any trout. On Vancouver, sort of, but really on Jeff.

So.

Anyhow.

That's how I met Jeff. And how we came to have a relationship. I'll call it a relationship, because I don't know what other term to use.

That was going on two years ago, and since then we've been visiting back and forth. Mostly, I come to visit her. Though she says she likes my patch of the country, it seems to me my life must be a total bore for her. She smiles and talks easily with my folks, my buddies, and everyone else she meets, and sometimes I think she could stare at wheat fields – summer green, autumn gold or blanketed in snow – for hours on end, but then I worry she's hiding yawns behind her smile.

Her own life is so dynamic. Take her friends. They're off ocean kayaking, or doing experimental theatre, or suing tobacco companies, or growing orchids.

But even among them, Jeff stands out.

We'll all be sprawling around in her loft, where the walls are this blue-grey colour that makes you feel like you're sitting in the mist that rises off a lake on an autumn morning. Drinking beer, wine, herbal tea. Ranjit will be playing his sitar, Whangbo will be sketching with flying fingers, Christina will be nursing her and Ruth's baby – and yeah, they're both gals!

Me, I'll be sitting and listening, and they'll all be talking.

City talk. Like, how horrible the traffic has gotten to be; there's gridlock at all the intersections from seven in the morning until seven at night.

And Jeff'll give her burbly chuckle and say, "Guys, you're nuts! Why do you sit in gridlock? Take the alleys, for Pete's sake."

That's her. She takes the alleys. She always finds her own personal way of doing everything. She sees different stuff from other people, and even if she's looking at the same stuff she sees it differently.

Like how she sees me. Everyone's always said how steady I am. Not brilliant but smart enough to get by. Responsible, dependable. Sometimes I feel like I'm an English sheep dog. Not an ounce of spontaneity in my body, my mom has said many times, with an affectionate shake of her head.

But Jeff lets me be someone different. If I forget to pick up groceries, she just flicks her hair back and says, "Hey, no big deal, so we'll go out." Then she says, "What do you feel like?"

Of course I say, "Whatever you want is fine with me," but she rolls her eyes and says, speaking slowly like to someone who's not so swift, "Bear, listen to the question. What do *you* feel like? And," she adds immediately, "don't agonize over it, just answer off the top of your head."

So I'll say something like "Thai" or "Greek" and she'll say, "Great! You've got terrific instincts when you trust them, Bear."

My life back home is fine. Just fine. But when I'm with Jeff, it's bigger and brighter. There's more potential. And no predictability.

Jesus Christ, what am I doing?

With hands gone suddenly shaky, I pull the car over to the side of the alley and turn off the engine. I am one block away from Jeff's place.

Around me, the apartment buildings are dark. There's a yellow window here and there, an insomniac or shift worker, someone up with a hungry baby. Lives, asleep or awake, going on behind those unrevealing panes of glass.

I wind down the truck window. The night air is crisp. I breathe deeply, smelling city and ocean. The West End is quiet, in its own West End way, which means there's a siren way off in the distance, and a rustle that's likely a squirrel in the branches of the horse chestnut tree beside me, and, if you listen harder, the hum of a car on one of the nearby streets.

A ping from under the hood of the truck.

The rustle and scrape of my clothing against the seat as I shift position. Clothing that's grown uncomfortable from having been worn too long.

My eyes are gritty. I squeeze them shut and rub them with my knuckles. I think of Jeff shaking her head enviously. "It's so unfair that you've got perfect vision," she says. "I haven't been able to rub my eyes like that since I got contacts. Can you imagine, Bear, not being able to rub your eyes?"

I smile, remembering the earnest expression that scrunches up her face.

And then I swallow hard.

What the hell was I thinking?

Like, I can just land on Jeff's doorstep in the small hours before dawn, and she'll welcome me with open arms? Like, I can say, "Jeff, I think it's time we bound our lives tighter and started talking about a future together?"

What if she gazes at me with pity in those melting eyes of hers and says, "Silly old Bear, you know I'm fond of you but..."?

What if she's not alone? Oh, we've talked around the fidelity issue. I know she's had lots of lovers in the past, which sure is different from the way I've been, back there in hicksville. She says she's grown tired of flitting from affair to affair, says it was fun once but now she's into something different.

That was good enough for me, cautious Bear that I am. I knew I wasn't going to be seeing anyone else – not when Jeff was filling my heart – and I hoped I might be her "something different."

But now I'm thinking that maybe I'm just another of her affairs and maybe her "something different" has yet to come along. Until it does, she'll mark time with the likes of me.

And maybe she's doing that right now. Maybe there's someone else keeping her company in her cozy brass bed.

I can't just drive up and park the car, reach into my jeans pocket for the keys she gave me, unlock a couple of doors and go waltzing in like I'm sure of my welcome.

How could I have even imagined it?

Guess it was that spontaneity thing she's been on at me about. Jeff's got me being spontaneous, and now look where it's brought me.

I could sit here in my car, beside the tree with the squirrel, until it's morning. Find a phone booth. Give her a call. That would be the sensible thing to do.

I remember Jeff saying, "You've got terrific instincts, Bear."

And I realize that taking the alleys sure as hell doesn't mean sitting in them until dawn breaks. I knuckle my eyes once more then turn the key in the ignition.

I've only driven half a block when I slam on the brakes. There's a figure walking toward me down the alley, emerging ghost-like from the pre-dawn light. But it's no ghost; I'd recognize that bouncy stride anywhere. I fling open the door. "Jeff!"

My voice stops her cold and my heart lurches into my throat.

Then, "Bear? Bear, is that really you?" Her voice is high with disbelief. And joy.

I swear it's joy.

Suddenly, she's running toward me, her arms high, and I catch her as she leaps at me, and her arms are tangled around my neck and mine are around her waist and, honest to God, I'm spinning us around in a circle like something out of a shampoo commercial.

When I put her down, all I can manage to say is, "What are you doing, out so early?"

"I woke up and a little voice told me to get up, that there was something special waiting for me. But, Bear, I never guessed it would be you!"

"Is it okay? That I came without calling first?" Is it okay, I'm really asking, that I had a sudden need for a future, with you?

She studies my face, and I'm sure she's reading everything in it, the words that I haven't dared speak. As I wait for her answer, I pray she doesn't say it's fine. Any word but "fine."

She touches my nose with a gentle finger. "Silly old Bear. Don't you know? It's perfect. Just absolutely perfect."

Biography

Susan Lyons' short stories have been published internationally in women's and story magazines. Her books are published by Kensington Aphrodisia; they're sexy romances that are intense, passionate, heartwarming and fun.

She grew up in Victoria, British Columbia and now lives in Vancouver, where many of her stories are set. She has degrees in law and psychology, and has had a variety of careers, including perennial student, grad school dropout, job creation project administrator, computer consultant, and legal editor. Fiction writer is by far her favorite. Writing gives her a perfect outlet to demonstrate her belief in the power of love, friendship and a sense of humor. Visit her website at www.susanlyons.ca.

Brushstrokes

by

Richelle Mead

Rating: Spicy

Genre: Paranormal Historical

Brushstrokes

Francesca thought the priest was a lost cause, but I still believed I could lure him into my bed.

"Help me, Father," I sobbed, falling to my knees before him. "I don't know what to do. I'm lost. I'm going to burn forever. There's no hope for me."

"Child, child," he murmured. "Of course there's hope. God forgives all."

He leaned forward, eyes kind, but he didn't touch me, thus forcing me to stifle a growl of annoyance. That was the whole point of this weeping spectacle. It was the perfect opportunity for him to gently pat my hand or—better yet—to hold me in a compassionate embrace. Then, perhaps, he might run a comforting hand along my cheek, perhaps down my neck, on to my breast...

Father Betto wasn't falling for any of it, unfortunately. As it was, I knew meeting with me in private unnerved him. He knew the risks—both to his own resolve and to his reputation. With the force of my money and power, however, I had insisted no one else would counsel me through the 'spiritual crises' that continually plagued me.

"I want so badly to be good." I continued to kneel, conveying just how much the pain of my sin ached in my bosom while also giving him an excellent view of said bosom. "But I'm weak. I can't seem to let go of my worldly attachments."

"That isn't true. You always give to the Church. And the hospital's still talking about your last contribution. God rewards such kindness."

"But is that enough?" I whispered. I knew my tears gleamed like jewels upon my face because I'd crafted them that way. Perfect. An enhancement to my beauty. No red eyes or blotchy skin here.

"It's a start. If you truly wish to go further, you will give up your earthly excesses. That dress, for example, is far more...elaborate than a woman of your station truly requires."

I glanced down at my gown. It was a thing of beauty, emerald green brocade over gold-colored silk. A perk of having a 'brother' in the silk guild. When I'd been a mortal over a thousand years ago, the emperor himself had worn nothing so fine.

Brushstrokes

"This dress?" To make sure we all knew which dress he referred to, I ran my hands over my body, sliding them carefully down my breasts and hips. With a small flare of triumph, I saw him reluctantly drag his eyes away. "But I...I couldn't..."

This signaled a well-worn argument between us. It was always the same. I would come to him, in tears over the state of my soul, and he would tick off the luxuries and behaviors in my life I needed to expunge. I would listen, cry a little more, promise to take his words to heart, and then change nothing.

"Fra Savonarola is urging the entire city to give up its vanities, you know. He plans to gather up all sinful items and burn them on Shrove Tuesday. You should answer the call. It could be a rebirth for you. A purging by fire."

I smiled and muttered something conciliatory. I'd throw myself to the flames before donating to Savonarola's madness. Father Betto was a fervent believer in the zealous friar's cause, and lately, it seemed the rest of Florence was too. The city's residents had turned into a flock of frightened sheep.

"There is, of course, another matter...one, perhaps, better discussed with your brother..."

Still smiling politely, I waited for him to continue even though I knew what he would say. It was another oft-discussed topic.

"You and your sister have both been widowed for some time—"

"It still hurts, Father. Francesca feels the same way. It's so hard...so hard to move on..."

At least, she and I continually tried to make it appear that way. My fellow succubus and I both put on good shows of mourning for our fictitious husbands, but she kept forgetting the name of her 'beloved,' which made us look bad.

"Yes, yes, I understand the need to grieve, but it's been years. Neither of you wear black anymore. A young woman without a husband is far more susceptible to sin—particularly considering your involvement in your brother's business. It isn't...appropriate. You interact with men so often...well, some might question your virtue. If you truly wish to remain unattached, then you should take vows."

When he started talking convents, it was time for me to leave. I rose gracefully to my feet. "I'll think about it. Thank you, Father."

He stood with me, his eyes again lingering on my body a bit longer than they should have. Hiding my smile, I left the church, knowing it was just a matter of time.

* * *

"I suppose you cried again," muttered Francesca when I arrived home later. She stood before the mirror in her room, trying on necklaces for the wedding we had to attend that night. Their brightly colored jewels contrasted dramatically with the creaminess of her skin, and I paused to admire the effect.

"I even got on my knees."

A smile quirked her lips. "A more blatant invitation than usual. I'm surprised. You must be getting desperate."

"Not desperate. Just trying new tactics."

"Tactics, hmm? You can call it whatever you want, but you're wasting your time. You're one of the best I've ever met," she said it both grudgingly and honestly, "but still, even you have limits. Besides, he's not that much of a catch. I swear, every time we go to mass, he has less hair than the day before. If you really want a priest, why not take that young one over at Santa Croce? He's terribly attractive. I'm sure he'd give in."

"I'm sure too, considering half of the city is filled with his bastards already. I want someone untainted. That's the whole point."

She rolled her eyes at me, saying nothing. Francesca was young for a succubus, only a couple hundred years or so. She was content to drink her fill of the life we needed from easy conquests: mortal men who needed little urging to commit adultery or some other sin. As for me, I held myself to a higher standard. A priest like the one at Santa Croce wasn't worth my time. I wanted good men, men with souls so pure that when I took them to bed, the energy that poured into me was like the Holy Spirit itself.

143

I left her to make my own preparations, changing to a dress dyed a brilliant red. It, like the gold of my hair, was much coveted by Florentine women. Unlike these poor women and their crazy fixation on dyes and other hair-lightening concoctions, I had the luxury of shape-shifting. A blink of the eye, and I had any color I wanted. A minor compensation for having sold my soul.

* * *

No expense had been spared at the wedding. The bride, a tiny thing of fourteen, shone like a small sun in her heavy brocaded dress, and the servants brought out delicacy after delicacy at dinner. Francesca and I dined with the women while the men had their own area on the other side of the room. Afterward, mingling and other festivities ensued.

"Bianca," I heard a voice say. Turning, I stared into familiar brown eyes.

"Signore Cristofani," I murmured, lowering my own eyes as was appropriate, but still managing to sneak a sidelong look at him. With those black curls and long lashes, he was worth taking several looks at. Lovelier still were his hands and the way they could stroke a woman's flesh...

He cast an anxious glance around, making sure no one noticed us. Addressing me alone was a breach of etiquette, particularly since he was married.

"Why haven't you returned my letters? I need to see you again."

"I can't see you again, Signore. What happened before...it was wrong. It was a sin I will not repeat."

It had, however, been a sin we repeated a number of times the night it occurred. It had been a good night, one that had left a taint on his soul and filled me with enough life to last a month. It had also left him drained and exhausted for days afterward, as often happened when men of good character lay with succubi.

"But...I love you." Naked desperation glowed on his face. "I can't live without you."

"You must go back to your wife," I said, still playing proper and demure. Handsome or no, I hated it when they clung like this. I'd gotten what I needed from him, and I daresay he'd gotten plenty in return. We were finished. Why couldn't he move on? "Please don't speak of this again."

I retreated into the crowd, knowing he'd hesitate to pursue me among so many witnesses. I'd just made it to the other side of the room when someone else stepped in front of me, nearly making me trip over him.

"Bianca Rinaldi?"

"Yes?"

I carefully eyed the man before me. He was young, handsome in a different way than Cristofani. Apparent time outdoors had given his face a weathered and tanned look. The sun had lightened his brown hair, and frank gray eyes appraised me. His common attire looked out of place among the other guests' opulence, and I wondered what he was doing here. There was a grand note in his voice when he spoke, like he was someone more important than he looked.

"I'm Niccolò Giordani."

I waited.

"You've heard of me."

I shook my head. His face fell.

"Oh. I'm a painter. I did the picture of the Annunciation over at the Palazzo Fazzi. Perhaps you've heard of it?"

Ah, an artist. That would explain the air of self-importance.

I shook my head again, amused and puzzled. "What is it you want from me, Signore Giordani?"

He still seemed stunned that I hadn't heard of him. Blinking, he recovered himself quickly. "Why, your patronage, of course."

"I'm not looking for an artist."

"Not yet. But that's because you haven't met me. Er, I mean, now you have...but, well, you understand." He took an inappropriate step closer. "You see, Signora, I've had a vision."

I stepped back uneasily. I didn't really want any crazy mystics in my life just now. "A vision from God?"

"No. A vision from the muses. A vision to create a fresco. A fresco the likes of which has never been seen."

"What of?"

"A Bacchanalia. The god Bacchus reclining among nymphs and satyrs who drink and dance to his glory. It will be amazing. A feast for the eyes. The muses have promised as much."

"That's...an unusual idea. And possibly immoral."

Recent years had seen a resurgence of the old myths in art, something I heartily approved of. I'd missed those glorious, decadent stories. But many modern interpretations were caged in terms of Christian symbols, or else they depicted relatively tame scenes. Although intriguing, what he suggested would both provoke and offend someone like Fra Savonarola.

Niccolò grinned. It was a delicious smile, one full of charm and mischief that made his lips look particularly appealing. "Which is why I come to you."

"I told you, I'm not looking for a—wait. Are you saying I'm immoral?"

"A bit. I mean, I've heard no concrete details about your behaviors, of course, but you have been a widow for an *extremely* long time. And everyone knows you've sponsored artists in the past who work with 'questionable' topics."

"I also sponsor a number of artists who portray proper Christian scenes."

He made a dismissive gesture, ignoring my prim tone. "Of course you would. How else would you get away with your other interests?"

This was the best thing to happen to me in a while. I lived for absurd moments like these. Everything about him was preposterous—and entertaining. Artists did not proposition their prospective patrons, particularly female ones.

"Signore Giordani, I'm 'flattered' by your offer and your regard, but I can't make a decision like this without my brother's consent."

Niccolò scoffed. "Don't play coy. Your brother's never here. Everyone knows who really handles the finances in his house and business. You have a man's mind in what is very, *very* much a woman's body."

It was true, I supposed. My 'brother' was a minor demon who traveled excessively and was far too busy brokering souls to be troubled with his silk trade in Florence. He was happy to let two succubi handle it. In return, Francesca and I enjoyed the relative freedom of unattached women who still technically remained under the protection of a male family member.

I studied Niccolò, working to keep a straight face as I considered his brazen offer. "And when could you start this masterpiece?"

"As soon as my lady likes. We can draw up the contract tomorrow. I think you'll be pleased with the quality of materials I plan on using."

"But probably less pleased with their price," I noted dryly.

"Brilliance has no price. And I know you can afford it. The final product will be well worth it. Your guests' mouths will drop in awe. Nobles and dignitaries will line up outside to see it. Besides, I offer outstanding speed and attention to detail with my price. And, once we're lovers, I'll even write a book of sonnets in praise of your beauty. No extra cost."

"Once we're—are you joking?"

He cocked his head at me. "About which part? The sonnets or the cost?"

"The lovers part."

He blinked, clearly confused. "Why, plenty of high-born ladies take their artists as lovers. And I've wanted a clever mistress for some time now." He sighed wistfully. "The stupid ones are so taxing. I can't get out of bed with them fast enough. With a learned woman though...ah, how marvelous a thing it would be to make love and then discuss the great philosophers. And then make love again."

Francesca was never going to believe this. Good lord, I wanted to laugh, but that would attract too much attention. My straight face grew harder to maintain.

"Signore, your proposition is completely scandalous, not to mention insulting. I'll overlook it this once, but it'd better not happen again if we're going to do business."

"'She wants to yield in her heart. Stolen love is as sweet to a woman as a man.'"

I rolled my eyes. "Don't quote Ovid to me."

That charming grin returned, underscored with something more suggestive. "Ah, you *are* clever. I can hardly wait."

* * *

Niccolò was as good as his word. We finalized the contract the next day, outlining scope, materials, payment, and timeframe. Once it was signed and notarized, he set about sizing up the wall in our salon, planning sketches and other preparations. In the following days, he arrived early and worked late, barely leaving in time for curfew.

My own days were busy with controlling the household and business finances—more of 'playing a man,' I guessed—but I still managed to spend a fair amount of time watching him work. I liked studying an artist's mindset, and he could chat fluently as he went along. To my surprise, he was astonishingly well-read.

"Are you saying it wasn't just jealousy?" I asked one day, watching him sketch with sinopia. We'd been discussing Ovid's *Metamorphoses*.

"Well, of course it was jealousy but not just because Arachne won. Children experience that kind of jealousy. This was bigger. Arachne wove better than a goddess. A goddess! Don't you see the implications? Humans surpassing gods, surpassing those who created them. It calls the whole balance of power into question. The gods do not like their progeny to be too successful or too clever."

I sifted through all the stories I'd heard in my long life. "Like Prometheus. He stole fire for humans, so they could advance themselves, and it angered the gods."

"Exactly so. Truly, you are as wise as you are beautiful."

I rolled my eyes at his melodramatic flattery and gave him a sly grin. "But these are only pagan stories, right? They mean nothing."

Niccolò paused in his sketching and sat back on his heels, cutting me a knowing glance. "You're smarter than that. Our one, true faith of today gives us the very same message. All of humanity is now condemned because Mother Eve sought to advance herself, and women in particular are discouraged to learn and study."

"You sound like you disapprove."

"As I've said before, I like clever women."

"Some might consider you a heretic, you know."

"Then I'm in good company, Signora."

I laughed. It had been so long since I'd had anyone I could discuss these kinds of topics with both frankly and intelligently. When I spent time with men, we usually had...other matters to attend to. And the women of this age were so ignorant and poorly educated as to bring me to tears. Knowledge and wit: those things almost meant more to me than my lovers. Men came and went in this world, especially to an immortal. But the wisdom they left behind...that was eternal.

Francesca found Niccolò less amusing than I did.

"You're wasting our money," she chastised after he'd left that night. She'd been with a lover earlier in the evening, and to my immortal senses, she glowed with his stolen life energy.

"I checked his references. He's good. And when he's done, we'll be left with a tribute to an age of decadence and debauchery. Besides, we could use a little excess around here. Father Betto told me Savonarola plans on gathering up the city's 'vanities' and burning them."

She made a disparaging sound, her disdain shifting to Savonarola. "Great. As if his laws and 'holy' gangs weren't bad enough. Now he wants our mirrors and clothes?"

"And any sinful books or art."

"Oh. Well, that's not such a loss. And don't look at me like that," she added, seeing my glare. "If you spent half as much time seducing men as you do reading, you could challenge Lilith herself. I don't care about the books. Just let me keep my silk."

"Is someone going to take it?"

We both turned around at the new voice. A surge of power filled the air. Savia, the demoness we both answered to, stood before us. She had materialized in the salon without warning, as she was accustomed to doing. Francesca and I curtsied.

"We were discussing Fra Savonarola."

Brushstrokes

Resplendent in black silk, Savia strolled around the room and settled on one of our low couches. The black of her hair flowed into her dress. Her aura burned around her. "Which one is he again?"

"That ugly friar with the hooked nose," offered Francesca. "The one who got the French out."

"I think it was the city's ransom that actually got them out," I muttered.

Savia favored me with an indulgent smile. "My darling Bianca, always so clever. Tell me what you've been doing. Have you taken your priest yet?"

Francesca and I dutifully reported on our recent activities. Savia was very efficient as demons went. She showed up every couple of weeks, listened to our reports, advised if necessary, and otherwise left us alone. Yet, despite this casual treatment, we both knew her power over us was insurmountable. Only a fool would anger her. Actually, only a fool would anger any demon, end of story.

Francesca finished citing her recent conquests, glowing like a prize pupil. My list had been much shorter, but I felt no shame. Savia listened impassively to it all and stayed silent when the recitation ended.

"You're taking the easy prey," she said at last, voice cold as she stared at Francesca. My colleague's gleeful smile faded.

"But I—"

"I do not want to hear about men who have sought *you* out, men who only wanted another mistress. I want to hear about monks and priests. I want to hear about guilty husbands and fathers whose souls you've lured to our side. If you want easy fucks, you can go join a brothel. Do you understand?"

"Savia, I—"

"*Do you understand?*"

The demoness rose to her feet. She was no taller than us, but her power crackled around her, making her presence loom over Francesca and me. The other succubus sank to her knees, trembling.

"Yes, Savia," she whispered. "I understand."

As I said, only a fool would cross a demon.

* * *

Weeks later, I sprawled across the couch in our salon, talking with Niccolò while he worked.

"Ovid didn't know anything about love," I told him. I should have been reviewing accounts from a recent shipment, but the lure of his charm and intellect continued to prove too strong. He looked up at me with mock incredulity.

"Nothing about love? Woman, bite your tongue! He's the authority! He wrote books on it. Books that are still read and used today."

I sat up from my undignified repose. "They aren't relevant. They were written for a different time. He devotes pages to telling men where to meet women. But those places aren't around anymore. Women don't go to races or fights. We can't even linger in public areas anymore." This came out with more bitterness than I intended. I'd adapted to these times as I had all others, but I missed the freedoms earlier eras and places had enjoyed.

"Perhaps. But the principles are still the same. As are the techniques."

"Techniques?" I repressed a snort. Honestly, what could a mere mortal know about seduction techniques? "They're nothing but superficial gestures. Give your ladylove compliments. Talk about things you have in common—like the weather. Help her fix her dress if it gets mussed. What does any of that have to do with love?"

"What does anything have to do with love anymore? If anything, those comments are particularly applicable now. Marriage is all about business." He paused, tilting his head toward me in his usual way. "You've done something with your hair today that's extremely pretty, by the way."

I paused in return, thrown off by the compliment. "Thank you. Anyway. You're right: marriage *is* business. But some of them are love matches. Or love can grow. And plenty of clandestine affairs, no matter how 'sinful,' are based on love."

Brushstrokes

"So your problem is that he's ruining what love is still left?" His eyes drifted to the window, and he frowned. "Does it look like it'll rain out there?"

The zeal of this topic seized hold of me, making his abrupt interruptions that much more annoying. "Yes—what? I mean, no, it won't rain, and yes, that's what he's doing. Love is already so rare. By approaching it like a game, he cheapens what little there is."

Niccolò abandoned his brushes and colors and sat down next to me on the couch. "You don't think love is a game?"

"Sometimes—all right, most of the time—yes, but that doesn't mean we shouldn't—" I stopped. His fingers had slid to the edge of my dress's neckline. "What are you doing?"

"This is crooked. I'm straightening it."

I stared and then started laughing as the ruse revealed itself. "You're doing it. You're following his advice."

He leaned close to me, wearing that dazzling and dangerous smile. "Is it working?"

"No."

He pressed his lips against mine. They were soft and sweet, and his tongue felt like fire moving into my mouth.

"What about now?" he murmured a moment later, breaking from me.

"Now it might be working."

I put my hand behind his neck, pulling his mouth back down to my own. When his hand began slowly pushing up the folds of my skirts, I knew it was time to retreat to my bedroom.

Once there, he abandoned any attempts at subtlety. He pushed me down onto the bed, the fingers that so deftly painted walls now fumbling to release me from the complicated dress and its layers of rich fabrics.

When he had me stripped down to my thin chemise, I took charge, removing his clothing with a brisk efficiency and delighting in the way his skin felt under my fingertips as my hands explored his body. Straddling him, I lowered my face and let my tongue dance circles around his nipples. They hardened within my mouth, and I had the satisfaction of hearing him cry out softly when my teeth grazed their tender surface.

Moving downward, I trailed kisses along his stomach—down, down to where he stood erect and swollen. Delicately, I ran my tongue along that shaft, from base to tip. He cried out again, that cry turning to a moan when I took him into my mouth. I felt him swell between my lips, growing harder and larger, as I slowly moved up and down.

Without even realizing what he did, I think, he raked his hands through my hair, getting his fingers caught up in the elaborate pinning and carefully arranged curls. Sucking harder, I increased my pace, exalting in the feel of him filling up my mouth. The early twinges of his energy began seeping into me, like glittering streams of color and fire. While not physically pleasurable per se, it sparked me in a similar way, waking up my succubus hunger and igniting my flesh, making me long to touch him and be touched in return.

"Ah...Bianca, you shouldn't ..."

I momentarily released him from my mouth, letting my hand continue the work of stroking him closer to climax. "You want me to stop?"

"I ...well, ah! No, but women like you don't...you aren't supposed to ..."

I laughed, the sound low and dangerous in my throat. "You have no idea what kind of woman I am. I *want* to do this. I want you to explode in my mouth. I want to feel it on my tongue, running down my lips ..."

"Oh God," he groaned, eyes closed and lips parted.

His muscles tensed, body arching slightly, and I just managed to return him to my mouth in time. Hot liquid poured into me as he found his release, and I drank greedily while his body continued to spasm. The life energy trickling into me spiked in intensity, and I nearly had a climax of my own. We'd only just started, and I was already getting more life from him than I'd expected. This would be a good night. When his shuddering body finally quieted, I shifted myself so that my hips wrapped around his. I ran my tongue over my lips.

"Oh God," he gasped, breathing labored and eyes wide. His hands traveled up my waist and rested under my breasts, earning my approval. "I thought ... I thought only whores did that..."

I arched an eyebrow. "Disappointed?"

"Oh, no. Oh God, no."

Leaning forward, I brushed my lips against his. "Then return the favor."

He was only too eager. After pulling the chemise over my head, he ravaged my body with his mouth, his hands cradling my breasts while his lips sucked and teeth teased the nipples, just as I'd done to him. My desire grew, my instincts urging me to take more and more and stoke my body's burning need. When he moved his mouth between my legs, parting my thighs, I jerked his head up.

"You said I think like a man," I hissed softly. "Then treat me like one. Get on your knees."

He blinked in surprise, taken aback, but I could tell something about the force of the command aroused him. An animal glint shone in his eyes as he sank to his knees on the floor, and I stood before him, my backside leaning against the bed.

Hands clutching my hips, he pressed his face against the soft patch of hair between my thighs, his tongue slipping between my lips and stroking the burning, swelling heart buried within. At that first touch, my whole body shuddered, and I arched my head back. Fueled by this reaction, he lapped eagerly, letting his tongue dance with a steady rhythm. Twining my hands in his hair, I pushed him closer to me, forcing him to taste more of me, to increase the pressure of his tongue upon me.

When the burning, delicious feeling in my lower body could take no more, it burst, like the sun exploding. Like fire and starlight coursing through me, setting every part of me tingling and screaming. Imitating what I'd done to him earlier, he didn't remove his mouth until my climax finally subsided, my body still twitching each time his tongue tauntingly darted out and teased that oh-so-sensitive area.

When he finally broke away, he looked up with a bemused smile. "I don't know what you are. Subservient... dominant... I don't know how to treat you."

I smiled back, my hands caressing the sides of his face. "I'm anything you want me to be. How do you want to treat me?"

He thought about it, finally speaking in a hesitant voice. "I want...I want to think of you like a goddess...and take you like a whore..."

My smile increased. That about summed up my life, I thought.

"I'm anything you want me to be," I repeated.

Rising to his feet, he turned me around, pushing me to my knees on the bed. I felt the hard press of his erection behind me, and then he shoved it into me, sliding almost effortlessly now that I was so wet.

Moaning, I arched myself up so that he could get a better position and take me deeper. His hands clutched my hips as he moved with an almost primal aggression, and the sound of our bodies hitting each other filled the room. My body responded to his, loving the way he filled me up and drove into me. My cries grew louder, his thrusts harder and deeper.

And, oh, the life pouring into me. It was a river now, golden and scorching, renewing my own life and existence. Along with his energy, he yielded some of his emotions and thoughts, and I could literally feel his lust and affection for me.

That life force warred with my own physical pleasure, both consuming me and driving me mad, so that I could barely think or even separate one from the other. The feeling grew and grew within me, burning my core, building up in such intensity that I could barely contain it. Seeing how close I was, Niccolò shoved into me with increased force, so much so that I nearly fell forward, my face pressed against the soft covers of the bed.

The fire within me swelled, and I made no more attempts to hold off my climax. It burst within me, exploding, enveloping my whole body in a terrible, wonderful ecstasy. Niccolò showed no mercy, never slowing as that pleasure wracked my body. I writhed against it, even as I screamed for more.

And more there was. Much more.

* * *

Niccolò might be immoral in the eyes of the Church, but at the heart of what mattered, he was a decent man. He was kind to others and had a strong character whose principles were not easily shaken. As a result, he had had a lot of goodness and a lot of life to give, life I absorbed without remorse. It spread into me as our bodies moved together, sweeter than any nectar. It burned in my veins, making me feel alive, making me into the goddess he kept murmuring that I was as we continued our lovemaking.

Unfortunately, the loss of such energy took its toll, and he lay immobile in my bed afterward, breaths shallow and face pale. Naked, I sat up and watched him, running a hand over his sweat-drenched forehead. He smiled.

"Those sonnets might be harder than I thought. I don't think I can capture this with words." He struggled to sit up, the motion causing him pain. "I need to go...the curfew..."

"Forget it. You can stay here for the night."

"But your servants—"

"—are well-paid for their discretion." I brushed my lips over his skin. "Besides, aren't we supposed to discuss philosophy and then make love again?"

He closed his eyes, but the smile stayed. "Yes, of course. But I...I'm sorry. I don't know what's wrong with me. I need to rest first..."

I lay down beside him. "Then rest."

* * *

"That fresco is the work of demons!"

I gave Father Betto a nigh angelic look. "It is?"

"Yes, of course. It depicts sin and hedonism. What were you thinking?"

Sitting across from him in his office the following day, I looked sheepishly down, lower lip trembling. It was another of our prayer sessions, and I wore a dress with a Milanese neckline so low, it was a wonder he couldn't see my nipples. "I thought the Church supported the arts. You commissioned a painting last autumn."

"It was of the crucifixion," he reminded me. "By paying for this monstrosity, you encourage the depraved creations so many painters are engaging in. This is what Fra Savonarola is trying to

156

get rid of. Many such works will burn in the flames. Botticelli is bringing his own abominations."

I jerked my head up, momentarily forgetting my mission to seduce him. "Sandro Botticelli?" As if there was any other. I had seen his paintings. Their beauty made my heart ache.

"He's seen the error of his ways and now repents—as must you. Savonarola's Bands of Hope will come to your house soon. You must yield your vices to them."

Thinking of Botticelli's masterpieces consumed in fire, I could only stare into space. Then, remembering my task here, I moved a hand over the priest's. He flinched but did not remove it as my fingers tightened around his. I looked up at him through my lashes.

"Thank you, Father, for your continued guidance. You're too kind to me."

* * *

Niccolò didn't show up the following morning. I lingered in the house for much of the day, waiting and hoping. No sign. Finally, figuring I should get some work done of my own, I went down to the lowest level of the building where we stored a great deal of our stock and conducted transactions.

"My darling Bianca."

Turning, I smiled up into the face of Giovanni Alfieri. A merchant of considerable wealth and influence, he traded and shipped with us regularly. He also wanted to bed me very, very badly. I waved away the clerk assisting him and wandered up to Alfieri's tall, bearded form, tossing my hair back coquettishly. I liked him fine for business but had no intention of ever doing anything more; his soul was too corrupt to even count as a prize for hell. Still, we enjoyed an excellent flirtation.

"Signore Alfieri, what a treat. You're visiting us in person. I figured you'd send one of your assistants."

He swept me a gallant bow. "And miss the chance of basking in your presence? Never. That dress, by the way, is particularly stunning. Lovely neckline."

I laughed. Nice that somebody at least appreciated my better attributes. I knew he had no illusions about my 'virtue,' nor did he hold its lack against me.

"You've been staring at my neckline?" I filled my voice with mock indignation.

"Certainly not," he said, pitching his voice low so the workers wouldn't hear. "I've been paying much more attention to what it contains. I've also been imagining what it contains."

"Well," I said dryly, "I trust you have a good imagination."

"It's excellent, but I wouldn't mind comparing to the real thing..."

I repressed an eye roll and beckoned my clerk back over. Alfieri's face immediately turned shrewd and attentive. Lascivious or not, he was a businessman at heart, and his ships had a huge shipment bound for England soon. He'd make us both a lot of money.

When we finally closed up shop, I returned upstairs, hoping to find Niccolò, but he still hadn't arrived. Finally, barely an hour before curfew fell, he showed up at last, a secretive look on his face and a large, wrapped bundle in his arms.

"Where have you been? What is that?"

Unwrapping the cloak, he revealed a stack of books. I sifted through them wonderingly. Boccacio's *Decameron*. Ovid's *Amores*. Countless others. Some I'd read. Some I'd longed to read. My heart gave a flutter, and my fingers itched to turn the pages.

"I've gathered these from some of my friends," he explained. "They're worried Savonarola's thugs will seize them. Will you hide them here? No one would force them away from someone like you."

The books practically shone to me, far more valuable than Francesca's stash of jewels. I wanted to drop everything and start reading. "Of course." I flipped through the pages of the Boccacio. "I can't believe anyone would want to destroy these."

"These are dark days," he said, face hard. "If we aren't careful, all knowledge will be lost. The ignorant will crush the learned."

I knew he spoke the truth. I'd seen it, over and over. Knowledge destroyed, trampled by those too stupid to know what they did. Sometimes it happened through forceful, bloody invasions; sometimes it happened through less violent but equally insidious means, like those of Fra Savonarola.

"Bianca?" Niccolò chuckled softly. "Are you even listening to me? I'd hoped to spend the night with you, but maybe you'd rather be with Boccacio..."

I dragged my eyes from the pages, feeling my lips quirk up into a half-smile. "Can't I have you both?"

Which is how, an hour later, I found myself straddling Niccolò in my bed, both of us sweaty and sated as I read passages aloud from the *Decameron*. I'd ridden him into exhaustion, taking him as forcefully as any man might conquer a virgin. He lay back, watching and listening with a small smile, happy and content.

* * *

Over the next few days, Niccolò continued to smuggle more and more goods to me. And not just books. Paintings accumulated in my home. Small sculptures. Even more superficial things like extravagant cloth and jewels.

I felt as though I'd been allowed to cross through the gates of Heaven. Hours would pass as I studied paintings and sculptures, marveling at the ingenuity of humans, jealous of a creativity I had never possessed, either as a mortal or immortal. That art filled me up with an indescribable joy, exquisite and sweet, almost reminding me of when my soul had been my own.

And the books...oh, the books. My clerks and associates soon found their hands full of extra work as I neglected them. Who cared about accounts and silk with so much knowledge at my fingertips? I drank it up, savoring the words—words the Church condemned as heresy. A secret smugness filled me over the role I played, protecting these treasures. I would pass on humanity's knowledge. The light of genius and creativity would not fade from this world, and best of all, I would get to enjoy it along the way.

When Savia's next visit came, she showed approval at Francesca's recent trysts, much to my friend's relief. The demoness was slightly less thrilled to hear about my continued delay with Father Betto, but her mood stayed optimistic. I'd proven myself on too many other occasions for her to grow agitated—yet.

"I have faith in you, Bianca. I've seen you work before." Her dark eyes cut to Francesca. "You should pay attention. You could learn a lot."

Francesca flushed angrily, upset at still being considered second best. "Bianca doesn't have much time for teaching anymore. She's too busy building up her horde."

Savia, curious, demanded an explanation, and I told her about my role in protecting the contraband. As always, her response took a long time in coming, and when it did, my heart nearly stopped.

"You need to cease this immediately."

"I—what?"

"And, you need to turn these items over to Father Betto."

I studied her incredulously, waiting for the joke to reveal itself. "You can't...you can't mean that. This stuff can't be destroyed. We'd be supporting the Church. We're supposed to go against them."

"We're supposed to further evil in the world, my darling, which may or may not go along with the Church's plans. In this case, it does."

"How?" I cried.

"Because there is no greater evil than ignorance and the destruction of genius. Ignorance has been responsible for more death, more bigotry, and more sin than any other force. It is the destroyer of mankind."

"But Eve sinned when she sought knowledge..."

Savia's lips turned up in a smirk. "Are you sure? Do you truly know what is good and what is evil?"

"I don't know," I whispered. "They seem kind of indistinguishable from one another."

"Yes. Sometimes they are." When I didn't answer, the smile vanished. "This isn't up for debate. You will yield your stash immediately. And to sweeten the deal, you'll give up some of that vast wardrobe you have. Perhaps that will finally endear you to Betto."

"But I—" The word *can't* was on my lips, and I bit it off. Under the scrutiny of her stare and power, I felt very small and very weak. You don't cross demons. I swallowed. "Yes, Savia."

* * *

Niccolò showered my neck and lips with kisses, their caresses both tender and fierce. "There is no way," he declared, "your skin can be so soft. It isn't possible."

I managed a smile I didn't feel. Part of me had died, despite how wonderful he felt moving in and out of my body. I stared up into his eyes without really seeing them, distantly noting he was about to peak. I made the appropriate noises when it happened, tightening my muscles around him as that ecstasy took over and his seed spilled into me. The lightning of his energy crackled through me as well, and he gasped at its loss, not knowing what had happened. He never realized I shortened his life a little each time we made love.

I had moved around in a daze since Savia's directive, despairing and depressed. She had the power to make my life very, very miserable if I disobeyed her, and I'd known she would check up with Father Betto and Francesca to make sure I'd indeed turned over my stash. What could I do? Nothing.

And then...yesterday, I'd thought of something I could do. But to make it work...to *really* make it work, I realized I'd have to make a terrible choice. I'd have to choose the lesser of two evils, just like the old cliché says, giving up something I loved to protect something else I loved.

Niccolò rolled off of me, exhausted but pleased. "Lenzo's going to bring me one of his paintings tomorrow. Wait until you see it. It shows Venus and Adonis—"

"No."

He lifted his head up. "Hmm?"

"No. Don't bring me any more." It was hard, oh God, it was so hard speaking to him in such a cold tone.

A frown crossed his handsome face. "What are you talking about? You've already taken so much—"

"I don't have them anymore. I gave them up to Savonarola."

"You...you're joking."

I shook my head. "No. I contacted his Bands of Hope this morning. They came and took it all."

Niccolò sat up, frown deepening. "Stop it. This isn't funny."

"It's not a joke. They're all gone. They're going to the fire. They're objects of sin. They need to be destroyed."

"You're lying. Stop this, Bianca. You don't mean—"

My voice sharpened. "They're wrong and heretical. They're *gone.*"

Our eyes locked, and as he studied my face, I could see that he was starting to realize that maybe, just maybe I spoke the truth. And I did. Sort of.

We dressed, and I took him to the storage room I'd hidden the objects in. He stared at the empty space, face pale and disbelieving. I stood nearby, arms crossed, maintaining a stiff and disapproving stance. I'd had centuries of practice making men believe any illusion I wanted.

Eyes wide, he turned to me. "How could you? How could you do this?"

"I told you—"

"I trusted you! You said you'd keep them safe!"

"I was wrong. Satan clouded my judgment."

He gripped my arm painfully and leaned closed to me. "What have they done to you? Did they threaten you? You wouldn't do this. What are they holding against you? Is it that priest you're always visiting?"

"No one's made me do this," I replied bleakly. "It's the right thing to do."

He pulled back, like he couldn't stand my touch, and my heart lurched painfully at the look in his eyes. "Do you know what you've done? Some of those can never be replaced."

"I know. But it's better this way."

With a last shocked look, he stormed out of the room.

Swallowing back tears, I watched him go. *He's just another man*, I thought. *Let him go.* I'd had so many in my life; I'd have so many more. What did he matter?

Ignoring the pain in my chest, I crept downstairs to the lower level, careful not to wake the sleeping household. I'd made the same journey last night, painstakingly carrying part of the horde down here, a feat that required several trips. It had been many years since I'd performed that kind of manual labor, but I couldn't trust anyone else.

Splitting the art and books had been like choosing which of my children had to live or die. The silks and velvets had been mindless; all of them went to Fra Savonarola. But the rest...that had been difficult. I'd let most of Ovid go. His works were so widespread, I had to believe copies of them would survive—if not in Florence, then perhaps some other place untouched by this bigotry. Other authors, those whom I feared had a limited run, stayed with me.

The paintings and sculptures proved hardest of all. They were one of a kind. I couldn't hope that other copies might exist. But I'd known I couldn't keep them all either, not when both Savia and Francesca knew my collection contained art. And so, with tears running down my face, I'd chosen those which I thought most worth saving.

Francesca had seen the shipment of chosen items go out with Savonarola's thugs this morning. She would report that to Savia. But I'd still technically disobeyed a demon, and I needed to cover myself. I needed a distraction to ensure that neither Francesca nor Savia would probe too closely and find out about the other stash. That was where Niccolò came in.

If he believed all of the treasures were gone, so would the others. His angry, abrupt split from me would distract Francesca and Savia while convincing them of my own devastation, giving them no reason to doubt my sincerity. Besides, if he knew about the secret goods' existence, the truth could eventually come out. I couldn't risk that, couldn't risk him knowing. I couldn't risk anyone knowing

Except for one.

Brushstrokes

Giovanni Alfieri had refused me at first when I'd asked him to smuggle the salvaged objects out of Florence. While not a pious man, he feared the Church just as we all did. He didn't want to court the kind of trouble that might ensue if he was caught. But I saw the glimmer of greed spark in his eyes as I increased the price he'd get for his assistance. And when I'd taken off my clothes and did all the things to him he'd long imagined—and a few he hadn't—he'd agreed to take the two crates of contraband to England.

The real irony here was that I was sending them to an angel. I didn't like angels as a general rule, but this one was a scholar, and when I'd lived there, we'd gotten along reasonably well. Heretical or no, the books and art would appeal to him as much as to me. He would keep them safe. How ironic, I thought, that I would turn to the enemy for help. Savia had been right. Sometimes good and evil were impossible to distinguish from one another.

Now, standing in the darkened storage area, I bid a silent farewell to the crates. Alfieri would come for them in the morning. I knew I was also saying goodbye to Niccolò, the expression on his face still haunting me. But his grief would save me—and the crates. The knowledge and the beauty I so loved about mankind would be saved. And inside of him, I knew Niccolò wanted the same thing. If I could have told him my dilemma, I think he would have understood.

Besides, he would still keep creating too, still making his wonderful, immoral art. He didn't need me for that. He would get over me. After all, I was just another woman to him, just as he was another man to me.

* * *

Father Betto glowed as he paced his office, afloat on his zeal and exultation.

"Fra Savonarola was so pleased. You can't imagine how wonderful this is. It is a blow to the forces of evil—an example to this indulgent city."

"Yes, Father."

Even he couldn't mistake the doubtful tone in my voice. Alfieri had safely taken my crates, but the loss of the rest still weighed heavily upon me.

Turning around, Betto knelt in front of my chair and placed his hands over mine.

"You are an angel, child. I'm so proud of you. You are peerless among women."

I studied the rapt way he looked at me, felt the warmth of his hands. Feeling sick inside, I slid my hands up his arms as I recalled my mission. Perhaps this fiasco wasn't a total loss.

"Thank you, Father. I owe it all to you. I couldn't have done this without your guidance. I'm grateful." My hands traveled further, touching his cheeks as my face moved closer to his. He took a heavy, shuddering breath, his eyes wide. I could feel the lust humming around him, feel how much he wanted me. "Very grateful."

Later, as his body moved clumsily into mine, I stared at the ceiling, thinking it funny that it took a renunciation of sin to finally lead him into it.

Good and evil were impossible to distinguish from one another.

* * *

Savonarola's Bonfire of Vanities was a great pyramid stuffed with fuel and sin. His followers threw still more items in as it blazed, seeming to have a never ending supply. Other citizens came forward, caught up in the moment, contributing dresses and mirrors and books. I watched as Botticelli himself tossed one of his paintings in. I saw only a glimpse of it in the firelight. It was beautiful. And then it was gone. Tears ran down my face, and this time, they were not contrived.

"Bianca."

"Hello, Niccolò."

He stood in front of me, gray eyes black in the flickering light. His face seemed to have aged since our last meeting. We both turned and silently observed the blaze again, watching as more and more of man's finest things were sacrificed.

"You have killed progress," Niccolò said at last.

"I've delayed it." Reaching into the folds of my dress, I handed over a purse heavy with florins. It was the last part in my plan. He took it, blinking at its weight.

"This is more than you owe me. And I won't finish the fresco."

"I know. It's all right. Take it. Go somewhere else, somewhere away from Savonarola. Paint. Write. Help others. Whatever it takes. I don't care how you do it. Just create something beautiful."

He stared, and I feared he'd give it back. "I don't understand. Why are you doing this now? I know you didn't want to give those things away. Why did you do it?"

I studied the fire again. Humans, I realized idly, liked to burn things. Objects. Each other. "Because men cannot surpass the gods. Not yet anyway."

"Prometheus never intended his gift to be used like this."

I smiled without humor, remembering the conversation that now seemed ages old. "No. I suppose not."

We said nothing else. A moment later, he walked away, disappearing into the darkness.

Biography

After a childhood filled with romance novels and mythology books, Richelle Mead's voyage into urban fantasy and paranormal romance was inevitable. She holds an M.A. in Comparative Religion from Western Michigan University and a liberal arts bachelor's degree from the University of Michigan. Her studies have included world mythology, religion, literature, and ancient and medieval history. She also has a particular passion for wacky and humorous things.

She is the author of two series from Kensington Books. The first, beginning with SUCCUBUS BLUES, is about reluctant succubus Georgina Kincaid and will debut in March 2007. Richelle's DARK SWAN series will be released in 2008 and follows the adventures of an Arizona shaman. She has also recently signed with Penguin/Razorbill for a YA series about a teenage vampire princess. It will be published in Fall 2007.

Richelle currently writes full-time in Seattle where she lives with her husband and four cats. Late-night musings and updates about her books can be found at: www.richellemead.com

Red's Merry Mischief

by

Debbie Mumford

Rating: Tangy

Genre: Fantasy

Red languished in his frame, too disconsolate to play tricks on the happy young couple currently coupling in the king-sized bed beneath his window. Life sucked, and immortality spelled never-ending suckiness. The little faery drifted to the bottom of his enchanted glass and reflected on the crime that had landed him in this abysmal prison. Fate had been unkind, to cause him to use his power against the Summer Queen. It had been a mistake; it never should have happened; and it had cost him his freedom.

All true, but it had also been deliciously decadent to watch the most powerful faery of Tuatha de Danaan allow herself to be ravished by a human male. Red's mouth curved into a lascivious smile as he remembered how his small magick had been responsible for Titania's monumental embarrassment.

* * *

Lysette.

The comely faery lass danced among the poppies unaware of Red's careful observation. He drank in the grace of her slender body as she pirouetted from one side of the meadow to the other. Her black hair shone with the iridescence of a raven's wing, a perfect contrast to the moonbeam shimmer of her creamy complexion. The leaf-green fabric of her gown flowed and swirled around the firm, lithe curves of her breasts and buttocks, drawing his eye to their promise while modestly concealing her secrets.

Lysette.

Handmaiden to Titania, the Summer Queen of Tuatha de Danaan. Red ached to possess the dark-haired maiden, but he hesitated to approach her again. His ego still smarted from their last encounter.

"Take you to my bed?" she'd laughed when he'd offered for her at the Beltane fire. "Not if you were the last male fae in the kingdom!"

But as he watched her dance among the red-gold blossoms, a daring thought occurred. What if he rescued her? What if the fair Lysette found herself besieged, and Red valiantly fought for her honor and her freedom? Would she still withhold her glorious treasure from the hero who swept her from danger and returned her to safety underhill? Red's heart raced and his eyelids drooped as he imagined running his hands over her soft curves, kissing her berry-stained lips, sinking into her warm, welcoming depths ...

"Attend me, Red!" Titania's sharp voice slapped him back to reality, and Red whirled to face his liege.

The Summer Queen was a vision of perfection—from her flowing platinum tresses, emerald green eyes, and porcelain complexion, to her reed-slim body with its delectable curves. Red dropped into a courtly bow before his over-stimulated imagination could carry those thoughts further. The Summer Queen, a formidable power in her own right, was accompanied by her husband. Oberon's blue-black hair and hazel eyes made him the perfect foil to Titania's pale glory. In unity, the Fae's royal couple dazzled the eye; at odds, their temper disrupted the order of the natural world. Fortunately, today the atmosphere was charged with nothing more sinister than bored condescension.

"My lady," Red said, not daring to raise his eyes. "How may I be of service to my queen?"

Amusement colored her voice when she answered, "Still coveting the fair Lysette, I see. Methinks you need a quest, young fae, to occupy your thoughts and give outlet to your energies."

Red straightened, his face hot with embarrassment. Titania glanced at Oberon, and her green eyes flashed in response to his indulgent nod.

"Go forth into the human realm and find me a knight. He must be courageous and bold and skilled with weapons of war. Tuatha de Danaan requires a mortal champion, and you will bring him to the glade beneath the Guardian Oak three days hence. I will meet you there to inspect your choice." She leveled a stare at him that froze his bones. "Go, and do not return underhill until I have accepted your knight."

Titania extended her bejeweled hand and Red bowed to kiss it. He straightened, saluted Oberon and said, "I shall not fail, my lady. Until we meet beneath the Guardian Oak."

He turned on his heel, stole a final glimpse of Lysette and vanished into the mortal realm.

* * *

Red reclined in the crook of an apple tree whose branches overhung the training field just beyond the castle's stagnant moat. He'd been watching the men-at-arms train for the better part of the day and despaired of finding a knight of any quality here. However, as this was the best fortified castle he knew of, he continued his vigil though his mind often wandered back to Lysette. Perhaps he could think of a way to combine his quest for a knight with his conquest of that raven-haired temptress. A clever fae could always find a way ...

A trumpet fanfare sounded, and Red straightened, his interest piqued. A knight in armor rode forth from the castle, across the drawbridge and cantered to the field. Unable to hear what was being said, Red grabbed a ripening apple and bit into its tart flesh while he leaned forward to watch the knight's actions.

The mortal raised his visor and gestured to the men-at-arms. They gathered to one side and watched as the knight demonstrated various weapons.

Red chewed thoughtfully. This fellow just might do. He certainly met the requirement of skill with weapons and the dents in his armor spoke of courage in battle, but how was Red to determine his boldness?

He handed the apple core off to an inquisitive squirrel and drew his knees up under his chin without a thought to the precariousness of his perch. Schemes chased themselves across his mind until finally one took root and grew. Yes. That just might work. Better still, he might be able to twist it to serve his pursuit of the fair Lysette.

The knight finished instructing the men-at-arms, and the training session broke up. Red dropped lightly from the tree, wrapped himself in the invisibility of a summer breeze, and followed the knight back to the castle. Once in his quarters, the mortal removed his armor to reveal a powerfully built physique—

especially through the chest, shoulders and arms—a face that remained handsome despite a nose that had been broken more than once, and sweat-soaked auburn hair clubbed at the base of his neck. Red nodded in satisfaction. Physically, this mortal would do nicely; now to test his character.

The evening entertainments of a mortal castle bored Red, but he stayed close to the knight and amused himself by stealing tidbits of food from the plates of the prettiest maidens. He toyed with the idea of stealing other, more intimate delicacies from them, but resisted temptation. He could always return when he wasn't on a quest for the Summer Queen.

At last, the mortal knight retired to his chamber and freed Red to complete his scheme. As the young man closed his eyes, Red worked an intricate enchantment, capturing the warrior's will and summoning Lysette from Tuatha de Danaan in the same spell.

When the faery maiden appeared, Red melted into the shadows and waited for the final element of his enchantment to come into play. Lysette turned in a graceful circle, clearly seeking the wizard who had successfully called her to the mortal realm. She frowned and approached the sleeping knight.

Red forgot to breathe, so intense was his desire not to disturb the working. *Yes, my lovely,* he thought. *Just a little closer. Touch his shoulder; you know you want to ...*

Lysette leaned over the knight's sleeping form and trailed her fingers across his bare arm. Her sharp intake of breath caused Red to grin. Caught! He'd done it! He loosed his hold upon the mortal's will and leaned against the wall, prepared to enjoy the show.

The maiden touched the sleeping man again, more boldly this time, massaging the firm muscles of his upper arm before sliding her hand up over his shoulder and down onto his chest. Just as her hand reached the auburn curls that covered his powerful chest, the mortals eyes sprang open and he captured her hand in a snake-swift strike of his own.

"Who are you?" he growled, pulling the dark-haired faery close. "Why are you in my chamber?"

"I don't know, my lord," she said, her voice a whisper of confusion. "I was summoned here, but I don't know by whom."

Against the far wall, Red bit his lip to keep from laughing aloud. The proud Lysette, in the grip of a half-naked mortal man. Oh, this was rich revenge, indeed. He hoped the knight would push his advantage, at least a bit. After all, if Red was to rescue his fair maiden, he just as well have the benefit of exposed flesh to accidentally fondle in the process. She'd hardly blame *Red* if that barbaric mortal tore off her gown!

He kept silent, wrapped in his glamour of invisibility and watched in avid delight as the knight registered the stunning loveliness of the woman he held captive.

"Give me your name, fair maiden," the knight said, "and I'll release you."

"I cannot," said Lysette. "I ... I'm not sure why, but I cannot speak my name in this realm."

The man straightened into a sitting position and pulled Lysette onto the bed beside him. His eyes narrowed as he studied her face. "What treachery is this? If you are not from this realm, whose kingdom do you claim?"

"The lord Oberon is my king," said Lysette, modestly lowering her eyes from the man's naked chest.

"Oberon?" questioned the knight. "I know of no king named Oberon. Who has sent you to test my loyalty, wench?"

Lysette's lip trembled, and she tugged at her hand in an attempt to free herself from the knight's grip. His reaction pulled her onto his lap so that his free arm encircled her waist while the hand that held hers released her.

Yes, thought Red. *Take her now! Remove her gown, free her firm round breasts. Let me see her rosy nipples before I rescue her from your savage advances.*

Lysette held herself aloof, touching the knight as little as possible. He turned his head toward her, and their eyes met. Red watched in heart-pounding excitement as the couple leaned together into a kiss that scorched the very air concealing his presence. A shudder of wicked delight ran through his loins when the mortal raised his hand to toy with the ribbons holding Lysette's gown closed across her bosom. The strings loosed almost of their own accord, and Red lunged forward anxious to feel those perfect globes with his own heated fingers.

A whisper of power stirred his concealment, and Red whirled to find himself face to face with an indignant Lysette. Confusion befuddled his brain, and he froze in mid-stride.

"What ..."

"Red! What have you done?"

He glanced from the angry faery maiden before him to the couple rapidly disrobing on the bed. Angry Lysette. Aroused Lysette. How had he mangled his spell? How could she be in two places at once? He knew which he preferred, but he also knew which he had to deal with, and quickly.

"Lysette, my sweet," he said. "You are Lysette, are you not?"

"I am, you idiot," she cried, her eyes blazing, "but *she* is not!"

Red turned to watch the lustful pair tussle playfully on the bed. A wistful sigh escaped his lips. Regretfully, he turned to face the storm brewing in the dark beauty's eyes.

"If you are here," he asked in as innocent a voice as he could command in his excited state, "who is there?"

"That, you monumental idiot, is Titania, and I suggest you get that unwashed mortal off of her royal ass before his majesty the king comes in search of his wife!"

"Titania!" Red's stomach heaved, and all thought, lewd or otherwise, fled his mind. "Why would Titania answer a summoning for you and in your guise?"

"Because she wanted to see the knight you'd chosen for her," sighed Lysette. "She wanted to check on your progress without alerting you to her presence."

Red closed his eyes and tried not to think what this little prank was about to cost him. He'd intended to rescue Lysette before anything happened, but now Lysette wasn't Lysette, and Lysette had interrupted him and he didn't know what the smartest move would be ...

"Red! Do something!"

The panic in Lysette's voice startled Red. "What?"

"The queen is about to be mounted by that mortal! Stop him!"

Red whirled to face the panting couple and saw a tangle of arms and legs—completely naked arms and legs—not to mention a very shapely ass. An ass that even now positioned itself to allow its owner to slide onto a very engorged male member. Red strode toward the bed only to rush headlong into a very solid obstacle. The King of all Tuatha de Danaan, Oberon, Titania's husband, shimmered into existence between Red and the lusty couple, with his back to the bed.

"Attend me, Red," bellowed the king. "Where is my wife?"

Red skidded to a halt and sketched a very shaky bow. "Your wife, my lord? I have not seen the Summer Queen." He lowered his eyes before Oberon could read the lie beneath the literal truth of Red's words.

Oberon frowned, nodded to Lysette, and said, "I was told Titania came to inspect your knight."

Sweat trickled down Red's brow, and he tasted bile as he watched the queen inspecting the knight's anatomy in intimate detail behind Oberon's back.

A squeal of pleasure from the bed caused the King of Tuatha de Danaan to swing around and face the couple mating in oblivious fervor. "Lysette?"

Oberon turned back to the handmaid who cowered against the wall. "Are you Lysette, or is that Lysette? And if that's not Lysette, who is it? And why in the name of all that's magic are the two of you standing here watching this couple … couple?"

Lysette sank to the floor, her hand clamped to her mouth. Oberon turned from her and glared at Red.

"I can explain, Sire," he said feebly, knowing his doom loomed over him.

"Cease!" roared the king, and the fornicating couple fell away from each other and lay quietly on the bed, to all appearances, sleeping peacefully.

* * *

Red knelt on a plush carpet of wood sorrel before the throne of the Summer Queen. Oberon stood a few paces away, his face swathed in a storm of violent emotion. Lysette waited behind Titania, ready to answer her smallest request.

Titania, resplendent in a gown woven of summer sunlight,

gazed at Red with detached disinterest. The mischievous fae shivered in the midsummer heat. Soon the axe would fall and this misadventure would end. It had to end. He couldn't endure much more of the court's cold silence.

No one spoke of what had befallen the Summer Queen, but everyone knew. The Queen's silent misery froze her folk, while the King's white-hot anger singed any unwary enough to venture near. And everyone knew that Red stood firmly in the eye of both storms.

"Be done with it, wife," growled Oberon as he strode to take his place on the throne at her side. "Condemn this miserable wretch, or I will!"

"No," she said, her words glacial and slow. "The violation is mine, as is the humiliation. Vengeance shall be mine as well. No one shall so much as speak to this creature without my leave."

Oberon glowered at Red, his fingers tightening to white on the arms of the throne, but his voice was clear and calm when he said, "As you wish, my love."

"Lysette," she called and waited while her handmaid stepped forward and curtsied. "His scheme was meant for you. Do you wish to advise me on his punishment?"

"Forgive me, lady," said Lysette. "He is rude and mischievous. He is unbelievably thoughtless and fickle, but I don't believe he meant me harm." She cast a sideways glance at Red and shame stabbed his heart at her words. "Please, lady, if you can find it in your heart, be merciful."

Titania sighed, straightened on her cushioned seat, and stared directly at Red. "Lysette makes a good point. You are thoughtless, Red. I would be within my rights to order your execution, but I bear some responsibility for this fiasco as well. You did not realize with whom you toyed."

The Summer Queen rose, glided across the deep green leaves to stand over the kneeling fae. "I sentence you to a hundred years' imprisonment," she said. With a wave of her hand she conjured a pane of glistening glass. "Use the time to consider your crimes. Learn to think before you return underhill."

Another wave lifted Red and slammed him into the glass. It liquefied around him, swallowed him, and digested him. He came to rest in the interstices within the crystalline structure.

Lysette.

At least he could still see Lysette. Perhaps she would take pity on him and place him in her chambers ...

The Summer Queen clapped her hands and the human knight knelt in Red's place on the sorrel. "Take this glass into the mortal realm," she commanded. "Place it carefully, somewhere quiet, that my errant subject's thinking may not be disturbed as he awaits his release."

The knight rose, picked up Red's prison and prepared to leave. The Queen stopped him with a gesture. She stepped forward, placed her fingertips on Red's glass and whispered, "Remember, master trickster, time runs differently in the mortal realm. A hundred years in Tuatha de Danaan will be an eternity there."

Lysette, cried Red, but his voice was swallowed in the glass' magic.

Biography

By day, Debbie Mumford works as a technical writer for a land-use / architectural firm, but her evenings and weekends are dedicated to helping her writing career take flight. She is a regular contributor to Flash Me Magazine and has been published in KidVisions and Dragons, Knights and Angels. Her e-books (available from Freya's Bower) include GLASS MAGIC, a duet of romantic fantasy short stories featuring a mischievous faery named Red, and SORCHA'S HEART, a romantic fantasy novella about her favorite creatures — dragons! SECOND SIGHT, a paranormal romance novel, will be available from Freya's Bower in early 2007. Visit Debbie at http://www.debbiemumford.com/

Baring It All for Mr. Right

by

Rhonda Stapleton

Rating: Sweet

Genre: Chick Lit

Baring It All for Mr. Right

I check out my hot new neighbor's tight body as he unloads a few boxes from the back seat of his white Camry.

Well-shaped legs? *Check.*

Broad shoulders? *Check.*

An ass tight enough to bounce a dollar bill off of? *Double check.*

With the last box in his arms, he pulls the front door with his foot to close it behind him.

Naturally, he piques my curiosity. For some reason, our Cleveland neighborhood tends to attract either older couples or single women. The closest we have to an eligible bachelor is 42-year-old Tom Hanson, whom my roommate Lily and I nicknamed "Ménage-a-Tom" —one night during a block party, Tom got wasted and asked us to be in a threesome with him. Needless to say, we pretty much avoid him now.

I rush inside. Lil is vegging out on the couch with a bag of chips, watching some reality TV show.

I'm bursting to tell the news. "Oh my God! You have to check out our new neighbor!"

She looks up at me, wiping an errant crumb off her t-shirt. Lil's not exactly the cleanest person in the world, but she's been a close friend for over 15 years, and she always pays her half of the rent on time.

She tucks a strand of shoulder-length brown hair behind her ear. "The guy who bought the Andersons' house? Is he a troll?"

"Hardly. Trust me. Just come and see."

We dart out the side door and sneak into the back yard. The sun already set, so the sky is getting darker by the minute. All his windows except the back kitchen window are tightly closed, shutters down.

I push up against the chain-link fence and strain to look in. It's the wrong angle, and I can't see a thing. Damn.

"We need a plan," I mutter.

"Like what?"

My mind scrambles to come up with a clever idea. *Think, Joanna!*

A flash of inspiration hits me. I whisper to Lil, "Go grab the Frisbee. We'll pretend to play, and oops—I'll accidentally fling it

180

into his back yard. If he notices, he'll have to come out and get it for us. If not, we can go back and get it, and just so happen to peek into his window."

Lil's eyebrow rises. "It's dark. Who plays Frisbee at night?"

"Who cares? It's brilliant. Trust me. It'll work."

She sighs and plods back into the house. A minute later, she emerges, a red rubber ball in hand. "I couldn't find the Frisbee, so I grabbed that ball your niece left over here last week."

"A ball? I don't think you're taking this seriously. Are you even trying?"

Lil squints at me. "This whole plan is dumb to begin with. So either make it work, or let me go back in and find out who got voted off!"

"Fine," I whisper. "Just toss the ball, but miss me."

She tosses it into his back yard. It bounces a couple of times and lands squarely in the middle of the grass. Perfect.

We wait with baited breath for a minute or two. Okay, so *I* wait with baited breath. Lil looks bored to tears.

Nothing.

I nod to Lil. "Okay, time to proceed. I'll hop over first and give you the all-clear."

She snickers. "Roger, Dodger."

I tiptoe to the fence and throw a leg over. As I straddle the fence, the other leg quickly follows.

I push myself forward to hop off the fence, but I don't move.

I think my shorts are snagged on the fence.

"Lil!" I whisper. "I think I'm stuck!"

I tug again, now feeling the frantic need to detach myself from this metal trap.

Rrrrrip.

I fall to the ground on Hottie Neighbor's side of the fence.

Oh God, please tell me that rip wasn't what I thought it was. I reach a hand to my backside. My fingers touch bare skin.

Lil starts giggling hysterically, doubled over until she's gasping for breath. "That was hilarious. You should've seen it!"

"Oh, hardy har," I mumble.

Hottie Neighbor's side door opens, and he steps out into the cool evening air, wearing a pair of faded jeans and black t-shirt.

He looks up at me, his dark brown hair slightly mussed and a huge grin plastered on his face.

I stiffen up and casually cover my ass with my right hand, feeling like a 6-year-old caught cramming an entire candy bar into my mouth.

He sizes me up, his dark eyes twinkling. "Well," he says, his voice low with an edge of amusement, "it looks to me like you've got a problem." With one eyebrow raised, he leans over and picks up the red ball, handing it to me. "Here you go."

I grab it with my left hand. "Thanks for your help. What's your name?" I blurt out, casually squeezing my shorts closer together with my other hand. Maybe he didn't see anything, and I can get out of this without looking like a total flake. I just need to play the nice, welcoming neighbor.

I hear Lil snicker behind my back on the other side of the fence.

"I'm Jacob."

"Hi. I'm Joanna. Sorry the ball flew over there. Lil has terrible aim," I say, trying to save face.

"Hey! Not cool!" she cries out.

He smirks at me, his dark eyes peering into mine. "Yeah, I saw that out the window. Quite a jump you made over here."

Oh, no.

He saw me rip my pants.

A flush works its way up my neck and over my cheeks. Time to make my exit. Keeping my back away from him, I glance around quickly, trying to find a way to escape. Damn it, his entire yard is fenced in. The only way out is back over the fence, or—

Jacob chuckles. "You can cut through my house. I'd hate to cause more injury to your shorts if you tried hopping the fence again."

I sigh. Guess there's no way out of this. Following him, I head through the kitchen and living room, filled with unopened boxes.

He opens the front door. "Thanks for...dropping by."

I stiffly nod, wishing the ground would swallow me whole. "Bye. Nice meeting you." I dart into the house before I can embarrass myself any further.

"Well," Lil said, shaking her head at me once we're back inside, "that was interesting. Although he was quite attractive." She pauses and stares at me for a moment. "Oh my God. You can ask *him*."

I stare in confusion at her, stripping my ripped shorts off. Lil and I have seen each other in undies so many times, it doesn't faze either of us anymore. The joys of having a roommate, I guess. "Ask him what?"

She rolls her eyes, picking up the bag of chips off the coffee table and cramming a chip in her mouth. "Duh," she says around a mouthful, "Ask him to go to the wedding with you."

"Are you kidding? I just committed a crime—I broke into the guy's backyard. And ripped my friggin' pants while doing it." A fresh wave of heat steals over my cheeks. God, I'm such an idiot! "Besides, he and I barely know each other."

She opens her mouth to speak, but I cut her off. "Wait. I need to grab some shorts that don't show my ass. Hold that thought." I fly to the kitchen to pitch my ripped shorts, then go upstairs and throw on a pair of knit shorts. I make my way back to the living room and settle into the lounger, kicking my feet onto the coffee table. "Go on."

"Who cares if you don't know each other or not? Some people get married on less than that. At least you'd have something in common to laugh about." She grabs another handful of chips and plops down onto the couch.

"Maybe he's in a relationship already. I don't need to hone in on some other girl's man."

Lil holds up her fingers. "One, no ring. Two, he just bought a house by himself. Three, if he was moving, surely his girlfriend or significant other would be helping him." She smiles in triumph.

Damn, she's right. "How'd you get to be so smart?"

She shrugs. "I'm just observant. Anyway, you'd better get cracking. The wedding's in two weeks, and you promised you'd bring a date. Remember our deal?"

As if I could forget. When Lil and I received invitations to her cousin Jenna's wedding, we decided to force ourselves to find dates by indicating on the RSVP that we'd bring someone with us. Lil just found her date last weekend, a friend of one of her coworkers, but I'm still solo.

I nod. "Okay, okay. Don't nag. I just need to get to know him better and see if we're even compatible."

Lil laughs. "I'm not telling you to pick out curtains with the man. Just ask him to be your date." With a wicked gleam in her eye, she says, "But if you really insist on getting to know him better, maybe we can work on making that happen."

* * *

I hate my job.

I know it's temporary until I finish my degree—I'm in my last year of earning my bachelor's in biology—but it still sucks.

Well, at least the rain dampened the spread of pollen and spores. On mornings when I run the leaf blower to clear debris off the courts, I wear a mask to keep my allergies under control. Yeah, that's so attractive.

I roll the huge, awkward squeegee across a tennis court, forcing the water off the sides of the concrete slats. We have to clear off the courts after it rains so that the customers, impatiently waiting in the café, can get back to playing on their rented courts.

One down, seven to go. Four of our courts are inside, which cuts down on my maintenance duties.

I glance at the domed courts. The half-completed drainage ditch running alongside the indoor courts taunts me. Another fun "tennis court attendant" job I have to finish soon.

Did I mention how much I hate my job?

After hauling ass and drying the courts, I run back inside to the cash register to help Eunice, my coworker. She started here a month ago after her husband died. Rather than sit home alone, she came out of retirement and got a job. When I work with her, I try to do all the hard labor jobs so she doesn't tire herself.

"Sorry," I say, dragging in deep breaths, "I just finished."

She smiles, and the wrinkles around her eyes deepen. She pats my hand. "It's okay. Sorry I couldn't help, but we got busy in here. You know how these people get about their Powerade."

I glance at the clock. Time for my lunch break. Hooray! "Hey, Eunice, I'm taking my lunch break now. My friend Lil packed a picnic, and she'll be here any minute."

"Sounds good. Go enjoy your break. You deserve it!"

Eunice is such a nice woman. She's about the only redeeming quality of working here. Most of the other attendants are crabby teenagers working their first jobs, too lazy to help out.

I step outside, avoiding eye contact with the tennis pros, and wait for Lil. After a few minutes, her dark blue Neon pulls into the parking lot. Thank God, 'cause I'm starving.

She flings her door open and scans the area, looking for me.

I wave and walk towards her. "Lil! I'm here!"

"Hey, lady. That little rain shower on the way over here was weird. Hope we can find a dry spot to sit."

"Well, maybe we can go over to the picnic tables, since the grass is still wet."

Her passenger door opens, and out steps Jacob, wearing his requisite jeans, a white t-shirt, and a baseball cap.

I hadn't noticed him in her car. My heart thumps in surprise, and I reach up as subtly as possible to smooth my hair and shirt, brushing off all the errant leaves that somehow found their way onto me.

"Hi," he says, that charming smile edging one side of his mouth higher than the other. "Lil invited me. I hope its okay I came along."

I glance at Lil, who offers me a wide-eyed shrug. "He was weeding, and I figured he'd be hungry."

She's so transparent. "Sure, it's no problem," I say, fighting down the butterflies in my stomach.

I help them carry the food, and we find the table farthest away from the tennis courts. While Lil drapes the blanket across the slightly damp picnic bench seat, I unload the familiar red-and-white-striped bucket of fried chicken, mashed potatoes and gravy, mac and cheese, and green beans.

Lil never was much of a cook, preferring to order food, instead. Which is fine by me; I'm pretty lousy in the kitchen, myself.

"Oh, Lil," I tease, "you shouldn't have slaved so hard."

"What can I say?" She shrugs and doles out plates, napkins and silverware. "KFC does chicken better than I do."

The three of us eat fast, wiping out the chicken and sides in record time.

Food coma sets in, and I moan as I pitch the trash. "Oh God, I'm so sleepy now." I stretch in my seat, willing myself to wake up, then glance at my watch. Break time is over. "Well, thanks for dropping by with lunch, guys. I appreciate it. I need to go finish digging a drainage ditch."

"You're welcome," Lil says. She shoots a sideways glance at Jacob. "Sounds like you got your hands full for the rest of the day, Joanna. That sucks."

Jacob looks at me quizzically. "You have to dig ditches?"

"Yeah. Apparently, I'm on the same employment level as 'prison worker'," I say with a grin. "I think my boss is a bit nuts."

"Who's helping you?" he asks.

"Eunice is handling the register, so I'm gonna finish it myself. No biggie." I get off the bench and hand the basket back to Lil.

Jacob stands up. "I'll help you finish it."

"That's nice of you, but it's okay. It's part of my job."

He looks me square in the eyes. "There's no way you should be doing that by yourself." He turns to Lil. "Thanks for bringing me. I'll hitch a ride home on the bus after I help her finish this ditch."

Lil smiles, her eyes twinkling. "Well, she's only supposed to work another couple of hours today, so she can give you a ride home when you guys are done. Can't you, Joanna?"

Me. Jacob. My tiny 1984 Chevette. Can he even fit in the car without sitting on my lap?

"Well?" Lil asks, both her and Jacob staring at me.

"Um, sure, I can give him a ride," I say, which prompts a naughty thought. I squelch it immediately. *Be a good girl.*

After saying goodbye, Lil heads for her car.

Jacob strips off his t-shirt, revealing his tanned chest, lightly speckled with hair. "Let's do it, then. I'm ready."

Oh yeah, this is going to be harder than I thought.

I peel my eyes away from him and swallow, trying to maintain some bit of calmness so I don't jump him right here on the picnic

186

table. "Wait right here." I pop inside to tell Eunice I'm back to working, then go to the shed and grab two shovels. I come back and hand one to him. "We're just digging it to run downhill, since the frequent rainfalls are causing flooding."

We work hard for the next two hours, but in all honesty, it's probably the best two hours of my life. We talk about family, friends, funny jokes we heard—everything under the sun. It's been a long time since I've felt so comfortable with a man. He tells me how his mom is constantly trying to matchmake him, even to the point of inviting strange women over for their Sunday family dinners just so he can meet new people. I laugh a little, but inside, feel a bit guilty. After all, Lil's working overtime trying to hook the two of us up. Guess that doesn't make us that much better.

After we finish, I clock out and we head home. I pull into my driveway and turn off the car.

I glance over at him from the corner of my eye. "Well, thanks again so much for helping with that ditch. I never could have finished it without you."

"No problem." He smiles, and my heartbeat speeds up. Even sweaty, he looks so freaking hot. And God, his lips are so sexy. I bet he tastes delicious—

Gah! Stop it! I shake my head, pulling the keys out of the ignition, and fly out of my seat. "I'll see you later!" I say, trying to keep my voice perky and not show the rush of desire I'm feeling.

I watch him enter his house, then smack my forehead. *Nice job*. Now he probably thinks I can't even stand to be around him, given that I jumped out of the car like my ass was on fire.

I stick my key in the door, but it flies open, my keys jangling loudly.

"So," Lil says, "did he say yes?"

"Nice to see you too, Lil," I reply in a droll voice. "Oh, I'm doing great, thanks for asking." I grab my keys from the door and toss my purse on the table in the foyer.

She rolls her eyes.

I suck in a deep breath, waiting for the inevitable tongue-lashing. "No, I didn't ask him. I got scared."

She pinches her lips and stares at me for a long moment. Then, her face relaxes, and she smiles brightly. "Oh, okay. That's fine. Don't worry about it. I'll just ask aunt Edie to scrape up someone for you since you seem unable to do so yourself. She loves to hook people up and always does such a great job."

A sudden vision of Lil's last matched-up date, wearing a tweed blazer and patting his toupee as he waited anxiously on the front step, pops in my head. Her aunt is the absolute worst at picking out men.

I glare at her, fighting back the shudder. "That's low."

Her eyes widen. "Well, you made a promise. I'm just helping you keep it."

I deeply sigh. "Fine. I'll go ask him. And by the way, I hate you."

She laughs and pushes me out the door. "I know. Ask him tonight, or I'm calling her."

I trudge over to Jacob's front door, lifting my hand to knock on the front door. I pause, breathing deeply for a few moments to calm myself down, then knock rapidly before I can talk myself out of it.

He opens the door, a surprised smile on his face. He's still shirtless, but holds a plush white towel in his hand. "Hey, Joanna. I was just getting ready to hop in the shower."

"Hi," I reply numbly, my brain freezing up at the thought of him naked, showering, and me lathering a handful of soap over his chest, which would slowly drip down his stomach, and lower...

I stare at him, unsure of what to say.

He stares back at me for a moment. "Um, would you like to come in?"

I mentally shake myself out of it. "Oh. Sure." I follow him inside.

Jacob tosses the towel on the corner of his dark brown leather sofa. "So, what can I do for you?"

This is it. Do or die time. I force myself to speak, blurting out the words. "Well, I know this is really, really last minute, but I figured if you weren't doing anything, maybe you wanted to go with me to Lil's cousin's wedding tomorrow evening. As friends, of course, because I wouldn't presume to think otherwise, and after all, we just met—"

"Sure, I'll go," he says, an amused smirk on his face.

"Really?"

He nods, shrugging. "Sounds like fun."

I shoot him a huge smile. "Great. It'll be fun." Duh, he just said that. "Um, meet me at my house at 5:30."

Oh my God, I have a kinda date.

* * *

Beeeep beeeep beeeep. The alarm clock drags me out of a deep sleep. I shut it off and glance at the time.

It's 3:40 pm. Oh God, Lil's going to kill me. I was only going to take a short nap, since I knew we'd be up late for the wedding and reception. I should have been up two hours ago!

Still groggy, I leap out of bed, grab my car keys, and dash out the door. How could I have napped for so long? Since Lil has to work late today, I promised her I'd grab our dresses from the dry cleaners before they close at 4. The place does great work, but closes early on Fridays.

I turn onto Rockside Road. The typical rush-hour traffic cars crawl slowly through the lanes.

"Come on, people!" I yell in frustration. I weave into the right lane, spy the dry cleaner's parking lot, and turn my car into the empty lot.

One minute to spare. I rule.

I step out and walk up. The door sign says, "Sorry, We're Closed."

AAAAH! I choke down the anger and frustration, then knock on the door, hoping to catch someone still there. No one answers.

Okay, calm down. There has to be a solution. I'm a resourceful person. Surely I can find something for us to wear to her cousin's wedding. *Tonight.*

I just wanted to look so hot, Jacob wouldn't be able to resist my feminine charms. And now, I'm going to look like thrown-together crap. All because the stupid store closes early on Fridays.

Hey, who gets married on a Friday night, anyways? That's just asking for trouble. Couldn't she have gotten hitched on a Saturday afternoon, like normal people?

I grab my cell and dial Lil's work.

"This is Lil."

Deep breath. "Hi. It's me."

"Hey. Did the dresses come out okay? I wish I had time to buy something better, but it'll have to do for now."

I swallow hard. "Um, well..."

"Oh, no. Something's wrong with my dress?" Lil's voice has the squeaky edge that always appears when she gets stressed. Which doesn't happen often—she's usually a pretty laid-back person.

"Um, not quite." *Another deep breath.* "I screwed up. I'm sorry. They closed earlier than I thought. And I-I didn't get the dresses. I'm so sorry."

Silence.

"Lil?"

"We don't have dresses?" More squeaking.

This is bad. "It's okay. I can fix this." My mind races. "We have several options. I can go buy us new ones. It's my fault, so I can just charge them." I'll be paying them off for a hundred years, but so be it. "Or we can dig through our closets and come up with something. Or, um, we can see if any of our friends have anything for us to wear."

She sighs. "I don't know. Jenna's getting married in two hours, and I'm barely gonna have time to get ready as it is. We don't have time to shop."

My stomach churns. I feel like such an ass. How do I always screw things up royally? "Okay, so we'll go through our closets. I'm sorry about this, Lil. I'll help find us something good to wear."

"I'm heading home in a couple of minutes. They're letting me leave early, so that's good."

"Okay, see you when you get there."

We hang up. I fly home and throw any of our clothes that could be useful onto my bed. A medley of summery dress shirts, skirts, and pants drape across the bedspread.

190

We're close enough in size that we can share clothes, so I work on mixing and matching outfits.

Lil's dressy white shirt would look perfect with my peach-striped skirt. I grab her brown sandals to complete the outfit. Not quite my style, but it looks like something she'd wear.

Or maybe these black pants would be good, instead. I put them right beside the skirt as an alternate. She could wear her low-heeled black dress shoes.

I glance over the pile of clothes and run a finger across my new shimmery silver shirt. I bought it a month ago, but I haven't worn it yet, since I've been saving it for the right occasion. This might be a good time to try it out with my knee-length black skirt and black heels.

The side door opens and closes. Lil calls out, "I'm home!"

"I'm in my room, getting clothes together."

She steps into my doorway, startled at the clothes strewn across the bed. "You've been busy."

Well, she doesn't look like she's going to stab me in the face for screwing up her plans. "You mad?"

"A little, but I'm trying to get over it." Her eyes stop on my silver shirt. "Oh, that's nice. How come I never saw that before?"

"It was hanging in my closet. Isn't it cute?"

"I like it." She picks up the shirt and holds it against her. "Yeah, this might work. It'll look great with that skirt."

"Oh. Well, actually, I put together several outfits for us to look at." I fight back a grimace. Why did she have to pick this one?

"I think I like this one the best." She looks at me. "Is it okay with you if I wear it?"

How can I say no? It's my fault we're in this mess.

I look away from her, studying the pile of clothes to hide my disappointment. "Sure. Go ahead." *Suck it up, buttercup. Don't be grumpy about it.* I offer her a small smile. "It'll look great on you."

She grins. "Thanks. I'll go get ready in my room."

After digging through the pile for a few minutes, I throw on a long, slim black skirt and cream-colored top. Then, I put on my black strappy heels, park my ass in the vanity seat, and start fixing my hair, which suddenly refuses to cooperate.

Oh, well. I'll try to do what I can. Plus, after a few beers at the reception hall's open bar, anyone can start to look good, including myself.

Dabbing concealer over a small blemish on my chin, I study my reflection. Ick. God help us all.

* * *

The four of us—Lil, her date Brad (who actually wasn't too bad-looking), me, and Jacob—settle into the back row of the church with about five minutes to spare. Jacob goes in first so I can sit beside Lil, who is followed by her date. She looks fabulous in my new shirt.

Jacob looks great, too. I swear, the guy looks hot in just about anything. He's wearing a dark blue suit and light blue dress shirt with a tie, and I try not to stare at him or think anything about his thigh, which is lightly brushed up against my leg. Heat radiates from him.

Biting back a sigh, I face forward, scanning the crowd. I don't know Lil's family too well, though I have met them at the occasional family picnic.

Lil leans over and whispers in my ear, "I hope this goes well. Jenna's been nervous as hell, and I'm sure Mark is, too."

The organ starts, and we all turn in unison to face the back double doors. The flower girl, no older than three, runs through the doors, flinging pink petals at the floor.

She stops halfway up the aisle, runs back, and grabs the petals, cramming them back into her basket. Snickers echo throughout the church as the little girl's mom tries to quickly guide her to the front of the church.

Jenna and Mark's parents and the rest of the bridal party step through the door and proceed to the altar, followed by the groom.

As the doors close, the music changes to the wedding march. My breath catches in my throat when the doors swing open. We stand, and Jenna walks through, arm-in-arm with her stepfather, Jim. Her bone-white strapless gown lightly hugs her figure, the raw satin fabric illuminated in the church's candlelight. Her bouquet of white rosebuds shakes as she heads down the aisle.

Aw, poor thing. She's so nervous.

Jim leans over, whispering in her ear, and Jenna reaches a hand up to wipe her eyes. When they reach the front, Jim lifts her veil and kisses her cheek, handing her over to Mark.

We sit again, and Brad whispers something in Lil's ear. She giggles slightly, and a part of me feels jealous that she's really getting along so well. Especially when I'm feeling so attracted to Jacob, and we're technically only here as friends. I don't even know how he feels about me. I mean, he's very friendly and helpful, but it's not like I'm getting special attention.

Jacob shifts closer, which presses his leg against mine. I swallow hard when his cologne, a light, spicy scent, wafts over to me. I don't know what he's wearing, but he smells fabulous.

The pastor, a tall, thin man with peppered grey-black hair, tells Jenna and Mark to face each other. Jenna's hand still shakes as Mark takes her hand in his. Her eyes aren't looking at Mark; instead, she's peering over his right shoulder.

"Dearly beloved," the pastor begins, "we gather here today to witness this man, Mark Williams, and this woman, Jenna Abramson, become lawfully wedded man and wife."

He pauses and looks out at the crowd. "A marriage between a man and woman is a—"

"I can't do this," Jenna cries out, yanking her hand out of Mark's grasp.

Several people gasp, and voices of confusion and shock ripple through the pews.

Lil whispers to me, "What's going on here?"

I shrug, barely able to peel my eyes away from the drama. "I have no idea."

Tears stream down Jenna's face, and she wipes at them furiously while glaring at Mark. "Mark, I tried to forgive you, but I can't. I'm sorry." She grabs her train and wraps it over her arm.

Mark grabs her hand again, whispering. The whole crowd leans forward, trying to hear. "We're right in the middle of the ceremony. Can't we talk about this afterwards? Or at least somewhere in private?"

"Private?" Jenna's voice squeaks in the same way as Lil's. Must be a family trait. "Maybe if you hadn't been thinking with your *privates*, we wouldn't have this problem right now."

My stomach lurches. I feel like I'm peeping in on a private conversation, but I can't stop watching. Out of the corner of my eye, I see Jacob's jaw drop. The rest of the church gets deadly quiet.

Jenna faces us. "I'm sorry, but there will be no wedding today." She swallows hard. "There's still going to be food and alcohol in the reception, which is right down the road, so feel free to have some. It's already paid for, anyway." Choking back a sob, she darts down the aisle and out the double doors. Her mom, Betty, jumps out of the pew and dashes after her.

Mark stands in shock. We stare at him. He clears his throat. "Um, this is just a misunderstanding. I'll go talk to her." He follows her out the doors.

The bridal party shifts uncomfortably, unsure of what to do, as the mumbling and whispering in the pews grow louder.

The pastor sucks in a deep breath. "Ladies and gentlemen, I want to thank you for your patience. These things can happen sometimes. Let's just wait for a bit to see if it will be worked out." He follows Jenna and Mark out of the main chapel, the bible still clutched in his hand.

"Oh my God," I gasp. "This is just...unbelievable."

"I know!" Lil says, shaking her head. She and Brad start whispering back and forth.

Jacob's face is etched with concern, and he slowly shakes his head, too.

At that moment, I feel a wave of guilt. This has to be the worst non-date date he's ever been on. After this, he'll probably be ducking inside his house whenever I'm around just to avoid me.

Fragments of Jenna and Mark's conversation in the hallway make it into the church.

"—lied to me!"

"—believe you're bringing it up now. I told you I was drunk—"

"—just can't trust you! You told me you—"

Oh, this is bad. "I don't think there's going to be a wedding today."

Lil sighs. "Poor Jenna. I *knew* there was something rotten about him."

We hear the front doors of the church open, and Mark cries out, "Jenna! Wait!"

A car door slams, and tires squeal.

Yup. It's over.

Lil stands. "I think we should probably go."

"Yeah, I think you're right." I stand, too, followed by Brad and Jacob. Several people see us standing and do the same.

We head through the Double Doors of Doom into the hallway. Jacob puts his hand on my lower back to lead me out, and despite the somber atmosphere, a small thrill shoots through me at the feel of his warm hand on me.

Mark is sitting in a cushy mauve chair, hunched over with his face buried in his hands. His body shakes, and tears plop down onto the plush purple carpet.

"I wanna smack him," Lil whispers to me as we pass, "but in a way, I feel bad for him. He really looks torn up about this."

"This is definitely awkward. It's probably better if we leave him alone."

I throw one last glance over my shoulder. The church empties out. Everyone is quiet, unsure of what to say. Mark's dad and the best man, Greg, grab Mark and drag him into a side room, closing the door.

"See?" I say to her. "They can talk to him. He'll be okay."

We stroll down the church stairs and to the car. Lil sighs. "I think we should skip the, um, reception." We get in our seats and buckle up, me and Jacob in the back seat. Lil shakes her head. "You know what? I really need a drink."

Brad laughs. "Actually, I could use a drink, too."

"Me, too," I say. Or ten. What a stressful situation, and it didn't even happen to me.

Yeah, there's gonna be a lot of people buried in the bottle tonight.

* * *

195

The taxi pulls out of our driveway and takes off down the street. Since we all had a few too many at the bar, we decided to hitch a ride home. Brad was already dropped off, after planting a huge kiss on Lil and promising to call her tomorrow.

Of course, no kisses for me. Jacob was friendly and chatty in the bar, but he was like that to Lil and Brad, too. Of course. I was too embarrassed over the wedding fiasco to even attempt flirting with him.

Lil giggles as she stumbles over a crack in our driveway. "Oops—didn't see that. It's so damn dark out here."

Jacob snickers.

Her clumsiness makes me laugh a little, too. I don't think I've ever seen her this drunk before. Of course, I'm kind of buzzed myself, so I can't make fun of her. Those chocolate martinis went down way too easily. "Shh! We don't want to wake anyone up."

She and I sit on the front porch, enjoying the balmy night air. "Poor Jenna," she said, her voice somber. "Men suck."

I sigh. "Good men are way too hard to find. They do suck."

"Hey, I take offense to that," Jacob said, standing in front of us. "Not all men suck."

Lil shakes her head and peers up at his tall, shadowed figure. "True, but it's the sucky ones who always seem to find me. I mean, Brad seems nice enough so far, but the risk is high that he'll end up being a dud, too."

Jacob laughs. "Yeah, dating is rough." He looks down at me. "What about you? Do the losers find you, too?"

"Sometimes." His cologne wafts over to me again, I suck in a deep breath. God, he still smells good, even after being in a bar. Amazing. "But you don't seem like a loser to me."

Did I really just say that? He's not even pursuing me, and after this so-called date, he'll never want to. I need to shut up now.

He grins. "Thanks for the compliment, I think."

Lil stands up, stretching and exaggerating a huge yawn. "Well, I'm beat. I should head in and give Jenna a quick call."

I roll my eyes. Ever so subtle as usual. "Okay, tell her to let us know if she needs anything."

She agrees, heading inside. Leaving me alone with Jacob and all his hotness.

He coughs lightly into his hand. "Well, this was an interesting evening."

A flush burns my face. God, he probably wants to duck out of here and get away from me as fast as possible. And who could blame him?

I stand, unable to bear the nervous feeling anymore. I have to scrape up some sort of dignity. "I just wanted to say I'm sorry about all this. Obviously, the evening didn't go as anyone planned." I paste a bright smile on my face. "Well, I appreciate you going with me. At least the rest of your night is free, so I hope you can salvage it. Maybe some of your friends are available, and you can make plans. Sorry again."

I spin around and grab the doorknob, my heart sinking.

He grabs my other hand, his thumb brushing the inside of my wrist. "Wait. Don't leave."

My heart races in my chest. I turn back to him, looking at the black flecks in his dark brown eyes, and lick my lips.

He pulls me down to the sidewalk, peering intently down at me and still holding my hand. "Even though it was a bit awkward, I had fun being with you."

My throat closes up. "Really?" I manage to ask.

Jacob nods.

Maybe it's time to grab the bull by the horns. I lean up and press my lips against his, then back away quickly, not quite brave enough to kiss him the way I want.

He slips a hand around my waist and pulls me closer, leans his head down, and rubs his lips against mine. He deepens the kiss, slowly darting his tongue in and out of my mouth.

I press against him, wrapping my arms around his neck, leaning into his warmth.

Jacob lifts his head and smiles, his dark eyes catching glints from the porch light. "Joanna, I think you're adorable. I hope we can get to know each other better. Would you like to come over and hang out with me for a while?"

I nod, unable to stop the smile on my face. Maybe this is the start of a great relationship. "Sure. Let me change into something more comfortable."

"Great." He winks. "Hey, why don't you put on those shorts? I really like the way your ass looks in them."

Biography

Rhonda Stapleton started writing a few years ago to appease the voices in her head. She has a Master's degree in English and a Bachelor's degree in Creative Writing. Rhonda works as a principal publishing specialist for a legal publishing company and enjoys freelance editing and offering editing workshops. She belongs to RWA, several writing chapters, and Romance Divas. She lives in Parma, Ohio, with her two children and boyfriend. Her first chick lit novel, STRIPPED, is due out in the spring 2007 at Freya's Bower.

The Wedding Policy

by

Bebe Thomas

Rating: Sweet

Genre: Contemporary

The Wedding Policy

The summer of 1941

Belle Stuart believed in dreams coming true. Especially on the warm June day when she secretly met her love for a box lunch picnic by the pond in the horse pasture. Although his faded dungarees were patched, Belle thought Charlie, with his dirty blond hair and jaunty smile, a most attractive man. Wading in the shallows of the pond, they playfully splashed, then raced barefoot back to the blanket, gasping for air and laughing. Charlie pulled Belle onto his lap, crumpling her crisp white blouse and freshly pressed skirt, and tucked an unruly curl behind her ear. From his pocket, he drew a small box. Inside sat a tiny pearl ring.

"Oh, Charlie," she said, kissing him. "It's beautiful!"

"It's not very big or fancy, I know," he said touching her cheek, "but when we're married, I'll have the resources to get you a better ring. I promise."

"It's perfect. Just perfect." The tears ran down her face.

"Sugar, please don't cry," he said.

She shook her head, dabbed at her eyes with a napkin.

"I thought you'd be happy," Charlie said.

"I'm so happy, Charlie. Really, I am," she sobbed, "but you know I can't wear that ring. If my father sees it..."

"I know." He pulled a thin cord out of his pocket. "I figured you could wear it on this until I talk to your father."

* * *

Belle's father, Theodore Stuart, owned Paradise, the prestigious horse farm, and was the richest, most powerful man in the county. When his eldest daughter, Rosalie, left her intended, a very respectable young man, at the altar and eloped with a Cherokee field hand, Father claimed her actions almost ruined his reputation. He promptly disowned her, forbade even an utterance of her name, and instituted the wedding policy to maintain his good standing in the community. Almost everyone in the Bluegrass Basin, and most particularly the residents of the neighboring counties, knew of this wedding policy. Mr. Stuart personally selected the husband of each of his unmarried daughters and forbade the would-be bridegroom to announce the upcoming nuptials to anyone, especially the bride. Thanks to a long-standing arrangement with the family minister, the county clerk, and a circuit court judge, none of his other daughters would ever embarrass him again.

Belle hoped her father would approve of Charlie. Only a horse trainer, he was thought an ambitious and clever young man by all of the community. Belle was twenty-one, almost an old maid. Her sister, Rebecca, had two offers of marriage already, but Father had said that Belle would be the next to marry. Since no other arrangements had been made, she was sure that Father would soon allow her to marry Charlie.

* * *

In a navy blue sailor dress with a boatneck collar, Belle attended the church social on Saturday night. She handed her blueberry pie to old Mrs. Simpson. As was the custom, each unmarried young lady brought an item to be auctioned at the bake sale. The highest bidder won the item and the baker's attentions for coffee and dessert. It was always the highlight of the evening. The Stuart sisters usually had a fair share of bids on their wares. Rebecca received many offers, as she was so pretty. Belle received many because she was an excellent baker. She was not a petite, fair-haired beauty like her sisters. The other girls took after Mother's family, the Webbs, but Belle looked like her father, with strong features and curly brown hair.

Belle looked forward to church events because Father relented a bit, letting his daughters flirt and dance – under his watchful eye, of course. Belle scanned the church hall for Charlie. This was the night he promised to speak to her father. At the far end of the room, Bob Smith and his band were setting up the instruments. A group of teenagers stood in one corner chattering away. Along the side of the room, the young ladies of marriageable age sat along the wall in folding chairs. Some girls had one or two beaus vying for attention, some had none, and Rebecca, holding court, was surrounded by several eligible young men from all over the county. In another corner, some of the men discussed politics and the Nazi regime in Europe. All the married ladies helped Mrs. Simpson set up the cakes, pies, brownies, and cookies and gossiped about the goings on. Not finding Charlie, she assumed he was talking to her father as planned and found a seat next to Betsy Hill.

When the band started playing, Belle danced with Bill Jenkins, Ralph Smith, John Treanor, and an older man, Mr. Hughes, a banker from Lexington, but she did not see any sign of Charlie.

After a time, Bob Smith announced, "The bake sale is about to start!" Several of the men bid on Belle's pie, but Mr. Hughes raised the price with each request.

Then Charlie yelled out from across the room, "A dollar and a quarter."

Belle spun around on one heel to smile brightly at him. She thought he looked pleased. Father stood behind him with a furrowed brow.

"One dollar fifty," Mr. Hughes said.

"One seventy-five," said Charlie. He winked at Belle.

"Two dollars," countered Mr. Hughes.

Belle knew that Charlie didn't have that kind of money and mouthed, "It's all right," but Charlie bid again. Mr. Hughes looked tired of the bidding war, and Belle figured that he would back off. People liked Charlie and would always let him win.

"Five dollars." Mr. Hughes waved a five-dollar bill in the air.

Bob Smith asked, "Charlie?"

Charlie just shook his head.

"Sold to Mr. Bartholomew Hughes. Our highest bid ever!"

Belle wanted to go to her beau, but she had to serve a slice of pie to Mr. Hughes. Charlie would wait.

* * *

"Here you go, Mr. Hughes." She handed him a slice of pie and a cup of coffee.

"Aren't you having any pie?" he asked.

"Oh, no. I'm not particularly fond of blueberry pie. I'll just have coffee," Belle said.

Mr. Hughes pulled out a chair near the end of a long table and motioned for Belle to sit down. He sat at the end of the table, next to her, at an angle. He tasted a forkful of pie and seemed to savor it. "Well, it is delicious."

"Thank you, Mr. Hughes," Belle said. She didn't know why, but the compliment pleased her.

"Please. Call me Bartholomew – Barth – Mr. Hughes, seems so...elderly."

Mr. Hughes was older, but handsome. Gray peppered his dark hair.

"Okay. Sure, Mr. Hugh...Barth, I mean."

He took a sip of coffee. "So, Annabelle, why do you bake blueberry pie if you don't like it?"

"It's Belle," she said. She had never liked her given name.

"Belle," said Mr. Hughes with a nod. "It suits you."

After an awkward silence, he asked about the pie again.

"Oh, it's Charlie's favorite," Belle blurted without thinking. She quickly glanced around hoping her father hadn't overheard.

"Oh?" Mr. Hughes raised an eyebrow. "What kind of pie do you like?"

"To tell the truth, I really like pineapple upside down cake. That's my specialty." Belle saw Charlie at the next table out of the corner of her eye. She felt his gaze upon her and she smiled to herself.

"I hope to try it sometime," Mr. Hughes said and wiped a crumb from the corner of his mouth. "What else do you like to cook?"

Belle looked over to Charlie, trying to read his expression. "The usual fare, I suppose, fried chicken, biscuits, pepper gravy, collards," she said, turning back to Mr. Hughes.

He smiled. "I'm surprised that more men didn't give Charlie a run for his money tonight. This is the best pie that I've ever eaten. Pleasant company, too."

Belle shrugged. "Most of them would rather talk to Rebecca."

"So," he said, "I get the impression that something is going on between you and Charlie. You two aren't going steady, are you?"

Oh dear. Belle wasn't sure how to answer this question. She already let that comment slip about Charlie. She took a long sip of coffee to give herself time to think before answering. Being engaged was not going steady. Also, Mr. Hughes was a banker and probably spoke to her father frequently. She wouldn't want to make Father angry. Not now, with her marriage at stake. "Ah...not exactly. And what about you, Barth?"

"No. I'm not exactly going steady with Charlie either," he said, raising his eyebrow again.

She giggled. "I know that. I mean, umm, well..." Belle was embarrassed and felt a hot blush on her cheeks.

"I know what you meant," he said with a grin. "I'm kidding."

"I'm a widower, Belle. My wife died in childbirth when the last baby was born. My aunt lives with the family to help care for the children and keep house."

Sympathy filled Belle. "That's sad."

Mr. Hughes leaned back in his chair. "Do you like children, Belle?"

"Sure. I usually run the nursery during services." Maybe she could help Barth Hughes. He might like Betsy Hill. After all, she was a spinster and nearly thirty. Belle determined to introduce them. She caught sight of Betsy and motioned for her to come over.

"Speaking of children, Mr., I mean Barth, have you met Betsy Hill? She's a teacher," Belle said.

"Pleased to make your acquaintance, Mrs. Hill. Please have a seat." He held out a seat next to Belle.

"Likewise," said Betsy as she settled into her seat. "Mr....?"

Betsy should correct him. They were awfully formal with each other.

"Hughes."

Belle wanted to scream. How could Betsy be so dense? But the music started, and Charlie walked over.

"Come on, Belle. Let's dance," he said.

It wasn't like Charlie to be so rude, but he probably couldn't wait to tell her the good news. Belle quickly introduced Charlie to Mr. Hughes and then practically ran to the dance floor, hardly able to contain herself. The night was almost over, and she hadn't spoken to Charlie yet.

"So," she asked, "what did he say?"

Charlie leaned in close. "He said that he'd think about it."

Squeezing his hand, she said, "That's good. It wasn't 'no'."

"I know, Sugar. It's just that I thought for sure he would say 'yes', and my problems would be over," Charlie said, leading her toward the edge of the dance floor.

"Your problems?"

"You know, our getting married," he explained. Charlie slowly slid his hand down her back, caressing her.

"I'll simply die if he doesn't say 'yes'." Belle sighed and moved in closer. She loved how she felt excited and warm inside when Charlie held her. She never felt this way about anyone before and knew she would never love anyone but him.

* * *

The wedding was to take place on the Saturday before Christmas.

"A holiday wedding. Festive, festive, festive," Mother exclaimed.

Belle looked across the dining table at her mother, a smart looking, petite, and usually refined woman. The dining hall was now Wedding Central much to Father's chagrin.

"You certainly are excited about my wedding, Mother," she said.

"Well, you are too, aren't you, dear?" Mother looked up from her paperwork.

"I'm really anxious. I know he talked to Father, but..." Belle worried aloud.

Mother sighed with a smile. "Dear, dear, Belle. You know your father's policy."

"I know. I just thought...maybe..." Belle's voice caught as she blinked back tears.

"Oh, dear!" Mother said. She put down her pen, took off her reading glasses, and went around the table to Belle. Patting her hand, she said, "Don't cry, dear. I know your father can be difficult, but he is a fair man and a good judge of character. You don't have to worry."

Belle wailed. "Why won't he tell me?"

"I don't know, dear. I don't know," Mother said. "After thirty-five years of marriage, I still don't understand how he can be so stubborn. But I think his good qualities outweigh the bad."

Belle took a few deep breaths and wiped her eyes. "I really don't have to worry, Mother?"

"I'm sure your father has picked a good man." She patted Belle's hand reassuringly and returned to her seat at the opposite side of the table. She looked at her notes briefly and said, "I thought we would have the wedding breakfast here at Paradise. What do you think, dear?"

* * *

Running against the chilly December wind, Belle touched the pearl ring under her coat, quickly glanced back at the main house and prayed that nobody was watching. In the spring and summer, it was easy to steal away to be with Charlie. Now that the days were short and the nights were cold, Belle hardly saw him. Reaching the horse stables, she looked around anxiously, cringed as the hinge squeaked when she opened the door and slipped inside the barn. In the dark, Belle reached up for a lantern and match, but was pressed up against the wall of an empty stall.

"Charlie?" she whispered, but she knew it was him by the touch of his callused hands, the clean smell of soap, and the taste of cherry tobacco mixed with faint hint of Jim Beam on his tongue. She slipped out of her coat, and he deftly unbuttoned her sweater, pulling her into the hay.

"I love you, Charlie," Belle said. She curled up beside him under a layer of horse blankets.

"Mmm... hmm..." he said, sleepy with his eyes half closed.

"I can't wait until we are married." Belle propped herself up on an elbow. "No more sneaking around."

Charlie opened his eyes and smiled, "Sugar, you know how your father is."

"I know. It's just…"

"You know, I'm thinking of signing up for the Navy. Fighting the Japs," he said sitting up.

"The Navy?" Belle asked and buttoned her sweater.

"Yeah," he said and turned away. "California. That's where you'd live."

She stood and lightly touched his arm. "I want to be with you, Charlie. It doesn't matter where."

"I know, Sugar." He kissed her on the forehead. "I know."

* * *

On Belle's wedding day, the main house buzzed with last minute activity and preparations. Her sister and mother fussed with her hair and fastened all the buttons in the back of the ivory silk gown.

"Look in the mirror," Rebecca said, turning Belle around.

Belle was beautiful in the formfitting lace bodice and full skirt embellished with hand-embroidery. Rebecca had helped straighten Belle's hair and fasten it into a chignon at the nape of her neck. Belle looked down at her hands and twisted the tiny pearl. Today, she would no longer hide her engagement ring.

"You look beautiful, dear," Mother said, dabbing her eyes.

"I hope Charlie thinks so." Belle smiled.

In the reflection, Belle saw her mother give Rebecca a knowing look.

"Um… I'll go check on the flowers," Rebecca said and quickly left the room.

Mother patted the bed beside her. "Sit down, dear. I need to tell you something."

"Oh, Mother," Belle said, exasperated. "I know about the birds and the bees."

"Annabelle. Sit down."

Something about the tone of her mother's voice and the look in her eyes made Belle very nervous.

Mother touched Belle's arm. "You're not marrying Charlie today."

A wave of nausea consumed Belle. She started to shake uncontrollably. This couldn't be true. Of course she was marrying Charlie. Tears welled up in her eyes. "Why?" she cried. "You said I shouldn't worry. You lied to me!"

She handed Belle a handkerchief. "I said your father would pick a good man, not that he picked Charlie Taylor."

Belle sobbed, "Well, I won't go through with it! I want to marry Charlie and I will marry him!"

"I'm so sorry you're hurt, dear, but Charlie doesn't want to marry you. He's gone." Mother patted Belle's hand. "I hoped he would at least say goodbye to you."

"He's gone?" Belle choked on a salty tear.

Mother stood and walked to window. "Your father... He didn't think Charlie would be..."

"Charlie can't be gone, Mother." Belle was incredulous. "I'm supposed to get married today."

"To Bartholomew Hughes." Mother turned from the window.

"Mr. Hughes?" Belle wailed. "Oh, no! No way!" Belle stood, shaking in shock and anger. "I hardly even know him. Besides, what about Betsy Hill?"

"Betsy Hill?" Mother asked. "What would a handsome man like Bartholomew Hughes want with that plain old schoolmarm?"

"What does he want with me?" Belle cried.

"He was quite taken with you at the church social. And his children, losing their mother at such tender ages. Why wouldn't he want a pretty wife like you?"

"Mother, he's ancient!" Belle wailed.

Chuckling a little, she said, "Belle, dear, forty is not ancient. You'll learn to love Bartholomew, just like I learned to love your father. He's a good..."

"Forget it. Just cancel everything. I won't do it. I won't!" Belle plopped on her bed, pouting. "I hate Rosalie!" she yelled. "If she hadn't run off with that..."

Mother put her hand over Belle's mouth. "Hush, Annabelle," she hissed. "Your father might hear you. This would make him very angry."

"But, Mother..."

"I agree with your father's decision, dear. Bartholomew is from a good family. Charlie is a horse trainer. He has no family. And now he's been..." Mother sat beside her, touching Belle's cheek. "You really don't know Charlie, dear."

"I know I love him," Belle said, quietly. "And I am not marrying Mr. Hughes."

Mother rose and walked to the door. She turned and said, "Charlie is gone. You've embarrassed yourself long enough by sneaking off to the stables with him. You will not shame your family today." She turned the knob and said, "Fix your makeup, dear. You don't want anyone to see you've been crying."

This was terrible. Belle had to find Charlie.

A knock sounded on the door. Rebecca peeked in. "Are you okay, Belle?"

"Mother says Charlie's gone, but he can't be. He would never leave me."

Rebecca hugged Belle as she cried.

Between sobs, Belle asked, "Will you go find Charlie for me?"

Belle quickly scribbled a note for Charlie. And waited. Had Charlie joined the Navy? Would he meet her at the church? Well, of course he would be at the church. He would be there to take her away, and they would run off to California together. He probably bought tickets for the train. But how would they get to Lexington? It was too far and too cold to walk almost thirty-five miles to the train. Maybe he would borrow John Treanor's pick-up truck. That made sense. They would take the train to California.

When Rebecca returned, she still had Belle's note.

"It's fine. He'll be at the church."

"I better touch up your make-up," Rebecca said and dabbed a little foundation under Belle's eyes. "No one was at the stable, and when I looked in the field house, two of the hands were talking and laughing. I couldn't hear very well, but I thought I heard them talking about Charlie. But they saw me and became very quiet." She put a little rouge on Belle's cheeks. "They said that they hadn't seen Charlie since last night."

Belle hoped Charlie was in town buying their train tickets. He would certainly be at the church.

The Wedding Policy

* * *

Belle looked for him as she approached the doors of the church. No Charlie. She frantically searched each pew from the back of the church where she waited with her father for the music to start. No Charlie. As she walked down the aisle, she looked for him at each pew. No Charlie. Maybe he was waiting for "speak now or forever hold your peace", but no Charlie. Belle thought about saying, "I do not" instead of "I do", but she knew that would merely stall the ceremony – not stop it. Father would see to that.

She realized that Charlie was being kept away, but as long as she didn't consummate her marriage, she could get it annulled. She thought it would be easy enough, that old geezer probably wasn't even interested in sex. She would become Mrs. Bartholomew Hughes, in name only. Until Charlie returned.

Later, Mr. Hughes brought her to his home in Lexington. "Belle, these are my children: Robert, Julia, and Amy, the baby. Children, say hello to your mother."

"Hello, Mama," they said, not at all cheerfully.

"Listen, Mr. Hughes—" she began.

"Barth."

"Barth, I am not their mother. These children must respect their mother's memory." It was best not to get attached to his children.

Barth seemed to think about that for a moment. "Okay. How about Mama Belle?"

The Federal style house had four bedrooms and a suite on the second floor. The kitchen, Barth's study, dining room and parlor were downstairs. It was the kind of home she and Charlie would have someday.

"You have a lovely home, Barth," she said and sat near the fire.

"It's your home now. Our home. Needs updating. Decorating," he said.

She agreed with him, but replied, "No, I think it's very nice."

"Well, I'm sure that you'll want to make some changes." He sat on the sofa and picked up the evening paper.

Belle felt a headache coming on. All she wanted to do was go to sleep. This had to be a bad dream and she hoped to wake up tomorrow in her own bed.

"Barth?" she asked, standing. "I'm feeling a little tired from all the excitement. Would you tell me which room is mine?"

Glancing up, he pointed. "Up the staircase. First door on the left."

Belle was shocked. "I thought that was your suite."

"It is. Now it's ours."

"Yours and mine?" Belle asked.

He walked over to her and touched her arm. "You're nervous. I'll be gentle; I promise."

"It's not that," she said, blinking back the tears, "It's just, well..."

"Charlie," Barth concluded.

"Well, yes. I thought he would stop the wedding today, but he didn't show up, and then I figured that Father sent him away until after I was married, and I didn't really think..."

"That I would be interested in...?" he asked, raising an eyebrow.

"Yes," Belle said. "And Charlie was planning on joining the Navy. What if he was sent to fight? It wouldn't..."

"Be fair for him not to have a chance," he completed her sentence again.

Belle wondered how he could complete her thoughts.

"I'll make a deal with you, Belle," Barth said, pacing the length of the room. "I will sleep on the davenport in our suite for the next three months."

"But...." Belle tried to interrupt.

"Please let me finish. We will sleep in the same room, and I promise not to touch you. If Charlie contacts you within three months, we will end this marriage, and you will be free to marry him. I think three months is ample time, don't you?"

"Well..."

"We'll see what happens. Let's discuss this again in a few months." He squeezed Belle's hand.

Belle instinctively felt that she could trust him. Bartholomew Hughes seemed like a fair man.

"Thank you," she whispered.

"But I have to warn you, Belle, he's gone for good. We'll grow to love each other."

In the following weeks, Belle met the postman at the door daily and sprinted to the telephone at the first hint of a ring. She scoured the newspaper, searching the lists of casualties for Charlie's name, and although she was relieved each time she didn't see his name, she was certain something terrible had happened to him. She started to think that perhaps Barth was right, that Charlie would not return. After several months, Belle concluded that Charlie must have died in battle.

Eventually, Belle did grow to love her husband. She took off the ring Charlie had given her and tucked it away in her bureau. She and Barth formed a true partnership, raising a family together. When Barth died after almost forty years of marriage, she was surprised by how intensely she missed him.

But she always had a special place in her heart for Charlie Taylor. She had kept the pearl ring, as a symbol of her true love. For many years, she had heard bits of whispered gossip that Charlie had been paid off, that he married into a rich Montana family, but she knew that he had been killed in the war, that he was unable to come back for her.

* * *

1982

At her youngest son's wedding, Belle thought she saw Charlie standing in the sunlight outside the doors of the church. She blinked twice and would have sworn that she'd seen a ghost if she believed in such things. Feeling faint, she sat down on the nearest pew.

"Mama Belle!" cried out the eldest, Robert, as he rushed up the aisle to her aide. "What happened?"

"I'm fine. Just need to catch my breath." She twirled the small pearl ring she wore on her right hand. Belle had tucked it away over forty years ago and had only started wearing it again after Barth died early last year. Since his death, the children had questioned her every misstep, cough and sneeze. At sixty-three, this was somewhat annoying, but Belle considered herself fortunate to have such loving and attentive children.

But the man from the doorway... surely, it wasn't her Charlie.

"Are you all right, Sugar?" he asked.

She nodded, numb, in a dream. She never believed that she would see Charlie again. That part of her life had died over forty years ago; indeed, she'd lost part of her heart. Yet, he was here, presumably an old family friend, introducing himself to her family.

"You're looking young, Sugar," Charlie said, sitting next to her.

She thought, *Hair dye is a woman's best friend*, but replied, "Thank you, Charlie. You're looking well yourself." It was true; he was still a handsome, charming man, lean, tall and tanned with silvery hair and ice-blue eyes. He wore a designer suit, a Rolex, and a fancy diamond pinkie ring - quite a contrast from the simple pearl she wore.

He touched her hand. "You still have the ring."

"Yes," she said. Odd. His touch seemed so familiar.

Charlie held her hand lightly and said, "Imagine that. All this time."

Forty years. He'd let her think he was dead. And he must have known she married another man and raised his children.

"What are you doing here?" she asked, gently pushing his hand away.

He whispered, "I wanted to see you."

"When you didn't come for me..." She looked around the empty church. It looked almost exactly as it had on her wedding day.

"That was a long time ago, Belle," he said. Funny, it felt like yesterday to Belle.

Growing angry, she said, "I thought you were killed in the war."

"Let me explain," Charlie pleaded. "I always wanted you. I planned..."

"My father gave you money to stay away?" she half stated and half asked, almost afraid to hear the answer.

"But, Sugar," he said with a placating tone. "What choice did I have? If you married me, your father would have disinherited you." He brushed a wisp of hair away from her face. "Don't you see? I did it for you."

She did see.

He smiled. "It's not too late for us, is it, Belle?"

"Oh, Charlie," Belle sighed. "I never believed what people said about you – until now."

Then she placed the ring in the palm of his hand, closed his fingers over it and walked out of the church to her waiting family. After all those years, she finally knew the truth, and from her heart, he was gone for good.

Biography

The Wedding Policy is the short story that inspired Bebe Thomas to follow-up her popular debut, AURORA'S PASSION, with her latest novel, AURORA'S PROMISE, both available at Freya's Bower. Bebe lives in Philadelphia with her husband and their one-eyed cat, Max. She can be contacted via her website: www.bebethomas.com.

Blood & Feathers

by

Emily Veinglory

Rating: Sizzling

Genre: Gay erotica

"You cannot help him now; he bears the mark of the vampire."

Paul did not respond to Augusta's gentle tug upon his shoulder. He stood, stooped forward, clasping his great wings tight against his back. He could not tear his eyes away from the body that lay so still upon the bed. "I was meant to protect him."

"The council called you away. Nobody can blame you for what befell him in your absence."

"*I* can." Paul turned to his fellow angel. Her eyes were fixed upon him with acute concern, and Paul knew he should heed his mentor's words. She'd passed into her second life generations ago, and everyone knew that Augusta would not be a mere guardian for very much longer. The armies of light had better uses for a woman like her.

Such grand destinies meant nothing as he stood before his former charge's bed. Terry French lay insensible, naked. His pose mimicked that of a corpse prepared for burial. His closed eyes and crossed hands suggested peace, but incongruous details marred the scene: sickly sweat on his tanned skin and two tiny marks upon his slender neck.

Terry wasn't exactly dead, but he wasn't alive either.

This man could have lived a long and celebrated life as one of Britain's preeminent conceptual artists. He could have been reborn as an angel; one of the few, the very few, who harbored such a soul. Now the very best he could hope for was that his life would end and go no further than a mortal grave.

Augusta's hand tightened upon his shoulder. "We must go."

Grudgingly, Paul obeyed. Spreading their wings, the mundane world faded, and the constant turmoil of the spiritual realms lifted them upwards. The veils of reality crossed and crystallized, and only from a distance did they look like clouds.

Augusta made her way upon spectral wings as if she was born to them and cut a direct path to her goal, no doubt old enough to be bored with the sight of white vapors of opal white twisting and fighting iridescent black. The endless storm. Paul had heard the rumors; the whole mortal world was created to resolve this storm and determine what would come after.

With a jolt, she brought them back to the grimy mortal world that nevertheless contained all the colors in between. Paul stumbled, 'finding' his feet – or at least getting them to recognize the sudden reality of the ground.

It was a shop, a common corner store. Small, cramped, jammed with booze, cigarettes and sugary goods with expiration dates some time in the next millennium.

"Why are we..."

"Vincent has been called up," Augusta said with a conspicuous lack of sentiment. "This man was his charge. Bryant Fry the manager of this place."

Paul felt his guts curdle at the sight of the tall, awkward man behind the counter. His cheap uniform shirt was creased up like a crumpled paper bag, his long face wrinkled and shadowed with stubble. He smiled as if by rote and reached to scan an old lady's purchases: a large block of cheddar and a newspaper. Even his hands were perversely broad, the backs dotted by faint freckles. Paul could not hide his distaste and he did not try.

"A shopkeeper! I am meant to spend the next God-knows-how-many years watching a *shopkeeper*?"

Augusta's expression hardened. "We are assigned our tasks by those who know humanity's needs, and ours. I make allowance for you, Paul, because you died so young. You have not had a full mortal life through which to learn patience or humility. Perhaps you are being given a chance to learn them now."

Knowing the futility of further protest, Paul clamped his mouth shut and glared at his mentor.

After a few moments, Augusta's expression softened, and she shook her head. "Watch diligently, Paul. And you may learn that there is more to Bryant than meets the eye. Come the day, you, he and I will all fight side by side. We can only hope, all of us, to be worthy of that responsibility."

And with a flick, her wings caught the winds between the worlds, and Augusta was gone.

Paul settled himself into a small space that existed between the beer fridge and the entrance to the back room, to accommodate the inward opening door. Paul stood there, wondering. Was Terry still unconscious? Was he alone? Was he afraid?

And as for living a short life...most of his mortal existence was spent in one school or another waiting to "grow up" and get out into the real world. He had been good, studied hard but never excelled, graduated and started a low paying job at a local agricultural supply store. Everything he did just seemed to be the prologue to real life. He'd still been living at home, beneath the heavy weight of his parent's disappointment, always being promised better things, good grades, promotion...only to end under the massive wheels of an SUV that drifted across the highway center line.

A young acne-afflicted man strolled into the store and slung a backpack over the counter. As he shucked off his heavy parka, he revealed another pinstriped work-shirt with enamel nametag attached.

Bryant was replenishing the colored rows of cigarette packets on the back wall. He didn't even look over. "Franky, tell me this, when you leave home and whatever it is you want to do with your life, are you going to be someone people can rely on; someone who is always there for his friends and family?"

"I guess."

"Then you should start practicing now because life is only going to make it harder for you to do that as the stakes get higher."

Franky belatedly got the point. "I'm not late," he protested too loudly, conspicuously consulting his wristwatch.

"I saw you winding your watch back as you came around the corner. I expect you to be behind the counter ready to work on the dot of six. That's what I pay you for."

"You don't pay me. Foodmart does."

"I may not sign the checks, but I can see to it that you never get another one."

Bryant finally turned and looked Franky in the face. It wasn't a stern look; more along the lines of fatherly disappointment.

"Yeah, okay," Franky mumbled.

* * *

In keeping with his obviously scintillating life, Bryant lived over the store that he managed. His studio apartment was still painted the same clean but scuffed off-white the builders must have chosen, on the assumption that later residents would personalize from there. Bryant had added a beige sofa that must have been secondhand when he got it because it looked older than he was, and a similarly colored computer that perched atop its own delivery box – positioned to be used from the sofa. A television sat on top of the bench that separated the main area from a kitchen that wasn't quite as roomy as an elevator.

Bryant flicked on the television, pulled a burrito from the fridge, and placed it in the built in microwave. He watched the BBC news idly, waiting for the "ping", and then settled down to check his email.

Paul stood by the window, looking out at an attenuated view of the buildings across the street. Two wide lanes of the road lead through this small inner city suburb to the main drag by way of this grimy stretch of asphalt. Groups of young people drifted along the sidewalks towards the pubs and bars a little further down.

He wasn't proud of the feeling, but as Paul looked at the laughing youths, he hated them. How dare they have good friends, trendy clothes, and the nightlife of London laid out before them? What had he been offered? A small Scottish town with one dingy pub, dour parents, underachievement and a dead-end job selling teat sterilizer and ear-tags to brain dead dairy farmers. Dying was the most interesting thing that ever happened to him, and it had just lead to this, another vigil, another promise that if he was "good", better things might be in store.

The only good thing that had ever happened to him was Terry. Terry was beautiful, graceful when he moved, witty when he spoke, passionate about everything he did. He almost seemed to know, somehow, that Paul was there. When he was alone, Terry spoke his thoughts aloud, and not quite as if he spoke only to himself. Paul knew he'd been infatuated with the man. He wouldn't call it love any more than one could "love" a movie star or a saint. Paul watched Terry but Terry never quite saw him in return, never quite spoke specifically to him – and how could he?

Unless the most dire of dangers required it, guardians did not directly intervene – a guardian's presence might vaguely be felt, but as individuals, they were almost never seen. And with that thought, Paul's tenuous hold on duty slipped free. Even now, he was meant to be a fucking angel – if not quite the sort superstition said existed – Paul was still invisible to those he admired, and at the command of indifferent powers who had far more important things on their minds than the happiness of Paul Nesbit.

Nineteen years of obedient life and seven months of obedient afterlife had brought him nothing but tedium and frustration. The only thing that had ever come close to making Paul happy were those rare moments along with Terry when, if he closed his eyes, he could almost believe this gorgeous, revered artist was speaking to him and him alone.

And if only for those accidental glimpses of what friendship might be like, I owe him. Or maybe this is just something I need to do for me.

With one last glance at Bryant, safely ensconced in his dull, domestic existence Paul spread his great wings and was gone.

* * *

Terry had pulled on his clothes, but they sat awkwardly on him, pulling and creasing. His habitually purposeful stride was broken into a stuttering gait, his hair not tamed into its usual product-enhanced sweep, stuck up in ragged tufts. Paul's heart lurched to see this epitome of confidence and style shambling down the street like a common drunk.

He only wished he knew more about how the change progressed. Would Terry already need blood? He followed nervously behind, unsure what to do.

After all, Augusta, and so presumably the powers that be, knew Terry had been bitten. If he was going to harm people, or pass the condition on, surely they would do something? But no, that was naive.

There had been a guardian nearby when that truck snuffed out Paul's life, a being capable of foreseeing and preventing the accident, who had done nothing. The angels did not concern themselves with the normal events of the mortal world. They were empowered only to prevent intrusions from the spiritual realm.

So how was it that the council called him away and in those few hours a vampire, a creature partially spiritual and aligned with the dark forces, chose to attack Terry within his home? Did they somehow want this to happen?

Terry's steps strayed into the quieter, more rundown sections of the neighborhood. There seemed to be no particular goal as he took a path that meandered and doubled back. Other pedestrians glanced at him nervously.

Paul moved up to walk intangibly by his side. It did seem as though the vampiric condition had a sudden onset. Terry's thin face was suddenly gaunt, his eyes glinted with ruby highlights, and his hands shook. A lady passed by in a small, sheer top, depending on her "beer jacket" to keep warm. Terry's eyes followed her. Misunderstanding his attention, she laughed flirtatiously as she hurried by. Her giggle ended in a nervous squeal, and she hurried on – frightened by what she saw in Terry's eyes.

How can I save Terry from becoming a murderer under the influence of this evil condition?

Terry stood still, watching the lone woman disappear down the street. He took one step after her but then stopped and looked around. Cars purred down the road sporadically, and small clusters of people drifted by or loitered outside shops and at the crossing. Terry shoved his shaking hands deep in his jacket pockets, then with a dim spark of his old confidence, turned down one of the darkened side streets leading down to the old canal.

The scene was set out with all the horrible and inevitable clarity of the set-up shot in a horror movie. Terry was still strung too tight, but no longer hesitant or confused, striding through the darkness as if it were daylight. The gloom down by the water was broken only by a fringe of up-cast light from beyond the backs of buildings that faced the street. A bright dot appeared further ahead, moving slightly, ruddy, a cigarette. A slight inhaled flare gave a glimpse of a man's face.

Paul stopped. This was well beyond the realms of coincidence surely?

Terry's eyes fixed upon the approaching figure, and his whole body was immediately electrified with the palpable energy of a predatory animal. His gaze flicked about the darkened scene, unmistakably scanning for potential witnesses. His fingers splayed and curled downwards, posed to seize his prey.

The man coming towards them was Bryant. He had a cell phone pressed to one ear as he gestured with his other hand, occasionally bringing the cigarette it held to his lips. "Oh jay-zus, Bill. Not the Black Bull again. Only old farts go there. Next, you'll suggest we take up dominoes and lament the end of the Thatcher years."

Bryant's eyes flicked up, but did not fasten on Terry, whose black apparel blended with the unlit and overgrown banks of the old canal. The rank grasses whispered in a slight breeze that blew towards them carrying with it the acrid scent of cheap tobacco.

With eyes that saw just a little more than ordinary light should show, Paul saw the expression on Terry's face, Bryant's inattention and inexorable approach – and he knew the moment of no return was approaching almost upon them all. Terry's mouth gaped, his canines extended in smooth white tines glistening with saliva. His steps slowed, and his neck dipped as his usual grace transformed into a serpentine stalk.

I can't allow it. Paul knew in a flash how he would explain it. Whilst following Bryant, he saw Terry about to assault him. Assuming that Terry, as a vampire, was now counted as a spiritual being, he intervened.

But, in truth, he knew it was Terry he wanted to save.

He approached close behind Terry's tall frame, flexing the sinews of his wings, he fanned them wide. Even in intangible realms, some laws of physics applied – it would be difficult to carry a double burden. He could of course have removed Bryant, but the angels favored subtlety, and Terry was the one who must by now already know there was some truth to the supernatural tales. Bryant would be left to continue on his mundane way, none the wiser. And besides…it was Terry he wanted to hold in his arms.

Bryant was drawing ever closer, almost within reach now. Terry tensed to spring, but Paul reached for him convulsively. Bryant jerked as he glanced up, but they were gone before he could have seen more than a blur. Paul's slender body strained to pull them from the physical plane just long enough to move from the isolated pathway to Terry's minimalist studio apartment. He managed it, but clumsily.

Terry sprawled forwards onto his huge rag rug, which took up the space between his scattered seating and a raised marble island on which the gas fire sat. The fire, set low, cast the only light. Paul collapsed awkwardly across Terry's body and had time only to gasp before he was grasped and thrust onto his back, his wings crushed awkwardly beneath him, feathers catching and breaking.

Terry's eye fastened on him for the first time. Paul had tried sometimes to stand in the path of Terry's gaze to be in the very place he looked, but he had never captured this, the real feeling of being seen. But what did Terry think of what he saw?

"So you are the one, my protector. I did wonder if I would ever be so fortunate as to see you." The hand that pinned him relaxed and crept up to touch Paul's cheek. "I did not expect you to look so young, or do all angels look like youths?"

Paul's heart thudded in his chest. He groped for some sensible words to say but could not muster the will to do anything but lie supine there in Terry's arms as he had so often dreamed of doing.

"Shouldn't you have left me by now? Now that I am cursed?"

"You… know?"

"This creature who did this to me took some pleasure in tormenting me with a few choice facts."

Terry relaxed, seeming content to lie by Paul's side, propped up on his elbow like some idle couple on a riverbank. He looked down at Paul fondly.

"He told me one thing that I think I already knew in my heart. That there was someone who watched over me, day and night, and was only gone for a moment."

"Too long..."

"I don't blame you. I swear I felt you there even when my rational mind knew that I was alone: my angel, my muse..."

His fingers trailed absently down Paul's loose, tawny hair. But then his arm convulsed, his eyes creased in pain.

"..And that monster told me this: that I would need blood, warm blood within hours or I would die. I tried to fight it, my angel. I truly did. But... I must have it."

Looking up into his tormented, sable eyes Paul knew what he would say next.

"I cannot say if I truly have blood anymore," he said. "But what I have is yours, if it will help you."

Terry cupped one hand around his face, and as he leaned forward, Paul braced himself for pain. But Terry simply kissed him gently on the lips. Soft pressure that grew slowly. Terry's firm tongue pushed between Paul's lips. Softly, prompting and instructing with every touch. Paul balked nervously, but then as pangs of sensation spiraled up within his body, he yielded, opened, followed...

Paul had always found the standard angel garb of a white knee length tunic to be frankly embarrassing. But there were some advantages to that simple garment as Terry's hand reached down, lay smoothly across his thigh, and slid slowly up, dragging the fabric with it. Unsure even of what was meant to happen now, he still wanted to feel Terry with his naked skin, every inch of it.

He fumbled with Terry's jacket, but the fabric seemed to conspire against him. Terry grabbed his hand and pushed it back against the fragile expanse of his wings. He stooped over Paul, paused, and ran his fingertips tentatively down the layer of brittle feather.

"You can't be very comfortable like that..."

"My wing is going numb," Paul confessed, worried that the passionate moment seemed to be waning.

Terry looked down at him for a long time, and then he bent and kissed Paul again, just lightly.

"Follow me," said as he stood and walked away.

Paul righted himself carefully. In a fully physical form, the wings were an awkward weight that shifted his balance and made even the most intuitive of movements feel slightly out of control.

He followed after Terry tentatively and found him in the bedroom. There before him was that very charcoal grey duvet on his beloved had lain like a corpse just a few hours before. Terry undressed in a matter of fact way, without embarrassment. Paul had seen his body hundreds of times. Terry trained hard, hit the tanning bed, and got exactly what he wanted out of his body just as he did out of the rest of his life. Paul had always admired that dedication and resolve.

He turned to Paul, torso defined like an anatomy model, broad cock half erect. Paul hesitated. His own form seemed as unformed as a Plasticine model in comparison, pale, slender and soft. Terry just stood and waited, then finally held out his hand, almost like he was asking to dance.

The tunic had two deep, hemmed slits to accommodate the wings, fastened at the top by laces that tied together to complete the simple, round neckline. Once Paul reached up and pulled the lose end of the ties, the whole garment drooped down, the front opening like a petal.

It dropped to the floor, and Paul stepped over it, trying not to look down at his own inadequate form.

"You're going to have to show me..."

"There are many things I have to show you, my angel." Terry stepped in close, smelling faintly of sweat, reaching his cold hands to slowly touched Paul on his neck, and then dropping down over his stomach to brush his cock. Paul felt himself blushing.

Terry lips moved slowly down his neck to the upper curve of his shoulder, first kissing, and then very softly dragging the points of his teeth over the skin. He shuddered.

"Not yet," Terry said with a rough voice. His cock hard, pushing insistently against Paul's stomach.

"You're perfect," Terry said. "I wish we had more time."

"We have as much time as you want. I won't leave you. I won't leave you again." Ever again.

"I want you to lie on the bed, my angel. On your front." He paused, noticing Paul's hesitation. "Go on. I promise, you're going to enjoy this. Put that pillow under your stomach."

Crawling onto the broad expanse of the king sized futon, he felt utterly vulnerable and a bit of a fool. He positioned the thick down pillow just below his belly button so his ass was offered.

"Close your eyes," Terry added.

Paul folded his arms in front of him, resting his forehead on his forearm and closed his eyes. In the darkness, he heard faint sounds, a drawer sliding open and closed again. The mattress sagged slightly to one side.

He kept his wings tight together and down the centre line of his body. Terry's hand rested on the small of Paul's back, a sudden spark of contact but not warm, as cool as the air. It reached up ruffling through the downy feather in the knotted muscles of his back between the bases of each wing, and then smoothly pressed the nearest one down and across.

The other echoed it by habit so that his wings spread out to his side, baring his body. He felt the muscles of his back clench with nervous anticipation.

"It's all right. Shhh." Terry's long-fingered hand stroked up and down Paul's spine from the base of his neck to the small of his back, slowly, evenly, venturing a little further each time until he ran, slowly, so slowly all of the way to the crease of Paul's buttocks and then further, teasing just short of his ass. Every ounce of Paul's awareness followed that fingertip in its languorous journey. All the way to his neck, all the way back. Then Terry pulled away. Paul waited, drowning in the darkness, adrift.

He started when the touch returned, wet and cold, trailing down from just above his asshole and then pushing casually in, just a little. Slowly, in and out, in and out.

Paul felt his cock trapped under his body swell, shifting nervously.

"You all right there? You've really not done this sort of thing before?"

Paul just shook his head.

"No, I didn't think so. You just tell me if you want me to stop, okay?"

And all the while that slender finger moved slowly, slickly in and out, venturing just a little further each time. Then moving in a soft circling motion. Paul felt his body gently cede to the unfamiliar intrusion, accepting it, and as the novelty faded, other sensations emerged. He thought of Terry's thick, hard cock, his desperate eyes, and felt his ass grudgingly allow two fingers now, tightly side by side.

For a moment, he wanted to be back in the living room just talking, kissing, making out, but he felt those two lubed fingers slide faster, fully into him and pressing down firmly. A warm wet sensation welled up within him, and Paul moaned. He wanted Terry to fuck him. Now!

Paul arched his back, easing his legs apart. Terry kept on teasing him, caressing the rim of his ass, running his fingertips around, and then slipping them in briefly before going around, around. Then he pulled away and moved off of the bed. Paul kept his eyes squeezed closed, waiting.

Terry's hand rested across Paul's buttocks, stilled, and then a wet touch. His tongue traced the path of his finger, around, slowly, pushing in just a little, probing. Paul felt love, lust, fear; his cock ached so hard he pushed it against the soft cushion, trying to ease it in small, grinding movements.

Finally, he felt Terry ease his weight onto the bed, one knee at a time. He thought he was ready for Terry's slow, cautious advances. He felt Terry above him, the mattress giving as he rested one hand just under Paul's right armpit, feeling slight movements as he did...something. But then he felt the rounded head of Terry's cock against his ass. Without a word, it began to slide into him, pushing him wider than before, a stretched ache as Paul felt his ass slide over the rounded head and grasp the shaft tightly.

Terry pushed into him in one smooth movement deeper and deeper, lowering his body at the same time until they were pressed tightly together. Paul clutched at the duvet beneath him, still and utterly swamped by the sensation of having another man inside him. He could feel the pulse of his blood, the sweat on his skin, the sweet ache...

As Terry began to thrust into him always full and slow and sweet, it felt like being fucked in a wound – raw but horrifyingly sweet, sliding, pushing — as if Terry's cock was splitting him slowly open. Then quicker, harder, striking and sparking warm, welling pleasure with each stab. Paul writhed on the bed, pinned down. With one hand, he reached out and grasped one of the chrome bars of the bedstead and felt it creak and begin to give.

His groin clenched up, on the verge of coming when Terry stooped down on him again and a sudden single, teeth striking the side and front of his neck and driving deep, plunging into his flesh.

A harsh cry, stifled as Terry's hand clasped over Paul's mouth lifting his chin and stretching his neck out. The fangs dug deeper, biting, questing, sucking. Arousal faded sharply away, but Paul somehow could not think to struggle, he felt helpless and even as his body began to shake and the world became so cold, so dim, he thought: it's all right. It's all right. He won't hurt me.

And then the darkness behind his closed eyelids rushed up to embrace him like a suffocating shroud.

* * *

Dawn was cold and empty. Paul's senses reported to him sluggishly, and reality coalesced. Alone. Weak. Thirsty. An empty bed, rumpled. On his side, light bodied. He uncurled slightly, winching and worked out finally what the nagging old sameness, new difference was – just as he felt something soft and light tickle across his shoulder blade.

Sitting up slowly, there was no weight of wings upon his back, and all around him a carpet of huge white feathers covered the bed. He swallowed painfully, raising one hand to his throat where dry blood crusted upon torn flesh and trailed down his chest. His fingers traced its path.

He eased around, stiff necked and afraid of breaking like a man made from half dried clay. The room was empty. Memories welled up but he would not address them, letting them float unresolved.

He would not have. He could not have.

Sliding one leg shakily off the bed he put his weight upon it.

Alive again, hooray?

Mortal again, boo hoo?

Who knew? How could he know how he felt, until he knew where Terry was?

Paul walked very carefully, each step experimental in nature, until he came to the doorway. The apartment was strewn with Terry's work, even one of the latest. Full casts of human models in different positions made into furniture. His eyes skated over the kneeling woman coffee table to the center of the room where Terry lay upon his back.

One tentative step after another, Paul drew closer. Terry was limp, pallid, still. The rug had been kicked aside, and a circle of invocation was engraved upon the floor beneath it. Not hastily chalked but precisely carved some time ago, awaiting use. It was a portal to the dark realm, the home of those who became demons in their second life.

A simple dagger protruded from Terry's chest, but there was very little blood, it had pooled in purposefully designed channels, no doubt to avoid smearing or distorting the circle.

Terry was dead, and there was really no other explanation. He had killed himself in his hurry to join the army of darkness, leaving Paul behind.

He stood, feebly turning the facts over and over in his head as if the tumbling would wear their cutting edges smooth. Terry had used him. He had known more, far more, than he pretended from the very beginning.

The coincidence of the vampire coming while Paul was away was explained. The vampire had come because Terry had called it. Terry had happened across Bryant because he sought him out. He sought him out to bring Paul to him. He brought Paul to him because his blood completed his transformation.

He stood and looked down at the grotesque corpse utterly unable to see anything he could do, any way to move forward, even to tear his eyes away. As far as he could see, his pitiful excuse for a life, post-life, existence in general, really needed to come to an end right here.

Before Augusta found him.

* * *

Paul sat in the apartment a short while. The smell of the stale corpse became stronger by slow degrees. They would be here soon, the angels, to investigate.

He had to leave. He struggled into one of Terry's interminable black T-shirt and suit ensembles. The legs were too long, and the jacket sagged slightly, but it was a tolerable fit. He wondered idly if some police analyst would have to deal with the riddle of Paul's DNA sample at a crime scene, given that he was already dead and buried. Or did the high and mighty angels "deal" with that sort of anomaly before human eyes ever saw it.

Terry's shoes fit, but tightly. Standing in the bathroom, looking at his reflection, Paul saw a frightened boy in a man's clothing; the shadows around his eyes, the darkest thing in his pale face. He had no plan except to leave this place, and so he did.

Even as he rode down on the elevator, he cursed himself for not searching the apartment for cash, or something to sell – but there was no way in hell he was going back.

He stepped out onto the sidewalk and began to walk. Fears curdled in his mind: did the bite alone make one a vampire? Could the angels find him by some... magic, no matter where he went?

He did not know the town well, only those places he followed Terry to and he had no desire to visit those haunts. He simply walked, taking turns at random until he came to a small park between two tall, brick buildings. There was a small fountain topped with a bronze figure gone green with corrosion.

A squirrel perched on the lip of the fountain and regarded him with nervous suspicion. Paul stumbled to a stop, reluctant to push the creature from his perch. He backed away and sat upon a wooden bench.

The day was cold and grey. The flat sky seemed to glare down at him.

Think of a plan, Paul. Think of a plan. But his mind remained as blank as the sky.

* * *

In aimless wandering, Paul whiled away the day. No matter how his mind gnawed at the problem, he could find no purchase upon it. He was hungry, and cold, sensations he had not felt since his death – or felt only in the most abstract of ways.

The streets were quiet in the mid afternoon when he noticed office workers coming out onto the streets alone and in small groups. A woman in a smart pantsuit walked up to the wall upon which he sat, set down her large brief case and opened it. She pulled some battered white sneakers from the case and eased off her high-heeled shoes – being careful not to put her stockinged foot down on the ground as she changed her shoes.

"This transit strike's a bitch, eh?" she said. "Do you live far off?"

"Yeah," Paul replied quietly. "A fair way." If anywhere at all.

"Your best bet would be to head up to the main road and try to thumb a lift. People are being pretty cool."

"Sure, thanks."

She strode off purposefully down the sidewalk swinging her briefcase with her heels rattling inside.

Almost immediately, another woman stopped. "Hey, cheer up. There's a bunch of people getting together over by the fountain, forming safe-walk groups and rental car-shares for people going further out. You should go check that out."

"I'm alright, thanks though."

"You sure, hon?"

"Yes, really..."

God knows what sort of vibe he was giving off. Paul got to his feet and started to head down the road again. The shoes were starting to rub, but he stifled any limp. The flywheel of his mind just kept turning without coming up with any kind of plan. In an hour or so, it would be getting dark, and even colder.

Blood & Feathers

As he walked, he was joined by a growing stream of displaced commuters plodding along with resignation that ranged from frustrated to surprisingly cheerful. Time hardly seemed to pass at all as the ranks of grey buildings slid by. He eavesdropped on dozens of cell phone conversations – each pretty much a copy of the next. 'I'm walking home, I'm going to be late.' The skin on his heels started to chafe, and he could feel the blisters rising and finally tearing wetly.

With a grimace, Paul hobbled to a stop and hopped over to sit on a concrete step. He eased the brogue off gingerly and peeled off the thin cotton sock. He flexed his cramped toes and inspected the raw skin of his heel.

"Well, I guess you won't get going much further tonight."

Perhaps it should have surprised him, looking up to see Bryant standing there with his key in his hand. Paul realized he was blocking the side door that lead up to the shopkeeper's apartment and had walked past the façade of the Foodmart without even recognizing it. But his emotional circuits just seemed too burnt out to respond, and he looked away blankly.

"You want to come up for a bit? I can give you some band aids for that, at least."

"Sure, yeah. Thanks," Paul muttered.

* * *

He limped up the grimy stairs after Bryant. The apartment looked somehow different through normal, mortal eyes. Simple, but clean and orderly. The frayed sofa was soft, and he settled onto it with a sigh.

"You walked all the way from downtown?"

"A little further than that, even."

"Do you want a Coke?"

"Sure."

Bryant handed him a cold can and vanished through a door into what must be the bathroom. His muffled voice called out, "By the looks of that, you oughtta soak it with a bit of disinfectant first and…"

234

He re-emerged again with a package of band-aids in one hand and a bottle of Dettol in the other. Leaning against the doorway, he gestured with the sloshing bottle of disinfectant. "You know this may sound a bit weird, but it would make just as much sense if you just dossed on that sofa there tonight. The buses will probably be running after work tomorrow."

"Um, well, I wouldn't want to..."

Bryant's cell phone buzzed, and he looked around for a moment before disappearing back into the bathroom, presumably to put something down.

"Yeah... Franky, Franky you what. Look you're meant to give a month's... Well, fuck you, too, then. No, well, I'm not your boss, so now I can speak to you any way I like rather than let professional courtesy get in the way. You were never on time, never polite, and the stock take is coming up way short on beer and fags – your favorite brands, too. Don't bother about the notice. You what? A reference? Are you really that stupid?"

After a brief period of muted swearing, Bryant came back in with a metal basin piled up with a few different packages. "Sorry about that," he said bashfully. "I really did my best with that kid, but working in a convenience store was obviously just too far beneath him. He'd rather go on to the dizzying heights of burglary and marijuana distribution. Bollocks. Now I have double shifts to work until I can get someone in for weekday lates."

He tipped the contents of the basin out and took it over to the sink. He looked over to Paul, and the frustrated scowl faded from his face. "Looks like you have the sort of job that doesn't require a classy outfit like this." He gestured vaguely to the mint green-striped shirt. "They actually added a bowtie to this ensemble, but I keep 'forgetting' to put it on." He sighed.

"Actually... um..." Paul felt awkward about it, but he saw a chance to have somewhere to stay just for a little while. "I got fired today. High powered jobs are just a haven for high powered bastards."

"Oh, well." Bryant didn't seem to know what to say. He brought over a basin of warm water full of something citrus scented. "Put your foot in that for a while."

"Thanks, look...I don't mean to..." He reached a hand across the gap between them on the sofa. "I'm Paul."

"Hey, Bryant...I mean I am, Bryant. And don't worry. It'll be good to have a bit of company, eh."

Bryant's hand was broad and warm, enveloping his own. They both seemed to hold on just a little too long.

Bryant's face flushed as he pulled away. "Of course I could, ah, call you a cab – there'll be one available eventually."

"No, it's good. If I'm not imposing."

"No."

"Good."

Paul immersed his foot in the tepid water of the basin, feeling vaguely foolish at the precaution until the sting of detergent hit the flesh beneath the open flap of skin. He hissed and tensed but pushed his foot flat down in the basin.

"Yeah, well, I don't know how you just kept walking until it got that bad. How's the other one look?"

"I'm sure it's fine."

"Yeah. Well, maybe you'd better check."

Apparently, Bryant wasn't going to leave it to him. He knelt down and unlaced Paul's other shoe like it was the most logical thing in the world to do. Peeling off the damp sock and wrapping his fingers around the instep, he peered around.

"Not so bad," he said. Paul felt Bryant's fingers run down the sole of his foot casually before releasing it. He stepped away and walked off towards the kitchenette. "So, was it your first job? You look like you can't be long out of school."

"My second job, I was there almost a year. I'm nineteen, you know. Some people think I look younger."

He heard the hiss of a soda can opening and craned around to watch Bryant return. "You look like you've been working too hard if you ask me."

He leaned over and then reached out with his free hand. "Did you cut yourself?" His fingertip touched the edge of a scab that showed at the neck of Paul's t-shirt. He started to pull the collar down to expose the ragged gash. Seeping blood had caught the cloth. More out of surprise than pain, Paul jumped away. His hand flailed out, knocking the Coke from Bryant's hand and pushing him back.

Paul jumped to retrieve the gurgling can. Feelings welled up suddenly, fear and anxiety churning. He curled his fingers, crushing down the sofa cushions. "I'm sorry."

"No, I am sorry. I didn't mean to hurt you."

Oh bloody hell. "No, uh, it was just an accident at work. I was careless. I am already imposing on you and now…"

Bryant just laughed. "We do seem to be having a little trouble communicating. But you are more than a little banged up, and I… well, I'm just being foolish. Perhaps you'd like to turn in early. Take a proper shower and turn in. There's a TV in the bedroom so you can watch that if you're not tired."

"I can't turn you out of your bed. I mean we've hardly even met."

"You know it's funny, but I have the strangest feeling like we've met before, or were meant to meet." Bryant's face froze with sudden embarrassment. "Don't pay any attention to me. Just go ahead. There's a clean robe on the back of the door."

* * *

The small bathroom was also stark and white with matching bland white towels hanging from white plastic hooks beside a white terrycloth robe. Some people just didn't care about design.

The cloth of the T-shirt adhered to his body. He stripped off all his other clothes and stepped into the small shower booth. The tepid water at its lowest pressure, dribbled over his body, washing away another less than pleasant return to normal mortality, a layer of greasy sweat from walking the city like a zombie.

So, plan 'A' – freeload off Bryant the shopkeeper for as long as possible. Plan B, there is no plan B, so stop feeling guilty about plan A until your neurons can come up with something better. What about, 'Hi Mom, I'm not dead'. I think not.

He banged his forehead softly against the tiled wall, but eventually, the demands of a mundane task pulled him back. He peeled the shirt off gingerly and dropped it out of the shower to make a sodden heap. His black, borrowed clothes sat on the linoleum like a sullen stain.

His fingers crept up cautiously. The edges of his deep bite marks were swollen and encrusted. They felt warm, and any infection he might have, well its nature hardly bore consideration, but at least it served to seal the wounds somewhat. He stood under the water until it started to cool, then hurriedly rinsed off the sluggish trial of blood from the torn scabs. He shut off the water and stepped out, patting the rest of his body dry and pressed a wad of toilet paper down on his shoulder.

He hesitated to take the robe, but with little other option, he slipped it on, the heavy cloth weighing down his ad hoc bandage. The bathrobe was a size or two too large for him, but its thick cloth was strangely comforting. It felt warm and soft under his fingers, a garment long accustomed to the shape of a body.

He tried to tidy up the room, folding up his sodden clothing and wiping the floor with the now pink-stained towel. But with every movement, he felt the collar shifting over his wound, and his mind skated over the thin surface of his problem, gingerly avoiding falling through.

With a night of sleep, perhaps he could think properly. He cracked the door open sheepishly. Bryant looked up from his perch over his computer.

"I really do feel like I'm taking advantage," Paul said.

"Well, if it doesn't worry me," he replied. "I don't see why it should worry you."

Paul felt himself smile faintly.

"The bed's made up fresh," Bryant added. "I'll take the couch."

Paul looked dubiously at the well-padded, but rather short sofa, in comparison to Bryant's lanky frame. But like he said...if it didn't bother him.

He shut the door quietly but firmly behind him. It's not that he wasn't suspicious. Paul settled into the crisp, cool bed made up with old-fashioned sheets and wool blankets, leaving the robe on. He lay for a long time listening to the muted sounds of Bryant moving around in the living room. The TV clicked once but was quickly turned down so low that it was nothing but a distant mumble.

He felt hungry but ignored it, curling up tight and pulling the covers up around his neck. He was already half asleep when he heard the door crack open, and his heart lurched. He lay still and waited. After a few moments, the door closed again, and the apartment fell still and quiet.

* * *

Paul found himself awake in the early hours of the morning and lay still listening to the city slowly rumble into life from the grumbling garbage truck and early buses to the first commuters. In the half-light of the early morning, he heard a gentle knock at the door.

Pulling the blanket up, he blinked to see the door still closed. "Yes?"

"Hey." Bryant leaned in. "I've gotta go open the store. I get a break at about nine-thirty if you want to come down and grab some breakfast."

"Um."

"Come on, my treat. I just put your clothes in the drier. It's in the kitchen."

"Okay."

"Okay."

Damned if he wasn't just the most cheerful guy ever. Paul peered at the digital clock perching on the bedside table, even at four-thirty in the morning. After a while, he felt weird and guilty just lying there. He turned over a few times, restless. He realized he'd rather assumed that the angels would have found him by now; they're angels, after all. And bloody hell, he hadn't exactly planned it this way, but he wasn't hiding in the very last place Augusta would think to look, surely?

Not that his angsting was going to change what they did. For all he knew, a whole chorus of angels was standing all around the room. If they wanted something from him, he was sure they'd let him know. He lay and watched the time tick away, one glowing

239

decimal at a time. Finally, he just couldn't stand being alone a moment longer.

He rolled slowly out of bed and crept across the room into the empty living room. Peering around the kitchen, he found a small-scale clothes washer-dryer unit tucked under the bench, his borrowed clothes still warm and tangled up inside. He felt vaguely sick at the sight of them – Terry's uber cool, always-black style of dress didn't have the same connotations that it used to.

Well, the least he could do was to go and see if he could help Bryant out in the store somehow, to pay him back for taking him in so easily and with so little question.

There was no way he was getting those shoes back on his aching feet, so Paul slipped on a pair of scuffed sandals that waited beside the door. He inspected the lock carefully, making sure he left the place locked.

Around the corner, the shop was lit up, and Bryant was behind the counter. The morning light hit his profile, giving it a sort of old style movie star quality. A gaggle of high school students filled the area before the counter, and a larger group waited outside.

"Not leaving us already are you?" Bryant called cheerfully over their heads.

Paul pushed his way though, very cautiously given the state of his exposed heels. "I just, ah, thought I might be able to help out down here."

"Oh, well. If you do the bagging, I'll get this lot out of here a little quicker and I'm sure we'll all be happier for it."

"Oh, I'm in no hurry," piped up a goth-styled girl with a uniform hemmed up as high as it would go.

"Ignore the girl child," Bryant said wryly as he raised the hinged part of the counter to let him in. Then he added in a sotto voice, "Far be it from me to suggest a minor child is in any way fast."

"I'm not a minor; I'm sixteen," she said with all the outrage of someone who has reached that milestone recently.

Bryant leaned forward. "Then you be sure to hand those crisps to Paul with all due respect. He's your senior by fully three years."

"Almost four," Paul added. He took the scanner from Bryant and found it was pretty much as easy to use as it looked.

They fell into an easy rhythm as a rush of people stormed in to grab their morning paper, coffee or junk food for their lunch (or breakfast). Most of them came and went with a scowl and a grunt, barely bothering to make eye contact. A few regulars meant the conversation became well rehearsed by the time a bulky lady in the distinctive green striped shirt and nametag combo came in.

"Hi there, Mr. March. And, who is this then. You've not gone and replaced me?" Her tone wasn't quite making a joke of it.

"No danger of that, Mrs. Prentice. Paul's just a friend visiting with me."

"Oh is he? Well he and you can both get out from behind my counter now. I've work to do."

Bryant raised his hands in mock surrender and got out of her way, so Paul followed suit.

"Come on down to the café with me," he said as they headed out the door. "The morning rush is about done now, and I generally grab breakfast, then head in to sort out paperwork, restocking and so on before helping with the lunch rush and then taking over for afternoon. Then I knock off when the late shift comes on, except I'm a little short now that Franky has followed the siren call of juvenile delinquency..."

And Paul knew exactly what he was going to do.

***

It was approaching one in the morning, and Paul was about to finish working his first late shift. Pretty soon somebody called "Robert" would be in to work "earlies." It was already feeling familiar. Bryant was still there, leaning on the counter.

"Aren't you sick of this place yet?" Paul asked.

"Oh, some things I don't think I'd ever get sick of." Bryant suddenly blinked and looked away. "Forget I said that."

His richly expressive face was creased with embarrassment, those broad, capable hands resting lightly on the counter.

"What if I don't want to forget about it?" The words came out without any real thought, but he found he meant them. Just a few hours after he felt like every feeling had been burnt from his body...

Bryant looked around. The shop was empty, but a guy was just coming in, trailing over to the fridge and lugging over two six-packs. Paul made the sale, his gaze flicking up to Bryant who assiduously avoided looking his way. As soon as they were alone again, Bryant leaned forward.

"Look, this job is yours for as long as you want it. You can crash with me as long as you like – no strings attached."

Bryant's face flushed. It was a face with character, and for all his protestations, Bryant must be, what, in his late thirties at the most, and hardly disfigured. Besides that, he was a solid, caring man – complex enough but certainly not secretly conspiring to join the army of darkness. Bryant didn't know a damn thing about fashion, but Paul found himself thinking that fondly. It wasn't all that articulate, but deep inside, Paul knew he was feeling something for Bryant, maybe no grand passion as yet, they only just met, but something real.

Paul just shook his head. "I'm beginning to get the idea that you have a low opinion of yourself, Bryant."

"Look, Paul. It's just that you're a handsome young man obviously going through some sort of a rough spot. I don't expect you're going to be working for a corner store and dossing with me for long. And..."

Paul just smiled. The convex mirror showed a big guy with the now familiar pinstripe shirt coming up the sidewalk. Robert, no doubt.

"Well, if it doesn't worry me, I don't see why it should worry you," Paul replied.

Paul felt pretty awkward as he followed Bryant up the stairs. Once they got inside, he said, "So you've had a pretty long day. Can I interest you in sleeping in your own bed?"

He wasn't totally sure what he was offering. Well, it was pretty obvious, but he wasn't totally sure how he felt about it.

"We don't have to do anything, you know," Bryant said.

Paul turned and walked into the bedroom, unbuttoning his new work shirt as he went and dropping it behind him. Bryant left the lights off and followed after him.

His presence behind Paul's body was electric, then a heavy hand fell upon his shoulder and all the tension drained out of Paul's body with a sigh. Bryant's touch lingered, trailing along the slope of his shoulder. Even by the indirect light of the streetlights through the blinds, the wounds Terry had left were clear to see.

"I saw those marks, like stab marks, when you changed. Are you sure you should...?"

Paul turned to him, standing in close. "You'll just have to be gentle with me."

"I think I can do that."

Bryant stripped off his clothes calmly until he was completely naked, then he leaned into Paul and kissed him softly. Paul reached out, feeling the solid barrel of Bryant's chest, warm and firm. As their kiss deepened, Paul closed his eyes, leaning back, feeling Bryant's hand splayed at the small of his back, leaning him slowly backwards onto the bed.

Bryant unfastened Paul's trousers and slid them and his underwear slowly down. He stood back for a moment. "You are so beautiful," he said.

"Don't..."

"Don't?" Bryant leaned over him, hands planted on either side of his body. "It's what I see. It's what I feel."

"So, what is this, love at first sight?" He felt Bryant's breath puffing against his cheek.

"Okay," Bryant said, now without any embarrassment. "Let's call it that."

"Okay." Paul felt himself smiling broadly. Let's call it that.

Bryant's lips traced down his neck and across his chest. He curled up but winced at the pain in his shoulder and lay back.

"Bryant?"

Bryant ignored him, his lips moving down further, brushing his inside thigh and sliding over his cock wetly. Paul clutched at the covers as his cock was tightly gripped, firm lips pulling down its length and reach up again each time harder and wetter. He moaned as the tension built within him. He tried to hold back, opening his eyes and staring up at the dim ceiling.

Bryant stopped and delicately licked the tip of his stiff cock, swirling the tip of his tongue around the sensitive head.

"Bryant," he moaned as he came suddenly. "Goddamn!"

Bryant crawled back up along his body laughing. "Why so annoyed?"

"I wanted... I wanted to..."

"I wanted to do just what I did. But we can do things your way next time..."

Bryant spooned up beside him, his cock hard, pressing against Paul's thigh. Paul reached over. It was so soft, the skin sliding slightly at his touch. He spit on his hand, leaning in so they lay face to face. As he caressed Bryant's cock, he felt his lover's breath catch, his body stiffened.

"I can think of so many things," Paul whispered, "for us to do."

But the simple repetitive act, caressing up and down, with this great, loving man so totally under his control. He could probably do that, just that, forever.

***

Some time in the night, Paul became aware that he was dreaming, and in that dream, he saw an angel.

"You knew where I was the whole time, didn't you?"

Augusta just smiled gently and pulled Paul into her embrace. Finally, she held him away from her.

"You could come back to us now. You just have to say the word."

Paul's heart thumped, hard. "Can't I stay?"

"With a shopkeeper?"

"With Bryant, for as long as I can."

Biography

Emily Veinglory is an ex-patriot New Zealander now living deep in the heart of Indiana, which is enough to make anyone want to write about werewolves, highwayman and inter-galactic prostitutes. She writes mainly gay romance with a dark twist, but sometimes something sweet or with a girl – just to mess with her readers' heads. If you have feedback, requests or would like to see a sequel, please email veinglory@gmail.com. For more information see http://www.veinglory.com

The Mirror

by

Sasha White

Rating: Sizzling

Genre: Contemporary

This story originally appeared in *Down & Dirty 2*, (Pretty Things Press, 2004).

The Mirror

I noticed him as soon as he stepped into the dingy pub. He wore faded jeans, a tight white T-shirt and a leather jacket, but it was the rough stubble on his firm jaw line and the shaggy cut of his black hair that gave his good looks that dangerous air most women, including myself, found so irresistible.

His eyes scanned the room, stopping when they met mine. Acknowledging my gaze with a slight nod of his head, he walked toward the bar. The way his body moved encouraged my eyes to travel over his broad chest and flat stomach to the impressive package under his belt buckle. I could feel my anger and frustration receding, lust replacing it.

A distraction, just what I needed.

He stopped next to the stool I occupied at the bar and ordered a beer from the pretty bartender. She gave him an obvious look of invitation as she opened the bottle and set it in front of him, but he ignored her and turned to me.

"What's a good girl like you doing in a place like this?" he asked, a blend of mischief and lust in his dark eyes.

"Thinking about what an asshole my boyfriend is," I answered honestly.

He raised an eyebrow inquiringly.

Needing no further encouragement, I unloaded all my pent up anger on him. How I was on my way home from a very important business trip that had kept me away from my boyfriend for three weeks, only to have my car break down. To make matters worse, when I called to tell Jamie that I would have to spend the night in this two-bit town on the side of the highway while it got repaired, he picked a fight with me. He'd made a special dinner for us and had planned a romantic evening in anticipation of my return and was mad because now his surprise was ruined. When I suggested he drive the hour to come and spend the night in the hotel with me, like a little boy sulking, he hung up on me!

"So I've been sitting here for three hours, alone, bored, and frustrated," I finished.

He shifted closer. "I have something that'll make you feel 100% better."

"Yeah," I asked derisively, "what could that be?"

The Mirror

He leaned in so that his warm lips brushed my earlobe as he whispered, "Me." The heat from the hand he placed meaningfully on my stocking clad thigh spread rapidly through my body.

A shiver ran down my spine as my mind went blank "YES!" my body screamed. "Let's go," my lips answered.

We quickly crossed the street to the old motel where I already had a room. My fingers trembled with excitement at what was about to happen, causing me to fumble a little with the key in the lock. We stepped inside, and I looked around the room. It looked and smelled clean, but was obviously a cheap motel room.

Perfect for a secret *rendezvous*.

I walked to the dresser by the wall and set down my purse. Turning to look at him, I slid the jacket of my business suit slowly down my shoulders and dropped it to the floor, revealing the skimpy camisole beneath.

I could tell by the look in his dark eyes as he stepped towards me that we both wanted the same thing. A hot, sweaty session of lovin' that would last all night.

Stopping in front of me, his hands gently cupped my head and brought his lips to mine in a slow seductive kiss that quickly changed to hot and hungry as our tongues tangled. I felt his cock hardening against me as his hands slid into my hair. Gripping a handful, he pulled my mouth away from his.

"Not so fast."

He smiled devilishly and turned my body to face the mirror over the dresser, stripping off his own jacket as he stepped behind me. Pressing his sculpted chest against my back and his hard package against my ass, he made eye contact with me. Watching my eyes, he then lowered the straps of my camisole over my shoulders towards my waist, momentarily hooking the lace edge on my stiff nipples.

"Look at yourself," he whispered. "How hard your nipples are. They're begging for attention. Your eyes are begging too. Don't worry. I'm going to give you what you want. What you need."

His hands cupped my breasts from behind, tweaking my nipples, pinching and rolling them causing me to gasp sharply. The sight of his hands on my pale skin made all the sensations rippling my insides that much stronger. My breath began to come in pants as his hands worked my body and his lips began to nip playfully on along my shoulder and neck. My hands reached behind and grabbed the firm cheeks of his ass, pulling him against me harder as I shuffled my feet further apart.

"Oooh, poor baby," he crooned in response to my urgings. "Things moving too slow for you?"

His hand slid down my soft belly skin to the front of my skirt, pressing against my pubic bone. Teasingly, his fingers began a walking motion that caused them to brush between my thighs at the same time as raising my skirt. When only my panties covered my pubes, he scraped his fingers along my crease and laughed softly. "You're almost ready for me."

I whimpered, and he pressed his fingers against me more firmly. My hips swayed encouragingly. His hand left me to join his other on the elastic at my hip. With a quick jerk, the elastic snapped, and my panties were gone.

The image framed in the mirror was so hot. The reflection showed me standing with both my camisole and skirt wrapped around my waist, black garter and stockings framing my pouting pussy. His firm, tanned arms surrounded me, his eyes burning brightly as he watched his hands glide over my body.

Me soft, him hard. Me light, him dark.

A study of contrasts.

Another groan escaped as I watched his hand reach my pussy lips only to spread them apart, causing my aching, swollen clit to thrust out rudely. His other hand hovered over my aching button, index finger pointing.

"Please..." The word trembled off my lips, my eyes searching his in the mirror.

He brought his finger up to his mouth. His lips parted, and his pink tongue darted to wet the tip teasingly. Our eyes meet as he lowered his finger again, this time stopping directly on my clit, and with firm circular pressure, I was off.

One touch was all it took to make my eyes slide shut and the fireworks to start. My knees buckled, my head rolled back, and my juices flooded his fingers and my thighs. His body stayed pressed to mine the whole time, keeping me standing. When I came back from the fireworks show, I was wrapped tight in strong arms and held against a hot, hard, very male body.

"O.K.?" he asked softly.

"Mm hmmm..." I purred.

"Good." He pressed his hips against me firmly. "Now we can get to it."

Those words made my body hum in anticipation of more pleasure. I tried to turn to him, but he resisted. Grabbing my hands and placing them firmly on the dresser, he commanded me to keep them there.

The posture thrust my butt out and made me aware of what he wanted. I watched in the mirror as he stepped back to rid himself of his clothes. When he was naked, I could see his throbbing cock straining towards me. My mouth watered, and I wondered how that angry, purple head would taste, knowing I would find out by the end of the night.

"Later," he stated, reading my desire in the licking of my lips. "Right now, I am going to fuck you so hard you'll be lucky if you can walk tomorrow."

I just spread my legs further apart and arched my back in invitation, showing him where to put that cock of his and daring him to do as he promised.

"Oh." It was his turn to groan. "You've got a fantastic ass, baby."

He grabbed both cheeks in his hands and began massaging them, spreading them apart, and then he bent over and gave one a sharp bite. Moving one hand from my ass, he dipped his fingers into my wet hole. Teasing me a little more, he added another finger when my hips began to match the rhythm of his strokes.

"Oh yea, your cunt is so hot and tight. My fingers aren't enough, though, are they? You want me to fill you up, don't you?" he asked in a harsh whisper. "Here it comes. All for you, baby."

He pulled his fingers out, one hand grabbing my hip as the other guided his meaty dick between my spread legs. Leaving himself at my entrance, both hands grasped my hips firmly and, with one quick, hard thrust, filled me completely.

I let my head fall forward as he closed his eyes and started thrusting in and out. His cock was hot and thick inside my tunnel, every move he made causing fantastic friction. Every few strokes, he'd swivel his hips sharply, thrusting even deeper, hitting a hidden pleasure point buried deep inside me. My panting shifted to whimpers of pleasure as he picked up speed. Soon, his fierce pumping caused my hands to slide from the edge of the dresser to the wall behind it, giving me leverage to push back.

"Oh, yeah," he growled. "That's it."

He leaned forward enough that he could grab a swimming breast. Palming it roughly, he pinched my nipple and felt the answering clench of my pussy walls around his cock. I could feel my insides coiling tighter as he did it again and again.

His hand left my tit to grab a handful of my hair and pull my head up so our eyes met in the mirror. I saw sweat beading on his forehead and lips stretched taut across his teeth, and I knew he was fighting his own orgasm, waiting for me.

"Yes, yes, that's it. There. Harder!" I cried out as my cunt clenched and another orgasm hit me. My insides began milking him, our eyes never separating. I saw sparks go off in his when he clenched his teeth, a final groan escaping his lips as his cum shot into me hotly.

My head fell forward onto the dresser, and I struggled to stay standing in the aftermath. A few seconds later, I felt strong arms pull me back up, turn me towards him, and snuggle me into a warm hug.

He placed soft kisses on my neck and whispered in my ear. "I wasn't sulking when I hung up on you. I just wanted to get to you as soon as possible."

Biography

Sasha White was born in Calgary, Alberta and raised all over Western Canada. The travel bug has stayed with her and ever since she left home, she continues to go wherever opportunity leads her: the United States, Scotland, Ireland, Northern Ireland, Nepal, Singapore, Mexico, South Africa, Mozambique, Swaziland, and Greece. When she's not writing sizzling erotica, she can be found tending bar, waitressing, traveling, or engaged in her hobbies of bookbinding, photography, and the martial arts.

Sasha is the author of BOUND (Berkley Heat, 2006), *The Crib* in PURE SEX (Kensington Aphrodisia, 2006), *Sex as a Weapon* in THE COP (Kensington Aphrodisia, 2006), and *Shift Change* in SEX IN THE OFFICE: WICKED WORDS (Virgin Black Lace, 2005), among many other stories. Her novella, *Watch Me*, will appear in the KINK anthology from Berkley Heat in February 2007. Her story, *Tempting Grace*, is part of the ALLURING TALES collection from Avon Red, to be released March 2007. Her single author anthology, LUSH, will be released in April 2007 from Kensington Aphrodisia.

The Reluctant Bridesmaid

by

Lois Winston

Rating: Sweet

Genre: Chick Lit

"Whoa! Those are some butt-ugly dishes." Nick Landry, editor-in-chief of *NJNow*, leaned over my shoulder and stared at the polka-dotted china displayed on my computer screen. "I figured you for better taste, Paige. That stuff reminds me of a loaf of Wonder Bread."

"Or dinnerware for a clown," I said, closing the web page.

Nick scrubbed the five o'clock shadow that sprouted from his jaw each day at exactly three-fifteen. "I thought you were working on the arts funding legislation."

I swiveled in my chair to face him. "I was checking out Tara's bridal registry."

Nick raked a hand through his perpetually tousled chestnut hair, combing it off his forehead, and scowled. "Why torture yourself?"

Why indeed? "Guess I'm just a glutton for punishment. Besides, I don't see how I can get out of giving them a wedding present, being that I'm in the wedding party."

Nick segued into protective Big Brother mode. "You're better off without him, you know."

"I know." The *him* Nick referred to was my ex-boyfriend, Gary Powell. Last Valentine's Day, Gary said he had something important to discuss with me. I anticipated a diamond and a marriage proposal; I received an oral Dear Jane.

Three weeks later, Gary showed up at a family gathering on the arm of my spoiled-brat cousin Tara Clooney – no relation to George, even though she's spent years pouring through Internet genealogy sites trying to find one. Tara is convinced she's got celebrity genes lurking somewhere in her DNA and has left no chromosome unturned in her quest to find the missing link.

Since our shared heritage comes from her mother being my father's sister, I have no hope of discovering that George is my twenty-seventh cousin, eight times removed, a fact Tara takes pleasure in voicing at every family get-together. Like I care.

"You only pretend not to care because you're jealous," she's said on more than one occasion.

Yeah, right. What I cared about was the two-carat sparkler that appeared on the third finger of Tara's left hand by Easter Sunday. That and the fact that I'd been branded the world's most naive fool after Tara let slip – accidentally on purpose – that she and Gary had been secretly dating since Thanksgiving.

Nick placed his hand on my shoulder and gave me a comforting squeeze. "Forget him."

He meant Gary, of course, not George.

I rose from my chair and paced the miniscule cubbyhole that was my home away from home nine hours a day, five days a week. "I'd love nothing better, but how do you forget a heel when his size tens will be showing up at every family function from now until death they do part?"

"I doubt Gary and Tara will last that long," said Nick. "And frankly, knowing Gary the way I do, I'm glad you're no longer a twosome. You deserve better."

"Got anyone in mind?" The wedding was less than two weeks away, and I still didn't have a date.

He held up his hands, palms outward. "Forget it. I'm the guy responsible for you getting hooked up with him in the first place, even if I never meant for that to happen. No way will I introduce you to any more of my frat buds. None of them are good enough for you."

Great. Not only did I have to attend Gary's and Tara's wedding, but I'd have to go solo. How pathetic was that? And knowing Tara, she'd probably seat me at the table with the other single cousins – the oldest after me being all of fourteen.

Tara had been jealous of me from the moment of her birth – exactly three days, five hours, and twenty-seven minutes after my own. I had arrived a week early, thus usurping her of first grandchild status, an unforgivable sin as far as the overly competitive Tara was concerned. I would have been my grandparents' favorite no matter how the birthing order panned out, though. Between them, Nana and Pops held three doctorates. My straight A's won out over Tara's C minus average hands down, no matter how many beauty pageant tiaras she acquired.

As children, Tara first stole my toys. Then my playmates. Now, she'd stolen my man. And she'd snicker all the way down the aisle, knowing how humiliated I'd be at the reception. Unless...

Nick read my mind. "Got a date for the wedding?"

I shook my head.

"You've got one now."

I stared into his shamrock green eyes. "Is this a mercy date?"

"Call it a *mea culpa* date." He started to leave but paused at the entrance and turned back. "By the way, I need you to cover for Jess Saturday afternoon at that presidential fundraiser in Princeton."

Jess Harrow was our weekly magazine's political reporter. My beat consisted of the New Jersey arts scene and an occasional human interest story, but being a small staff, we often helped out each other. "This Saturday?"

"Yeah. Problem?"

"Tara's bridal shower is Saturday."

"And?"

"And gee, I guess I'll have to miss it."

Nick grinned, his eyes twinkling with mischief. "A real shame," he said, stepping into the corridor.

Nick Landry. What a guy. But we'd always maintained nothing more than a big brother/little sister relationship. Pity. If ever a girl needed a knight in shining armor to ride to her rescue...I shook my head as I turned back to my keyboard. Some things just weren't meant to be.

I valued our friendship, though. Besides, I'd agree to muck out the horse stalls at Monmouth Race Track to avoid Tara's shower. Spending an hour or two listening to blowhard politicians? Piece of cake.

* * *

Later that evening, I dropped my bombshell news during a fitting at Chez Bride

"What do you mean you're not going to the shower?" asked Bari-Lynn, my step-mother. "You have to go, Paige. You're a bridesmaid."

I stared at myself in the full-length mirror. Tara had chosen cinch-waited, full-skirted bridesmaid gowns in yards of daffodil yellow chiffon. I looked like a jaundiced Holstein. "One of the *ten* bridesmaids," I said. "I won't be missed."

She waved her skeletal arms like an anorexic, platinum magpie. "But how will it look? What will people say?"

By *people*, Bari-Lynn meant Tara's mother. Bari-Lynn and Aunt Sybil sprang from the same Short Hills-Ladies-Who-Lunch-on-Lettuce-and-Cosmos mold. No wonder, considering Aunt Sybil had introduced Dad to Bari-Lynn after my mother died. In my opinion, marrying Bari-Lynn was not one of Dad's brighter moves, but as air-brained trophy wives go, she was benign. She and I might not agree on much, but we did get along. Most of the time.

I shrugged. "What did *they* say when Tara stole Gary from me?"

She rolled her eyes and let loose one of those what-am-I-going-to-do-with-you sighs before slumping onto a nearby ivory satin chaise. "Gary broke up with you before he started seeing Tara."

I raised an eyebrow overdue for a waxing. "Really?"

"Paige, please. As a bridesmaid, you have certain obligations."

My other eyebrow lifted to join the first. I wasn't a bridesmaid out of any long-standing bond between Tara and me. As far as I was concerned, my only obligations were to show up and not make any horrible faces during the photographs. This was all about one-upmanship, but Bari-Lynn would never see why I didn't get along with Tara. Being a former beauty queen herself, she thought Tara was perfection personified, and I needed all the help I could get. I saw little point in explaining the facts of life – my life – to her.

"My work obligations come first," I told her. "People will have to understand. If they even notice I'm missing."

Bari-Lynn frowned. At least I think she frowned. It's hard to tell when someone gets monthly Botox injections. "They'll notice. And I'll never hear the end of it." Then she changed the subject. "We should head over to Quakerbridge Mall after your hem is pinned."

"Why?"

"You still need to pick out a wedding gift."

"Already taken care of."

Her eyes widened. "You went shopping without me?" Bari-Lynn considers shopping a holy experience. I'd rather muck out those stables at Monmouth than spend an hour at the mall.

"With a click of my mouse. Tara and Gary are now the proud owners of one overly-priced, uglier-than-sin, polka-dotted bone china serving platter."

Bari-Lynn raised her French manicured hands to the heavens. "Oh, Paige, what am I going to do with you?"

"Hey, don't blame me. I didn't pick the pattern."

* * *

The next day, Nick called me into his office. "Want to have some fun?" he asked.

"What did you have in mind?"

"A little *quid pro quo*."

I dropped into the chair across from his desk. "I'm listening."

* * *

The day of the wedding, Nick and I arrived at the church together. He took his place with the rest of the ushers while I headed for the Bride's Room. I found the other nine bridesmaids fluttering around Tara like a flock of silly yellow chicks. Aunt Sybil and Bari-Lynn performed Mother Hen duty while the photographer snapped away.

"There you are, Paige," said Bari-Lynn, noticing me observing from the sidelines. "We were getting worried. Hurry. We need pictures of you with Tara and the other girls."

I strolled over to the group and allowed the photographer to place me in the tableaux.

"Stand here, hold this, and place your hand like so," he said, demonstrating how he wanted me to hold up a silver hand mirror to reflect Tara's profile.

I reached out for the mirror with my left hand.

Tara gasped. "Where did you get *that*?"

Eleven pairs of eyes followed her gaze to my hand.

The Reluctant Bridesmaid

"My God!" said Bridesmaid Number Three – Tiffany, or Lindsey, or Brittney. All of Tara's bridesmaids looked the same to me. I was the only one without a perky nose job, a perfect salon tan, and a diet that consisted of more than a leaf of romaine once a week.

"It's at least twice the size of yours, Tara," said Bridesmaid Number Seven.

"Four point two carats," I said.

Tara grabbed my hand and glared at the ring, then me. She wrinkled her rhinoplasty nose. "It's not real," she said, tossing my hand away like a soiled tissue. "It can't be. You're not even dating anyone."

"Oh, it's real," I said, fluttering my fingers. "Van Cleef's will vouch for that. And before you hurl your next insult, no, I didn't buy it for myself."

Bari-Lynn pushed her way through the oohing and ahhing yellow gaggle. She clasped my hand between both of hers and studied the ring. "Stunning," she said. "Paige, darling, you've been keeping secrets from us."

I noticed Tara scowling at her own ring. Two large crimson blotches had sprouted on her cheeks. "Secret relationships seem to be something of a family tradition," I said. "I'm just following in Tara's footsteps."

My cousin's blotches deepened to purple.

* * *

Throughout the ceremony, Tara forced a tight smile that didn't reach her eyes or her new husband. During the reception, I caught her periodically glaring at Nick and me.

"Think she's demanding a bigger chunk of ice?" asked Nick, nodding toward the newlyweds who seemed engaged in a heated exchange. Several people standing near Gary and Tara darted glances at each other before edging out of earshot. Others crept closer to eavesdrop.

I chuckled. "You were right. Those two deserve each other."

"So you're finally over the louse?"

"Definitely."

"Good." Nick raised a glass of champagne. "Here's to new beginnings."

I clicked my glass against his. "To new beginnings." I nodded toward the diamond ring. "And your very generous grandmother. Please thank her for the loan."

"I will. The next time I visit the cemetery."

I stared at him. "I don't understand. I thought—"

Nick placed his hand over mine. "My grandmother willed me the ring, Paige. To give to the woman who captured my heart. And I have."

Biography

Award-winning author Lois Winston writes humorous, cross-genre, contemporary novels. She often draws upon her extensive experience as a crafts designer for much of her source material. Her first book, TALK GERTIE TO ME, a combination chick lit/hen lit/romantic comedy with a touch of the paranormal, was an April 2006 release from Dorchester Publishing. LOVE, LIES AND A DOUBLE SHOT OF DECEPTION, a mom-lit romantic suspense, will be a June 2007 release from Dorchester. When not writing or designing, you can find Lois trudging through stacks of manuscripts as she hunts for diamonds in the slush piles for the Ashley Grayson Literary Agency.

Visit Lois at http://www.loiswinston.com/.

The Forge:

Jezren Dark Sky

by

S.R. Howen
Writing as
Shaunna Wolf

Rating: Tangy

Genre: Futuristic/Dark Fantasy

Prologue

"Why?"

Jandra looked down at the small human child walking beside her. The girl's eyes were too large for her face. Her green eyes and pale skin with its sprinkling of freckles gave her an impish appearance—her flaming red hair added to the illusion. But this child wasn't a cute little imp. She was the most annoying street child the charity house had taken in.

"Because I said so," Jandra snapped back through her voice box.

"My mother says you should never do anything unless there's a good reason to be doing it." The girl picked up a stone and threw it across the street. It winged off a fence and a dog began to bark.

"Oh, and tossing that rock had a reason?" Jandra asked. Her mandibles clacked together in irritation despite her attempt to hold them still.

"Sure did."

Jandra's antenna flicked back and forth, a showing of her exasperation. "Like what? You like to get yelled at by irate dog owners?"

"Like to know which houses have dogs—so's I won't get bit." The girl skipped away from Jandra, her thin bare feet throwing up dust. Jandra looked down at her exoskeleton—now covered in fine grey grit. She hated water, and this dust wasn't going to simply brush off.

"The dog can't get out and bite you." Jandra was supposed to keep a hold of the girl's hand. Jandra couldn't stand to touch her, didn't like to touch any of them, humans especially, their oily skin made her squirm—so once she was out of sight of the orphanage, she let their hands go.

The girl brushed at her boney knees and smoothed her hands down the dingy grey dress she wore. "You know," she said and tilted her head to one side—toward the fence she'd pinged the stone off of. "I might need to borrow something sometime."

"For god's sake," Jandra said. Disgust colored her words and then she saw the smirk on the girl's face. The little bitch had baited her on purpose—again. Jandra glanced up the street then back down it. The afternoon heat had chased everyone indoors.

In two quick steps, she had a hold of the girl's hair. She yanked it. The girl grabbed for her hands, but didn't yell or cry out. Jandra yanked harder.

One of the girl's feet connected with Jandra's leg. Jandra pulled her hair with a hard tug, this time eliciting a satisfying yelp.

"My mother will . . ."

Jandra lifted the girl off her feet by her hair, jerking her around so she landed in the dirt. "Your mother? Your mother is a street whore. Cheapest trash in the red zone. She isn't doing anything to me—she didn't even want you."

"Not true," the girl cried. Tears glazed her eyes. Jandra had never seen this little bitch cry. The prospect excited her.

"She left you on our steps, only reason she got you was because she's too cheap a whore to afford an abortion. Too cheap to buy a permit. Illegal or she'd of been sterilized—wouldn't be contributing to the overpopulation of humans who can't control their breeding."

The girl's tears vanished. Jandra blinked. Hatred blazed in the child's eyes. The bitch sprang to her feet and rammed her head into Jandra's mid-section—into the one section on her body not protected by her hard shell. Her breath whooshed out of her. She fell back into the dirt. When they got back to the house, the little bitch would get tossed back out in the street.

Jandra's legs waved in the air, and her arms flailed until she was able to turn on her abdomen and climb to her feet still gasping. The little bitch had vanished. Panic closed around Jandra's insides. Where could she have gone? If Jandra lost her, the director would have Jandra's head in his jaws. She was already on probation.

"Jezren," Jandra screamed, using the little girl's name for the first time. "Jezren, get back here. Jezren. This isn't funny."

The dog inside the fence barked—other than that, even the breeze seemed to be holding its breath as Jandra screamed the little girl's name again and again.

Chapter One

Jezren hoisted herself up onto the fence. She kicked the boards again. No barking dog, nothing—not a single guard creature to be seen. Taking a quick inventory of the yard, she saw what she expected.

The day before when she'd been out begging door to door, she'd walked past this fence and looked between the boards. The sun had glinted off the crystal wind chimes. Given the quality of the light and the soft sounds, they would fetch quite a bit in the market—not what they were worth, but with winter coming, she needed every coin she could save. Voices on the street made her drop back down outside the fence. She moved along the boards until she stood in the shade of a large tree.

She sat on the ground with her back against the boards. A law enforcer glanced down the pathway between fenced yards. She dug in one of the woven sacks she'd filled with the days begging. Locating a couple pieces of fruit she bit into one of them, making it look like she'd stopped in the shade for a quick snack. Begging wasn't against the law—theft was. She had the microchip in her arm to prove she'd paid her fee for the season. The apple didn't have a good hard crunch to it—it would have made great applesauce, but she chewed it with enjoyment.

The lawman kept watching her. Had he seen her looking over the fence? She leaned her head back against the hot wood. If he had, he would have been staring at her butt. She knew he would have. Jezren tugged her shirtfront up, pulling the edges together over her breasts. In the last year, begging had gotten difficult—and less profitable. In the past ten years of street life, she'd managed to do pretty well. There were beggar houses that she could pay a few coins to stay in when it got cold or too hot to be out—but now they wanted to put her in with the adults. And the cost had doubled, tripled for the better places.

She guessed she was an adult—she'd never menstruated and never would. Part of street life involved voluntary sterilization if you wanted a permit. And if you didn't have one, you didn't do very well—few small sections of Earth allowed street people, those who didn't have a permit—and who the hell wanted kids if all they had was what the streets offered anyway?

The lawman still stood at the mouth of the path. His back to her. She dug in her other bags. A couple of shirts—flannel, with long sleeves. One looked almost new. A sweatshirt with a picture of an owl on it, an awful shade of bright green—she wondered if it would glow in the dark it was so bright. The inside felt smooth and silky—brand new. That would come in handy. One pair of worn shoes, but they looked to be about the right size. Several pairs of socks, old, but without holes. A blanket with one edge chewed on—but most of it was serviceable. There were a couple of huge pants and a belt to go with them. She'd sell those.

Drawing the string tie shut, she opened the other bag—her sell for sure bag. Inside, she had a plastic bowl, a plate, several bent spoons, and a glass dish wrapped in paper. She set the paper aside, being careful to tuck it under her leg; she didn't want to get nabbed for littering. Not a chip in it—clear with high edges and a triangular cut to the pattern. It weighed a lot. Laughter escaped her—an ashtray. She'd seen them in the antique stores—why would someone give away something so valuable?

Using the oversized pants, she rewrapped it—if she could get a set of those crystal chimes, she'd have enough for half the winter. The paper went back in the bag with the ashtray. The other sac held the food she'd gotten. Some canned, most of it dehydrated stuff—the best stuff to get. She'd make it last, maybe trade some, sell some if she wanted something at the market.

The lawman left without looking back at her.

In one quick motion, she hoisted herself over the fence. She dropped into the mostly silent yard. The wind blew in a soft breeze that stirred the chimes—their sound a calming shish in sharp contrast to the pounding of her heart. No matter how many times she did this, she always lived in a womb of fear until she got away clean.

Walking over the stones of the pathway to the back patio, she hummed in tune with the chimes. Get them, wrap them in the other pants, over the fence—walk away calmly. The stones were smooth under her feet, but, here and there, crisscross lines marred the surface. What in all the worlds would someone drag over the expensive stone to make that sort of a mark?

At the overhang to the patio, she stood on a chair and took one set of chimes down. She wrapped them in some of the paper from the bag. Her keep bag and the food bag sat outside the fence. All she had to do was get the other set of chimes. Odd, the patio door stood open a bit. She'd rung the front doorbell, and no one had answered—could someone have come home while she ate that apple?

A shadow crossed behind the door. Jezren's gaze darted to the scratches in the stones, then back to the shadow—no longer a shadow. The Slither glided out of the door and looked at her. Jezren swallowed hard, grabbed up her bag, and made for the fence. The Slither right behind her, its four-inch claws raking the surface of the stones when it crossed them—its hot breath on her legs.

She leapt for the fence. The Slither caught her pants and tugged. She tossed her bag over the fence and, before it could grab flesh, she let her belt loose. Hanging by one arm she almost fell back into the yard when it grabbed a greater mouthful of her pants, no doubt expecting to get a mouthful of her.

Jezren dropped down on the other side of the fence. She didn't have time to catch her breath. The Slither had figured out she wasn't in the pants. Its teeth grabbed at boards. With a crack, a loose worn board popped off—almost enough space for it to get out.

Jezren grabbed up her other bags and ran out of the alley. And smack into the law man.

Chapter Two

"The Slither," she gasped. "Thing tried to get out and eat me." Her heart hit the insides of her ribs so hard she was sure the lawman could hear it or feel it.

He kept a firm grip on her upper arm and looked over her head down the pathway. Jezren stayed very still, leaning against him, playing scared little girl. She didn't have to fake shivering. Slithers were ending up everywhere. From a planet of reptile-like people, they were a transparent pale green. They could blend in everywhere—lay on the dirt, they looked like dirt; lay on the grass, they looked like grass; lay on stones... only way you really saw them was when they moved—they were a shadow. They could stretch out thin, and yet bunch to leap at you. Their long jaws held several rows of pointed teeth that re-grew like a shark's. They were making supplementing a beggar's wage almost impossible.

"Well, now," the lawman said. He still kept a flesh-bruising grasp on her arm. "You sure you wasn't inside that fence?"

"Was sitting there eating my lunch—you saw me. I pitched the core over the fence." The idea came to her very quickly—Slithers were well trained, some said sentient—so why would it come after her? If she irritated it, it might come after her.

"Your begging going so well you can afford to be tossing food away?" He eyed her with a stern look. She knew the look. It said I know you are lying. "Maybe I should be switching jobs—I can't afford to toss food away."

Jezren tensed her arm, testing his grip. She drew in a deep breath, let it out. "You like worms and moldy food? Damn apple had a rotten core, so rotten it was moldy."

"Then you won't mind me searching your bags," he stated.

Jezren couldn't refuse. If a beggar were stopped by a lawman, they didn't need a reason to search them. Some of them even stopped beggars regularly—took anything they had of value. He'd find the ashtray—a financial loss, and he'd find the wind chimes—worse.

"Please, let me go. You didn't see me do anything." She twisted her arm a bit after she relaxed it. He didn't fall for the ploy—his fingers tightened.

His arm came up, and before she could protest or agree to the search, he touched his stunner to her. The drug shot into her system. Her will vanished.

"Follow me and bring those sacks with you." He let go of her, turned and walked down the street.

Jezren tried to refuse. She watched from some distant place inside herself as she picked up first her food bag, her keep bag and her sell bag. She shouted at herself when she walked behind him like a loyal puppy.

People moved out of their way—Jezren saw several others whom she knew. Beggars who scampered away as fast as they could without attracting attention to themselves. When the law station came into sight, Jezren swallowed the bile rising in her throat. They'd take everything from her, including her chip. She'd be on the street all winter—for the rest of her life. She wouldn't be able to get any kind of permit ever again. Well, at least this winter she wouldn't be on the street, when they found the chimes, she'd be in a work compound. Tears tried to well up in her eyes, but with the drug, she couldn't do anything he didn't tell her to do.

Her heart beat in her throat. Maybe he'd take what she had of value and leave her in the alley to sleep the drug off. She could go out begging, get one of her friends to beat her up a little—get some coins to pay for medical attention she wouldn't get, make up for the loss.

He took out a small key and put it in the lock of a wooden door. A small panel sprang open, and he touched his thumb to the glowing blue glass. The door opened into a wood floored hallway. Once inside, the door slid shut behind her, engulfing her in cool air. Solar light lit the hall all the way to the end. Along both sides of the hall, doors marched in a line. The lawman moved to the very end of the hallway and stood waiting for her to catch up. Once she stood next to him, he produced yet another key and opened another Ident panel. The door slid open with a faint hum.

Jezren tried to will her feet to stay still, tried to will her mouth to work. She wanted to scream. Beggars were killed everyday. And this lawman wasn't going to rob her. He wouldn't take her to an apartment to do that. She'd be found raped and murdered, and no one would care. Her mother wouldn't care—not in ten years of looking had Jezren found her—and no one knew anything about her either.

When the lawman stepped inside, she couldn't stop herself from following him. Tears came to her eyes—she grasped that small amount of control and tried to multiply it. Concentrated on expanding it. Worked hard at moving her fingers when he ordered her to give him her bags. While he pilled through them, dumped them on the huge leather sofa, she managed to move her hand, then one foot and the other, enough that she knew she could will herself to disobey him—maybe even fight him.

"Well, now." He turned to face her, and she went slack jawed and stone still. He held up the ashtray. "Looks to me like you were inside more than that fence."

Jezren wanted to tell him she'd gotten it begging. She had the location penned in her logbook. Most beggars didn't keep logbooks; most couldn't read or write. Jezren had taught herself. She stayed silent. Learn his game—every action had a reason.

"And these?" he asked holding up the chimes. They made a soothing sound in the almost dark room. He shook his head. "Looks to me like I have enough here to put you in a camp for maybe two seasons. Think you can do two seasons—beggar girl?"

Jezren clamped her tongue to the roof of her mouth. He hadn't commanded her to answer him—so if she were still drugged, she couldn't offer an answer. He opened a tall narrow closet door and dug in a box. He came out with some silver spoons, a gold ring, and some other jewelry she couldn't see very well the way he had it clasped.

"Maybe enough in these bags to do a full year—or longer. Maybe even get you York camp."

She almost let out a squawk. York camp was where the worst offenders went. Of the few women who went in, none came out—alive.

"I see you understand my dilemma. I turn you in, and a bunch of convicts get the spoils. I let you go, and you'll steal again—so what should I do?"

In her mind, Jezren told him he should go fuck himself. On the outside, she stood still, while her heart raced. He wanted sex. She'd guessed that already. So why didn't he rape her? His gaze rested on her chest where the curve of her breasts showed above her shirt. Prostitutes made a lot more than beggars, and there were laws that protected them—they had a right to health care as long as they were registered.

Maybe rape didn't turn him on—he wanted willing. But at what cost? Other beggars coupled on a regular basis. She didn't have any sex drive to speak of as far as she knew. Maybe being sterilized before you were an adult did that. One of her friends had told her it was because she hadn't met the right man yet—told her some women only liked it with the right man.

Well, this lawman—no matter that he was fit and muscular looking with dark hair and a chiseled face—eye candy as some would have said—she felt nothing but fear and annoyance. Tempered with anger. But no desire—apathetic at best.

How long was the drug supposed to last? Could she bargain for her food at least? Bargain to keep her chip?

"You know what I want?" he asked. "Answer me—yes or no."

"Yes," Jezren said unable to lie.

"How many men you been with?" he asked next. "Answer in number form."

"Zero," she said. She had some physical control of her body, but very little mental control.

His gaze raked up and down her body again. He set her bags in the closet and closed the door, pressing his thumb to the lock. He wasn't going to let her keep any of it.

From a drawer in a side table, he withdrew a syringe. A quick injection in her arm, and she fell on the thickly carpeted floor twitching.

"I'm willing to bargain," he said. Jezren twitched. "Let you keep your chip, let you go in the morning."

"No," Jezren managed between clacking teeth.

"To the law station, and we process you." He sounded disappointed.

"More," Jezren said. Her limbs felt on fire. She'd seen someone wake up from the zombie drug before. It felt far worse than it looked and it wasn't a pretty thing to watch.

"You think you're worth more?"

"Virgin—yes," she said this time.

He squatted next to her—touched her hair. His fingers tugged at some of her tangled curls. She thought she should have been repulsed. She felt nothing. A tool to collect money—at least her looks could earn her that, maybe earn something better than being a dirty beggar.

"Ahh, but, little beggar, I hold the keys here—I could offer you nothing. Take what I want and give you nothing in return but the camps."

Could he be playing with her? She concentrated, said, "Camps then. Pay me—willing."

He continued to touch her hair. "Your chip, your freedom, and the bag with the food."

Her legs jerked. She shook her head, almost told him yes. If he refused, she'd go to the camps and die, and if she didn't die, her life would amount to the same thing. Free she could at least change her chip in the spring—make more money as a whore, maybe escape earth.

He grinned at her and touched her breast, now exposed by the jerking and twitching of her body.

"Tell me what you want," he said. He played with her exposed nipple—his face flushed—his hand hot.

"My chip, my freedom, all three of my bags—full of my stuff," she said almost clearly. The twitching stopped, and almost all feeling returned to her body. When his hand slipped into the top of her underwear and touched her slit, she managed to make herself stay still.

"Yes," he murmured.

"And . . ."

"And?" His fingers didn't stop their probing.

"The silver spoons you showed me."

"For those, you stay all night."

Jezren thought of the money they would fetch—she could afford a clean place all winter and decent food in the beggar's zone, and if she did some winter begging, she could change her chip in the spring.

She nodded her head.

Chapter Three

Jezren leaned against the bar. Her long red hair hung in freshly washed and dried curls down her back. Her milk white skin and her green eyes reflected back at her from the bar mirror. The man next to her had gone to middle age spread. He drank his drink in gulps, and his voice shook. His hands would as well. He'd huff and puff and squirt almost as soon as he climbed on top of her. He'd stint her on any tip blaming her for his ill performance.

In the past five years, she'd had too many men like him. She'd learned quick enough to take payment in advance, and to make sure her account got credited before she even rented a room—or they had to pay her in coin.

"I want the back door," he sputtered.

Jezren gazed back at him. "No. Told you I don't do kink, even minor kink. Straight—maybe you pay extra some oral—nothing else. You don't like it, go elsewhere."

She didn't need the money today. Had a considerable savings in her guild account and in hidden, tax-free and guild dues free, coins.

He glanced around the room. He wouldn't find many who would do anything but straight, not the legal anyway. With a grunt, he pushed away from the bar and moved across the room.

"Wish I could afford to turn them away," her friend Molly said. Molly picked up the man's mostly full drink and gulped it down. She flipped a few crumbles from the crunch bowl into her mouth and chewed while watching Jezren's rejected client plead with a big boned blond woman.

"You keep doing kink, and they'll take your chip." Jezren sipped her wine.

"Stupid law. Who says we all get the same anyway? Know your tips are twenty times mine."

Molly's dun brown eyes and thin limp hair didn't make her glamorous, but she was pretty in a farmer's daughter kind of way.

Jezren stared at her wine. The red liquid looked oily in the glass. She waved smoke away from her face. Sighed. Molly lit a cig and drew on it, blew the smoke away from her friend—real cigs, ones that made you sick.

She waved more smoke away. "I want more than this, Molly."

"You could be a kept woman—maybe do a term, six months, a year."

"I want a real life."

"Doesn't get any realer than this. Neither one of has any school, we don't have a thing to offer but our body."

Jezren watched the boy clearing tables. He pocketed a few small coins left on the table. He made less than a beggar on a poor day, but even a bus person's job was closed to them. Once you became a member of any of the under guilds—forget ever getting out.

She'd been offered a term, six months by the same sort of man now walking out with the big-boned blond. Some days, it seemed everyone did kink but her. And term, that's all any of them talked about—do one guy for a term easy, easy, easy. Jezren tuned out the conversations on set up funds transfers and possible marriages for those who wanted out. Marriage was another form of prostitution except you had to clean a house, cook, and care for kids on top of the sex and you didn't get paid for it.

The thought of some overweight guy, the same portly "gentleman" doing her every night for six months or worse the rest of her life made her shudder.

"Gadds I hate sex," she said.

Molly sputtered on her drink and laughed so loud that several people in the bar stopped talking and stared at her. She kept on laughing until she snorted and gasped. Jezren let her go on and on until she couldn't stand it anymore—she whacked Molly on the back.

"Fuck, bitch, that hurt," Molly said. She rolled her shoulders and made her back pop. At least her laughing stopped.

"Well?" Jezren demanded.

"Well the fuck what?" Molly took out a coin and slapped it on the bar. The barkeeper made his way to them and poured Molly a large mug of beer. Molly lit another cig and leaned back against the bar, tugging one side of her blouse down to almost expose one nipple.

"You like it? Find fulfillment and joy in it?"

"Christ," Molly spat. "Get yourself some whiskey and go drink this mood off."

"Answer me—you like it? This your dream life?"

"Shit." Molly turned away from the door and faced the bar. She sat on a bar stool and pinched the bridge of her nose. "What else you going to do? Wait tables? Think pimple face there likes cleaning up other people's leftovers? The great Jezren, reader and writer among us—you figure you can become a teacher, a doctor, a lawyer . . . the butcher, the baker, the candlestick maker? Huh? What you think—they like their jobs? Bet they think their jobs suck—but they do them—do them 'cause that's what they know, what they can do, what they're good at."

"I could be good at other things, so could you."

"Like what? Go back to begging? Maybe one of the other under guilds—how about toilet cleaning—that sounds fun."

The door banged open, followed by the loud boom of already intoxicated voices. Two men stood in the doorway surveying the room. They were average height, but their bare arms bulged with muscle. They wore belted pants and crossover tunics. Leather and expensive fabrics with boots that glowed with off world material made them stand out. But the thing Jezren saw among the riches were the swords strapped to their backs. Down their arms tails of feathers were tattooed into their glowing skin. On their faces, they had tattoos as well.

"Money on the hoof," Molly said and slid off her barstool. After she arranged the cleavage on a display, she made her way across the room and looped her arm with one of the men. He smiled at her, winked at his friend and allowed Molly to lead him to the far side of the room.

Jezren couldn't make her feet move. Her mind whirled. She hadn't thought they were real—a fiction, a story.

"Your daddy, he's a warrior, baby girl. Some day he'll come back for us."

"What's a warrior?"

"He hunts bad people, across the twelve worlds, does service for his guild—one day he'll be a Night Bird—one of the few who earn that honor—no better guild in all the known worlds. None with more money—every night you'll have a full belly, have meat to grow on."

"Is that where he went, Momma? Daddy left us to become a bird?"

"Go to sleep now. No more stories tonight."

"Momma, I want to know. I want to know where Daddy went."

"Well, now, what have we here—a diamond among the river rock?"

Jezren startled out of her memories. She looked at the man standing next to her. He smelled of fresh soap and leather. The feather tattoos on his arm were vivid—like fresh wet paint. And he had scars, one on his face, another long thin one down his arm—but, on him, they looked in place—they belonged, a badge of honor.

"We could go somewhere, and you could see more of it?" His blue eyes sparkled, and, for the first time in her life, Jezren felt curiosity about another's body. She didn't think it was desire, but it was something.

"Are you really a Night Bird?" The words felt strange in her mouth. Night Bird Bounty hunters and warriors were like the tooth fairy, a story told to children to make them behave—they weren't real. Something her mother had made up to explain to a child why she didn't have a father.

The man laughed. He sounded happy, nothing of the mundane life creeping into his laugh—he knew his place and he liked it.

"I am a member of the Order of the Night Bird," he said. "But I am as human as you are—only true Night Birds are the Ix Chel'n."

"Must be fascinating to be off world—to meet *others.*"

"Anyone can travel off world," he answered. He waved to the barkeeper and inclined his head towards her.

"Whisky," she said. "Straight."

The barkeeper nodded and moved off without a word.

"I've met a few aliens—bugs mostly."

That made him laugh. Jezren thought she sounded worldly. She realized she sounded ignorant and foolish. Heat burned in her face—something that rarely happened.

The door to the bar opened. A chair toppled over, and the man next to her drew his sword in one smooth motion. His partner suddenly stood at his side. They vanished out the door—apparently after the two scruffy looking men who'd come in.

"Fine, fucking fine, fucking peachy, fucking great . . ."

"Molly, shut up," Jezren said. She slapped a few coins on the bar to pay for her whisky. Drank it down in several quick gulps before she hurried back to her guild room.

She pulled out the small box she kept hidden under her bed. She carefully removed the paper inside. Time had yellowed it a bit, and the wrinkles made it feel as soft as old worn cow hide. It seemed a lifetime ago that she'd gotten that ashtray wrapped in this chunk of paper.

She smoothed it carefully. It wasn't a page out of a fantasy book—a book she thought perhaps her mother had gotten the Night Bird storybook father from. Newspapers often had novel sections in them, and Jezren had always thought that's what she had—her mother's fantasy lover taken from a page a day novel.

Become a Night Bird warrior—earn honor and respect. The page went on to describe the life of a bounty hunter as something glorious and fulfilling—a way to earn not only wealth but respect as well. It advertised a warrior's school that guaranteed placement in a Night Bird Order—well not guaranteed a placement, but promised a try out.

The date at the top of the page was seven years in the past. Did such a school even exist, or still exist?

Jezren used a pen and wrote the number on her hand and put the page back in its place before she went to the public communications terminal.

Chapter Four

"How the hell did you ever talk me into this," Molly asked.

Jezren pushed a stray wisp of hair out of her face and lunged after her friend. Molly landed in the dirt of the practice arena with a whoosh of breath. Jezren leapt on top of her. She managed to avoid Molly's palm in her face and, with a quick twist, flipped Molly on her stomach and pinned her arm behind her.

"Call, end. Jezren," the instructor said. Jezren didn't want to let Molly go—she could hold her this way—and Molly couldn't do anything about it—she could hold anyone in her class—even the men.

"Jezren . . ." her instructor said—his tone a warning.

She let Molly go and helped her get to her feet.

Molly looked at her arm. "Fucking great," she said. A large bruise already discolored her forearm.

The instructor moved away from them with a look of disapproval marring his features.

"Damn," Jezren said softly. She slapped Molly on the back of the head. Molly flinched and let out a yip before she leapt on her friend. Molly's counter caught Jezren by surprise, and they both crashed into the dirt.

"Fuck'n stop telling me to clean up my mouth," Molly said and smacked Jezren's head into the dirt.

"You talk like a toilet," Jezren said between breaths. She pushed the heel of her hand against Molly's chin.

Molly twisted her neck and sunk her teeth into Jezren's arm. She called Jezren a garbled bitch and whore.

Jezren grabbed a handful of Molly's hair and yanked. Molly let go of her arm and twisted her body so that she landed on top of Jezren. She held Jezren's wrists and banged her head into Jezren's. Bright points of light exploded in Jezren's brain— before their instructor said:

"Call, end. Molly." The instructor's voice seemed filled with surprise.

Molly slowly let go of her and got to her feet. Molly stood looking at her hands as if they had acted on their own. Jezren climbed awkwardly to her feet and spat blood out of her mouth.

Molly had never in the last year done more than defend herself—
and she had only put a small amount of effort into that.

"Interesting," the instructor said before he moved away from
them.

"I need a drink," Jezren said.

Molly sat on the ground and started to laugh. "You should
have seen your face." She laughed again.

"Bitch," Jezren said.

"Whore," Molly said back. Jezren sat on the ground near her.
They looked at each other, then away and started to laugh at the
same time.

"Tell me again why we're doing this," Molly said. She held her
arm out in front of her and turned it, examining the array of
bright spots forming into one large bruise.

"I was too chicken to do it by myself." Jezren lay back in the
dirt watching the clouds race by. Winter training had been
awful—brutal cold, ice, mud, slush—and the men who were
training here. She and Molly were the only women. Molly made
good money on the side—Jezren refused. She hadn't even had
sex in the last year. Her savings were almost gone. She'd paid
both her tuition and Molly's—only way she could get Molly to do
it with her. She got room, meals and drab baggy clothes. The
food was hot, and there was always meat and once a day fresh—
no bruises or rot—fruit. The room was a spare little cell with no
window, but it had a thick rug on the floor and heat, heat that
came up right through the floor. No cold spots and before it even
got cold enough to need them, blankets had been placed in her
rooms and wool sleeping clothes with them.

Molly had kept her room in the whore's guild—and kept the
one at the school. Everyone who'd started with them had moved
on—been granted the elusive application to the Night Bird Order.

"We're not what they want," Molly said as if she could read
Jezren's thoughts.

"No dangly bits," Jezren said back. Jezren became aware of a
sore spot on her back—earlier in the day the instructor had
soundly connected with her shoulder using a wooden training
sword. Jezren had been angered, but had stayed restrained

enough to manage to whack him back—she'd even kept her gloating to herself.

She struggled to her feet. "I need a shower and some food."

Molly trudged along beside her. The year would be up in only a few days. She didn't have the tuition for the next year or even for another month—Molly might have, but she doubted it. She should have kept selling flesh till . . . She held in tears. There wasn't going to be an offer—they wouldn't be a physical application to the Night Bird Order.

The schoolmaster met them at the door to the shower rooms. His gaze briefly met Jezren's.

"Pack your things and be in my office to check out in fifteen minutes." He turned on his heal leaving Jezren to stare at his back in both anger and sadness.

**

Jezren stood with Molly and several others—men whom she thought were better than her at the sword work, men whom she couldn't imagine would be kicked out. What had they done? Molly's incessant swearing and foul mouth? The small fight they had gotten into? The fact that the next term registration was due already and she had been trying to put off the headmaster, telling him she would get it to him "soon?"

"Good thing I kept my other guild room," Molly said.

Jezren gave her a foul look. Molly squeezed her shoulder.

"It was a good try. At least we'll be safer now—able to protect ourselves."

"I don't even have money to pay whore's guild dues," Jezren said quietly.

The school headmaster walked out into the yard, wearing his formal long robes. Next to him, a tall human moved with practiced grace. The sword ridding his shoulder glinted in the afternoon sun—the purple gem stone eyes of a Night Bird Sword mocked her—laughed at her.

"Guess they need to make sure we go quietly," Molly muttered.

"This is David—good luck," the headmaster said before he walked away.

"You know not all make it to the Academy as warriors, doesn't mean you end up on the streets—there are other options. The academies—we have the same needs as other cities—law workers, cleaners, cooks and so on—we don't have any of the under trades." His gaze swept over them, and Molly moved back a step to stand behind Jezren's shoulder.

"There are Warrior Trainees, Trade's people, and Servant class. All are paid positions—as I said, no under guilds whatsoever." Again, his gaze landed on Jezren.

Jezren crossed her arms over her chest. He was kicking them out—and the others standing with them—were they also at one time members of an under guild? "So the Night Bird warriors do lie."

Molly kicked her. Others in the crowd gasped. David studied her—with amusement?

"Lie?" he asked.

"I didn't hide what I was when I came here. My friend didn't either. But yet they collected our fees and dues, took my money the same as everyone else's, knowing that we would be turned away in the end because of what we came from."

"And, if I said that you were offered a chance but simply couldn't make the cut—would you fight that decision?"

"Enough, Jezren, let's get out of here," Molly whispered to her. She clasped Jezren's elbow.

Jezren jerked her arm away and took a step closer to David. "Yes."

"You don't think you've gained anything in coming here?"

"Yeah a lot of damn bruises," she spat back.

David drew his sword, and everyone stepped back several paces . . . everyone except Jezren. She raised her chin and glared at him.

"Out of the thirty of you standing here, how many of you think you can make it on the Academy Home World?"

Jezren didn't take her eyes off him and when he held his sword out to her hilt first, she clasped her arms to her sides.

"Afraid of my sword?" he asked her.

Jezren snorted and hugged herself tighter.

He offered his sword to Molly next. Jezren squeezed her eyes shut and whirled around to face her friend. Molly stood frozen to the spot. Jezren let out a long breath. He went to each of the thirty—offering his sword. Most reached for the sword only to have him snatch it back before they could grasp it.

Molly picked up her packs and slung them over her shoulder. "Come on, whore, I've been abused enough today—I'll pay your dues for the next year—you owe me."

David walked back through the crowd and touched the shoulder of one of the men who hadn't tried to touch the sword, he touched the shoulder of another, touched Molly and lastly he reached for Jezren—she flicked his hand away.

"Please exit out the side left gate," he said.

"Like good puppies," Molly said.

Others in the group not singled out whooped and whistled. Jezren knew she couldn't fight the choice this arrogant warrior had made—she was nobody, a beggar and a whore. She followed Molly out the indicated gate.

Much to her surprise, it opened onto a vast field, and, in the center of that field, a small spaceship sat. She'd never seen one on the ground before. It must have been the way David had gotten to earth—she thought of that, enough wealth to travel in space in his own ship.

"Tell me something," David said behind them.

"Are you savoring this?" She turned to glare at him.

"Very," he said.

"Figures," Molly said.

"Why didn't you try to touch my sword?"

Jezren looked at the others. She shrugged. "The mark on your hand, means you have a soul bond to your sword. I might not be happy at the moment, I may never be happy, but that doesn't mean I want to fry."

His gaze fell on Molly. "And you?"

Molly looked at Jezren before she answered. "Jezren didn't."

"Fair enough," David said.

The two men answered the same as Jezren.

David turned toward his ship. "Quarters on the ship are cramped, but it's a hyper-ship. Five days, and we'll be on Ix Chel'n II."

Jezren was the last to pick up her packs and follow David onto his ship wondering if she could possibly have been accepted into the Night Bird Academy or if she would spend the rest of her life as a paid toilet cleaner.

Chapter Five

"Jezren," Molly whispered in the dark. Molly would be leaning over the edge of the bunk in the room they shared with four other women—they were the only females out of over five hundred students. Molly and Jezren were the only human women.

"What?" Jezren hissed back. One of the others in the room stirred. The woman had huge ears. She would hear every whispered word Molly said.

"Are you scared about tomorrow?"

Jezren sighed and tugged her blankets up. Nights on Ix Chel'n II were cool and rainy, days warm and breezy all year round.

"What good, human, does it do to be frightened of something you can do nothing about?" The voice came from the woman with the big ears.

"I wasn't talking to you," Molly growled.

"Good thing or I'd eat your tongue for your assumption of my fear."

"Molly, go to sleep—you'll do fine." Jezren turned over on her bunk. Tomorrow marked the end of their third year in Warrior's training. It marked the test—the real test. If you passed tomorrows judgment, you became a first level Night Bird.

If you failed, you left Ix Chel'n to train on other worlds with non-Ix Chel'n Masters. Jezren had only seen them at a distance. The founders of the Night Bird Order—not so very tall, but powerful looking, with wings that, if unfurled, would have filled a sport's court. The Ix Chel'n masters watched them from the edges everyday.

"What if we don't pass?" Molly whispered to her, this time Jezren could see the shadowed outline of Molly leaning over the top bunk.

"Are you stupid as well as ugly? You leave this world and become a law enforcer, or perhaps a ship's guard." The big eared woman gave three sharp barks—laughter and added, "Or maybe you can go back to earth and demand a higher whore's price for the scars you've earned here."

"Kie-im-ik, please. She only meant to speak with me," Jezren propped herself on her elbow and gazed in the direction of the alien woman. "We humans do that when faced with a test or an unknown."

Kie-im-ik made a gagging sound then hissed, "She insults you—and you let her."

"It is how we are," Jezren said.

"Fold your fucking ears up—I wasn't talking to you."

Would this be the night one of the others would lose control and beat Molly? Kie didn't climb out of her bunk—she wouldn't risk getting barred from the Master's Judgment.

"Molly, right now I can't think past tomorrow. Go to sleep. We don't have to fight, just sit there while they read our names."

"What if they send us to separate places?"

Jezren sat up almost knocking her head into Molly's. She got to her feet.

"Where are you going?"

"Out."

"You can't . . ."

"I can't stay here right now."

"They catch you out, and you'll not even get a lesser Order," Kie said.

"I'm not going past the boundary." Jezren moved across the room and slid the patio door open. Cool fragrant air greeted her. Misty rain covered her quickly, making her hair curl and raising goose flesh on her arms—arms hardened and defined by time with a sword. Down a narrow stone path and around a bend, she came to some empty warrior's rooms. Outside one of the back ones, she'd discovered a small garden. A bench sat on one side of it, and flowers hung in Mother Nature's version of leis. She took a deep breath. The air smelled of indulgent fragrance, and in moments, her tensions melted away.

In the daylight, the cliff dropped away to a dizzying depth. In the dark, it seemed she could have walked over the edge and stood on the air. She moved her body in some of the relaxation forms, staying clear of the edge until the last of the tension in her muscles drained away. Sitting on the bench, she heard movement on the path—brush being pushed aside.

286

She sat very still—she was within the boundary—well almost. Any of the human instructors would understand her need to be out here. She could claim a spiritual need.

One of the Ix Chel'n emerged from the path. She couldn't dash away from him. Her trip out here now seemed a foolish risk. He partly spread his wings and shook them. He folded them neatly against his back and ran his hand over his bald head. The light of three moons let her see his talons and the small horns growing out of his head.

"Humans don't see well in the dark. The edge marks the start of a long drop."

His voice sang over Jezren's nerves. Smooth like fine whiskey but with the promise of sensual and slow arousal.

He looked at her over his shoulder. The moonlight playing in his purple eyes. Making his gray-green skin glisten. The muscles of his chest were well formed, and his shoulders looked impossibly wide. Here and there, the silvery light played off his elaborate Night Bird tattoo.

"I needed to clear my head. My roommates like to word spar and . . ." Jezren stopped speaking when he turned to face her directly.

He tilted his head toward her at the same time one of his wing tips dipped. In the moonlight, his features suggested he thought her excuse amusing.

"You came to this place seeking answers—which future path to take?"

" I guess so."

Jezren felt foolish. Words came so easy to her, yet this master held her in thrall. He was elegant, strong, mesmerizing, and she wanted to listen to him speak all night long. With a jolt, Jezren realized what she felt, sitting in this fairy tale garden with this man who could have been a demon if he'd been on Earth, had a name.

"You're fascinated with my appearance?" he asked—this time the sparkle in his eyes and the head tilt definitely said he found her amusing.

She felt heat burn up her cheeks. She had looked him up and down—what was she going to say—I think I've discovered what lust is? "I haven't had a partner of any race in over three years"

He laughed this time—a deep throaty laugh that settled in his chest and made her nerves dance with as much lust as his voice.

"And you think I would be a suitable partner?"

Was he flirting with her? She was outside the boundary and alone with a male whom, by his appearance, could have raped her and tossed her into the abyss. She drew in a breath, smiled at him. Fear had no part in it—she wasn't afraid. She wanted to touch him.

"I have no idea—would you be?" Once the words were out of her mouth, she wanted to draw them back in. When the breeze came up again, the scent of cinnamon filled the clearing.

"Do not tempt me, Lady Jezren. Humans do not have a monopoly on lust—and attraction."

"You followed me out here."

"I have gotten to know your reactions to things very well. Knew you would seek silence this night. But this place, no, I did not expect to find you here."

"I should go back," Jezren said.

In two easy steps, he barred her path. He clasped her hand and brought it to his face. Jezren felt a twinge of fear. It melted away. The cinnamon scent came from him—stronger now, swirled with the floral scent it spoke of another kind of indulgence. She let her fingers touch him. His flesh felt baby soft. Yet under it, a current of energy made her squeeze her thighs together. Why did he stir her in such a way?

He clasped her face in his hands. His fingers explored the contours of her face. Jezren reached for his shoulders and touched his upper wing bones. He jerked back from her shaking his head.

"I'm sorry," she stammered. "I didn't mean to . . . hurt you?"

He drew in ragged breaths and stepped back further. "Not hurt. You should go. Now."

This time, his tone frightened her— urgent lust in his voice. She hesitated only a moment before she raced down the path. When she heard voices, she stepped into the brush.

"Din'arik? What happened? Was the seer right? Did she come?"

"Brother," Din'arik said, "she came."

"No," the newcomer said. "Why would she refuse if the spirits called her to this place?"

"I didn't ask her."

"What?"

"Lin'arik, the one the seer spoke of—she's human."

The newcomer drew in an audible breath. "How? Perhaps she hasn't come yet, perhaps the seer was wrong."

"I felt it. She felt it. Humans, they don't understand what they feel most of the time and this woman . . . I do not think she knows what love is much less past spirits finding each other again—and across worlds."

Confused and sure her translator had garbled what she heard, Jezren bolted to her room.

Chapter Six

"He's coming isn't he?" Molly asked.

Jezren stood in the small clearing near the edge of the cliff. She stared into the dizzying dark. "Molly, go back inside."

"For Christ's sake," Molly said. "You have a death wish?"

"He's not going to hurt me any more than that guy you slept with last night."

"Human—not, not some creature."

'Din'arik isn't a creature." Jezren stayed calm. Never waste energy on words or anger that is best used to defend yourself. She didn't need to defend herself—physically anyway.

"The entire school is talking about it." Molly moved to stand next to her. "Fuck, he could be the devil incarnate. You can't even cut their hide, imagine what his dick is like—spines or worse—he might want your blood."

Jezren let out a small laugh. "That Miltorik, he had spines— you didn't object to him. The stitches weren't fun."

"He looked human—thought he was until you told me. Wasn't some gargoyle crossed with Lucifer."

"Four years—you ever going to get over your xenophobia?"

"I can work with them, train with them, doesn't mean I have to lust after them."

She moved back into the garden area. Small lanterns now lit the underbrush. The lei like flowers were in full bloom, the apartment hers now. She'd moved ahead of Molly. They were both Night Bird Warriors in training, but Jezren had passed the final test. She would leave on her first Order-given assignment in only a week. She would have a hunt partner—it wouldn't be Molly.

Or Din'arik. Din'arik was an instructor. He'd have to give up that status to become a hunter again. She sat on the bench.

"He'll use you," Molly said.

"So he uses me."

"They could toss you out for it."

"They can't toss me out anymore—remember? I'm no longer a student."

"You act like you want to still be here getting the shit beat out of you. The real fight, think I heard that enough times." Molly sat next to her.

"That was before."

"Jezren Dark Sky, I don't like sex and love is a myth—dick blind."

"Bite me," Jezren said.

Molly started to speak—stopped. "What if they kick him out—the entire Order will be after you. Blame you."

"He won't sacrifice his career over me." Jezren drew in a deep breath of scented air. Din'arik stood close by. She could detect the cinnamon scent of him. "I leave in less than a week—let me be on this. Can we agree to disagree?"

Molly glanced back at the trail. "If you weren't the only family I had, I'd turn your dumb ass in." She got to her feet and stopped at the mouth of the trail. "Think hard on this Jezren. We've clawed and chewed to get this far—don't throw it out on some stupid tryst with a *thing*." She vanished into the night.

Din'arik melted out of the greenery.

"Ignore her," Jezren said.

"They do speak of us often." His voice always sang over her skin, made goose flesh raise and warmth spread through her.

"Does it bother you?" She kept her back to him. He moved past her.

"Some. There is much to consider. I can't take an alien woman as my wife—our ceremonies won't permit such a thing. And my family . . ."

Jezren laughed—the sound hollow and sad. She'd found love, found lust, and it would have to be forbidden. Seemed a fitting form of irony—Jezren always knew what she wanted, but obstacles always stood in her way. There wasn't any trick, any twist, any turn around this one.

"And there is Molly. She is not my blood, but we are sisters of a sort . . . friends."

"There are ways around this," he said. "There is a way for you to become a citizen of my world."

Jezren got to her feet and rubbed her arms. "Some of the other humans have told me about it."

291

"Will you listen to your friends?" Din'arik asked her. "They have no idea what they are talking about—no sacrifice or blood dances involved."

"Your career means more than a fling with a human woman—doesn't it?"

"My career means nothing without the true meaning of life—love and a mate for eternity."

She laughed. "Molly is right on that score."

"Molly isn't right about much of anything," Din'arik told her. "Least of all about me."

"She told me last night that you should have been a pick-up artist—you know all the right words."

"Apparently not. My words have no meaning on you."

"I hear them, Din'arik, I hear them. But I have heard so many words from so many men." How she wanted him, wanted the love she felt returned. "How will you feel when they kick you out of the Academy, maybe the Order—I won't seem so attractive."

"I'll resign," he said.

"You can't do that."

"I already have."

Jezren laughed. "There you go again. You wouldn't resign over a night of sex, that may or may not work, any more than I believe you could fly off this cliff."

"My life is nothing without you, Jez," he said. He leapt off the cliff. Diving straight down, it looked as if he would collide with the ground. She screamed. Fell to her knees at the cliff's edge.

"Din'arik," she screamed. How could he have taken his life? He . . .

Wind washed across her, and she heard his wings before his form blotted out the moonlight. Hovering in the air, he held his hand out to her.

"Come, Jez, let me show you all that is forbidden in sight of other races. Take this flight and become one of us."

Jezren climbed to her feet. In the air, his form was incredible—his wings beat slowly, yet he hung in the air. An angel or a demon.

"Have you forgotten—I don't have wings."

"I can support both of us."

292

"And if we crash to the ground?"

He laughed. His wings pulsed. He swooped toward her, grabbing her arm and dragging her off the cliff. They dipped toward the ground before he flew straight up. She clung to him, burying her face in his chest, feeling his muscles work.

"I have resigned, Jez. I will be your hunt partner—if you will have me, if you take this flight willingly."

"Fucking damn, don't drop me."

Din'arik laughed. "You are Ix Chel'n now. And if you think the talk was bad before—it will be worse now, but now they can do nothing about us."

Us. Us. The words rang in her soul. "And us means?"

"We have each other this night."

"I won't need stitches will I?"

Din'arik laughed. "Not this night or any other night."

Jezren laughed again. Let them talk and Molly be damned. Jezren Dark Sky had found the true meaning of life.

Biography

For more than seven years, S.R. Howen has been an editor at Wild Child Publishing. She also runs workshops on how to craft a winning synopsis and query letter. This past year, S.R. Howen has been editing (and writing) for the newly created Freya's Bower.com. Her most recent work, THE FORGE, an erotic e-novella written under the pen name Shaunna Wolf, was released in July 2006.

A former military brat, then military spouse, and a traditional naturalist, S.R. Howen currently lives in Texas, with eleven cats (three of them the non-domestic sort) three rabbits, and four fish, one husband and her daughter. She is working on a sequel to THE FORGE and on several more traditional fantasy novels. For more info on her and her works please visit her agent's web site: www.zackcompany.com <http://www.zackcompany.com/>

Secret Valentines

By

Kit Wylde

Rating: Sweet

Genre: Contemporary

Val pulled the memo out of his coat pocket and stared at it for the fourth, or more, time. He still couldn't believe the company would make them do this. When did they expect their employees to have the time? He sighed. What did it matter? Either they did it or found themselves on the company's short list, which seemed to grow longer every day.

"Will that be all?" A bored voice from the other side of the counter interrupted his thoughts.

Val looked up at the convenient store clerk and nodded.

"It's 85 cents." The slightly nasal voice irritated him further.

Eighty-five cents for a candy bar. One lousy candy bar. But what was worse than the money was the time it took away from his work, and personal life, to do this. He hoped she liked chocolate.

Snowflakes caressed his hair and face as soon as he stepped out of the store. Slate gray clouds covered the sky from horizon to horizon, not a whisper of blue to be seen anywhere. Everything seemed muffled, distant and surreal. It suited his dark mood. Of all the holidays, he disliked Valentine's Day the most. Christmas was over commercialized, but bearable. Halloween had been his favorite as a kid, but that had become as commercialized as Christmas. Easter didn't mean much in their house, for all his mother spouted Biblical phrases. But Valentine's Day had meant relentless teasing for a good two weeks proceeding the actual day because his mother named him Valentine. And being a boy named Valentine compared to being a boy named Sue. He'd heard every bad pun anyone could possibly come up with since the day he'd started kindergarten. Scratch that. Since the day he started to walk. Maybe before, but he couldn't remember that far back.

Now he had to be someone's secret valentine for an entire week. They expected him to find out about this – he withdrew the memo from his pocket again – Cliodhna O'Cleirigh, a name he couldn't even pronounce, and give her little gifts and notes. This stupid charade was supposed to promote a "community within the company" so everyone "becomes better acquainted with co-workers outside their department." Heck, he didn't even want to be that familiar with those in his department let alone some unknown clerk with an unpronounceable name.

He drew his scarf closer about his neck and watched his feet disturb the peaceful snow. Nothing bothered it. Many people hated snow, but as many people loved it. No matter how any one felt about it, the snow didn't care. It floated down from the sky or sometimes whipped around wherever the wind propelled it. Wherever it landed was where it landed. It didn't matter. What would it be like not to care?

Shrugging, he entered his office building and, avoiding the overcrowded elevator and masses of curious people, climbed the stairs to his office. His feet were inches from entering his office when a voice stopped him.

"Hey, Valentine, who'd you get?" Richard asked.

"It's supposed to be a secret, Dick. Uh, oh, sorry, you like to be called Richard, don't you?"

Richard laughed, reminding Val of a braying ass. "Well, I got Vivien. I have no problems being her secret valentine." He leered. "I know exactly what I'll give her. And it won't cost a dime."

"Yes, well, that's nice." Val laid some files on his desk and sat down, hoping Richard would take the hint and leave. Poor Vivien. Beautiful and smart, she got stuck with the dick of the office. Since Richard's mind never rose above his belt buckle, Val didn't imagine it would be too hard for Vivien to cut him into little pieces. Val wanted to be there when it happened at the annual office Valentine's Day party because it would happen. He smiled.

Absentmindedly, he pulled the crumpled memo out of his pocket and set it on top of the files along with the candy bar.

Richard snatched up the memo and read it. He crowed. "Oh-ho! You got Cliodhna O'Cleirigh. Isn't this rich! The most unsociable person in the company is the secret valentine of the most mysterious one. This should be interesting. I can't wait to see what you do for her. Since no one knows much about her, this could be very interesting. Do you know no one has ever even seen her eat? Oh, she leaves for lunch, but no one knows where she goes. I asked her out once, but she just looked at me with those gray eyes of hers and politely said, 'No, thank you.'"

The same thing I would say if I was a woman. Richard chased anything in skirts. Any woman who said 'yes' to him needed a lobotomy.

Richard must have seen Val's expression because he tried to defend himself, "Hey, she was lucky I asked her. As mousy as she is, I can't imagine she gets many takers." He leaned in closer and whispered loudly, "Anyway, don't worry. I won't tell anyone." Having accomplished his mission, he sauntered out of the office.

How had Richard pronounced her name? Cleo— whatever. He didn't have to pronounce it because he would drop the candy bar off with a note. Maybe at the party others would say her name and he'd be saved. One could always hope.

Writing a hasty note, he checked the memo once more for her department, stuck the candy bar in his pocket and made his way to the archives.

An elderly woman with iron gray hair sat at the first desk next to the door. A plate with her name, Eloise Goodman, sat on her desk. She looked up at him over horn-rimmed glasses. He must have seemed hesitant because she smiled kindly.

"Can I help you?"

"Yes, I'm Val Bryan from the accounting department. One of my co-workers asked me to come by and drop off something for a..." He hesitated. How did one pronounce this name?

"You must be looking for Cliodhna." Humor twinkled in her eyes.

"Clee-ona?"

"Yes. Her desk is in the third cubicle on the right. Oh, and she just stepped away from her desk. Your secret is safe."

"I'm not..." He started to protest, but from the look on her face, he knew any protestations were pointless. "Thank you."

Looking around furtively, he set the chocolate down on her desk. He scanned the desk, searching for anything that would tell him about her, but it was bereft of any personal paraphernalia. No clues. *Damn!* How would he find out what she liked and disliked if she didn't leave hints in the regular places?

He turned to leave and bumped into a slender, sylph-like woman with large gray eyes. Hair the color of moonbeams draped over and below her shoulders. For a moment, Val could only stare, speechless. "Excuse me."

"What are you doing at my desk?" Her voice was soft and lilting.

"I came to..." He cleared his throat. "Your secret valentine asked me to drop off your first gift."

Her nose crinkled in distaste. "Oh."

"You don't approve of the secret valentine?"

She shook her head. "No."

Her hair shimmered under the light. Val lost his train of thought at the sight of her hair brushing her pale skin. Skin that looked incredibly soft.

There was a gasp, bringing Val back to his senses.

Cliodhna moved quickly away from her desk as if being pursued by a swarm of bees.

Bewildered, Val hurried after her.

"Get it off my desk!" The soft voice became the piercing cry of a threatened bird.

"What? What's wrong?" He tried to touch her, but she flinched and started scratching her arms.

"That chocolate bar." Loathing filled her voice. "I'm allergic to chocolate. Just the smell of it gives me hives." She pushed back one of her sleeves to show him the small red bumps already beginning to form.

Val grimaced. "I'm so sorry. I... he... she didn't know."

"Obviously." Eloise stood behind her, an accusing expression on her face. "Here, Cliodhna, I've called the hospital." She put a comforting arm around her before turning to look at Val. "Remove the chocolate so she can get her purse."

"The hospital?" Had he heard them correctly?

"Yes, the hospital," Cliodhna said. "If I am going to get rid of this quickly, I'll have to get to hospital right away for some treatment."

"Oh, right." He moved backed to the desk and pocketed the candy, feeling stupid and in the way. "I'll tell your secret valentine not to get you any more chocolate."

"You can tell them not to get me anything." Cliodhna grabbed her purse. Eloise bustled her off before he could respond.

Val looked around the quiet room relieved that no one else saw his humiliation. The experience didn't sit well with him, and he decided that the next gift he gave her — and yes, there would be one - would make her smile.

He waited to see if anyone would arrive who could answer some questions, but no one did. After a few minutes, he gave up and wandered back to his office, his mind firmly focused on their encounter, looking for some thing that would tell him more about her. What color was she wearing? Was she in pants? Skirt? Sweater? He shook his head, embarrassed. And here he prided himself on his observation skills, even boasted that his surpassed those of most women, but he couldn't recall one thing beyond her beautiful eyes, silver hair, delicate rose petal skin, and that magical flute-like voice. On top of that, he didn't remember how to pronounce her name.

Damn!

When he returned to his office, he found a small, bulky package on his desk. Excitement coursed through him. While part of him balked at the thought of secret valentines, he admitted that receiving a surprise gift certainly added spice to the day. He reached for the package then paused. Did he really want to know? Gingerly, he fingered the clasp. What if the gift was as thoughtless as his? What if he didn't like it? But what if he did?

Decision made, he ripped the envelope open. Crumpled newspaper, five scratcher tickets, and a note tumbled onto his desk. He grimaced. Val didn't care to gamble, and scratchers were gambling. It wasted money. Money better spent on something else. Unfolding the note, he read the bold letters scrawled across the page said: If you're good, maybe you'll get lucky.

Great. Another come on. Which of the women, besides Cliodhna and a few older, married women, hadn't already hit on him? Who said it was a woman? A little voice whispered. Val shuddered, not wanting to entertain such a thought. People could do whatever they wanted as long as the other person was so inclined. He was not. He preferred his dates to have curves and no Adam's Apple.

Setting the scratchers and note aside, Val sat and pulled up an Internet page, intent on finding more information about Cliodhna, or at the very least, the origin of her name. He found a search engine and typed in her name. A few sites on Irish names and legends popped up. Curious, he clicked on one of the Irish name links. A long list of Irish names for women, their pronunciations and meanings filled the screen. He scrolled the page until he found her name. CLEE-ona, that was how her first name was pronounced. At least people could say his name. He wondered how many times she'd suffered the thrashing of her name. And did she go by Cleo?

Cleo. Now that was a short, sweet name. No one could tease you about a name like Cleo.

He skipped to another page, wondering what legends were connected to her name and discovered they had something else in common. The poor girl had been named after a legend, too. At least this legend was unknown in the States. Still, he knew what it was like to be named after a legend. No wonder she kept to herself.

So, she was Irish. More appropriately, her name originated in the Gaelic/Celtic culture. Maybe he could give her something that related to this. Not something corny like the Irish Blessing that everyone would think to give, no something a little more special and unique, like her.

He clicked on another link, and a smile broke through the frown. It was perfect.

Early the next morning, he went directly to the archives department to leave Cliodhna's second gift. Most of his co-workers would have arrived by now, but this room was empty, like yesterday. He wondered if anyone in this department ever worked. It suited his purposes, though, this empty space. As much as he would like to see her again, he couldn't chance it. After one more look around, he walked over to her desk and set the small shamrock on it. He leaned a note against the emerald green flowerpot and stepped back to survey his handwork. With a satisfied nod, he turned and collided with a warm body. His heart leapt when his eyes locked with large, gray ones.

"I thought I told you to tell my secret valentine not to get me any more gifts." A smile belied the harshness of the words.

For the first time, Val saw a hint of warmth in those wary, gray eyes. "I did, but I... they didn't listen. They were appalled when they heard about your allergic reaction. I... uh, they wanted to make it up to you."

Cliodhna fingered the note before picking it up. Her gaze scanned the short simple message. The smile that had teased the corners of her mouth bloomed in full, transforming a solemn visage into one of ethereal beauty. Silver sparks shimmered in her eyes when she looked up at him.

Val stared, enchanted. She placed one slender hand upon his arm and leaned toward him. Her touch sent an electric current shooting through him, and all thoughts spun away. Whatever words fell from her lips floated into the ether, disappearing before his overheated brain could decipher them.

Taking a deep breath, he focused his mind. Embarrassment overcame him, and heat crept under his collar. "I'm sorry. I'm afraid I didn't catch what you said."

She laughed. The sound tinkled through the room like a chorus of tiny bells. "I asked you to thank my secret valentine for me. It was very sweet of them to do this." She caressed the leaves, her face alight with joy. "It reminds me of home. Even the leaves have the striated white and green stripes like the shamrocks of home. It was very thoughtful of them."

"So, you are from Ireland?" he asked.

"Yes, I am from Munster, in Cork County." Sadness crept over her features.

"You miss it?"

"Very much."

"Perhaps it will produce a four leaf clover," he said, hoping to coax another smile from her.

It worked, albeit a rueful one. "Ah, now that is very rare. But if it did, perhaps it would bring me the luck, faith, love and hope rumored to go along with one."

"Well, how could it fail such a fair one as you?"

Her laughter rang out. "Oh, I see you've been kissing the Blarney Stone."

"Alas," he replied, "I've never been to Ireland, but part of my family tree could have kissed it."

Interest sparkled in her eyes. "Your family comes from Ireland?"

"A few generations back, but, yes, they do."

"Ah, now I know why I like you, Val." She graced him with another smile before turning her attention back to the shamrock. She stuck her finger in the soil and shook her head, tsking. "It's dry as a bone. I'll have to water it." Picking it up, she started walking off through the row of cubicles.

Val trailed behind her, loathe to let her leave his sight.

She stopped and looked at him, laughter lighting her features. "I don't think you can come with me." When he didn't respond, she said, "I'm going to the women's loo." She flashed him another smile and opened a door in front of her that he hadn't noticed until that moment.

He shifted from one foot to the other, embarrassment coursing through him once more. "Oh, yes, well, I'll be going back to my office then."

"Will you be delivering my next gift?"

The smile she turned on him left him speechless. He nodded.

"Good. I'll look forward to our visit tomorrow," she said, disappearing into the bathroom.

Disappointment and elation rushed through him on his way back to his office. It wasn't until Val reached his desk that his brain registered she'd called him by his name. He'd never told her his name. The woman she worked with, the one who'd alternately been nice then cold to him yesterday, must have told her. What was her name? He shook his head. Once again, he couldn't remember something he normally would have. But it didn't matter. Tomorrow, he would see Cliodhna. Although he'd only seen her twice so far, he found that those two times didn't fulfill the need coursing through him.

Now, how would he surprise her tomorrow? Cracking his knuckles, he sat down at his desk and pulled up an Internet window.

Secret Valentines

* * *

The next two days passed in a blur. Val knew that much of his work still sat upon his desk undone, but the desire to find new ways to make Cliodhna smile and laugh consumed him. The gifts his secret valentine gave to him became more crass as Valentine's Day grew closer. Thursday, the day before Valentine's Day, a red bag sat on his desk. He didn't want to look inside, but curiosity got the better of him. Cinnamon massage oil wrapped in cellophane accompanied a note that said: To add spice to tomorrow night.

Val grimaced. *Yeah, in your dreams.* Uncovering his secret valentine held no appeal. However, using the massage oil on Cliodhna did... if she'd let him. Somehow, he didn't think it would happen too soon.

By the time the Valentine's Day party arrived, he struggled to contain the anticipation pulsing through him. In his right hand, he clutched the final gift; the one he hoped would convince her to go out with him at least once.

Red and white ribbons and balloons festooned the walls and hung from the ceiling. Someone had stuck a cupid to the back of the door. Val barely had time to register everything before Richard sidled up to him.

"So, I heard you've been making progress with Cliodhna. You hoping to get some?"

"Richard..." Val never finished the sentence. In the doorway stood Cliodhna. Over one arm draped her heavy winter coat; a black, practical purse clutched in the same hand. In the other was a brown paper bag. The silvery blue glitter sweater enhanced her otherworldly look. He almost believed she could be the fairy queen from the legend. For a moment, he thought he saw shimmering light around her, but Richard's low wolf whistle drew his attention.

"Man, I never knew she could look so..." Richard leered, "luscious. I might have to try a little harder."

Val ignored him and crossed the room to greet her. "You look beautiful. Like your namesake."

Cliodhna smiled mysteriously, a pale pink blush coloring her high cheekbones. "Thank you." She looked around him as if searching for someone. She gripped a small paper bag in her left hand.

"Who are you looking for? Maybe I can help."

"Richard Simpson."

Disgust filled Val. That the company would pair someone as delicate and sweet as Cliodhna with Richard made him angry. "Well, I can help you with that. If you want, I can introduce you to him."

"Oh, no, I know who he is. He asked me out once, but I was really hoping to avoid him. He's the main reason why I didn't want to participate in this whole secret valentine thing. When I found out I had his name..." She paused.

"No need to say more. I understand. My first introduction to you was from Richard." Val bit his tongue. Damn! That sentence just gave him away. He tensed.

She chuckled. "Don't worry. I know you're my secret valentine."

"How?" Chagrin filled him. He thought he'd been so circumspect pretending to be the deliverer.

Her laughter rippled through the room, drawing the eyes of everyone else. One of the many things he discovered about Cliodhna was that she rarely laughed. Something he hoped to remedy. She appeared unaware of the effect her laughter had on the others.

"Oh, I've known it was you all along. Eloise told me after that chocolate fiasco," she confessed.

He looked away, ashamed of that first gift. "I didn't know."

She touched his arm. "It's okay. The second day when you gave me the shamrock, I forgave you. Each gift has made me ashamed of mine to him, but I couldn't bring myself to give him anything remotely personal for fear of encouraging him. From the way he is looking at me now..." She shuddered.

"Here." Val handed her the final gift. Hope battled with fear in his chest.

Cliodhna took the gift, smiling up at him. Reaching into the bag, she withdrew a beautiful illustration of a fairy. Beneath the drawing was the name: Cliodhna, the Faerie Queen of Munster. She gasped, delight erasing any lingering distaste on her face. "She's lovely."

He grinned, relieved. "You resemble her. Your silvery hair and gray eyes, like the mists of Ireland that come in off the sea, I imagine. You are certainly as beautiful."

"Oh, no, never as beautiful." She leaned forward and kissed his cheek. "Thank you. I shall cherish her."

Val beamed. If only they were alone.

"Oh, here is your last gift."

He looked inside the bag. Red silk boxers with little white hearts were inside. Heat prickled along his hair follicles. "Uh..."

"Don't worry. They're from Eloise. She got mad at you for that chocolate bar and decided to tease you. She couldn't make it tonight and asked me to give it to you." She winked at him. "Would you hold this for me? I want to get mine over with." She handed the gift back to him.

Cliodhna moved off toward where Richard stood getting dressed down by Vivien. Anger radiated off of Vivien. Val could almost see the sparks flying as Richard obviously got singed. He didn't need to hear what she said to know Richard wouldn't go near her again.

Val followed her, curious to see how she handled Richard. Would she flail him with her words like Vivien or freeze him out? Ice seemed more her forte, but one never knew.

Richard's face brightened when he saw Cliodhna approaching. "I see you've changed your mind."

Val didn't see the expression on Cliodhna's face, but he saw her stiffen.

"No. I just came over to give you your final gift and let you know that I was your secret valentine." She held out the brown paper bag. "Here."

Richard opened it eagerly. "Oh." He pulled out five scratchers. "Well, maybe I'll get lucky this time." He leered at her.

Val wanted to plant a fist in his face. The jackass.

"You'll have to play them to find out." Ice dripped off the words, but Richard didn't take the hint.

"You want to play them with me? We could go to this nice little motel I know of and rent a room tonight." Richard reached out to touch her.

Cliodhna retreated, bumping into Val. Their gazes met. He squeezed her hand. She smiled then looked back at Richard. "I'm sorry, but I'm already spoken for tonight."

A zing of happiness spun through Val, but he didn't say anything. Instead, he placed his hand on her shoulder.

"Oh, I see." Richard shrugged. "So I was right, you are getting lucky tonight." His laugh was ugly. "No big deal. I'm sure Donna will fit the bill," he said before slithering away to a woman over in the corner wearing a bright red, skin-tight outfit with hair straight out of the 80s.

Val turned to Cliodhna, hope dancing wildly within him. "Are you really?"

She smiled up at him. "Am I really what?"

"Spoken for tonight?" he asked.

"Yes, I am."

Still not sure she really meant him, he persisted. "With whom?"

Her silver eyes shimmered. "My secret valentine."

Joy percolated in his veins. "Really?"

"If he doesn't mind having his saintly legend mixed with that of a fairy queen?"

For the first time, Val saw doubt dim those beautiful eyes. "Only if she'll be my Valentine."

She nodded and placed her hand in his, and they walked toward the door. As they reached the building entrance and stepped out, snowflakes floated from the pewter sky overhead. Val smiled. Maybe caring wasn't such a bad thing. And maybe, just maybe, being named Valentine wasn't so bad either.

Biography

Kit Wylde fell in love with romance during her teenage years. She didn't pen her first story until well into her thirties. She sold her first story and has been writing ever since. Recently married, she finds that writing romance helps keep hers fresh.

Her works have appeared in *Wild Child Publishing*, *Love Notes Zine*, *Under A Full Moon*, and *Coffee Time Romance*. Currently, she has one novella available through Freya's Bower, LAST CHANCE, a paranormal erotic romance. She has another due out in spring 2007 titled THE WHISPERING HOUSE, a paranormal erotic romance tinged with horror.

Printed in the United States
69176LVS00003B/4-21